ENKINDLE IN ME
Chalice Book 2

By Erin Lewis

Full Quiver Publishing
Pakenham ON

Enkindle in Me(Chalice Book Two)
Copyright 2023 Erin Lewis

Published by
Full Quiver Publishing
PO Box 244
Pakenham, Ontario K0A 2X0
www.fullquiverpublishing.com

ISBN Number: 978-1-987970-58-6
Printed and bound in the USA
Cover photo: Erin Lewis
Cover design: Erin Lewis and James Hrkach

NATIONAL LIBRARY OF CANADA
CATALOGUING IN PUBLICATION

Published by FQ Publishing
A Division of Innate Productions

Dedicated to all young adults discerning the vocations
God wills for their lives.

"The blessedness of temptation is twofold. It reveals the weak
spot in our character, showing us where to be on guard; and the same
temptation gives us an occasion for gaining merit by refusing to submit
to it."
-Venerable Archbishop Fulton Sheen

LOST AND FOUND

The nearly forgotten smell of burgers sizzling on a griddle wafted through the air. The curve of the booth's seat behind him, the faint Pink Floyd notes from an overhead speaker, the slick plastic menu in his hands... all were alien to Dallas. The strange weight of his jeans against his legs made him squirm as he grappled to remember these sensations. Sunlight blazed through the large window panel beside him where cars whizzed by along the road. Staring through the glass at a couple of sparrows pecking and squabbling for stray crumbs along the parking lot's edge, Dallas's eyes were wide. *This is real. I'm actually here, in the real world again.* He wanted to harness this feeling and retain it for the future. *Everything is a gift; everything's amazing in its own special and detailed way...*

"Are we ready to order?" The waiter's voice broke his trance.

"Another minute," replied Father Benedict from the seat across from Dallas.

Dallas snapped his head away from the window and back to the overwhelming list of choices. He really got to decide what he would eat for lunch today. Father Benedict had insisted he order anything he wanted. It was surreal to be out in public again, and Dallas consumed everything around him with hungry eyes, ears, nose, hands.

And now for taste. He wanted a cheeseburger and fries, nothing more. Father Benedict picked up the beer list and insisted on one for Dallas. "You're two years overdue," the priest ribbed him.

"Yeah, well," Dallas said, ears growing warm, "I've tried it before, at a neighbor's house when I was like 15 years old. I felt terrible about three cans in. Channing's parents were drunks—mean ones, too—so I never touched the stuff after we started hanging out a lot." His mind flashed to his mother, drink in hand in their tiny kitchen, sullen and withdrawn, staring at nothing.

"I was only going to offer you one." The priest smiled, unbuttoning the sleeves of his black shirt and rolling them up. "This is a special day that deserves celebrating. Not to get drunk, of course. Jesus turned water into wine for a wedding feast, so alcohol has long been a way of celebrating in a group. We sometimes take it to extremes in our present culture."

Dallas nodded. "Yeah, three beers in a row for a teenager was definitely taking it to an extreme. Okay, I'll have one. It's so weird to suddenly be a 23-year-old adult."

A few sips in, Dallas held his glass in front of him and stared into the clear golden depths. He cleared his throat. "Um, Father? About discerning this possible calling for my life..."

"Yes?" The priest's gray-green eyes met Dallas's.

"Now that I'm free, I'm really eager to start figuring things out. Move forward. I need to know if my past is going to stand in my way." He took a sip of the beer and clunked the glass down on the table.

"Remember how many changes you've undergone in such a short time," Father said in a gentle tone. "One step at a time, Dallas. Ease yourself back into the real world first, and God's purpose for you will unfold over time."

Over time — hadn't he already wasted enough time in prison? Dallas nodded, but he put a hand to his stomach to quell the simmering sensation. Was it his desire to plunge headlong after this unshakable something, or was it just the alcohol?

When they finished, Father Benedict refused to let Dallas help pay the bill or even the tip. "Let's go see about finding your old car." He dropped his wadded napkin on his plate and pushed up to a stand.

The chance at finding his car surged like electricity through him, and Dallas followed Father Benedict outside. He was impressed by the 75-year-old's energy level. The priest had driven himself from Denver to Oklahoma for their monthly visitations over the past three years. He hadn't imagined Father outside of those prison visits, other than the one time Dallas and Channing had met him in his church.

Dallas was itching to drive as Father Benedict put his car in reverse. He'd almost forgotten how much he loved to sit in that seat, controlling the movement of a vehicle though space, the natural feel of the steering wheel in his grip. The priest directed him to pull a road map from the glove compartment. Dallas comfortably studied the map and directed the route towards the remote part of that North Texas lake.

The countryside around them became vaguely familiar as Dallas's mind went back to that evening almost four years ago. He instructed Father Benedict to take the next left, and then they were crossing the bridge where he'd disposed of the evidence in the Wichita River. Dallas's heart sped up, and he saw the dirt road where they had left the paved highway that day. It was deeply rutted with dried mud, and they followed it for about a half mile. Father Benedict braked at Dallas's motion, and he stepped out of the car while the priest waited, idling. Dallas strode along the road's edge, straining for a reminder of where his former self had gone next. *Is this even the right place?* A wider area between some of the low, gnarled trees was his best guess.

"I think it's that way." Dallas leaned in the window, pointing off to the right. "It was winter, so there were fewer leaves on the trees, and now it's more overgrown. I'm not sure if we can get your car through there or if you even want to attempt it."

"Should we go on foot?" asked Father Benedict. "About how far is it, do you think?"

"Probably no more than a half mile, if that."

Father Benedict turned off the engine and got out.

The vegetation was dense, but there was an opening between the trees large enough for a car to have passed through. Dallas wiped his brow with the back of his hand, warming in the mid-70s autumn Texas weather. As the two men picked their way over tangles of plants run wild, they ducked to avoid thorn-covered branches. The path between the trees narrowed again, and it was less obvious how Dallas could have managed to get a car through. The priest commented on this.

"Yeah, I went through some tight spots," Dallas said, "because I wanted to be really hidden. But all these trees look the same, so I don't know if I'll recognize the exact spot." Biting his lip, Dallas wished Channing were here. Channing would've remembered better. And being back here unsettled him. His eyes darted across his surroundings. Nobody was watching him, but he couldn't convince his mind that his routine was no longer controlled by correctional officers.

Dallas and Father Benedict pressed forward, wading through tall grasses and pushing aside crooked branches. *A car couldn't have fit through here.* Dallas retraced a few steps. *But between these trees... yes, maybe this is it.* A sinking sensation in the pit of his stomach had Dallas becoming less confident and more concerned that he was leading the elderly priest through this overgrown wilderness for nothing.

Suddenly, dull silver metal flashed through some leaves. Dallas pressed towards it, breaking through branches and breath held. He froze and blinked. There it was: *his car.*

The Isuzu sat where he'd parked it, underneath and nearly against one of the low, twisted trees on the passenger-side back door. The tires were dry rotted, the paint a little more faded than it had been. A thin blanket of dead leaves covered the roof, hood, and windshield. Dallas stood tingling, mouth hanging open. "My car," he whispered. "I found it..."

Father Benedict approached the vehicle and brushed off some of the leaves, glancing back at Dallas with bright, dancing eyes at the discovery. The priest knelt and freed one of the back wheels from a thick vine growing up it.

Dallas was frozen. He wasn't even sure how to feel. He took a step forward, staggered with weakness in his legs, and dropped to his knees, closing his eyes and gulping deep breaths. He felt a hand on his shoulder.

"Do you want to open it, see if it starts?" Father Benedict encouraged.

Dallas withdrew his keys from his jeans pocket as he stumbled back to his feet. He walked to the driver's door and inserted the key, the familiar motion a part of him. The lock popped up. He pulled the handle and felt the sensation of a door stuck due to not having been opened in a very long time. It broke free and creaked open to his yank. Dallas slid into the driver's seat and put his head down on the steering wheel, swept up in a wave of regret.

Why did I abandon the car and run? Why? Dallas's body trembled. This was the site of one of his terrible and impulsive decisions, but it was too late to change his mind now. He couldn't take back his choice and take another route, one that wouldn't have Channing dead at the end of it.

Aware that Father Benedict was waiting, Dallas slid the key into the ignition and whispered a prayer of thanksgiving for finding the car, and one of pleading that he could get it out of here somehow. He turned the key and wasn't surprised when the engine wouldn't start. The battery was probably dead. He turned to face the empty passenger seat. Last time he'd sat here, Channing was right there. Sitting in that very spot and terrified, yet completely loyal. Dallas swallowed the lump in his throat and forced his gaze away, sliding back out of the seat. He opened the hood and looked over the insides. He circled the car, inspecting it from all angles. Then he scooted underneath on his back, brushing away sticks and leaves, to check out the underside. Everything looked as good as could be expected after so many years.

Father Benedict had watched in silence. Dallas turned to him and explained his take on the Isuzu's condition.

"No problem, I'll call a tow truck," Father Benedict offered.

"I'll pay for it." Dallas ran a hand through his cropped hair. "We can get it towed to whatever garage is nearest. I think it'll run okay after it gets some attention. Man, I loved this car. I thought of it as my ticket to freedom..." He swallowed. The meaning of the word had changed so drastically for Dallas that his former usage of it was like the reasoning of a very young child to someone older and wiser.

"I have a cell phone in my car," the priest said.

Dallas raised his eyebrows and detected amusement in Father's eyes.

"Everyone has one now. I'll call Triple A to send a tow truck. Since I still drive myself at my age, I have the insurance to cover it if needed. Do you want to stay here and look over the car some more?"

Dallas was grateful for the privacy. "Yeah, thanks, if you can find your way back to your car alone."

"I have a good sense of direction, something the two of us clearly have in common." The priest was already picking his way back between the stubby trees.

Dallas turned to the Isuzu. A flood of mixed emotions that comes when you encounter an old friend who you last saw on bad terms washed over him. His car had been sitting here for the past four years, waiting for him. If a car could feel, what would it have been thinking?

The Isuzu had remained alone among the trees, motionless. It hadn't made it to Ericsburg and couldn't have known where Dallas and Channing had gone. It still sheltered all their belongings since the day they had frantically abandoned it, bits and pieces of both Dallas and Channing: their lives, hopes, dreams, failures — everything. The car knew their secrets; it held details revealing them as more than wandering strangers along the lonely roads and the small towns. But Dallas and Channing had no longer been there to add memories to the car's vast collection. It was a fragment of their past, sitting in those woods to be forgotten. But Dallas could never forget the story it held.

He shook himself, scoffing at his sentimentality. He resisted the magnetic draw of his car. *I'm afraid because I know exactly what I'll find inside.* He'd assumed he would never see the contents of the car again, and the idea of it now, staring him in the face, tied his stomach in knots. The car was as much a time capsule of Channing as it was of himself. He had to force himself to confront it, alone.

He opened the driver's door again and got in. He gripped the familiar smoothness of the steering wheel with damp palms. Eyes closed, he leaned his head back, willing himself to go on. Dallas studied the passenger seat, deciding how to begin. His hands in protest refused to move, didn't want to change anything since Channing had last touched it. Tears slid down his cheeks. *I can't do this; it's too hard!*

A few Sharpies beckoned to him from the passenger seat floor, Channing's favorites for drawing. Dallas retrieved the one closest to him and uncapped it, immediately hit with that strong permanent marker smell. How was it not dried out? Why did a stupid marker get to outlast its owner? Dallas flung it back on the floor and then groped under the passenger seat. The box of cassette tapes. He slid it out and took off the lid. All their old music, the tapes they'd played over and over on road trips. *I haven't heard any of this music for a lifetime...* He closed the box and hugged it to his chest for a moment.

In the glove compartment, Dallas found a few folded-up maps, some CDs, his Discman and headphones, and an empty Band-Aid box. As he clutched the empty box, motionless, his stomach clenched as if he might vomit.

"This is impossible!" he yelled, pounding a fist on the dashboard. "How am I supposed to handle this? Channing's dead; he's really dead!" Dallas felt like a fool, paralyzed by an empty Band-aid box, unable to cope with what should be a simple inventory.

Dallas shoved the empty box back in the glove compartment and jumped out, slamming the door behind him. He paced, a mess of frazzled nerves, then froze. *Channing's kiln. It's in the trunk. Or, it should be…*

Dallas unlocked the trunk of the Isuzu. There it was, undisturbed. Channing hadn't uttered a word about it after they'd had to abandon the car. A bag of broken glass was wedged beside the kiln, materials the two of them had collected for Channing's future projects, artwork that was never to be. He lifted the toaster to reveal the coffee maker they'd brought from Dallas's old house—the two parting gifts his mother had bestowed upon him by not taking them herself. A smile tried to flicker across Dallas's face as he remembered brewing coffee outside the library with this coffee pot—the last time it had been used—and then the memory came crashing down in flames at his feet, the reason for that event stabbing him in the gut as to why they had no food and had been so desperate to fill their bellies with anything. He bit a quivering lip and tightened his grip on the toaster. That forever-gone moment in time, before he'd been caught shoplifting, when he could have found other options… Instead, Dallas had continued along the path of self-destruction, taking Channing down with him, running him to his death.

Dallas dropped the toaster back into the trunk, resisting the urge to slam it against the ground, then collapsed against the back bumper of the car, giving in to hot, bitter tears that choked him with heaving sobs. Through the blur, the empty place where the license plate had once been kicked him in the gut. This was that same raw anguish from his first months after Channing's death, those awful dark days of his early incarceration. Despair poured from Dallas, a desperate attempt to heave out the hot, thick feeling and get to the end, but the end wouldn't come.

Father Benedict found him a half hour later, still clinging to the car's bumper. The kind man knelt beside him on one knee and put an arm around him. Dallas could neither acknowledge his presence nor pull away, drowning in self-blame and memories. *This car hasn't seen me since 1997, when Channing was still alive…* Dallas irrationally tried to will himself back in that moment so that he could save Channing's life instead of gambling with it recklessly.

Finally, Dallas stopped, eyes raw, throat hoarse, temples pounding with a headache. Father Benedict wasn't there. Concerned eyes darting side to side, Dallas forced himself up. He pocketed his keys, closed the trunk without glancing in at the kiln or coffee maker lest they set off his rollercoaster of emotions again, and half-jogged in the direction they'd come. He caught a glimpse of black up ahead—the priest's shirt. Calling to him, Dallas pressed forward through the branches.

Father Benedict turned to wait as Dallas caught up, head hung over his behavior. He opened his mouth to apologize, but the priest cut him off.

"You don't have to explain yourself in any way. Do you want to come wait for the tow truck with me or stay back with your car?"

"I'll stay with you, thanks," Dallas muttered. They made their way back through the woods to where the priest's car was parked on the dirt road. They sat in silence on the hood, Dallas sniffling occasionally and trying not to think. When the tow truck appeared, Father Benedict took over with an explanation and then led the way through where the gaps between trees were wide enough for the truck to pass through. Dallas followed slowly at a distance, hands in his pockets. The tow truck tore up some of the undergrowth, making it easier to get back through the woods again to the Isuzu.

The car was loaded while Dallas watched. He was still numb a few minutes later as he sat in the priest's passenger seat, allowing everything to happen to him. As they pulled in behind the tow truck at the mechanic, Dallas turned his head and lifted his eyes towards Father Benedict. The priest was doing for him what he was incapable of making himself do.

"Father, thank you," Dallas said. "Seeing my car again is such a shock. It's just like we left it. I'd convinced myself the car would be gone, and that I'd never find out what happened to it, never see our stuff again—Channing's stuff. Each thing in there is stabbing me with memories. I wasn't expecting the harsh, painful grief again."

The priest put a hand on Dallas's left shoulder. "I'm sorry it is so difficult. Your pain had dulled to an ache over your years in prison. This is what I mean about adjusting to life again before pursuing a deeper calling. You need time, but also just to get the practical logistics in order. When you mentioned the slight hope of finding your car, I could tell how much you loved it. So, I plan to help you by paying for the repairs, if it is salvageable. If not, I'd like to buy you another car this week, before I have to go back to Denver. You will have a much better chance of keeping a job if you have transportation. I know it's important from my past work with men who have been newly released. It makes reintegration a smoother process when you own a vehicle."

Dallas's throat tightened with words that wouldn't come right away. "Thank you," he mumbled, staring at his hands in his lap. "And here I am, acting like a spoiled child because we actually found my car and it tears me up inside to look at it and the things inside."

"Dallas, no," Father Benedict reassured him. "Your feelings are so raw right now because of the precious memories that this car holds for you. You will have to work through those feelings, but in the end, I pray they all lead you to where any of your other memories lead you—back to a gratitude for having had a friend like Channing in your life and reminders of happy things the two of you did together."

"Dang, I hope it gets easier, but it's so hard." Dallas shut his eyes. "I haven't even looked in the back seat yet. And then our stuff up in Minnesota — that's waiting for me too. I hafta go get it and confront those memories too." He quivered as a heaviness settled in his gut, thinking of Channing's grave that he'd need to visit there. Regrets over his best friend's death weighed him down. "I know God forgives me and that Channing wouldn't want me to dwell on it in despair. I need to focus on offering up this pain for Channing's soul. I know it's my burden to bear."

"And sometimes you'll bear it well, and other times it will seem to be all you can do to not be completely overpowered by the weight of it," the priest said. "You have come so far already, but the road never ends. Not until we reach our heavenly home and can rest in the fullness of God's presence. The world is not our true home, therefore, we will never be fully comfortable here."

The Road goes ever on and on… Dallas let the priest's wise words sink in and mingle with the mental quotation spoken in Channing's voice, then took a deep breath and got out of the car. He straightened himself up and squared his shoulders with a new energy. *I can do this. I'm my own man again, and I've got Father Benedict's support.* And he was in his element here. This was his car, the car that he knew inside and out, and he could speak mechanic language about what it needed. He remembered that his toolbox was also in the trunk, another reassurance. He had this. But he had to make himself take charge. Dallas took confident steps into the shop.

"Hi there," he spoke to the man behind the counter. "That's my Isuzu that just got towed in. Hasn't been driven in almost four years, so I just want it looked over to double-check whether there's anything major wrong with it. I know it needs a battery and tires."

"Sure, we can look over it," replied the man. "Four years, you say? It might need a lot more than just battery and tires."

"I've checked it over myself." Dallas's stance was straight, voice firm. "I drained the gas tank before they got it on the truck. I'll change the oil myself. Otherwise, I'm not seeing anything obvious. Tires were about five years old already last time I drove it, and they're getting dry-rotted. I don't need anything fancy, just low- to medium-end tires."

"So, you know some about cars." The mechanic rounded the end of the counter.

"I do; used to be an assistant to a mechanic a few years ago." Dallas crossed his arms. "And I know this car well. Got it when I was 17, and I've tried to take good care of it."

"Leavin' it sitting outside for four years isn't exactly good for it." The man raised an eyebrow.

"W-well," Dallas faltered, "that part wasn't exactly within my control."

The mechanic was silent, then turned away. "I'll take a look, then get you prices on a couple different tires."

Dallas returned to the waiting area. Father Benedict had already helped himself to the complimentary coffee and offered to get Dallas a cup.

"Sure, thanks." Dallas followed Father to the nearby table and grabbed three creamers while the priest poured him a Styrofoam cup.

"Think I should ask if they have any job openings here?" Dallas asked suddenly. "It's not in Wichita Falls, but if they have something available…"

"Wouldn't hurt to ask," Father Benedict responded. "You are quite confident about cars and seem to know yours well. I'm really glad we found it."

"Me too." Dallas peeled the foil lid off one of the creamers and dumped it in his cup. "Even though the memories are hard, a different car would feel strange. If I can't have Channing alive, then still having the car he rode around in with me—well, is it weird that I'm starting to find that comforting?"

"Not at all," the priest answered.

The mechanic came back into the room and handed Dallas a few tire prices jotted on a slip of paper, then returned to the bay where the Isuzu was already up on the rack.

Dallas scanned the details, then walked to the window. The old satisfaction of mechanical work tingled in his hands as he watched them work on his car. He'd have his hands back on it soon enough.

"Sure you don't want us to change the oil?" asked the mechanic when he returned to inquire about the tires. "It'd only be another twenty bucks."

"No, thanks," Dallas responded. "I'll do that myself."

A short time later, the car was down, and Dallas was at the counter. "You were right—nothin' else wrong with that car," the mechanic told him. "Seems pretty solid. Put some gas in it, and the engine sounds good."

Father Benedict moved close. "I'll be paying for this."

Dallas, humbling himself rather than arguing, stepped aside with his thumbs hooked in his pockets.

After the receipt was handed over, Dallas cleared his throat and met the man's eyes. "You don't, uh, happen to need another mechanic right now?"

The man studied him for a few seconds. "No, we've got everything covered pretty well. You lookin' for a job?"

"I am, either working on cars or a construction job."

"Well, I hope you can find something," the man responded.

Dallas and Father Benedict exited the building. "Oh well, I really would like to be in a larger town anyway. And I kinda got the feeling that he didn't really trust me when he heard I let my car sit unused for so long." They stopped beside the Isuzu, parked in a space outside the bay. Dallas caressed the hood with one hand. "I can't believe I'm about to drive it again," he murmured.

"I'll follow you to the Walmart we passed," Father Benedict said.

Dallas nodded and got into the driver's seat. He slipped his key into the ignition and turned it. The engine roared to life, the car vibrated beneath him, sound came from the speakers. The last song Dallas and Channing had been listening to as they fled picked up where the cassette tape had left off, and it hurtled him back in time, against his will. The song's eerie vocals whined into Dallas's ears, finally continuing from his last paranoid moments in the car. Now he shuddered as he remembered his demand that Channing turn it off. His friend's scared, pleading words invaded Dallas's mind: *"Dallas, we love this album, our very favorite one between the two of us... we can't let this ruin it for us!* Dallas willed himself not to drown as he put the car in drive and twisted the volume knob down. He couldn't handle hearing it yet.

Walking into the Walmart was like another world. Being inside a big store again after three and a half years made Dallas feel like an ant under a microscope. Did he look as out of place as he felt?

Father Benedict noticed. "If you think people are staring at you, it's because you're walking around Walmart with a Roman Catholic priest wearing his clerics."

Dallas chuckled and admitted this was probably true, glancing down at his jeans and boots that, in his mind, didn't appear obviously dated. How much could have changed in casual dress for men in the past few years?

After they checked out with the oil, filter, and oil drain pan, Father Benedict said, "Since it's getting late, I'll get us a hotel for the night. Can you do an oil change there?"

"Sure." Dallas shifted one bag to his other hand and dug for his keys. "I'll just jack it up and do it in the parking lot."

At a nearby hotel, Dallas got to work under his car. It was all still in his muscle memory: he breezed through the steps until he was staring at the disgusting-looking oil draining out of the Isuzu.

He finished up and shimmied out from under the car. Opening the glove compartment and pulling out a rag, Dallas had a split-second moment of wondering how he knew to look there—he usually kept rags in the trunk. The one he held in his hand had blue stains on it and smelled faintly of turpentine.

"Channing's feet," Dallas whispered and made himself crack a smile at the memory. He wiped his hands on the rag, eyes closed, picturing that morning when Channing had jumped into the car with his feet painted blue. Suddenly, Father Benedict's approaching footsteps broke Dallas's train of thought.

"Are you hungry?"

"Ravenous." Dallas shoved the rag back in the glove compartment and went into the hotel room to clean up. Splashing cold water over his face, he glimpsed himself in the bathroom mirror: Dallas Malone, in his street clothes, free. He pulled the baggie holding his earring from his pocket. With a little fiddling and pressure, he got it into his old piercing easily enough. Dallas stared at his reflection, as if willing himself back in time as that teenager from nearly four years prior.

Channing suddenly stared back at him in the mirror from behind his shoulder, wide-eyed in horrified curiosity as 14-year-old Dallas held up the shiny needle flashing in the light, a drip of rubbing alcohol falling from the sharp tip into the basin below. The tiny droplet splashed in his mind like the roar of whitewater rapids, and Channing's sucked-in breath came from behind him, the younger boy's pounding heartbeat like a drum in Dallas's own head, and he drew his lips together in a hardened, tight line. The thick embroidery needle gripped in his right hand, the left going to his earlobe and firmly grasping, pulling taut, the flash of the steel and Channing's hands clapping over his eyes, unable to watch Dallas mutilate himself. The boy in a tiled Nevada bathroom showed no mercy or hesitation, and the needle was thrust through his flesh, a quick puncture, a few drops of blood with a wince and grin of satisfaction. The needle was withdrawn and discarded on the counter, and now Dallas's voice, "It's over now, Chan, you can look. Hand me the earring, would you?"

Dallas shook his head and blinked rapidly. He stared at the small silver hoop in his ear as if Channing had just handed it to him for the very first time. The piercing throbbed hot, and he put a hand to it to quell the impossible physical response. *That was a decade ago, a decade ago…*

Hours after Dallas had prayed the Memorare as usual while falling asleep, he jolted awake. After years of sleeping on the thin, stiff mattress of his prison cell, he tossed and turned in the foreign luxury of a strange bed. Moonlight streamed through the window, and he rose to peer out: the Isuzu, a glimmering enticement, with the contents he'd have to face sooner or later. *Just go out there now and get it over with.* Drawn by a quivering in his gut, Dallas jumped out of bed. He'd take care of it now and push through the pain before he'd have to unload it all into wherever he'd be living.

Dallas stepped into his boots and slipped through the door, grabbing a key card on his way out and half-wondering if he could figure out how to use it to get back inside. He unlocked his car and climbed in. He grabbed the old disposable cups out of the cupholder and made himself stuff them into a bag snatched from the back seat floorboard. He and Channing had already reused the cups a disgusting number of times. The Styrofoam one felt brittle from age in his grip. Dallas gathered old napkins and other garbage from the front seats.

Next, he put Channing's Sharpies in the glove compartment. As he was about to shut it, a pale green object caught his eye, tucked back in the corner. His chest tightened, and he took it up between his thumb and index finger. *One of the glass rings Channing made.* Dallas turned the smooth perfect circle over in his hands as tears welled up in his eyes. He slipped it onto the middle finger of his left hand, where it fit exactly. Dallas closed his eyes and murmured thanks for this unexpected gift. Only a few of the glass rings made in Channing's kiln had turned out this well: the one he had sold, one he had always worn himself, and this one. It was like Channing had left it there as a gift.

Picking up the empty Band-aid box he'd found earlier, Dallas felt a smile flicker at the edge of his mouth as he remembered Channing's Band-aid "art," stuck to the dashboard in a geometric pattern. The plastic surface still bore traces of the once-sticky residue. He flattened the box and tucked it into the garbage bag, then had second thoughts and pulled it out again. He slid it back into the glove compartment, feeling silly about it. But Dallas couldn't throw it out. *It's not like it took up much space, anyway.*

The notebooks under the passenger seat were Channing's: one a sketchbook and the other a lined spiral notebook. Unable to look inside them, Dallas thrust them back under the seat.

Between the seats, Dallas found the cassette tape case belonging to the album that was still in the player. He put it in the shoebox and then climbed into the back seat. A dried-out marker and empty peanut butter jar went into the garbage bag.

All the clothing they'd had no room to bring when they'd left the car to hitchhike was jumbled on the back seat, a combination of his and Channing's. He folded each piece methodically and made a neat stack. Dallas pulled several of Channing's books from under the empty cooler—he would add them to the box he knew sat in the trunk. He swiped under the driver's seat from the back for anything else and pulled out his old house key from Nevada. How had it ended up under the seat? If Channing were still here, he would've turned it into some piece of artwork. Dallas pocketed it.

His lonely moonlit inventory continued with the trunk. Dallas dropped his old key in the bag of glass bottles and other art supplies. Channing had only brought the most interesting colors when they'd left Nevada. *Wonder if I can even work the kiln correctly without Channing... Do I even want to?* But Dallas couldn't throw out the glass. A lot of time and effort had gone into procuring it.

The few books from the back seat fit into the cardboard box already crammed with Channing's library. Dallas skimmed the titles: *Oliver Twist, Around the World in Eighty Days, Paradise Lost, Augustine's Confessions,* a calculus text, a child development book, a thick poetry anthology, *The Princess and the Goblin*... He couldn't look anymore. As he pushed the box aside, a paper sleeve caught his eye: photographs. Dallas glanced inside and then shut the flap quickly. At least he had some pictures so that Channing's face would never be lost to him. *But I'm not ready to look yet.* A tear trickled down his cheek.

The can of turpentine behind several empty gas cans made Dallas's breath hitch in his throat. He'd always been responsible for Channing— it was why he'd brought the turpentine for Channing's feet when they'd left Nevada. *Responsible...* the word rang in Dallas's mind as he fought back tears.

Their camping supplies were deep in the trunk: the propane stove, a couple of pots and bowls, a can opener, a blanket. Mitchell would have a few more blankets, their sleeping bags and tent, and additional sheets and towels at his house. Dallas paused and murmured a grateful prayer for some of these necessities that he wouldn't have to purchase.

He paced beside the car, sorting complete. Dallas wanted to drive, that old restless longing creeping back into him. *But I can't just leave in the middle of the night—Father Benedict might wake up and worry. And my license is expired, so I'd be an idiot to do it.* Driving the car to Walmart and the hotel from the mechanic's shop was all the risk he needed to take. Dallas sat on the hood and leaned back against the windshield, hands folded behind his head, legs sprawled out comfortably, as he and Channing had so often done on the evenings of their spontaneous road trips. He closed his eyes and imagined driving, just driving away, for miles and miles, running far away... *Don't be selfish*, came a voice in his head. *You have a greater purpose than that.*

Dallas squinted up at the stars. "Okay, God, what is it?"

Don't be selfish; give of yourself to others. Don't run and hide. Give until it hurts.

Dallas folded his arms across his chest. How were these thoughts coming to him so suddenly? "Okay, I'm not actually gonna run and hide somewhere, although that sounds real nice. But I've already been hurt terribly," he grumbled, eyebrows lowered at the sky. "Is it really that selfish of me to not want to hurt anymore?"

Help others who hurt. Trust.

Dallas sat silent, squeezing his head in his hands to clear these uninvited thoughts that barged into his mind. "I couldn't help Channing!" he choked out, tension rising in his body, face flushed. "I led him to his *death!* Some kind of person *I* am to help anyone!"

Channing doesn't need your help anymore, but you can bring me to others. Give of yourself and trust.

What was *that* supposed to mean? Dallas slid off the car hood with a huff. "Are you talking to me, God? Or am I going crazy or something?"

Silence.

"Ha ha, nice joke." Dallas threw his arms out at his sides. "What the heck am I supposed to do? I haven't even been out of prison for 24 hours. I can't exactly walk into a seminary and say, 'Hi there, I just got out of jail yesterday for involuntary manslaughter, but now I'm supposed to become a priest.' Not right now, not yet. I want it, yeah, so bad it burns inside sometimes. But am I even good enough? And Father says to wait. I'll still help other people in the meantime. I need to get settled down before figuring out if you're really calling me, but being patient isn't exactly a strength of mine." The thought of running off to a hidden monastery as a monk entered his mind, and Dallas cracked his knuckles and sighed. "I'm sorry, God. I just need a little space to get my head on straight, is all. I'm still so confused, and it's like I'm in a foreign land —"

A door closed behind him, and Dallas spun to see Father Benedict leaving the hotel room and coming towards him across the parking lot.

"Sorry, Father, did I wake you up talking to myself out here?" Dallas tucked his hands in his pockets, face flushed.

"No, I didn't hear you," the priest answered. "I just wake up sometimes in the night, and I saw you weren't in the room."

"Couldn't stay asleep," Dallas muttered. "Different bed, different room..."

"It will take some getting used to," Father Benedict commiserated as they walked back to the motel room.

Father sat on the edge of his bed and opened his black leather-bound prayer book, moving a satin ribbon marker. He crossed himself.

"Are those the prayers priests say every day?" Dallas eyed the book.

Father nodded. "Yes, the Divine Office."

"So, that was what you were reading earlier in the mechanic waiting room," Dallas observed.

"I prayed the midday prayer then. This is Compline, the night prayer. When I find myself awake in the night, I consider it may be the Holy Spirit prodding me to pray. It doesn't have to be time wasted. Your patron saint, Cyprian, had something to say along those lines, although I can't remember the exact quote. Something about praying in the night. You may join me if you wish."

Dallas's hand went to the two saint medals, given to him by Father Benedict earlier, now strung around his neck on the chain with his crucifix. He wasn't sure he'd been praying out there or just trying to have it out with God.

"Sure, I'll listen and pray along with you." Dallas settled back on his bed and crossed himself as the priest said the words. The hymn, the psalm, the beautiful prayers falling from the lips of the old priest soothed Dallas. *"Let your servant go in peace..." yeah, I could use some of that right now. Maybe I should start praying these myself, get my own book...* He yawned and rubbed his eyes. *I'll need a new routine, a regular rhythm now that nobody's gonna force one on me...* His eyelids drooped.

When Father finished, Dallas had fallen asleep leaning back against his pillow in the same position he'd been in while sitting on the car hood. He was oblivious to the blessing for a peaceful night's rest Father gave with extended hand forming a cross in Dallas's direction. Finally worn out from the transitory day, Dallas slumbered deeply until the morning sun was well into the sky.

Dallas woke the next morning and stared at the red digital numbers on the bedside clock radio: 9:00. It had been years since he'd slept in so late — literally. He sat up and stretched. His back ached and he felt guilty for not appreciating the plushness of the bed. Father Benedict wasn't in the room, so Dallas took a shower, a strange self-pampering ritual, controlling the water temperature and time limit himself in this small, private hotel bathroom instead of in the locker-room-style showers of the prison. He pulled his jeans back on and went out to the car to get a shirt off the back seat. As he tugged it over his head, Father Benedict approached, carrying a paper bag and two cups of coffee.

"Breakfast." He held the bag out to Dallas. "There's more in the lobby, but I brought you two bagels and cream cheese."

"Thanks."

After eating in their room, Father Benedict said, "I think the next thing to do is to take you to get a current driver's license."

"Can I do that with no home address?" Dallas furrowed his brow. He'd thought of this the night before: how to drive the car to Wichita Falls with no license, and how to get a license without first getting an address. Everything was so complicated.

"I hadn't thought of that," the priest responded, "but no, you probably can't. Hmm. Maybe we should ask the local DMV about it."

After verifying that he needed an address to get a current driver's license, Dallas and Father Benedict left for Wichita Falls together in the priest's car. After getting things squared away there, they could come back for his car. Dallas checked with the hotel owner to ask if he could leave his car in the lot for a few days. His hands shook as he got into Father Benedict's car and stared at the Isuzu, left behind again for the forty-minute drive. *I'm coming back for it for sure this time*, he reassured his nerves.

Dallas stared at the blank walls of his apartment: his new home, his own space. He ran his hand along the small kitchen counter. The refrigerator and cabinets were stocked with the minimum basics, his old toaster and coffee maker sat on the counter, and he had a small table and two chairs. The single bedroom was furnished with a bed and small dresser in which he had put his and Channing's few articles of clothing. The living room was bare except for an old sofa that had been purchased at the Salvation Army thrift store and a pile of books, CDs, and other stuff from the car, stacked in a corner next to Channing's kiln. Dallas's Isuzu sat parked outside with a temporary tag, and a new driver's license was tucked in Dallas's wallet. And he had a job lined up—not his first choice, but the work would be steady as part of a construction crew doing commercial demolition work under the supervision of a foreman. His muscles tightened in anticipation of the physical labor: hard work would relieve the stress, as he knew from his vigorous prison workouts.

None of it would have gone so smoothly without Father Benedict. The first month's rent, the groceries, the furniture, the mechanic bills for the car, the hotel stays and restaurant meals: Father Benedict had paid for them all while keeping Dallas company over the past eight days. When Dallas had asked how he could afford all this— "Don't priests have a vow of poverty or something?"—Father had replied, "We receive a salary that is modest by today's paycheck standards, but I have tried to be frugal so as to put the extra money to good use. Helping a sincere young man get back on his feet is what I'd consider to be good use."

Work started in a week, but first: a trip to Minnesota to get his other belongings from Mitchell. It would be the first step Dallas would take alone at reintegrating himself into society—without relying on Father Benedict. A longing mingled with queasiness inside him as he anticipated visiting Channing's grave.

Dallas sighed and flipped off the kitchen light. He brushed his teeth in the small bathroom of his apartment and stuck his toothbrush and toothpaste into his bag, already packed for tomorrow's trip. Staring at himself in the mirror and running a hand through his short hair, he didn't look that much older. *I sure feel like it, though. Will Mitchell think the same?*

Dallas couldn't fall asleep right away. Dread gnawed at his gut as he thought about going back... back to where Channing had died. It wouldn't be easy. Dallas shifted on his mattress, still acclimating to sleeping in a place other than a prison cell. He had declined Father

Benedict's offer to buy him bedsheets since there were two sets waiting for him in Minnesota. He couldn't be excessive or wasteful.

Reaching for Channing's Memorare prayer card under his pillow, Dallas couldn't shake the emptiness of his new life. He'd been keeping it there every night since his release; often in prison, he had felt the card was safer in his locker where nobody else could get it. Now he kept it on him constantly, just as Channing had done. *I'll be taking it back to Channing's grave and reciting it there.* The thought gave him chills and a nauseated sensation. *Will I be able to handle it?* He brushed his fingers across the card and begged God to calm the worries in his head. He fell into a repeated recitation of the prayer until he finally fell asleep.

Dallas awoke and stood up from the floor, picking up his blanket and stretching to get the crick out of his neck. By the middle of the night, he'd been unable to stand the feel of the bed any longer. After a quick shower, he locked his apartment door, coffee in hand and bag over his shoulder. As Dallas pulled onto the highway, the exhilaration that a long drive had always evoked in him stirred in his heart. *I'm driving, free, the whole world around me outside the glass windows of my car.* Only one thing was missing, and its obviousness was like a hole in his heart. Dallas offered up the pain of Channing's absence aloud as he drove: "Lord, please help me unite my pain to yours. Please help me focus on you, and on doing good for you here on earth and not wallowing in the past. Thank you for allowing me to have Channing in my life for that short time. Please give me strength when I visit his grave... I can't do this on my own. I know I'm too weak."

Dallas finished his last bite of breakfast, the loneliness of a solitary road trip dragging his spirits down. "I'm coming to you, Channing," he whispered. Dallas glanced at the radio. The tape was still in the cassette player from their final trip together. He turned up the volume of their joint favorite album. Channing had selected this cassette and put it in before the shoplifting-gone-wrong incident that had changed their lives forever. *No way can I take it out — Channing was last to touch that tape.* Dallas drowned himself in sentimentality as the old familiar songs played.

The next evening, Dallas arrived in Ericsburg. The drive had dashed his expectations. "Camping" overnight in the car had lost all of its old appeal without Channing's enthusiasm, and waking in the driver's seat for the first time post-prison only to discover his dead-and-gone absence was like a knife in the gut. Dallas pulled into Mitchell's driveway before he was ready.

He remembered the older brick ranch house from their few days' stay when they'd been kicked out of the shelter before renting a place. A light dusting of snow crinkled under his boots as he stepped out of the car. A door opened. Mitchell bounded down the front steps, smiling broadly. They met at the front walk, and Mitchell clapped Dallas on the back. Mitchell was twice Dallas's age but had always treated him more like an equal than his employee.

"Hey, you made it! Come on in out of the cold."

"Thanks." Dallas hoisted his bag onto his shoulder and followed Mitchell through the door.

"I'm about to throw some steaks on the grill," he called over his shoulder. "Nancy, you remember Dallas," Mitchell addressed his wife as they came into the room where a TV garbled at a low volume and a woman stood and crossed the carpet.

"Nice to see you again, Dallas," she said warmly. "How was your drive?"

"It was good, thanks." Dallas rubbed the back of his neck. He hadn't spoken to a woman in years, other than a quick word with the cashier at Walmart a few days ago. It was a strange realization.

"We haven't had dinner yet, so I hope you're hungry," she added as she went into the kitchen.

"Uh, yeah," Dallas answered, "Mitch told me he's about to grill some steaks. Sounds great, thanks."

"Help yourself to a beer," Mitchell offered as he paused at the back door in the kitchen.

Dallas murmured another thanks and opened the refrigerator. He was going to have to get used to people offering him alcohol. The reminder that he was a full-fledged adult now was still sudden. He grabbed a can, then followed Mitchell out the back door to the patio.

Mitchell opened the grill and set four T-bone steaks on the grate.

Dallas's mouth watered. "Wow. You didn't have to go to any trouble for me, though."

"No trouble," Mitchell replied, "just figured you hadn't had a good steak recently. I mean..." He trailed off.

"It's fine." Dallas recognized Mitchell's hesitation and maybe embarrassment. "It doesn't bother me for you to talk about it. You're right; they never served steak in prison. Except country fried steak, which is kind of an insult to steak, like a T-bone's black sheep cousin or something." Dallas grinned up at him.

Mitchell laughed aloud, the tension broken. "Where'd this sense of humor come from? You always seemed so serious."

Dallas shrugged. "I think I was just so uptight with the worry in the back of my mind that all I could focus on was survival. In prison, I didn't have to worry about those basics anymore. Somebody else fed me and checked up on me constantly for over three years. Nothing was within my control. But God's in charge, not me. Accepting that has taught me to relax more, and just be better to other people around me."

"You've grown up." Mitchell turned a steak over. "I can tell already. I mean, there's a kind of old soul feeling I'm getting from you. I always thought we could start to get to know each other better if I could just crack your tough outer shell... Didn't know how serious the secrets inside you were. But I had a good feeling about you, that you were a good kid, and I still think so now. Man, I wish I had the need for another guy in the shop. I'd hire you back in an instant."

"I appreciate that." Dallas's gaze fell on his shoes, and he bit his lip. How he wished he could go back and do everything differently. "Not everyone wants to hire an ex-felon. I didn't get the mechanic job I applied for in Texas. It was my first choice, but I start work with a construction crew on Monday. It pays good; it's honest work I can do with my hands, so I'm grateful the contractor hired me despite my record."

"With your work ethic, you'll knock it out of the park." Mitchell slipped the steaks onto a waiting platter.

Dallas's cheeks warmed with the praise. "Nah, it's football season now." He grinned at his own joke.

Mitchell burst out laughing.

Dallas was filled with the lightness of having everything out in the open. Mitchell could finally see his full personality instead of the one covered in fear and the hiding of a terrible dark secret. He could truly be a friend with his former boss.

And now he was a normal person again, sitting at the dinner table with friends. Years of prison meals had almost erased his memory of how real food tasted. He devoured Nancy's homemade macaroni and cheese, declaring it the best he'd ever eaten, and the medium-rare steak practically melted in his mouth. Conversation turned to Dallas's plans.

"You can stay as long as you want," Mitchell said, "until you have to go back for work. You know we have the extra room. Is there anything else you need to take care of up here, other than picking up your stuff? Anything I can help you with?"

Dallas examined his empty plate. "I'm going to visit Channing's grave," he said slowly, "but I need to be alone to do that; was thinking I'd go by on my way out of town. I need to go to the county coroner's office and find out where he was buried. They keep records on that sort of thing, I've been told."

"I know where the office is. Want me to come with?" Mitchell offered. "I understand you wanting to visit his grave by yourself; I wouldn't intrude on that. I'm still so sorry about what happened to Channing," he finished softly.

"Thanks." Dallas's voice was strained. "I don't want to inconvenience you any, but if you can spare the time tomorrow, I guess I'd appreciate you helping me with going to the coroner's. You can tell the idea makes me uncomfortable, huh?" Dallas lifted his head.

"I figure you could use the moral support." Mitchell stroked his chin with his fingers. "You wanna go through your stuff after dinner, or are you too worn out from your drive?"

"Yeah, I think I need some sleep." The reality of what he had come to do was setting in and overshadowing what had been a happy reunion with Mitchell, and Dallas felt heavy all over. "I really appreciate you saving everything for me, before the landlord trashed it all."

Mitchell showed Dallas to the guest room. Three large Rubbermaid bins of his and Channing's things stood stacked in one corner. On top of the bins were two pillows, two thick blankets, and Channing's Airwalks. Dallas's breath caught in his throat at the sight of the shoes. On the floor next to the bottom bin was their microwave, the one they'd bought at a yard sale soon after renting the little house not far from the mechanic shop. Their sleeping bags lay alongside.

"You know, you were so good to us," Dallas said, remembering. "When you paid me a month in advance, that helped us to rent the house sooner. Living in the shelter that first month was rough, and who knows where we'd have been if not for your willingness to take a risk on me and trust that I'd keep working for you."

"It was the right thing to do." Mitchell clasped Dallas's shoulder. "I knew you needed a little leg up to get on your feet. I only wish it didn't all go south for you a few months later. Wish he was still here with you, man. I know he was like your brother. The way you talked about him when you applied, how you needed to take care of him — that's what convinced me to take a chance on you. And I'm still glad that I did."

Dallas swallowed. "I'm real sorry I let you down."

"I know. Get some sleep." It was all Mitchell had to say.

Dallas closed his eyes and let out a deep breath, accepting the grace given by his former boss. Then he washed his face, brushed his teeth, and changed shirts. The guest room bed had been made up neatly, and he crawled in between fresh sheets. He reached down, groping for Channing's shirt that he'd been wearing earlier. Dallas tucked it under his pillow beside the Memorare card before he could even reason with himself about what he was doing. He mumbled his prayers and tried to push aside the fear of what he had to do tomorrow, but all he could picture was Channing's last night alive in the little house a couple miles down the road.

"I've gotta go check on things at the shop before we leave for the coroner's," Mitchell told Dallas over their raisin bran.

Dallas's spoon paused halfway to his mouth, and he gulped. "Uh, I'd like to take a shower first, anyway. Maybe you could swing back by here to pick me up?" His chest tightened at the idea of going to the shop, right near the scene of Channing's death.

Silent understanding registered in Mitchell's eyes. "Sure, that works. I'll be back in thirty minutes."

Several hours later, Mitchell and Dallas were climbing back into his truck. "Well, that was grueling," Mitchell commented, "but we finally got it figured out."

Dallas blew out a sigh. "I feel bad you've driven all over the county. Let me pay you for the gas."

"No need." Mitchell glanced through his window before turning out of the parking lot of the main records office. The building in the next town over from the coroner's office was the end of what had seemed a wild goose chase. "We finally found the information, and now you know exactly where he's buried."

"The pauper's section," the words of the woman at the records desk rang in Dallas's ears. It sounded terrible.

By the time they got back to Ericsburg after a stop for a late lunch, it was nearly 4:00, and Mitchell needed to go back into the shop to finish a few things and close up at 6. A tug deep inside forced Dallas's attention. He wouldn't be back here any time soon. Maybe he should go along and face being back in that place. *Is it wrong to avoid the scene of Channing's death, like I'm dishonoring his memory? Could I make it a fruitful opportunity to pray for his soul? Or will it all just provoke and haunt me in my memories?*

"Do you need help with anything?" Dallas stuffed his anxiety with his rushed question, eyes aimed through the window. "At the shop, I mean?"

Mitchell paused, brow furrowed. "If you want to come along, I'm sure I could find something for you to do." He eyed Dallas.

Dallas swallowed. He should just be a man and go. "Yeah, I'll come with you."

As they approached the main street in Mitchell's truck, Dallas focused his eyes straight ahead, hands clenched in his lap. There it was: the street corner where Dallas's life had changed completely and Channing's had forever ended. Mitchell drove through the intersection and turned to park behind his shop. He glanced at Dallas out of the side of his eye but said nothing.

They entered through the back door. *The one I fled through when the cops came in the front,* Dallas remembered bitterly. Everything looked about the same. Two people sat in the waiting room, and Mitchell's assistant in the garage looked busy, while the young man at the desk, around Dallas's age, worked at the computer.

Mitchell greeted the customers, one of whom was waiting for an oil change while the assistant mechanic finished up on the first customer's car. Glancing at the empty coffee maker, he asked Dallas to make a pot and then headed into the bay. Mitchell emphasized being hospitable to his customers through his always-available complimentary coffee.

Dallas got the coffee going, then gave a friendly smile to the two people in the waiting area seats and told them to help themselves when it was finished brewing. Then he stepped out the front door. The jingling bell attached to the door handle jolted him, and he wobbled with dizziness, a flash of black in his vision for an instant. Those same bells had been alarms when the officers had entered the shop that afternoon, the May afternoon in 1997 that he was reliving in his mind right now. Dallas's ears were suddenly assaulted with innumerable jingling bells: at the mechanic in Texas, on a radio commercial, at Mass in the church he and Father Benedict had attended last week. He sprinted down the sidewalk to outrun his visceral gut reaction to the sound, but the bells were in his brain.

Dallas halted halfway to the corner and closed his eyes, breathing in the gasoline fumes from the street, heart thudding in his head. He opened them again and sucked in a breath, then took determined steps down the concrete and stopped at the corner. This was where he'd stopped as the truck hit Channing, the spot where the police had wrestled him to the ground and handcuffed him. Dallas put one foot up on the hydrant, laces of his boot dangling as he surveyed the scene blankly. Imagining this empty place on the asphalt as the location of Channing's last breath, his last moment on earth, threatened to crush Dallas. Nauseated, he sank down on the sidewalk, back against the brick wall of the building behind him. Echoes of his past self screamed out, *"No!!!"* Rosary beads pressed into his fingertips in his pocket, and he bowed his head to his shaking, drawn-up knees.

Dallas prayed the Rosary mechanically through misty eyes, the terrible section of street framed between his knees. When he'd finished, he sat in silence, chasing thoughts from his mind, threatening to punish them violently. *I just need to be here, just to be…* Eyes focused on his own knees, Dallas stared at his jeans — the same jeans he'd worn that day, the jeans he was arrested in, the jeans he wore out of prison at his release. *And of course, my same shoes…* Dallas shut his eyes to his boots thudding down this same sidewalk, hitting those same places he had now been walking in them again. Channing's shoes, back in Mitchell's house, only belonged to Dallas now because of Channing's barefoot race to his death. What about his clothes, the paint-stained ones? Was he buried in them? The morbid thoughts rampaged through Dallas, having their way with him. The lump in his throat held in his weeping. Trance-like, Dallas reached into his back pocket and slipped out Channing's Memorare card. He held it up, viewing it and the scene of the accident side by side. Chills came over him at the slim chances of his recovering it and then bringing it back here, to the very place where he'd begged the officer for it, knowing it was on Channing's body at that moment. *Please, God… please…* Dallas poured out his regrets and longed to go back in time.

Dallas glanced towards Mitchell's shop. He should probably see if he could help instead of… this. Feet like lead took him back to the door. The strong smell of coffee hit him as he entered the shop, and he winced at the bells. Dallas went into the garage, where Mitchell worked with his assistant on a vehicle. "Need any help?" Dallas offered, banishing his emotions back outside.

"If you want to, sure. Dallas, this is Chad." Mitchell motioned to his assistant, who wiped his hand off on a rag and extended it in greeting. They shook while Mitchell added, "Dallas is an old friend, visiting for a few days. Which do you want, engine or oil change?"

"Either's fine with me." Dallas grabbed a pair of coveralls from the hooks on the wall.

"I'm kidding; of course, you want the engine." Mitchell grinned. He put Chad on the oil change and had Dallas help him with the engine work. The job was mostly finished, and Dallas's hands flew as it all came back to him. He'd been so lucky to have landed this job. Gazing wistfully at the rows of tools along the wall of the garage, he warmed at the wish of repairing cars full-time again. He savored the next hour as they worked together as in days of old.

As they were closing up the shop, Mitchell worked at the counter while Dallas swept the waiting area. He paused to pour himself the last of the coffee before shutting off the machine, not bothering with the powdered creamer. He'd learned to drink it black in prison on days when there wasn't any real milk to add to it. He took a sip and suddenly saw Channing, standing there at the table by the coffee pot, pouring copious amounts of sugar into his Styrofoam cup as he waited for Dallas to get off work. His hands trembled, and Dallas shook his head to clear the memory. Mitchell had teased Channing that he was going to have to take the cost of the sugar out of Dallas's next paycheck.

"Like old times," Mitchell called out to Dallas.

"Yeah," muttered Dallas, recovering his near-drop of his cup, aching that nothing could ever truly be like old times again. The ghost of Channing's presence here almost smothered him. "I wish…" He set the cup down and told himself to keep breathing through his clenched teeth. "I wish I hadn't totally screwed up!" He flung himself around and paced to the door, but his anger threatened to burst forth right in front of Mitchell. The metal bells taunted him silently from where they hung perpetually on the door's inside handle, and Dallas swiped at them with an open hand. The jangle retaliated with its raucous noise and set his teeth on edge. *Deal with the trauma,* it jeered at him. *You deserve it!*

Mitchell came around the counter with his hands extended. "Hey, hey." His voice was soft but guarded. "You did what you thought was best at the time. I know I sure couldn't think straight when I was just nineteen. Your heart was in the right place, trying to take care of him like a brother."

Dallas swallowed and willed himself not to cry under the steadying pressure of Mitchell's heavy hands on his shoulders, and he remembered coming into work with the black eye his boss had scrutinized in silence. He wasn't that same person anymore. "I hate that I was so impulsive. But I know I can't change it now." He took a slow breath, the rush of desire for God and his holy priesthood riding into his lungs on the air, and he gulped it as urgently as the oxygen.

As Mitchell released his grip, Dallas's shoulders relaxed at the reminder of his calling. "Sorry, Mitch." He scrubbed a hand across his face. "I go back and forth from frozen to pissed off lately. I know I can only go forward trying to see the good that came from my mistakes, like meeting the priest I told you about who helped me really change my life. I don't know if I would've found God otherwise. I was still skeptical of Channing's growing faith right before he died and don't know when or if I would've come around to it. You know, the night before he died, Channing decided to become Catholic—and then I became Catholic in prison instead. It's all mixed up. I'm not totally sure what to think of everything sometimes… but I just keep clinging desperately to God."

Mitchell stooped to retrieve the dustpan. "Do you feel like your faith is a gift Channing gave you?"

Dallas fiddled with the crucifix on the chain around his neck. "Yeah, I do. On my good days. On the bad ones, I feel like it's something I robbed from him, along with his life itself. Not that only one of us could have had faith, but… but we *both* could've had it, together, if I hadn't caused his death."

"Sounds like he did have faith, though," Mitchell mused. "Just hadn't made it official."

Dallas bit his lip rather than going into Channing's rapid faucet baptism.

"You both have it now," Mitchell continued, "except you're still here struggling with it. I get it. When Nancy and I couldn't have kids, it tore her up, and I was mad at God for a long time. I finally decided I just had to get through the pain in life as best I could. I still doubt God sometimes. But there's gotta be something better after this, and that hope is what keeps you going. That's where Channing is now."

Dallas knew that Mitchell and his wife were Anglican, but he hadn't ever heard him discuss matters of faith before. He nodded. "I pray that he is. And I think those of us left here have to support each other in our faith, remind each other not to lose that hope. I didn't realize that about you and Nancy. I'm sorry it's been painful for the two of you. I get being angry with God over it. I've struggled back and forth with being mad at God myself, and sometimes that's hard to admit. I'll offer prayers for you and Nancy, and you know, if you hit a rough patch and need to talk through struggles with faith, I'm always here. You have my number."

"I appreciate it, man, and we'll pray for you, too," Mitchell offered in return. "I don't know that I can recall another man being so upfront about it with me. It can be hard to talk about God, but… I don't know; there's something that makes it a little easier for me to talk to you. Like I said, I can just sense something that's grown in you — like a spiritual kind of maturity or something."

Dallas still hadn't grown accustomed to the comments from people who were drawn to something spiritual about him or said that he was "wise beyond his years." *I'm not being obvious, or pushy, about my conversion, am I?* His dream of the priesthood came to him yet again. He closed his eyes as it washed through his mind, then he put away the broom.

They silently finished in the shop and headed out the front door, locking it up. The jingling bell and the sight of the intersection a few doors down triggered a shudder in Dallas's heart again. Mitchell stood at the door as Dallas solemnly walked down to the spot once more, paused, and crossed himself at the scene of Channing's death.

Mitchell waited for him in silence.

"I'm sorry, Chan," Dallas whispered, tears burning behind his eyes. He turned to follow Mitchell to the truck.

They drove home in the dark. "You sure you can't stay another day or two?" Mitchell asked.

"Wish I could, but I need to get myself ready for work." Dallas drew his lips shut. He had to prove himself. The only way to do that was to move forward with his life now.

"Hope you'll have breakfast with us first," Mitchell invited him. "You sure you can remember how to get to the cemetery on your way out?"

"Yeah, and I've got my road atlas," Dallas replied. "I'm gonna stay old school; don't think I want one of those new computerized GPS thingies."

"They're a pain in the rear to repair, I can tell you that much," Mitchell responded. "Anything computerized is, though. Give me mechanical all the way."

Conversation about the changes in the automotive world over the past few years continued over dinner with Nancy. Dallas went to bed soon after, adding prayers of gratitude for Mitchell's loyalty to him: Dallas Malone, friendless and with no family to speak of at the time of his arrest. At least he had a few compassionate people in his life, however far away they lived.

Dallas tossed and turned, his stomach tied in knots in anticipation. *I've been waiting for over three years to visit Channing's grave. Now I'll be there tomorrow morning.*

Dallas drove southwest towards the cemetery, bins of belongings packed in behind him and stomach revolting against the send-off breakfast Mitchell and Nancy had provided. Should he stop and buy flowers somewhere? *I have no clue about cemetery etiquette.* He sighed. He'd have to do whatever came naturally once he found Channing's grave.

He turned in at the cemetery's entrance drive and followed the narrow lanes that led to the back left of the property. A squirrel suddenly darted out in front of him, and Dallas slammed on the brakes. Something hard hit him in the heel, hurled forward from under his seat, then lodged itself under the gas pedal. Dallas reached down and retrieved a small blue Matchbox car. Channing's BMW—he must've missed it when cleaning under the seats. A lump rose in his throat as he clutched the metal token of Channing's past. Dallas tucked the little car into the pocket of his flannel shirt.

When he saw the tombstones had given way to small metal stakes, he pulled over on the side and turned off the engine. Dallas sat frozen, gripping the steering wheel until his fingers turned numb. He willed himself to get out of the car and search for Channing's grave. *It's one of these… I'm so close now.* Dallas's heart pounded in his chest.

He grabbed two of Channing's old books and slammed the car door, the sound echoing through the empty surrounding greenery. Dallas hesitated and chewed his lower lip, surveying the rows and rows of simple metal markers spanning before him. Only occasionally was there one that had been replaced with a real plaque or that had flowers or some other tribute laid there for the deceased. *Were all these people forgotten, buried here as a last resort because nobody claimed their bodies?* Anger surged up in Dallas at the thought of Channing's mother. *She* could *have claimed his body, but she refused! At least that meant the Catholic officer and his priest had come to Channing's grave,* Dallas relented. *That wouldn't have happened if she'd brought him back to Nevada for burial.*

Dallas stalked towards the tree line at the edge of the cemetery, branches of ancient oaks overhanging the shaded graves. He walked along the top row of markers, reading each name. Then he saw it: Channing's name etched in block print. His breath hitched in his throat.

Dallas dropped to his knees on Channing's grave and read the name and the date of death again and again. This was it—the place where he was in an agony of longing to be during those early weeks of imprisonment. Channing was here, right under this dirt. He collapsed face down on the ground and sobbed hard, shoulders heaving as he lay on Channing's grave, cool grass and patches of rocky dirt pressing between his fingers. He laid a cheek against the ground. This was as close as he could get to his best friend. All the things he'd wanted to say, everything Channing should hear, were all stuck in Dallas's throat. He'd said it all before, but maybe Channing could hear it best now that he was so close. Dallas clung to the irrational thought but could not speak for several minutes.

"I wasn't here for you, Channing!" he finally cried out through his outburst. "You died practically beside me, and I couldn't even go near you, couldn't help you, couldn't make sure they treated your body with respect! I couldn't help bury you. I let you down... my best friend! And you've been here alone for years, *alone!*"

The torrent of misery coursed through Dallas's body and shocked him with a pain so immediate, so intense, so stifling. "I'm finally here, Channing," he sputtered through the tears beyond his control. "I'm here, and I'm so sorry!"

As his grief flowed, memories burned through Dallas like a wildfire. He cried harder when he thought of Channing's childhood, beat a fist against the ground with a snarl when he remembered Channing's father, sighed with tenderness when he recalled some of Channing's childlike mannerisms and his optimism about life, and was struck with awe when he contemplated Channing's intelligence and his seeking of truth, of the strong faith he had gained despite all the troubles in his life.

The gut-wrenching sobs tore him apart again when he remembered the events that had led to the end and his own role in it all. "Y-you were *right*, Channing!" The words choked Dallas as he hitched them out between ragged breaths. His voice rose, and he threw an angry power into it. "Right about God, about faith, because you were *always* right about *everything*, and I was a damn *fool* to try doing everything *my own way!*" Dallas stopped himself short before he let his fists fly — at what, he didn't even know, but he'd probably end up with gashes in his hand if he took out his anger on the grave marker stake. He squeezed his fists to his face instead, exhaling tight, jagged sobs until he had to clutch his middle, willing himself not to throw up. Sprawling face down on the grass, he forced slow breaths. *I am forgiven by God, I am… But Channing's still dead; he's really, really dead!*

Dallas awoke in the afternoon. He shook himself — how long had he been asleep? His face hurt from the strain of crying and his head pounded with a headache. His watch revealed he had been at Channing's grave for several hours now, but his heavy heart anchored him with a need for closure, to *do* something. Dallas glanced side to side for anything to mark the place with more love and compassion than that sterile little metal tag. When he had money, he'd buy him a real grave marker. Inadequacy gnawed at Dallas's heart that Channing deserved so much more than what he could give, had ever given him. *"You can offer prayers for his soul,"* the words of Father Benedict rang in his mind: the best gift, the only true gift, that he could give to Channing now that he was dead. *Leaving him a cross or flowers or a fancy grave marker would only be to make myself feel good.* Dallas bit his lip. Drowned with a sudden vision, he was standing in this spot, arms extended as he read prayers for Channing from a book. He was dressed as a priest.

Dallas forced himself upright, chasing the image from his head, and took a deep breath. He picked up the books and extended them at arm's length in front of him, imaging Channing holding them again. He lifted his gaze to the sky and felt the surge of involuntary desire swelling inside him. He could've talked this through with Channing — his friend would've given guidance on this crazy unrelenting calling. Dallas flipped open Orthodoxy and stared at the notes scrawled in the margin. "Thank you, Channing," he whispered. A warmth crept into his soul. His Catholic faith and Father Benedict's fatherly presence were all because of Channing.

With words stuck in his throat, Dallas opened the other book, *Mere Christianity*. He started to write in the back cover: "Hey Chan — wish I'd read this book when you first told me I should. I finally read it in prison. It was you that planted the seed, and I hate that you died before you could see it. But I made it *home*, Channing. Home to the Church! I told Father Benedict how I'd baptized you. He knew you wanted it, too. He said it counted, that I gave you a *real* sacrament. At one of the worst moments of my life, God let me be the way his grace got to you." The pen stopped moving, and Dallas stared at the grassy grave beneath him. "I'm sorry for everything," he murmured. "I still hate myself for it sometimes. I know God forgives me, and Father said that you'd forgive me too, and that you'd want me to forgive myself. I'm trying, Channing, but it's *hard*. I'm gonna live with it for the rest of my life. Things will never go back to how they were before. I hate that you missed out on the rest of your life, or what it could have been."

Words flowed from Dallas now: about prison and his conversion, about finding the car and his upcoming job, about the Catholic parish near his apartment where he was going to join. He talked himself hoarse until darkness cloaked the cemetery. Dallas shivered without the sun's warmth, and his stomach rumbled. He hadn't eaten since breakfast. A sudden panic washed over him at how late it had gotten, and he half-considered the insane idea of sleeping there overnight.

Dallas jogged to his car in the dark and pulled out the thickest blanket—the one he'd always given to Channing on the coldest nights when they'd slept in the car or camped out. He opened one of the bins. The scented jar candle—yes! And right under Channing's favorite shirt. The soft fabric in his hands was a pleasant reminder of Channing's love of its cozy warmth. Dallas pulled it over his head, grabbed his bag of snacks, and walked back to Channing's grave.

"I can't leave," Dallas mumbled as he wrapped up in the blanket and sat down. "Not yet." He ate a few handfuls of trail mix. *I'll just sit up late praying.* A fervency gripped him. Channing would benefit from prayers uttered right above his body. Dallas lit his makeshift prayer candle. Its small flame danced, creating shadows against the nearby trees. He began with the Rosary, then spent a long time alternating between reciting prayers from memory and pleading with God: for Channing's soul, for release from his own guilt, for the pain to not consume him.

Brr, it's cold. Dallas clutched the blanket tighter under his chin. *Bet it's illegal to build a fire in a cemetery, though. Just a little longer...*

An hour later, all the prayers his lips could utter exhausted from him, Dallas stared at the flickering flame. This was nuts, being in the cemetery so late. His brain said he should have some sense and go, but his heart threatened to shatter if he left. *And where should I go this late?* Dallas pictured himself showing up back on Mitchell's doorstep at midnight.

His face flushed at the thought of explaining himself. He began the Rosary again as his eyes grew heavy. He snapped them back open and shook himself. *Don't fall asleep. You'll leave soon, get a hotel.*

Dallas's chest was sore where Channing's Matchbox car was pressing against him through his pocket. He rolled to his side and fumbled under layers of clothing, retrieving the small metal car. He set it gently beside the metal stake marking the grave, then had second thoughts. What if somebody took it, or if they mowed the cemetery and ran it over? But it was just a toy car. Dallas scowled at himself. The things of this earth are passing. He shouldn't be so sentimentally attached to things. But he pulled his hands into the cuffs of his shirt—Channing's shirt—and savored the warm feeling. The sense of connection with Channing swelled within his heart at wearing it. In his current state, he'd take material reminders as a small comfort to his otherwise bottomless pain over the loss of his friend.

Using a nearby stick, Dallas dug the earth beside the grave marker down a few inches, then gave the Matchbox car one last lingering look in the candlelight. Pressing it into the hole and covering it with the tightly-packed dirt, he said aloud, "Here's your car, Channing. I brought it back to you." Dallas tamped the dirt down until the spot appeared undisturbed. He snapped the stick in half and laid it on the grass in the shape of a cross. *There. Channing died with the faith of the Church in his heart under the cleansing waters of baptism, with a firm belief in God.*

Dallas glanced at his watch—11:30. *Just a little longer...* He drew his knees up to his chest, rested his arms on top of his knees, and pressed his face against the fuzzy gray sleeves. The shirt even smelled like Channing, however faintly. The olfactory memory made Dallas dizzy as he unwillingly breathed Channing in with his senses while tears streamed down his cheeks once again.

I'm being idiotic! He swiped a fist at the nothingness with a scowl. He couldn't be near Channing again on earth no matter how he tried. Nothing would ever be the same again. Being at Channing's grave wasn't really being with him. *Is this supposed to be some weird way of fulfilling the corporal act of mercy that I couldn't do before, to bury the dead?* Dallas pictured himself back at the scene of the truck accident, lifting Channing's body himself, like a soldier would have carried a fallen comrade off the battlefield with him...

"I need to go, but how can I just leave him alone here, God?" Dallas asked aloud. A slight nudge seemed to say, "It's okay. I'm with him now. I've been with him all this time when you haven't been able." Dallas let out a long, shuddery sigh.

"I promise I'll come visit again, Chan," Dallas murmured to the ground beneath him as he picked up the candle and pocketed his empty snack wrappers. He mentally prepared himself to walk away, back towards his waiting car, towards his new home and his waiting job, but guilt like an empty hole inside weighed him down.

"Please, God, please, help me!" he cried, burying his face in a forearm against the ground. "Channing, I wish you could tell me it's okay for me to leave you. It's felt like you were out here waiting for me that whole time I was in prison. Like it was *me* who had left *you*, not the other way around. Now that the proof's staring me in the face that you've really and truly been dead all these years... I just don't know what I'm gonna *do* with my life! How do I start over again, and *without* you?"

Dallas jerked his head up at the growl of a car engine nearby. He swiveled around to face headlights moving in his direction. Then blue lights flashed. *A police car.*

Dallas's pulse quickened and his throat went dry as the car stopped, and an officer with a bright flashlight got out and approached him. He sat up and ran his fingers through his hair. He must seem deranged to the outsider's eye. Scrambling to his feet, he greeted the officer.

"Good evening." Dallas adjusted the blanket on his shoulders, praying he didn't look as awkward as he felt.

"Evening? It's nearly midnight. Just wanted to check and see if you were okay." The officer scanned Dallas cautiously. "Got a call from one of the caretakers saying somebody had been hanging around this section of the cemetery for hours now. Your car?" he asked, motioning to the Isuzu with his patrol car parked behind it.

"Yes, sir, that's mine."

"Are you in any kind of trouble, or homeless... Can I help you somehow?"

"No, I'm not homeless," Dallas put in quickly. "I just needed to visit the grave of my friend. I hadn't been able to come here since his death until now, and... it's just been really hard for me to do," Dallas finished with a swallow.

The officer was silent a moment, then sighed. "Well, I'm really sorry about your friend. I can see that visiting his grave has been important to you. However, I have to inform you that it's technically illegal for you to sleep here overnight."

Dallas's insides tightened up at the word "illegal." He told himself to stay calm and not be an idiot.

"I don't think you mean any trouble, though, so I'm just going to tell you to go ahead and move on. You can come back and visit during the daytime in the future, but you're not allowed to stay overnight. Do you understand?"

"Yes, sir," Dallas responded. "I'm sorry, I didn't even think about that. I just found myself unable to say goodbye... Guess I needed a little prodding."

"I'll walk with you down to your car, then," the officer offered. "Do you need a private moment to finish up?"

Gratefully, Dallas nodded. "Yes, thank you."

The police officer stepped aside and waited, the beam of his light trained on the ground.

Dallas turned back to the grave and knelt down one last time and whispered, "Channing, did you ask God to do this, like a sign to help me leave? Okay, I'll go now. Thank you for everything—for your whole life—and for being a gift to me." Dallas flicked on his lighter with one hand and brushed his other across the marker with Channing's name on it. "I'm sorry, and I'll always be sorry, Channing." Dallas's throat felt as if he'd swallowed sawdust, and he wiped away a trickling tear. "I'll always pray for your soul. And I'll be back again, I promise. I... I love you."

Dallas stood to go for real this time. He stepped to the foot of the grave and stared down at the grass covering its surface, what could have become tonight's morbid sleeping accommodations.

"Bye." Dallas made the sign of the cross, then followed the officer down to his car. Opening his door, he gave one more glance up the dark incline of earth towards Channing's grave as he got in. Dallas started the engine and drove away.

"Has it been difficult, Dallas?" Father Benedict asked the question point-blank. "It's okay to admit if it has been so."

The two men sat in the rectory kitchen at the basilica in Denver on Sunday morning. Dallas had finally taken a long weekend to visit and attend Mass with Father after several weeks of dedicated labor on the construction crew.

He didn't respond right away. Dallas suspected that his mentor wanted a different answer than his mind was preparing, thinking over the time since his release. Going through Channing's belongings from the bins had been mentally exhausting. In fact, he'd put it off until finishing his first week of work. Facing a weekend with nothing to do, he'd decided to at least dig out some sheets for his bed—not that he'd made it through one night without moving to the floor or getting up to pace the apartment for a couple hours until he wore himself out enough to crash. Nearly two months post-prison, and he was finally staying in bed all night most of the time.

"Work's been good, strenuous but satisfying," Dallas began, cracking his knuckles. "I feel it in my muscles at the end of each day—tearing out cabinets and carpets, knocking down walls. I'm picking up on everything the boss asks of me. He seems happy with my work. And there's a certain dignity in doing a job well and supporting yourself."

The priest pursed his lips and studied Dallas a moment. "You are able to pay all your expenses with your paycheck?"

"Oh yeah, I'm making it work," Dallas replied. "I'm not wanting for anything."

"How about your life aside from work?"

"I've really just been trying to focus on the basics." Dallas avoided the priest's gaze, suddenly interested in the pattern on the tablecloth. "In my downtime after work, I'm doing a lot of reading, and I started praying the Divine Office. There's a nearby park where I've been walking and jogging. And, of course, I'm going to Mass on Sundays, and I've made it to daily Mass a handful of times, too."

"But has it been difficult?" Father repeated. "I mean, the actualization of returning to life in the outside world and how everything has changed for you since Channing's death?"

Dallas ran his fingertips across the thick texture of the knee of Channing's maroon corduroys he wore, under the table where Father couldn't see. Good thing Channing had liked his clothes loose and baggy or else they wouldn't have fit. He thought back to unloading the bins, lifting each piece of Channing's clothing, preserving them all in his bottom dresser drawer, and wearing certain articles while leaving others untouched. He'd seen it as some weird form of self-inflicted therapy: holding each item, remembering, crying over a half-empty bottle of vitamin C tablets, his pathetic attempt at keeping Channing healthy...

Father Benedict reached across the table to touch Dallas's arm, and he started. He met the priest's concerned gaze.

"You know..." Dallas paused, chewing his lower lip. He knew better than to bring up his potential vocation again—it was too soon. "Going to Minnesota and visiting his grave—that was hard. But since then, I've just been trying to move on. To not think about much of anything. I'm working, saving, saying my prayers, reading, going to church, exercising. So, I guess I'm doing all right."

Father Benedict looked Dallas in the eye. "Are you content? Do you have peace?"

Dallas blinked and then looked away. "I don't know. Maybe." Inside, he criticized himself. He was really just going through the motions. The pull towards the priesthood had persisted since his release. If anything, it was growing more insistent. But Dallas would keep himself occupied so as not to confront the kinds of questions Father Benedict was asking, hoping that the old adage of "time heals all wounds" would hold true if only he could pass enough of it to distance himself from all that had happened. But deep down, a restlessness swelled within him that he was ignoring.

An hour later, Dallas sat in a pew near the front, listening to Father proclaim today's Gospel reading and wishing he didn't have to drive back to Texas today. The words enunciated from the old priest's lips hit him: "No one who prefers father or mother to me is worthy of me. No one who prefers son or daughter to me is worthy of me. Anyone who does not take his cross and follow in my footsteps is not worthy of me. Anyone who finds his life will lose it; anyone who loses his life for my sake will find it."

Dallas bit his lip as the words hung in his mind. Was he preferring Channing to God? Yes—he was, by his actions, by his inability to let go of the past. He'd been ready to lose his life for Channing, but would he give his life for God? He read the verses from the open missal on his lap again before adding a silent plea. *Please, help me put my focus in the right place, to not despair when things and people and situations aren't perfect in my life.*

"But that's what makes me human, right, God?" Dallas whispered to himself. "I fall short, I fall into despair, and I'm broken. I want to use my time on earth to work towards heaven, eternity. Please help me." Dallas stared as Father Benedict lifted the book high, proclaiming, "The Gospel of the Lord." That image of himself as a priest floated again through Dallas's mind, a peacefulness like the calm of a still pond at sunrise. A warmth crept from his toes to his head, and he closed his eyes and sighed. *Can it be true, God? I promise, I'll explore that possibility down the road, once I prove I'm really okay here in the real world again, okay with Life After Channing... but I'm not ready yet. I'm still picking up his favorite strawberry frosted Pop-tarts in the store before I catch myself, and...* Dallas gulped as he gazed at the stained glass window to his right, the same one Channing had stood beneath in awe that lifetime of four years ago, enraptured by the antique chalice Father had shown to him. A tingle ran down his neck—that golden cup hadn't been a premonition for Channing. It had been meant for him, Dallas Malone, left behind. Then the doubt fought against the certainty: *You're only a couple months post-prison—no way are you cut out for this. Not yet, anyway.*

Back at work on Monday in Texas, Father Benedict's words echoed in Dallas's mind. The priest had told him to please seek him out, or another priest closer to home, if he needed to talk. But talking it through wasn't going to change anything. Dallas bit his lip as he stared at the flames of his debris fire, burning itself down on the pavement. He stuck his hands in his pockets and reentered the building. *Gotta just plow forward now, and stop focusing on my feelings about the past.*

His stoic personality had become obvious to the rest of the crew. One of the guys, two years younger and the same height, watched Dallas return mechanically to the skeleton wall and pick up a saw. "You like fire, huh?" he asked.

Dallas shrugged slightly and gave a little nod, pulling back and forth to slice through a two-by-four.

"You're so quiet, man. I worry about you."

Dallas paused and smiled warily. "Thanks, Mike. I'm okay, though."

"Maybe you need to loosen up and have some fun with us sometimes," Mike went on. "You said you just moved here when you first started this job, right? Do you know anyone around here, got any family nearby?"

"Nope." Dallas yanked a stud out of the wall and started a new pile on the floor. "It's just me." He hesitated, glancing at the open expression in Mike's slate-blue eyes. "Actually, to be totally upfront with you... I'm just trying to rebuild my life. I was in prison for a few years before this. I grew up a lot while I was there. But if I'm quiet, it's just that I'm concentrating on moving ahead and doing my job. I'm quiet by nature, anyway."

Mike was silent a moment. "Hey, no problem that you were in jail. Doesn't bother me. But man, you're *so* quiet. This is like the most you've ever talked. Maybe you should come to lunch with us sometimes. You're not really so new here anymore — it's been what, like six or seven weeks? It's time we all got to be friendlier with you!"

"I appreciate it," Dallas replied, "but I'm trying to save every penny right now, which is why I never go out."

"You can just bring your lunch from home into McDonald's when we go. No problem."

Dallas was intrigued by Mike's constant "no problem" attitude. His laid-back style was inviting. Dallas relented.

"Okay, sure. I'll come today."

"Come where?" Rodrigo, another guy on the crew, had just walked in. "You comin' to lunch with us?" He mopped his brow with his forearm, making his dark hair stick up.

"Yeah." Dallas shrugged. "Mike just invited me. If you guys don't mind, that is."

"Hey, the new guy can join in, sure!" Rodrigo slapped him on the back. "We didn't know if you were interested. Be glad to have you."

"Thanks." Dallas added, "I know I don't always seem very approachable. I'm just trying to get back on my feet right now, so I'm really focused on the job, is all."

Mike tossed a nail in the air and tried to keep it aloft by batting it upwards with his palm. "He just got out of prison before getting hired."

Dallas cringed. *So, maybe too laid back.*

"Hey, cool," Rodrigo said.

"It's not something I'm proud of." Dallas's eyes fell to the floor as heat crept up his neck. "I'd prefer not to talk about it."

"Sure, no problem," Mike said again.

Just then, their other three co-workers joined them.

"So, we're all going to lunch?" Alex elbowed Rodrigo. "As soon as Bossman says so?"

The foreman overheard his crew from the next room, where he was assessing what needed to be done next. "You guys at a good stopping point?" he called. "Head on out if you are."

"Yep," replied Mike, who Dallas had noted was the unofficial leader and the main line of communication between the foreman and the rest of the crew. "Let's go." The others all fell in behind him in exiting the building.

"Wanna ride with us?" Rodrigo asked Dallas. He always brought Alex, who was his brother, and one other guy, Julian. Mike and the remaining member of the crew, Stan, usually rode together in Mike's pickup truck.

"Sure." Dallas slid into the back seat of the Toyota Corolla.

As requested, nobody pried into Dallas's prison history over lunch. Sitting at the table with a bunch of other guys in their early to mid-twenties, Dallas should fit right into this, his peer group, and yet the atmosphere seemed impenetrable. Maybe he should let his guard down and try to make some friends. It sure had taken him long enough in prison, and now he was starting all over. In a way, being in prison was simpler, where everything was done for him. Fewer choices made for an easier life. Dallas pushed the thoughts aside. He didn't really wish he was still in jail, of course.

At a lull in the conversation, Dallas asked the guys if they'd always lived in the area. All of them had except Julian, who had moved from Mexico two years ago and mostly conversed with Rodrigo and Alex in Spanish.

Mike took a slurp through his straw. "Where are you from, originally —Dallas? Is that why it's your name?"

"I've never actually been there." Dallas shrugged slightly. "I'm from northern Nevada."

"Your family still there?" asked Stan.

"Nope," Dallas said. "I never met my father, and my mom… well, I haven't seen her in years, since I was 19. She always taught me not to rely on her, to be independent. So, it's just me."

"Man, that's kinda sad," Alex said. "But me and Rodrigo, sometimes we feel like our mom's in our business *too* much. And our grandmother… like, we're grown up now."

"But we live with them." Rodrigo snagged the last French fry from his brother. "So, that's that. Family is family, for better or for worse."

"We'll move out sometime." Alex sat up straighter.

"Sure, pipsqueak," added Mike, and the others laughed. "You'd be runnin' back to your momma in a heartbeat."

The trials and pleasures of living within a big family were as foreign to Dallas as it must be to the crew that he had no family to speak of. Other people had mothers and fathers and even grandparents, all thinking about them and involved in their lives. *Does my mom think of me, wherever she is?* He pushed down a pang of jealousy. Dallas's grandparents, the only ones he'd known of, were dead. Channing had been his only substitute for family. At least he had Father Benedict and Mitchell, and even Smith and Pedro from prison — as far away as they all were — as sort of stand-ins now. But real family ties were something Dallas had never given much time to thinking about before.

The quietest of the group, Julian, spoke up. "You have girlfriend?" he asked Dallas.

"Nah." Dallas's gazed flickered to the window.

"Duh, he's been in prison." Stan drummed his fingers on the table. "Maybe we can find him one."

"Julian's the one with a steady girlfriend." Mike leaned closer on his elbows and threw in, "She's hot."

Dallas felt that the conversation was taking an uncomfortable turn but didn't see what he could do about it.

"Yeah, Julian likes his girlfriend, but the rest of us just like girls," Mike continued, laughing. "Hey, speaking of—look at her!" He nudged Stan, nodding towards a girl who had just entered the restaurant. As she passed their table, Mike gave a low whistle, and Alex called out, "Hello, beautiful!"

The girl glanced their way and rolled her eyes, continuing to another table. The guys all laughed and jabbed each other with their elbows. Dallas kept his eyes on his sandwich and concentrated on chewing.

"Come on, Dallas, lighten up," Mike said in a playful voice. "Yep, guys—we need to find him a girl for sure! You're outta practice right now, huh?" He nudged Dallas, and they all laughed. Dallas tried a faint smile to keep the peace. They were just trying to include him. Maybe this was an isolated incident, just them showing off in front of the new guy.

Back at the worksite, Dallas hoisted debris onto his shoulder and carried it out to the dumpster. He heaved the broken pieces of boards and drywall over the side. A sense of shared camaraderie settled in the atmosphere as Dallas jumped in to help the others with the remaining tasks and then wished them all a good evening as they headed for their cars at the end of the day. "And thanks for inviting me to lunch," he added.

"Let's do it again tomorrow," Mike replied. "You can have some fun with us, man." He smiled.

Dallas opened his apartment door later that evening and picked up his prayer book first thing, dropping onto his couch. He concentrated on vespers, then shut the book and his eyes. "I want to be friendly to people," he murmured, "but God, please help me do it in the right way. Help me remember to keep close to you when I'm in the midst of worldly things."

Dallas went to his room and picked up the brown scapular and accompanying pamphlet from his bedside table. He'd bought it along with his prayer book at the gift shop at Sacred Heart, the parish he was attending. He turned it over in his hands. Opening the pamphlet, the words leaped at Dallas from the paper: *"Fireproof—Our Lady's Armor against Hell. Whosoever dies wearing it shall not suffer eternal fire. It shall be a sign of salvation, a protection in danger and pledge of peace."* Dallas read on. *"The brown scapular should be worn with a sincere devotion to Mary and imitation especially of her virtues of humility, chastity, and prayerfulness." Fire... protection from danger, growth in virtue – that's what I need.* Wearing it would be a physical reminder, on him always. Dallas tucked the scapular into his pocket and pledged to get it blessed by the priest after morning Mass tomorrow so he could start wearing it.

The next day at the jobsite, Dallas watched for opportunities to connect with the other guys on the crew. *They want to be your friend.* The assumption felt weak when put up against his shyness. *Everything I think of saying sounds dumb.*

Right after lunch break, he forced a question in the lull between the screech of the circular saw. "Hey, did I hear you guys talking about lifting weights a few minutes ago?" He turned to face Mike and Alex, scanning each face.

"Yeah, why?" Mike set aside the board and reached for another. "You too? Do you belong to a gym?"

"No, costs too much." Dallas lined up the tape measure as Mike held the board steady. "But I have some weights and a bar in my apartment, one of those that fits in the doorway to do pull-ups on."

"You any good at pull-ups?" Alex nudged his way between them and marked the line to cut with a pencil. "Mike's the pull-up king here." He jerked a thumb towards Mike, who puffed up his chest and feigned a modest wave of the hand.

Dallas smiled. "I'm pretty decent," he said, guarded. "I've liked doing them since I was a kid."

"How about a friendly wager?" Mike released the board and stepped back in between Alex and Dallas. "There's some bars over in Hamilton Park. What do you say?"

"You're on," Dallas answered with a firm handshake. "I don't want to show you up or anything..." Adrenaline tingled inside him at the chance for a friendly man-to-man competition. The gleam in Mike's eyes returned the sentiment of eagerness.

"How much?" Alex put in.

"I don't want to bet for money." Dallas raised his hands, palms out. "You guys know I'm trying to be frugal and keep myself out of trouble. I'd just do it for sheer fun."

"How is pull-ups fun?" Julian asked with a frown, joining the group.

They had a laugh over this. Julian made it clear that he wasn't a fan of manual labor, although he did do his share of the work.

"So, after work tonight?" Mike asked, eyes dancing. He flexed his arms and combed a hand through his thick dirty-blond hair. "Hey guys, you wanna come watch me cream Malone in a pull-up competition?"

Dallas smiled to himself as he turned back to the saw.

At 5:00, they headed to the park together in three cars. Alex rode with Dallas and made him laugh by attempting a pep talk.

"Mike, he's real strong," Alex cautioned. "I mean, you see his arm muscles, right? He can do lots of pullups. But you, Dallas, you're, like, real determined. You work hard. So maybe you can beat him. I'll keep count of you, and Rodrigo, he's gonna count for Mike. What really matters is the final number. So don't go too fast, that doesn't matter. Final number is what counts." Alex's serious enthusiasm was catching, and Dallas was getting psyched up. *Maybe I can fit in with this group after all...*

They arrived at the park and got out of the car. Rodrigo yelled to his little brother, "My guy's gonna beat the crap outta yours!"

"Like hell he is!" retorted Alex.

Julian and Stan were each going to keep count silently, as backups. Mike grinned cockily as he strutted up and extended a hand towards Dallas. "Good luck."

"Likewise," Dallas replied, eyes full of steady confidence as he shook on it.

At first, the pace was dead even, both men doing sets of fifteen reps between rests. It was clear to Dallas that they'd competed before to determine Mike as the best. He prayed that if he did win that Mike wouldn't feel threatened by it.

After a while, Dallas slowed his pace. He fell a few counts behind, settling into a steady rhythm. A few minutes later, Mike slowed as well. Dallas pulled ahead by one, the stretch of rigorous work tightening his arm and chest muscles.

Alex, ever excitable, danced around beneath them, counting loudly and cheering for Dallas. Rodrigo, not to be outdone by his brother, belted out Mike's current number. Both were over a hundred now. They had agreed to a final time limit of an hour, if neither quit before that. From the sound of it, Dallas figured none of them had ever done pullup sets for an entire hour before. He smiled inwardly.

Now Mike struggled to pull his chin above the bar, his sets growing smaller and his rest times lengthening. He had fallen behind by almost twenty and was only managing two or three pullups per set. Finally, at forty minutes, he couldn't manage one more. "I think I'm done in," he groaned as he dropped to the ground, shaking out his aching arms. Alex cheered like a maniac as Dallas pulled up again and again, completing a set of ten before dropping for a short rest.

"Now you're just showin' off," Stan scoffed.

"No, let's see if he can really go for a whole hour!" Rodrigo encouraged as Dallas jumped to grab the bar over his head again. "Want to, Malone?"

"Sure," grunted Dallas as he did another pullup. He lifted his body mechanically, the usual rush of endorphins thrilling him. He closed his eyes and saw himself doing pull-ups on the tree branch with Channing hanging onto his feet, trying to playfully pull him down. Dallas smiled and reveled in the memory, even as a pang pricked him in the heart. This wasn't a betrayal to Channing—of course, he was irreplaceable. *But this is reality. I can still have fun again.* He pressed on, heart thudding and arms straining.

Finally, they began counting down the last minute. Dallas was somewhere far away; he couldn't even tell how many pull-ups Alex was calling out as nothing but his own pulse reverberated in his head. They all started cheering, and even Mike wore a huge grin as he called out, "You win, man. And you didn't just *win*. You *clobbered* me!"

Dallas had paused so he could hear what they were saying and was able to understand Alex, who was screaming, "Seven hundred twenty-nine!" over and over again. Dallas, smirking, pulled his chin over the bar to make it an even number before dropping to the ground. The crew crowded around, congratulating him.

"New champion!" Mike declared, lifting Dallas's weary arm up in victory. "Man, I don't know how you did that!"

Dallas shrugged, examining his raw palms. "Dunno, I've just always been able to." The open blisters would sting like crazy later, but it was worth it.

"Hey, celebration at the bar! What do you say?" Mike offered. "Dallas's drinks are on me!"

"Let's do it Friday," insisted Stan. "When we don't hafta get up early for work the next day."

A hearty affirmation went around the group.

"You game for Friday, Malone?" Mike punched him in the upper arm with mock aggression. "Late night parrr-tay!"

Dallas returned the punch. "Yeah, let's do it." He ran a blistered hand through his sweaty hair and grinned, riding the high of acceptance in the group. Maybe friendship wouldn't be so difficult after all.

The next morning, Dallas was sweeping debris from the floor when he noticed Mike pull out a magazine. Blinking, he suddenly woke from his tunnel vision of the previous weeks. *I've made myself so focused on work and blocking out my feelings that I've been oblivious that those magazines Mike and Rodrigo are always goggling over are porn.* Now seeing him as a buddy, Mike sauntered over and stuck the magazine under Dallas's nose.

"Don't want to leave you out." He grinned up at Dallas.

The image had already assaulted Dallas's mind, but he forced his gaze away. "I, uh, don't really go in for that stuff."

"You're not gay, are you?" Mike's jaw dropped. "You sure don't seem like it."

Dallas felt his face redden as he recalled similar insults being hurled at Channing when they were in school. "No." Dallas tried to keep his voice cool. "I just think it's wrong to look at women that way." The newly-blessed scapular felt obvious to Dallas under his shirt, and he imagined the Mother of God's disappointment at his co-workers' immoral hobby.

"Ain't hurting anyone just to look," Mike said, "but if you don't wanna see it, no problem. The other guys will enjoy it just fine." He motioned to Stan, Rodrigo, and Julian, who were just coming back in from a smoke break. Showing them the picture and making lewd remarks, Mike commented, "See, Dallas? Julian likes it even though he's got a girlfriend. She's hotter than your girl, huh, Julian?"

"No, my girlfriend, she is better," Julian said in his heavy accent, "but this one, she is nice."

Mike laughed raucously and flipped to another page.

"What, Dallas doesn't want to see?" Rodrigo's eyes flitted between Mike and Dallas as he picked up on the tension between them. "Like, seriously?"

Dallas crossed his arms over his chest and tried to look firm. "Yeah. Pornography is wrong."

"Too bad," put in Stan with a laugh, "I guess we can't make any Porno for Pyros jokes about Mr. Head Pyromaniac here." The others burst out laughing.

Dallas bit back a snort at the reference to a band Channing had hated, recalling his diatribe about how Deconstruction had been so much better.

"Malone thinks he's too good for us." Stan nudged Mike, who flipped a page in the magazine and showed Stan.

"No problem, more for us." Mike chuckled.

A sick feeling gnawed at Dallas's stomach. *I want out of here. Maybe I should tell the boss, but will he care?* In a moment, his hope was deflated when the foreman entered the room.

"Okay, okay, put away your girly magazine, Mike," he drawled. "You've stared at it long enough today, haven't you?"

"But you wanna see this chick, Bossman." Mike held the open magazine up to him.

"Real nice, Mikey, thanks." The foreman stared at the photograph with a grin. "But I might just have to keep it myself if you don't get on with bustin' up that wall."

"I read ya." Mike rolled up the magazine and stuck it into his back pocket.

Dallas surveyed the scene as if outside himself, juxtaposing the image of Channing with *Orthodoxy* sticking out of his back pocket with the reality before him. *Am I really here? Are these my friends now? How did I end up with* this *as my life?*

Friday afternoon arrived. Dallas had kept his mouth shut and his eyes on his work the rest of the week any time a magazine had been passed around. He'd managed civil conversation, even a few jokes otherwise, sensing Mike's respect for his win in the pull-up challenge in spite of Tuesday's mocking of his moral stance. And the excited discourse about Friday's trip to the bar built over the week, letting Dallas know he hadn't totally botched the attempt at friendship, at least. Maybe eventually he could even get to know them well enough to influence them for the better, or else just keep ignoring their porn habits.

At 6:30, Dallas and the rest of the crew walked into the bar. Mike clapped him on the shoulder. "Whaddaya want to start with, Pull-up Champ?"

Dallas, reluctant to admit ignorance of beer varieties, told Mike to choose. A few minutes later, they were all drinking and talking.

Alex's voice had become a loudspeaker once he finished his second beer, blaring in Dallas's ear. Stan raised an eyebrow and leaned over to Dallas. "We don't just refer to Alex as the baby because he's the youngest. He's also a lightweight when it comes to drinking!"

"Whatever, man!" shouted Alex, turning towards the bar to order his third.

After 8:00, the bar got busier. Alex started pulling Dallas up to strangers, staggering.

"This guy can do seven hundred pull-ups in one hour!" Alex broadcasted repeatedly to everyone. "Isn't that amazing? He's amazing!!"

Dallas shook off Alex and the attention he was attracting. He wove through the noisy room towards the other members of the crew. Rodrigo, Mike, and Stan were at the bar getting more drinks, and Mike offered Dallas his second. His low level of experience gave him pause. He wanted to be social but didn't want to overdo it, either. He would just nurse the second one until they left.

As Dallas accepted the beer, Mike nudged Stan and jerked his head towards the end of the bar. A young blond woman, a short skirt accentuating her full hips, stood chatting with the bartender. She caught their looks and flashed a smile. They whispered lewd comments to each other as they sized her up.

Uh-oh, this sounds like trouble. Dallas turned to scan the room for the safety of Alex's ramblings, but Mike grabbed his shoulder and pulled him back.

"Hey," he said, as if he'd just struck upon a great idea, "let's go get her for Dallas!"

Stan nodded, eyes wide and grinning.

Dallas resisted, shaking his head. "I'm not interested."

"What? She's *gorgeous!*" Mike glanced over again. "How can you *not* be interested? I've seen her in here before, and she seems pretty easy. Hey, she's looking at you again!"

Again? Dallas couldn't stop himself from stealing a glance and, catching the woman's eyes, pulled his gaze away, cheeks warm as the color rose in his face.

Stan nudged him. "Don't you think she's pretty?"

"Um… well, yeah," Dallas admitted, scuffing a toe of his boot against the floor, "but…"

"Then what's the problem?" Mike asked, arms crossed.

"Like you said, I'm out of practice with women," Dallas tried to talk his way out of their plotting.

"And that's why we'll help you!" Stan leaned in close. "Haven't you noticed she's been looking at you off and on since she came in?"

Mike got her attention and beckoned her over. Dallas searched with panicked eyes for a place to slide away, if only he could locate Julian, Rodrigo, or Alex. He spotted them on the other side of the room, but now Mike was in between Dallas and the approaching woman. *Too late.*

Mike and Stan were used to talking to women like this. They fell into easy conversation with her, and she hung on their words and giggled at everything they said. Dallas kept silent. *She really does keep looking at me…* His heart raced, and he self-consciously ran a hand over his close-cropped hair.

"Hey, lemme introduce you to Dallas Malone." Mike nudged Dallas forward a step towards the woman. "He's still kinda new in town."

"Dallas — what a great name!" It rolled off her tongue, reverberating in his ears and paralyzing him as he stared at her red-tinted lips pronouncing it with emphasis. "I'm Samantha Stanton."

Dallas was stuck now. He nodded. "Nice to meet you, Samantha." His eyes roamed down her entire body, clothed in a quantity of fabric measurable in square inches, and he fought to regain custody of them. He forced a polite smile as he made himself focus on her eyes, heavily rimmed with makeup.

Stan leaned close to Samantha. "He thinks you're pretty." He turned and winked at Dallas with a smirk, and Mike chuckled beside him. Dallas wanted to sink into the floor as Samantha's smile grew.

"Well, Dallas, since you're new here," Samantha's singsongy voice danced in his ears, "I'd be *more* than happy to help you get comfortable in town." She slipped closer, staring him down intensely with bright blue eyes.

Did she mean what he thought she meant? Dallas froze and gulped.

"We'll let you two get acquainted!" Mike said gleefully, pulling Stan along with him towards a group of three women.

Dallas raised both eyebrows at Mike at this abandonment and then shot him a contemptuous glare, and he caught the mischievous merriment in Mike's eyes. *They've left me right where they want me!*

Dallas was a deer in the headlights as he turned back to Samantha, who smiled up at him coyly. He glanced side to side and shifted his drink to the other hand but saw no easy way out of this.

"You're real cute, Dallas," she gushed. "Your face is so expressive! So, are you actually *from* Dallas?"

He mentally sighed. Why had he decided to live in Texas with a name like his? He cleared his throat and commanded himself to relax his posture. *Just be normal; have a conversation with her.*

"Actually, no. I don't know why my mother gave me the name. I think she just liked the sound of it. I'm originally from Nevada." Dallas took a sip of his beer.

Samantha giggled. "You sound so funny when you say it like that: Nuh-*va*-duh!"

Dallas furrowed his brow. "Why, how do you say it?"

"Nuh-*vaw*-duh." Samantha's full lips exaggerated each syllable as she leaned in close to Dallas. "But if you're from there, your pronunciation must be the correct one. What brought you to Texas?"

Dallas examined his beer, turning it round and round in his hands. "Uh, I just drove here." *Stupid, that sounds stupid!* "I, uh, like to drive, and this is where I ended up." *Shoot, that sounds even dumber…*

Samantha laughed. "So, you're a mysterious wanderer who came from Nevada. You like to gamble? I've been dying to see Vegas! I've always hoped somebody would take me out there one day!"

Is she dropping hints? "I lived further north than that," he said quickly, rubbing the back of his neck with his free hand. "I've only been through Vegas briefly, never been to the casinos."

"Oh, really?" Samantha locked eyes with Dallas. "You'll have to go back and hit Vegas sometime. You know, there's not much to do in this town. It'd be a great trip to take…" She slipped her hand into his and gave it a little squeeze.

Dallas swallowed and gave her a nervous smile as a warmth spread throughout his body. "Uh…yeah, I just started this job recently, in construction. Mike and Stan, and those other guys over there," he said, nodding towards Julian, Rodrigo, and a very loud and drunk Alex, "we're all on the crew together, and—"

"So, you like to work with your hands?" Samantha studied the one she held, rubbing it gently with her thumb. Did she notice the scars? Surely the still-healing blisters were obvious. "I bet you have to be really strong for construction work. I'm not surprised; your virility has been calling to me from across the room all night!" She shot him a flirtatious smile of admiration.

Dallas's mouth fell open at the big word. He quickly clamped it shut again. The only time he could recall its verbal use was when Channing was acting out the role of Odysseus meeting the Sirens. *"It comes from 'vir,' the Latin word for man,"* Dallas heard Channing's authoritative explanation, and Samantha's compliments had him feeling more like a man than ever. He squirmed at the conflict between his discomfort and the gratification of his self-image wrapped up in her flattery. And the way she was holding his hand... It felt... nice.

"So, do you guys do renovations?" Samantha swayed from side to side as she spoke. "Tell me about it."

"Uh, we really just destroy stuff..."

Samantha's laugh rang through the air. "You're hilarious, Dallas!"

Dallas set down his drink and pulled at his collar with his free hand, hoping the other one wouldn't start sweating. He considered how to politely drop her hand but couldn't conjure the method—or desire. "Well, we remove walls, tear out carpet, cabinets... that kind of thing."

"I've seen the others in here," Samantha commented, "but I've never noticed you with them before."

"No, this is my first time here. So..." Dallas racked his brain for something conversational. "You come here often yourself?" He cringed inside at the lame question. "I mean, is it a decent place to hang out?"

"I'm here most Fridays." Samantha squeezed Dallas's hand again. "And I think your first visit tonight has made this *more* than just a decent place to hang out." She stared deeply into his eyes.

Dallas felt his throat going dry. "Umm... anyway... since I just started this job, I don't have time for much else. So, uh, I definitely won't be going to Vegas anytime soon." Dallas stared into his drink, trying to steer the conversation back to more stable ground. "I've gotta earn some money and get ahead." *There, closed that topic.* He exhaled.

"Well, you seem so responsible, Dallas," Samantha practically purred. "You save up awhile, and we can go explore Vegas together. It'll be an adventure!"

Dallas took a swig of beer, fighting the urge to pace like a caged tiger. Samantha pressed up closely to him, and he took a step back. "W-well," he stammered, blushing, "we only just met…"

"And isn't that why you're at a bar, to meet people?" Still attached to his hand, Samantha had followed his reverse step with a forward one of her own. Dallas inched back again, bumped into a bar stool, and sat down on it, nowhere else to go.

"I guess so," he muttered, "and to have a drink with my friends…" He freed his hand from the warmth of her grasp and set his glass down on the bar, tucking both hands into his pockets. Maybe they weren't his friends at all, setting him up like this. He desperately wished for Channing, a hopeless wish.

"Well, I'd *love* to get to know you better." Samantha ran her hand along his thigh.

Dallas shot up from his seat, nearly overturning the barstool as Mike, Stan, and Rodrigo sauntered alongside him.

"Your friend's shy." Samantha turned to Mike with a giggle.

"He sure is," Mike agreed, "which probably makes him all the more intriguing, right?" Mike sidled up beside Dallas and nudged him in the ribs with his elbow, throwing him an encouraging side glance.

"*Very* intriguing." Samantha stared Dallas down again.

He broke away from her gaze, noticed her smooth legs and short skirt, and jerked his eyes back up again. Not knowing what else to do, he tried a desperate angle.

"I'm really not intriguing." He shrugged. "Unless you think getting to know an ex-con is interesting. Really, I'm not that great a guy." He crossed his arms across his chest, but Samantha ignored his standoffish posture.

"*You* were in *prison*?" Samantha fawned over him. "That's even *more* intriguing!" She slipped a hand between his chest and his arms, hanging on him. Mike put a fresh beer in her other hand.

Stupid! What makes you think a woman acting like this would be turned off by a criminal record? And they were all way too enthusiastic over something he wasn't proud of. Dallas's mood darkened.

Samantha noticed. She stared up at him, studying his expression. "I'm sorry," she whispered in a tender voice amidst the laughs and raucous talking. Her wide eyes softened. "Was it really bad there?"

Dallas's heart did something funny inside his chest, but then he tensed as Stan threw an arm around his shoulders.

"Dallas is the nicest ex-con you ever did lay eyes on!" Stan's tone was sickly sweet. Dallas squirmed and slipped his hands into his pockets, freeing himself from Samantha's clinging, but they still had him against the bar. "He don't even objectify women, you know." The other guys laughed.

"Well, that sounds real sweet, now, Dallas," Samantha cooed. "Maybe you can show me how much of a gentleman you really are. Finish your drink, and you can drive me home."

Dallas's eyes widened, and his heart pounded in his chest.

Mike was in his ear now. "Take her, Dallas! She's practically *throwing* herself at you!" The others hooted and jeered, sounds that made Dallas think of a pen of pigs.

"You won't be sorry," Rodrigo was telling Samantha. "Dallas, he's real smooth. Once you get to know him, he's not so shy. He's just not so used to women, you know, after bein' locked up so long. We could tell you had the hots for him the second you walked in here."

Dallas closed his eyes and wished he were anywhere else—even in prison. At least this couldn't happen there. He gave up a quick prayer. This had already gone too far! He opened his eyes again to the scene he had to end, now at the risk of offending Samantha, alienating his co-workers, and denying his own hormones. The priesthood dream suddenly burned a trail through his mind like a shooting star.

"Look, what Stan said is true," he said boldly, voice clear and low. "I *don't* objectify women."

Everyone went quiet and turned towards Dallas. He faltered at the undivided attention, eyes darting from face to face and landing on Samantha's delicate features. His stomach twisted, and with a deep breath, he took her wrist and pushed between Rodrigo and Mike. "Excuse us a minute."

Dallas led Samantha to the end of the bar where no crowd was gathered, glancing back over his shoulder at the crew. All eyes followed, staring with raised eyebrows. Stan and Rodrigo's mouths hung open. Out of earshot, Dallas dropped her wrist and turned to her. "Samantha, I'm not going to take you home. I'm not that kind of guy." He paused and took a breath. "You're extremely beautiful, which is a gift God gave you. But you're misusing it. You probably think I'm crazy, but... you're worth more than that."

Samantha's eyes changed from confused to an expression Dallas couldn't read. She opened her mouth, but only a stutter came out before Mike was at her side, casting Dallas a mocking grin.

"You finished, Malone?"

Dallas fought down a sneer. His tough guy exterior, built up over his whole life, displayed itself with no effort.

"He turned me down." Samantha sidled closer to Mike. "Guess I'll have to find another ride home."

"Well, that's no problem, Dallas." Mike took a swig of his beer as Rodrigo and Stan inched closer behind him. "There's plenty other guys around who want to, uh, fully *appreciate* Samantha's beauty." He leered at her and winked, and she giggled in return.

"I'm sorry you'll be missing out, then, Dallas." She turned to him with icy eyes, then tossed her head. "You're absolutely adorable, with all your little principles and morals. Makes you sound so… oh, I don't know… old-fashioned, like a knight in shining armor. But that's the stuff of fairy tales. You're a real man underneath, and I know what you *really* want. Your friends here can let you know where to find me again when you change your mind." She smiled up at Mike.

"Too late—he's missed his chance." Mike slid an arm around her waist and yanked her close. "You want another drink? Hope you can settle for me, even though I'm not quite so *cute* as Dallas is." He smirked. "He's *crazy* to turn you down." Mike gawked at her up and down with consuming eyes that made Dallas clench his fists at his sides. Samantha elicited an indiscernible fawning comment back to Mike, but she glanced back at Dallas, her round eyes reflecting something deeper even as they burned him with their split-second look. He bit the inside of his lip as his heart lurched in his chest, then turned his head away.

Mike brushed past Dallas with Samantha on his arm. He paused, a little too close, and the two men exchanged a steely stare in that frozen moment. Samantha tugged impatiently at Mike's sleeve.

Dallas didn't wait to see any more. He turned on his heel to stalk out of the bar, weak-kneed and red in the face from the disdain of a beautiful woman. He almost ran right into a staggering Alex.

"Hey, how's it going with that babe?" he slurred. "Hey, lady," he called in Samantha's direction, "did this guy tell you… he can do, like… *thousands* of pull-ups in one hour?"

Dallas pushed Alex towards Rodrigo. "Hey, man, watch out for your brother, okay?" He shook his head and stalked through the door.

Outside, the cool night air hit Dallas, and he drew in a deep breath. His body shook all over. *I should walk back in there and punch Mike in the face! But that would be stupid.* Samantha wasn't resisting Mike's advances, so fighting him would be futile. He couldn't defend a woman who didn't want to be defended. Scanning the area for something to punish, Dallas kicked over a garbage can next to the building and regretted it even as he watched trash spill to the ground. He flung himself around with a huff.

At his car, Dallas evaluated his sharpness. His second beer sat inside on the bar, half-full. Feeling no tipsiness, only pent-up rage, he slid into the driver's seat and started the engine. It was only a two-minute drive home from here, anyway.

Dallas let himself into his apartment and slammed his door, wishing for a punching bag. He burned off the aggression with fast, furious pullups at the doorway bar. *I'll show those guys!* He gritted his teeth. *I could beat the crap out of them all if I wanted!*

Finally cooled down, Dallas dropped to the floor and pulled off his shirt. He slipped out of his jeans and into sweatpants and flopped on his bed with his prayer book. This kind of thing had never happened when he was hanging out with Channing—not even that one uncomfortable time when those girls had approached them at the beach and had triggered a big argument could compare to this. In prison, even when despicable language was used about women, nothing more could happen since there weren't any women there, and any pornography was confiscated quickly by the guards, so situations never escalated beyond talk.

Instead of opening to the evening prayers, Dallas stared at the ceiling with lowered eyebrows. Why couldn't Samantha see that she wasn't gaining any respect from those pigs in the bar? Didn't she *want* respect? *It's like the only attention she knows from men is lust, like she's satisfied with them only admiring her body.* Disgust simmered in the pit of his stomach at the insulting thought that it was all she'd expected of him either, just because he was a man. Shame suddenly burned at his ears—he had entertained the idea briefly. *But you wouldn't act on it*, he reminded himself. Only a few short years ago, he might have welcomed her advances, but he understood the truth about human dignity now, of the real purpose of attraction between men and women, about how all are created in the image and likeness of God... What might he have done tonight had he not experienced his conversion? Thoughts of his own origins flew into his mind, but he locked out the unanswered questions about his father. Channing's mother had gone through one boyfriend after another, but would hearing from Channing about the resulting fallout and damage and tumult have been enough on its own to deter him from taking advantage of an opportunity such as he'd had this evening? Thankfully, Dallas didn't have to find out. Now that he knew what was right, he was steadfast in his convictions.

Dallas flipped to Psalms in Channing's old Bible for a passage he'd read in prison. Running his finger down the page as he scanned the words, he found it: "Hear the case I bring before you, Lord, listen to my plea. Lend your ears to the vice of my pleading; on my lips there is no deceit. Give judgment yourself in my favor, let your eyes see that justice is done. Search my heart, inspect it by night, test me with fire—in me you will find no wrong. My speech is not turned aside towards the works of men: and because of your words I keep far from the ways of the violent. Keep my steps from leaving your paths, so that I may never stumble." Dallas paused and closed his eyes, murmuring thanks for his ability to control his temper lately—in front of other people, anyway. He would still use his fists in defense, but it was hard right now to see clearly, and while he knew it would have been wrong to get into a fight in the bar, failure still gnawed at him. *But Samantha wasn't asking for protection,* he reminded himself. *Test me with fire...* it was definitely accurate. Dallas burned over Mike's behavior.

He consulted the clock—too late to call Father Benedict. He should sleep on it, anyway. Thankful that there was no work tomorrow, Dallas finished up his prayers and got ready for bed.

Dallas dreaded facing the guys on the crew again after he'd stood up to them in the bar the other night. He managed to let go of it on Sunday with confession and Mass and prayers for Samantha—and all women who thought their worth was merely physical. He prayed too that his co-workers might understand how to treat women with true respect. That afternoon, he had called Father Benedict and vented his frustrations.

"This is part of your cross of entering back into society as a Catholic and trying to truly live as you believe," the priest had said. "The temptation presented to men by women like that is very powerful and hard to resist, but we must be in the world yet not of the world. You are having to balance being in the world and getting along with your co-workers while not letting them draw you into the sins of the world, those that are only concerned with short-term pleasures."

Monday morning, Dallas pulled up at the worksite tightly guarding himself. He was going to have to show that he wanted to do his job and do it well alongside these guys, and yet he would also have to make it crystal clear that he'd take no part in their womanizing. A small part of him held onto the hope that they'd gotten his message already and wouldn't even bring it up.

The foreman was instructing Julian, Rodrigo, and Alex on some electrical work, and he added Dallas to the job. They started disconnecting wires while their boss moved on to put Mike and Stan on another task. Dallas exhaled—he wouldn't have to work alongside Mike right away.

The other guys made occasional small talk with Dallas as they worked but mostly spoke in Spanish among themselves, and Dallas couldn't help but wonder if they were talking about him. He poured himself into focusing on the job, wire strippers and electrical tape in hand. When the foreman checked on them, he pointed to Dallas's work, wire nuts wrapped neatly with the black tape, and told the others to do the same. They mumbled apologies, and Rodrigo cast an ugly glance Dallas's way. "Sure, 'cause he's *perfect*," he muttered as the boss walked off. "Quit hogging the tape, Malone." Dallas passed it off in silence and swallowed down a snappy response.

The boss had just left when they broke for lunch. Dallas was following, but Stan stepped in his path, smirking. Mike caught up to them before Dallas was out the door.

"You comin' with us to lunch, Malone?" asked Stan.

"No, thanks, I want to take a long walk instead." Dallas struggled to keep any hint of hostility out of his voice.

"Dude, you really missed out the other night," Mike teased. "Not only are you the head pyromaniac and the pull-up champ, but apparently, you could be the champ with the ladies, too, if you wanted to. Poor Sam had to settle for me!" He and Stan laughed and high-fived each other.

"I really don't want to talk about it." Dallas sidestepped them and headed through the door as heat rose in his throat. They followed right behind.

"Maybe you wanna *hear* about it, though," Mike quipped. Rodrigo trailed alongside them, hanging on Mike's words. "And I guess I should thank you," Mike continued, turning back to Dallas, "for passing off such a sexy girl to me like that. Thanks, bro."

Dallas faced Mike, eyes narrowed and body tense. "I did no such thing," he said, voice low. "She can make her own decisions."

"Well, you rejected her, so what else was she supposed to do?" Mike lifted his hands, palms up. "But that was no problem, really. I made her forget *all* about you!"

"Bull," put in Stan, looking critically at Mike. "Hey, Dallas, she told us before we left her place that she still hoped you'd change your mind, maybe come along with us next time. She wants you, man. She wants you *bad!*"

Dallas recoiled. *Both of them went home with her?* He didn't want to hear any of this. He spun on his heel, heading for his car.

Mike shoved Stan as he spoke, saying, "Shut up, man, she doesn't need Dallas! She only wants him because he won't let her have him." They were on Dallas's heels until all three were at his car. "You know you want to hear what happened," Mike added to Dallas's back.

Dallas gritted his teeth and used all his will to push any temptation out of his mind. Their comments were only further engraving the image of Samantha into him. *See them as children of God… all of them, even these jerks.*

Mike stepped in front of Dallas's car door, blocking his way. "Man, I don't get you!" He threw his arms out to the sides. "You rejected the girl I tried to get for you! That was your prize, you know, for being Pull-up King. Lemme tell you what you missed out on."

"She's a person, not a prize to be won, and I told you, I *don't* want to hear it," Dallas growled, straightening up, "and if you try to make me hear it anyway, you're gonna find out that I can also be the king of beating the crap outta you." He regretted it as soon as he'd said it, but Mike backed down, eyeing Dallas's clenched fists.

"Okay, okay," he said, hands up and backing away from Dallas's car. "No problem, man. Really, we just wanted to help a fella out, get you used to the ladies again after your jail stint. It's just hard to believe you're really serious that you don't want her."

Dallas looked him squarely in the eye. "I'm serious." He got into his car and slammed the door. He backed out, turning the volume way up so that the rage-filled song erupting from the speakers echoed his own mood.

The next day went better. The guys didn't mention the bar incident again, and any comments made about women were kept strictly among themselves. Dallas pushed himself to be cordial and get the job done alongside them, but he was seldom spoken to, and the atmosphere was tense. *I can't relate to them at all.* He sighed.

That Friday, he overheard their plans to go to the bar again. Dallas tried to block out the boisterous camaraderie. As they cleaned up the tools before leaving, Alex asked him, "Hey, you wanna come with us?"

"Huh?" Dallas raised one eyebrow. Alex could be densely oblivious sometimes in a way that was almost endearing but not quite.

Before Dallas could say anything more, Mike called, "Don't hold your breath, Alex." He turned towards Dallas, arms crossed. "Have fun all by yourself, Malone. I'll make sure Sam's not *too* disappointed over your absence." He strutted past, smirking. Dallas clenched his teeth to suppress the urge to hit Mike.

Driving home alone in the rain, Dallas fought off visions of himself instead of Mike with Samantha. His rationality told him he absolutely didn't want to hang out with any of them. *But I'm lonely. I don't fit in.* Still shy about putting himself out there among strangers, Dallas hadn't gotten involved in any groups at church. That nagging thought about becoming a priest hammered in his head again. "Is that really where I belong, God?" he asked into the air. "I'm making an honest living here, trying to move forward, but I don't think this job's good for me. Look at what it's trying to pull me into!"

Another solid week had passed, and Dallas was rounding out a Sunday afternoon in preparation for work the next morning. A sudden ringing broke the peace. Dallas silently counted three more pull-ups to stop at an even ninety and dropped to the floor in his bedroom doorway. He shook out his hands and rotated his wrists as he trotted to the phone.

"Hello?"

"Dallas!" came the enthusiastic voice on the other end. "Hey, it's Samantha, from the bar. I hope you don't mind me getting your number from your co-workers."

Dallas did mind. As his stomach jumped into his throat, he paced to the window with the cordless phone and swallowed, still trying to catch his breath from his workout and wishing he'd checked the caller ID. "Uh, I…"

"You see, I wanted to apologize to you," Samantha broke in.

Dallas walked back to the kitchen counter, running his right hand through his hair. "Apologize? Um… for what?" *For hitting on me?*

Samantha cleared her throat. "I'm just sorry for how I reacted after you said you'd been in prison. I didn't mean to make light of it at all—"

"No, I could tell you didn't mean that," Dallas answered quickly. "I mean, when everybody else was laughing over it, and I could see your face change, and… so yeah, don't worry about it."

"Oh, Dallas—you're so intuitive to have noticed the meaning in my expression!"

Dallas wrinkled his nose. *Intuitive?* "But you said you were sorry right then. I believed you."

"I just wanted to let you know that whatever happened in your past doesn't bother me. I mean, I can tell you're a good guy, despite whatever you did wrong, so I was just surprised. That's what I meant by my reaction, but I saw that it probably came across as way too casual a response to something that was probably painful for you."

Dallas strode to his pull-up bar and eyed it, words stuck in his throat as his emotions over his incarceration tumbled around in his brain. He forced them in deeper and locked the door to those memories. "Uh, yeah, it's fine," he managed.

"So," Samantha's tone turned flirty, "since I don't have any problem with your history, I was wondering if you might want to see me again sometime?"

Dallas could almost feel her eyelashes batting at him through the receiver. He walked to the front door and stepped outside to pace the sidewalk to escape the caged feeling.

"I, um, well… I'm really focused on putting my life back together right now, is all. Getting back on track is all I have the time… uh, and ability, for." He bit his lip, unwilling to mention his potential vocation to her.

"How long since you got out of jail?" Samantha asked.

"About three months."

"Only three months, and you already seem to have it together!" Samantha complimented him. "I mean, you have steady employment, you have friends, and you seem like you're a really nice guy, like deep down inside… but, well, if you feel like you aren't back on track yet, like something's bothering you, then if you ever want to talk about it…"

Her silence prompted Dallas to speak. "Uh, talk about prison?" *No way.* He paused in front of his car and put his foot up on the bumper.

"Mm-hmm, if it would help," Samantha murmured. "I'd love to be a listening ear if you need one. I hate that you had some bad experiences and wish there was something I could do—"

"I really don't want to talk about prison." Dallas drew his lips together.

"Oh, I understand." Her voice was like butter, and Dallas felt like he could see Samantha's simpering, and he closed his eyes and turned away from his car to stride back up the sidewalk. His throat was dry as he guessed her real purpose for calling.

"Still," Samantha continued, "I do hope we can see each other again, maybe somewhere a little more private than the bar—"

"But aren't you seeing Mike?" Dallas blurted, suppressing the pins and needles sensation Samantha was giving him. "The other day at work, he mentioned seeing you last weekend. If you're committed to him…" Dallas struggled to explain and felt his face growing warm. "Well, you shouldn't ask me to see you. I'm not like that." Even as he spoke, the memory of Samantha pressed against him in the bar flooded his mind.

"Oh, I'm not *really* committed." Samantha giggled. "I guess I'm sort of dating Mike, but that could change. I like to keep my options open, you know… and he might not be my best option…"

Dallas spun around and walked back through his apartment door. "I… uh…" Silence filled the line for several seconds.

"But I get what you mean, Dallas," Samantha continued. "I don't want to be the cause of tension between you and Mike, especially since you work together. So maybe you want to come to the bar again one Friday night, hang out as a group? If you don't think one on one is appropriate, then I'd still like to get to know you somehow."

Dallas shook his head. "Hanging out at the bar's not really my thing." He scratched his head and paced into the kitchen, heart rate increasing. "Um, hey, I've gotta go. Uhh… thanks, about what you said…"

"You're welcome, Dallas," she interjected. "You're really nice to talk to."

"Uh, thanks. So… uh, maybe later. Bye."

Dallas pressed the red button on the receiver and thrust it onto the counter. His stomach reeled, and he leaned against the counter to take slow, deep breaths. He was nice to talk to? But he hadn't really said anything! Dallas stared at the phone, a small dose of pleasure at her attention mingling with his overall confusion and revulsion. *Oh well — you're not going back to that bar, so you won't have to see her again.* He reached for a glass of water and took a few swigs before returning to the pullup bar. Thoughts of the priesthood flashed through him with each pull-up. *No, I can't pursue a romantic relationship anyway, even if she wasn't seeing Mike — uh, wasn't sort of seeing Mike, or whatever…* Dallas sighed. *I don't have the ability.*

At work, friendly interactions had become a balancing act. Dallas grew weary of formulating excuses for avoiding lunch with the crew so it didn't seem like he was looking down on them. "I want to go for a jog," he said, and then did. He needed to burn off some nervous energy anyway. Dallas wrestled with himself, not wanting to be a hypocrite. *I've been convicted of manslaughter, for goodness's sake! How can I judge them as being more sinful than me? But I can't let myself get pulled into their behaviors.*

One day, Alex passed by while Rodrigo was ogling yet another pornographic magazine with Stan. "Hey, I thought Grandma threw that one out?" he asked his brother.

"Yeah, I got it back." Rodrigo shrugged. "You sure you don't wanna see this chick, Dallas?"

Dallas leaned against the wall and fought not to let the sigh he was feeling escape his lips. "No, man, I really don't. You guys should listen to your grandmother. You know the girl you're leering at in there; she's probably going to *be* somebody's grandmother one day."

The guys howled at Dallas's comment. "Hey, Alex, could you picture Grandma wearing *this*?" Rodrigo pointed to a page. All three of them doubled up with laughter.

"You're too much, man." Stan gave Dallas a critical smirk and a shake of the head. "Hey, Mike, did you hear what he just said?" Stan relayed Dallas's reprimand as Mike walked into the room.

Mike joined in the laughs and rolled his eyes at Dallas. "One thing I can tell you—Samantha ain't no grandma, that's for sure!" The others cracked up over Mike's gibe and exchanged high-fives.

A tightness clenched throughout Dallas's body and heat rose in his cheeks at Mike's callous attitude.

"Our grandma is fighting a losing battle!" Alex waved the magazine in the air. "She doesn't know how much there is on the internet. That's where this industry's future is!"

"Thank goodness she can't throw away the internet!" Rodrigo jibed amidst the jeers.

Dallas swallowed down the sick sensation that was creeping up his throat. He'd lost all hope that he could change the subject to some positive commonality with these guys. The heavy atmosphere of his workplace was becoming unbearably stifling.

Dallas and Mike worked to remove sheetrock from a ceiling one afternoon. An invisible tension held the silence between them as pieces came down in large, heavy sections, and they were struggling under the bulk of it when Dallas lost his footing on some debris on the floor. The brunt of the weight fell momentarily onto Mike, throwing him off balance. The piece of ceiling dropped to the floor with a crash.

"What the crap, Malone?" Mike wrinkled his nose and glared. "That almost landed on my foot!"

"I'm sorry." Dallas wiped his brow with a forearm. "I just slipped a moment. Maybe we need to pull somebody else over here to help us."

"We shouldn't need anybody else, *Pull-up Champ*." Mike's voice had an edge to it. Just then, their boss walked in.

"Is there a problem between you two?" He crossed his arms. "Seems there's something more that's been going on..."

"Nah, Bossman, there's no problem," was Mike's ever-predictable reply. "Dallas and me, we've found out we're just very different people."

"Oh?" The foreman raised an eyebrow. "I like how my crew works well together. Is this going to cause trouble here, or can you keep it outside?" He glanced from one face to the other.

"Oh, yeah, we're fine," Mike answered for them both. "It's in the past now. Me and the guys, we were trying to help Dallas get this girl at the bar. Turns out he didn't want her, though. I was offended at first, but hey, that left her to me the last two weekends, so who's complaining, right? She's old news by now anyway." He grinned in that cocky way of his.

"Well, lucky you." Their boss began to walk away, then paused and glanced back over his shoulder, adding, "Don't want any fights over girls in this workplace, you know."

"No, sir, there won't be," Dallas said, clenching his fists inside his pockets. Inside, a storm raged over Mike's nonchalance over the whole thing. A part of him wanted to gloat that Samantha had called him, that she liked him over Mike, but he continued to keep her phone call to himself, a vague sense twinging inside him that she wanted them to fight over her.

"Especially if Malone just gives 'em to you," the boss added to Mike with a mischievous glance. Looking back to Dallas, he said, "Mike here's quite the ladies' man, at least he fancies himself so. He's got enough of them so he's not really gonna be upset if you get one of them yourself, ya know. Right, Mikey?" He threw a playful glance back at Mike.

"Ha, you know it!" crowed Mike. "But Dallas don't want a girl, really. He wants us to stop bugging him about it, anyway."

The foreman raised an eyebrow as if he couldn't quite believe it. "Okay, whatever. You're a good worker, Dallas, and just so you know, it doesn't make any difference to me what you do in your spare time so long as you continue to be a good worker. Don't let this guy make you think he owns the town, ya know. Plenty of girls at that bar to go around if you want one."

Dallas's stomach twisted inside at the idea of women being obtained as objects even as a warmth crept over him at the remembrance of Samantha's attentions to him.

The foreman gave Mike a knowing look as he left the room.

Mike turned to Dallas, suddenly appearing serious. "Really, man, I'll leave you alone about the girls. Okay? I just feel like you think you're, like, better than us or something, you know?"

Dallas sighed. *This again…* "You do remember I was in prison, right? I'm far from perfect. I just don't want to treat women that way."

"Okay, no problem." Mike shrugged. "They seem to like the treatment, but we'll leave you out of it."

Mike made good on his word and excluded Dallas from any talk about women. Even Alex seemed to have gotten the point. Yet with each passing day, interactions with the crew grew more uncomfortable. A chasm yawned between Dallas and his peers. He still overheard bits of their crass comments and stories and couldn't help himself from listening in concern for Samantha's name. She'd called him three more times, and it had taken every ounce of his will to resist answering the phone the last two times.

Dallas had worked with the crew for almost four months—surely that was a good test run. He'd banked a lot of money. There had to be a better environment for him. *I'm listless; I don't fit in. Is this job just me spinning my wheels but getting nowhere?* His fingers itched on the steering wheel on his drive to work every morning now, a desire to flee, that old pull of the open road, when he would just grab Channing and head out on a random road trip.

Dallas spent a long weekend with Father Benedict, who had come to visit him for the first time since he'd picked Dallas up from prison and helped him to get settled in.

"I'm considering quitting my job." Dallas made the admission as he picked at the crust of his sandwich at his kitchen table. "The noise of my secular, and at times vulgar, workplace is drowning out the voice of God I'm trying so hard to hear. It's impossible to sort out everything in my head."

Father Benedict paused, sandwich suspended in midair. "It's only been a few months. You're doing good work, and your boss appreciates that in you."

"The thing is, the foreman's so nonchalant about the lewd speech and pornography that gets passed around." Dallas met Father's eyes. "These guys bring porn to work nearly every day!"

"I see," Father Benedict said, finger to his chin. "If your boss is enabling this, then I understand the negative impact it would have on the atmosphere."

Dallas nodded vigorously. "And I don't know if it's just my own wishful thinking, or finding a way to escape what my life's become… but I still hear that little nagging call. Also…" Dallas elicited a sigh as he glanced off to the side. "Well, Channing's absence has been even more apparent to me after spending a lot of time around these guys who are so superficial. It makes me long for his friendship again. I can't just continue with putting one foot in front of the other. I'm stuck, and I'm growing resentful that I can't make a new life for myself. The world out here just isn't the same without Channing, and it's such a challenging place for Christian morals, too." He thought again of Samantha's offer for him to take her home.

"It's wise to be mindful of your mental and emotional health," Father encouraged. "The transition to life outside of prison isn't a quick and easy adjustment, and you've undergone more changes than the typical man who serves a three-year sentence."

"Maybe I need to take some kind of action." Dallas cracked his knuckles. "If I have a heart-to-heart conversation with my boss, see if there's any way he'll discourage the demoralizing behavior towards women… It's such a topic of discussion for the crew on a daily basis, Father. I'm bombarded by it."

The conversation was broken by Dallas's phone ringing. He stood from the table with a frown and looked to see Samantha's number popping up on the screen. With a sigh, Dallas dropped back into his chair and covered his face with both hands.

The answering machine picked up, and Samantha's smooth voice filled the room. "Hey, Dallas, it's Samantha again. I was really hoping you'd be at the bar with your friends last night, but you sure seem to be Mr. Elusive, now, don't you?" Dallas's face warmed under his hands as her sultry voice spilled out for Father Benedict's interpretation. "Anyway, I sure would enjoy a change of pace, so if you're interested in doing something tonight, give me a call back. We could go out somewhere or just hang out at my place—I don't have a roommate, you know. Sure would love to spend some time with you, Dallas." Click.

Her spoken iteration of his name ran in circles through his brain: *Dallllas…* He snapped his head up and motioned towards the phone. "And that's another thing—my co-workers tried to set me up with this girl. I said no thanks, and she's been seeing one of them instead. So why isn't she just content with him? I've not been answering her calls since the first two times, but she keeps calling!"

Father Benedict pursed his lips. "I see. You are being presented with many challenges and temptations. This young lady is interested in both you and your co-worker, and so you do not wish to get to know her more closely?"

Dallas pushed his plate away. "I think it would be a bad idea. She seems to want something, um, physical."

Father Benedict gave Dallas a pointed stare. "What did you say to her when she called before?"

"The first time, I didn't say much." Dallas shrugged. "She did most of the talking. She asked to see me again then, too—I've only seen her that one time at the bar—and I told her no, since she's seeing Mike, but she told me she's not really committtted to him. The next time she called, we just chatted about random stuff for a few minutes first…"

Dallas stared at the phone on the counter behind Father Benedict and replayed the second call in his mind. He'd answered the phone against his better judgment that time—he couldn't be so weak again! Samantha had gotten him comfortable by asking him about Nevada, and he realized afterward that he'd fallen into the trap of casual conversation that may have misled her regarding his intentions. He cringed as he heard his voice smoothly relating the fact that Reno was actually farther west than L.A., his brain sizzling with his nerdy geography obsession.

She'd hung on his words, all astonished giggling, and he had chuckled a few times himself. But when she'd started probing with personal questions about his family, he'd clammed up. *But I was starting to like talking to her…*

The priest, leaning forward with crossed arms on the table, brought Dallas back with his expectant gaze. "Random stuff? Nothing inappropriate?"

Dallas shook his head. "Not really, except that I feel like she's wanting to get to know me too much for a woman who seems to be dating another guy. She told me a little about her background — she grew up in Fort Worth. Made a big deal about how it's right next to Dallas, just like my name…" He shook his head and heard her bubbling over the coincidence. "Told me how her parents divorced when she was in middle school and that her mother raised her alone after that. But I didn't tell her much of my own background. I don't want her chasing after me while I'm trying to discern my future."

Dallas closed his eyes. *"You're still seeing Mike, right?"*

"I saw him on Saturday, so I guess so. But if you don't want me to see him…"

"If you're seeing him, we shouldn't be talking like this. I can't… I mean, uh, I gotta go."

"But, Dallas, wait — "

"No. I can't — we can't — I'm sorry, I gotta go."

Dallas saw himself smashing the hang-up button and thrusting the phone across the counter as if it had been a snake about to bite him. He scrunched his eyes closed tighter and took short breaths to accompany his heart rate.

Father Benedict's hand touched Dallas lightly on one shoulder, and he jumped.

"Nothing about my life is going right!" Dallas pounded one fist on the table. "I'm talking to my boss on Monday. I can't surround myself with people like this when I'm trying to discern whether I have a call to the priesthood."

Father nodded slowly. "I believe in you, Dallas. I admire your desire to place yourself around good influences. You will determine the right course to take, and perhaps your conversation with your boss will bear good fruit." He patted Dallas's hand and gave him a confident smile.

Armed with Father Benedict's encouragement, Dallas steeled himself for a confrontation. At the end of the next workday, Dallas swallowed down the butterflies and spoke to his boss.

"Malone, if you don't like it, you don't have to look or listen." The boss crossed his arms. "I'm not going to tell the crew what they can and can't talk about. I don't mind them bringin' pornographic magazines as long as they still get their work done, and so far, that hasn't been a problem. In fact, it seems to make them work better, keeps up the morale. There's no harm in them."

Taking a deep breath and mustering up his courage, Dallas replied, "Then I need to give you two weeks' notice that I'll have to quit. I know the work is good, and you've been a great boss to me, but… I just can't be a part of listening to the kinds of things that are being said about women among the crew."

Dallas's last two weeks were tense. *He probably thinks I'm harboring a superiority complex*, Dallas realized when the foreman's attitude towards him became cool. The other guys said little to him, as well.

On his final day, however, his boss approached, hand extended holding Dallas's final paycheck. "You've been a solid worker, and I'm going to miss that. You never complained and always got the job done well. I'm sorry this hasn't worked out for you. I hope you can find what you're looking for. Don't hesitate to ask if you need a letter of recommendation, because I'd be glad to vouch for your abilities and your work ethic."

"Thank you, sir. I appreciate that." Dallas shook hands with his boss, a lightness coming over him. He turned to go, and Alex and Rodrigo looked wistfully his way.

"Bye, man," they called. "Appreciate all your work."

Mike stood in the doorway, looking Dallas in the eye, an expression on his face indicating his inability to fully understand the man before him. "You're a good guy, Dallas," he said slowly. "We'll miss having you on the team, truly." He stepped aside, and Dallas walked out the door.

For nearly two weeks, Dallas had hunted for another job. After getting no good leads during his final week on the construction crew and a frustrating solid week of unemployment, he was starting to doubt his decision to quit. *Was I too sensitive?* Certainly, he may have been too hasty, quitting without having something else lined up. Worst of all, the stagnancy of Dallas's days had become a slow and tortuous despair.

Today was a new low. He'd dragged himself through his morning prayers and had skipped the others. He'd eaten lunch but nothing else. Coming back to his apartment that evening from another afternoon of looking for a job and then picking up a few groceries, Dallas couldn't make himself do anything. He stared at the pile of laundry on his bedroom floor and half-considered taking it to the apartment's communal laundry area, then thought about how that meant he'd have to dig up some quarters for the machines.

Not really hungry, he stood in front of the open fridge and deliberated on whether to eat something anyway. Rubbing the stubble he'd failed to shave off his chin that morning, he sighed and closed the door and, with a pang, considered how, had things been different, he and Channing might be unwinding right now on this Friday evening. Instead, he was jobless, alone, and facing a weekend of nothing but laundry and putting away his measly amount of Walmart purchases. And Mass on Sunday, of course... Standing in the middle of his apartment and staring sullen and sloth-like at nothing was in stark contrast to his former self, the one that relished his downtime. Loneliness had spread through him like a disease since his experiences of not fitting in with his former co-workers. *Another way prison changed me: I had no privacy there, so I never really felt lonely.* A dull, aching emptiness of being a lone survivor in a foreign land left Dallas more isolated than ever before. Channing's sketchbooks beckoned to him from their place on the shelf. Dallas bit his lip. *I could look through those, just sit and wallow...*

There was a sharp knock at the door. Dallas started, temporarily jolted out of his apathy. He straightened himself up and went to answer it.

Samantha stood in the doorway.

Dallas's heart fluttered as he gulped in air and froze, a wide-eyed expression replacing the stoic one, and he wrestled with his instinct to shut the door as self-protection.

"Hi, Dallas!" she said, eyes sparkling. "I hope you don't mind me coming to find you. I asked Alex and Rodrigo where you lived, and I saw you come in this door a few minutes ago, and so... well, I thought I'd stop by and say hi."

Why had he told those guys which apartment complex he lived in? Dallas gaped, his brain tripping over itself, unable to respond.

Samantha flashed an enticing smile, her eyes outlined in heavy makeup and her low-cut, too-short sundress accentuating her curves.

"Aren't you going to invite me in?" Her tone was simple and innocent. "I'd love to keep you company for a while—"

"I don't think that's a good idea," Dallas blurted. "I told you before, that's not the kind of guy I am." Forcing a tough exterior while suppressing the reactions Samantha's presence was setting off inside him was a kind of sick agony for Dallas. *She knows exactly what she's doing!* He held his breath, fuming inside. *She's trying to use her power against me, and just when I'm at my loneliest, at that.*

"No, no," Samantha responded, eyes round, "you're taking me the wrong way!"

"Then what are you here for?" Dallas blocked the entrance to his apartment with arms crossed.

"I was over at the bar before coming here." Samantha mindlessly traced a finger up and down the doorframe as she avoided answering the question directly. "Mike's such a major jerk, you know." She rolled her eyes. "Really, I just wanted to come by and talk to someone different, and you just seem so… *nice*. I don't meet that many nice guys, if you hadn't guessed."

Dallas's heart softened. Maybe she was starting to realize the emptiness of letting guys at the bar treat her like a piece of meat…

"I was talking to Alex and Rodrigo, though, and they told me you'd quit work. So, I thought I'd check in on you. Have you found a new job?" She fluttered her eyelashes, gazing at Dallas as if he were a lost puppy she'd just found.

Unsure of how to respond, he just stood there saying nothing, but a strange warmth kindled in his chest. Did she really care?

"You seem all alone, Dallas." Samantha's eyes were tender.

His heart ached as she named his weakness, and his defensive posture slackened.

Samantha took the opening. As she peeked past Dallas, her eyes brightened. "Wow, you have a great place here! Looks clean for a single guy's apartment."

She hadn't seen his disaster of a bedroom. Dallas rubbed the back of his neck. "Uh… thanks." After a few more seconds' hesitation, he added, "So, you really just want to talk? That's it?"

"Yes!" Samantha bubbled. "Oh, Dallas, like your friends said, I can tell you're different from most guys. It'd be a breath of fresh air to just get to know somebody as nice as you seem, who has no other intentions…"

As she was speaking, she slipped past Dallas into his apartment, the entrance slightly wider as he let down his guard. *Too late.* Immediately, he turned, opening his mouth to protest, but no sound emerged from his lips. He took one step towards her and then paused and fell back, flustered.

"I love your place!" she repeated, eyes scanning the room. "I just love seeing the interior of people's homes. I think it tells a lot about the person who lives there, the way they arrange their living spaces."

Dallas scratched his head and managed a response. "Oh?"

Samantha nodded with a wide smile. "For example, just by looking at your place, I can tell you value simplicity and function, you're thrifty, and you're strong and independent."

Dallas gaped at her accurate assessment and finally found his tongue and his resolve. "Umm, wouldn't you rather go out somewhere, like maybe a nearby restaurant? I haven't had dinner yet." It was the quickest way he could think to get her out of there. His heart pounded now that she had gotten inside his apartment.

"Oh, I don't have any money," Samantha said. "I see you just went shopping." She flitted to the bags on the kitchen counter.

"It would be my treat." Dallas forced the offer from his mouth.

"Aww, that's sweet," Samantha said in that purring way of hers, "like you want to take me on a date! But I know you're trying to save up. I couldn't let you buy me dinner when you're out of work. I'm not hungry, but I don't mind at all if you have something for yourself."

Dallas grimaced as his conscience urged him to bolt. But he couldn't just leave her here in his apartment. Samantha was unloading Dallas's groceries now, putting boxes of cereal in a cabinet. She set a jar of peanut butter alongside the cereal. Crunchy peanut butter—Dallas didn't even like crunchy, but he'd bought it because it had been Channing's favorite…

"Hey, you don't have to do that," he said, approaching her.

She ignored him and kept unloading the bags. "Just making myself useful. Want me to make you a snack? You can go put your feet up."

Dallas was bewildered. Samantha was crafty. Now that she was in here, how could he get her out? He didn't want to be rude, but neither did he want to encourage her. What were her real intentions here?

"No, really, don't go to the trouble. I'm just going to have a bowl of cereal, is all." Dallas sidled up alongside her in the tiny kitchen, shrinking back to avoid brushing against her, and took a box down from where she'd just placed it. Racking his brain for what he could do to change the situation, he tore open the cereal and poured some into a bowl. Turning, he almost bumped into Samantha, who had already retrieved the milk from the fridge and stood offering it to him with a big smile. Now that she had gotten the ball in her court, it was clear she wasn't going to give it back to Dallas.

"Thanks," he said stiffly, receiving the half-gallon jug from her outstretched hands. Face flushed, he poured the milk over the cereal, carried it to the table, and sat down. He reached across the table and grabbed a banana and started slicing it into his bowl with his spoon. Samantha kept up her frenzy of activity in the kitchen, washing Dallas's dirty dishes that he'd left in the sink after she put away the last of his groceries, all while keeping up a friendly bantering.

"You seem to like to eat pretty healthy — good for you. Hey, why do you have two coffee makers?" She pointed to where they sat side by side on the counter.

"Long story," Dallas responded between bites. "But the short answer is that I really like coffee."

Samantha laughed as if he had said the wittiest thing ever. Then she came around the counter, seating herself across from him at the table. Maybe they could just talk a bit.

"So," he said, glancing up from his Cheerios, "you're getting sick of hanging out at the bar?"

Samantha rolled her eyes. "Absolutely. I mean, it's fun and all, but it starts to be the same after a while. I had a good time with your old co-workers, but, well… Mike talks big, thinks he's cooler than he really is. Stan's okay, I guess, but not really my type."

Dallas wondered what "her type" was. He certainly didn't think he fit the description himself, and yet, here she was of her own free will.

Samantha bubbled on. "The other three, they're hilarious, especially Alex. Not exactly the kind of guys you'd want to take you home or anything, but fun for some laughs together at the bar. Alex is practically a kid, isn't he?"

"Yeah, he's just 21." Dallas took the last bite of his cereal. It was sticking in his mouth like cardboard. "He's the same age as Mike."

"What!?" shrieked Samantha. "Mike told me he was 25! The liar!" Her voice was fuming despite a flicker of amusement in her eyes.

"Yep." Dallas pushed his bowl away and leaned back in his chair. "He talks big, like you said."

"And how old are you, then?" Samantha leaned forward, studying Dallas's face.

Figuring he had nothing to lose, he revealed his age to her. "23."

"I'm 24, so really, Mike's too immature for me anyway. You know what? Stan told me Mike's jealous of you!" Samantha's eyes twinkled as she slid her chair closer to Dallas's. He stood abruptly and carried his bowl to the sink, her gaze following him. "I think he's right, too."

"Mike doesn't have anything to be jealous about." Dallas washed his bowl and spoon, his back to her. A funny, warm feeling rose inside him. What else had they said about him?

"Sure, he does," Samantha retorted, flouncing into the kitchen. "He's all talk. Of *course*, he's jealous of you. He knows I really *did* just settle for him, that he'd never be my first choice on any given night. He acts like it's all a joke, but he knows he's below you. And," she added, "you can do, like, *thousands* more pull-ups than him, as Alex is always raving about after he's had half a drink. That boy can't hold his liquor, can he?" Her eyes were dancing with mirth.

Dallas chuckled, half-consciously allowing his ego to be stroked as he leaned against the counter. "So, Alex is still going on about that, huh? I didn't think it really bothered Mike that I beat him, but maybe it does and he just won't let on." Catching himself, Dallas continued more modestly, "It's no big deal. I'm sure there's other things he can do better than me."

"Oh, I wouldn't be so sure about that." Samantha's response glided smooth as silk from her lips as she stared him down.

Dallas edged out of the kitchen and cleared his throat, his eyes everywhere but on her.

Samantha reverted to her previous tone. "So, what kind of job are you searching for? Anything in particular?" She flopped down onto Dallas's sofa.

Pulling the chair out from the table again, Dallas sat facing her across the room. "Auto mechanic job would be my preference. But it looks like I'm gonna have to settle for something really basic, like a checker at a grocery store."

"So, why did you quit?" Samantha leaned forward, chin in her hand.

"It just wasn't a good fit for me." Dallas fidgeted with his hands in his lap, eyes off to one side.

"Why not?" Samantha pried.

Dallas stood and walked over to the window and pretended to look at something outside. "I didn't quite fit in with those guys. It got to be too awkward working with them." He racked his brain for some excuse he could make to get her to leave but came up with nothing. Maybe he didn't really want her to leave yet. He paced back to the table.

"You seem to have a lot of pent-up energy," Samantha cooed. "There's room for you here on the couch." She patted the cushion next to her. "I won't bite," she teased.

"I'm fine, thanks." Dallas leaned back against the wall across from Samantha. Goodness, she was beautiful, though. An urge crept up from deep inside to just give in and take the bait, his feet begging his brain permission to cross the floor to her. *With how my life here in the real world is going, does anything really matter, anyway?*

The persistent beckoning of that potential call to the priesthood barged into his thoughts like a trumpet's blare. Dallas took a slow breath. He knew the truth. Samantha was a human being, made in the image of God. He reached into his back pocket and touched the prayer card there, begging God for self-control, and the weight of the rosary he'd missed praying today was heavy in his lefthand jeans pocket. *Keep your cool and do what's right, no matter what. She doesn't exist for your gratification, even if she's offering.* The pathetic weakness of his own will was painfully obvious. What would happen if he made no effort to ask for supernatural help against his carnal impulses? Only the imagined weight of the sacramentals he'd armed himself with cemented his feet in place.

Samantha rose and flitted over to Dallas's cinder block and scrap lumber shelf. "Love your setup here; it's so rustic!" she said with sugary enthusiasm. She rummaged through the piles of CDs and cassettes. "And I love that you still listen to tapes! You're so old-school, Dallas!"

He shifted from one foot to another, watching her make herself at ease in his space. It was wrong for her to look through his things, uninvited, and yet he couldn't explain why or figure out what to say to make her stop.

"I just love music. I've written some lyrics myself, but I don't know enough to set them to music. I have this half-crazy dream of being a musician, but it'll never happen. Ooh, I know this one." Samantha held two Led Zeppelin CDs in her hands. "It's my favorite of theirs!"

"Yeah." Dallas shrugged. "*Four* is everyone's favorite because it has *Stairway* on it, but—"

"Oh, no, I mean *this* one." She waved the other album for Dallas to see. "My dad used to play this record." Samantha's voice was soft. "I don't see him much, not since the divorce when I was eleven. It takes me back to a better time…" She looked up at Dallas. "How about you? Are your parents still back in Nevaw—I mean, Nevaada?"

Dallas shifted. "I'm not sure where my mom is right now, but she was in Nevada last I knew."

"And your father?"

The reminder that they were both only children from broken homes prodded at Dallas's heart. "I don't have a father." He stared at the floor, hands in his pockets.

Samantha studied him closely, then gazed back at the album in her hand. "Yeah, everybody loves *Stairway*, but my very favorite is *The Rain Song*."

Dallas raised his eyebrows in surprise.

"What, don't tell me that's your favorite Led Zeppelin song, too?" Samantha wore an excited smile.

Dallas scratched his forehead. "Uh, yeah. Actually, it is..."

"Amazing!" Samantha laughed. She picked up a stack of cassettes. "I've never heard of some of these. For Squirrels? Spacehog? Loud Lucy? What genre of music are these?"

Alarms went off in Dallas's head about protecting Channing's old tapes. He prayed she wouldn't put in the For Squirrels album, shivering as he shook hauntingly prophetic lyrics from his mind and recalling that half the band had been killed in a car accident. *Like Channing...* Dallas stepped over to her and squatted to take the cassettes. "They belonged to my best friend years ago. I guess you'd call them alternative or indie rock, something like that."

Samantha glanced up at Dallas, who had stood again quickly after retrieving the tapes and noticing just how short her dress was as she crouched down at the shelf. Diverting his eyes from her, he cleared his throat, about to say something about feeling tired and that she should be going.

Samantha's questions cut him off. "So, why do you have them? Where's your friend now?"

"Dead," Dallas said evenly. He winced, wishing he hadn't said it.

"*Dead?*" echoed Samantha, shocked and pitying. "Oh, how sad! You poor thing," she crooned. "What happened to him?"

"Don't really want to talk about it." Dallas turned away. He walked into the kitchen and tried to look busy.

Samantha followed him. "You certainly are a man of mystery. I'm sorry about your friend, and prison. It sounds like you've been through some hard stuff."

Dallas was failing at appearing to do anything productive and knew he must look like a fumbling idiot. Certainly, she saw this. But he'd be a jerk to kick her out if she really just wanted to talk. Maybe she craved respect but couldn't articulate it.

Unwilling to talk about either Channing or prison with her, Dallas nodded towards the stereo. "You might recognize the first song on that Spacehog album. It played on the radio a lot when it first came out." *Anything to change the subject.*

"Okay, put it in." Samantha threw herself back down on the sofa again and drew her legs up beside herself. "How long ago was that?"

Dallas avoided looking at her and crossed to put the tape in. "I guess it was about 1995 or 6. Back in the good ol' days."

She erupted in laughter at Dallas's remark. "You're too funny, old man!" she fawned. "Ooh, yes! I *do* recognize this song! Hey, do you have any beer? It'd be fun to drink and hang out listening to music."

"No, I don't," Dallas answered truthfully.

"I'd go home and grab some," Samantha teased, "if I wasn't afraid you were going to run away before I got back. Really, Dallas, you're not *afraid* of me, are you? You seem so on edge."

She had hit the nail on the head. Dallas *was* afraid of her; that was the problem. And afraid of his own reactions to her temptations, too. Here she was, lounging on his couch after dark, listening to Channing's old music, with who knows what kinds of plans running through her mind… The longer she stayed, the less he trusted himself.

"It's getting late, and I'm just tired." Dallas knew his explanation was lame.

"But the night is young!" Samantha waved her arm dramatically. "It's only, what, 8:30? And I don't have to work tomorrow morning, either."

Dallas was quiet, shuffling his feet. "Uh, where do you work?"

"I'm a waitress at the truck stop by the interstate," she responded. "Kind of pathetic, I know. One day, I'll do something more ambitious. But it pays good. And the old guys who come through there appreciate a pretty smile and flirty attitude. Know what I mean?"

Her attempts to bait him made Dallas flinch. Even the way she had positioned herself on his sofa seemed intentionally seductive. *And Channing liked truck stops… no, was obsessed with truck stops for some strange reason.*

He sat again in the chair next to the table and focused on polite conversation. "So, have you worked there long?" Dallas drummed his fingers against his thighs. Maybe she'd realize how boring he was and leave soon.

"A year," she answered. "Before that, I lived in Houston and worked at a swanky nightclub." Samantha's gaze flitted across the room. "Hey, want to play cards?" She hopped up and retrieved the deck sitting on Dallas's shelf.

"Uh, sure." Dallas found himself agreeing. Playing cards seemed a safe way to be friendly. He motioned to the table and took the cards from Samantha's outstretched hand, and she sat across from him.

"So, the nightclub…" Dallas studied the cards as he shuffled them. It'd been months since he'd had anyone to play against. "How was that?"

"Oh, it might sound glamorous, but it wasn't." Samantha watched his hands. "I'd much rather be the customer at a nightclub. Gives you more control. You can't just walk away while you're working if some guy starts talking to you like a jerk, you know?"

How bad must it've been for her to consider anyone a jerk? The repulsive way in which Dallas's former co-workers had talked to her was something she didn't seem to mind, even though it left him wanting to punch something. But she *had* called Mike a jerk tonight…

"Hey, I asked what we're playing." Samantha's voice broke into his thoughts.

"Oh, um… you know how to play Spades?" Dallas started dealing, the muscle memory returning of the game that had occupied many of his evenings in prison.

"Sure, although I might be a little rusty." Samantha picked up her cards as they were dealt. "It's been a while."

As they played, Dallas fumbled over attempts to make small talk. He wasn't good at this. Samantha spoke freely about anything and everything, gushing over how Dallas was so sweet to take an interest in her. And she didn't seem to care how boring he was, either. Maybe that was just his self-deprecating side — maybe she really didn't find him boring at all. The ease with which they played slackened the tension in his neck and reminded him of his earlier loneliness, now alleviated. He admitted to himself that he was actually having fun.

"Beat you again!" Samantha's eyes danced as she laid down her final card and took the last trick.

"I thought you said you were a little rusty?" Dallas cocked an eyebrow and smirked. "One more game? I'm getting tired."

Samantha laughed. "Sure, likely excuse." She swept the cards towards her and stacked them neatly in two piles. "You just don't want to admit your defeat."

Dallas leaned on one elbow and gave a crooked grin. She was right. He hated to lose. "I must be rusty myself. Used to kill at this game, but I haven't played since—" He caught himself in time.

"Since when?" Samantha kept her eyes on the cards as she dealt.

Dallas tensed up and pressed his lips together in a line. He couldn't just ignore the question. "Uh, we used to play in prison a lot. Me and a few other guys." He retrieved his cards without looking at her. He wasn't going to say that he and Channing used to play, too.

"So, you've never played against a girl before."

Dallas furrowed his brow. "Guess not."

"That must be it." Samantha's face held back a teasing laugh.

Dallas finally won the last game. Maybe this was a good place to end things — on a friendly note, and before anything else could happen. It was after 9:30 now. He slid the cards into their box and stood up. "It's about time to call it a night, I think."

"Oh, drat, it's raining!" Samantha announced with a glance through the window. "I can't get these shoes wet; they'll be absolutely ruined!" The leather high heels lay where she'd discarded them on the carpet next to the couch soon after her arrival.

"I'll be glad to walk you to your car with an umbrella." Dallas moved towards the door to retrieve his umbrella.

"That *won't* keep my shoes dry," Samantha said decidedly. "So, unless you want to carry me" — she giggled like a little girl at this comment — "then I guess I'm stuck here awhile longer. Might as well make the most of it. Hey, let's dance!" The Spacehog album still played in the background.

Dallas dragged his feet back into the room. He half-considered offering to carry her out and then decided against it. Where could he even put his hands on her that wouldn't be touching skin?

Samantha glided towards him, taking his hands and pulling him into the middle of the floor. "That Zeppelin album has *Dancing Days* on it, you know…"

With a blush, Dallas broke away from her grip and retreated. "No, thanks. I said I was tired, remember?" He slid his hands into his pockets. "I don't know how to dance, anyway."

"It's easy with slow songs. Here, I'll show you." Samantha wrapped her arms around his shoulders and swayed her hips with slow, rolling movements. Dallas allowed himself to be rocked, commanding his hands to stay stuffed deep in each pocket. He shut his eyes as his heart rate increased. "Now you hold my waist and just move like this. And then after we practice, we can put on something slow…"

Dallas broke free and shook his head. Samantha appeared unfazed and danced by herself for a moment while he stood by miserably. He'd been about to tell her he'd enjoyed her company for the card games, but now he was second-guessing himself for not being more firm about her leaving before that. At least this whole thing would snap him out of his self-pity from earlier.

Samantha was back at Dallas's shelf, thumbing through his inherited library. "Heyyy, you must be smart. You read all these?"

Dallas sank down on the sofa and rubbed his eyes with his fists. "Yeah, most of them. Or, half of them, anyway." He bit his tongue to keep from saying they were Channing's books. He didn't want to talk to her about the history involved with his best friend. A weird fictional scenario of Samantha cornering Channing in a booth of a truck stop diner grew in his mind, his friend's voice whimpering how he only wanted to look through the souvenirs and get a cappuccino from the machine as she inched closer to him on the seat… Shoot, he really was tired. Borderline delirious.

Samantha had the thickest volume in her hands now, Channing's copy of the *Summa* by Thomas Aquinas. She paged through it with wide eyes. "Whoa, intense stuff!" As she stood flipping pages, something brown fluttered out of the book. Dallas froze, then he rose and crossed the floor, but Samantha had already crouched to retrieve it. Dallas hesitated. It was a delicate leaf skeleton, the tip of it now crumbled. Samantha picked it up carefully, breathing out in awe, "This is simply beautiful, Dallas! I'm sorry I dropped it—I'm going to try my best not to crush it… there!" she finished with triumph, the fragile leaf resting on the open page of the book laid on the floor beside her. She stood back up with it, rapt with attention to the leaf's lacy details. Dallas saw Channing in her actions, and a lump grew in his throat. Why couldn't he stop thinking about him?

"Did you put this in here?" she inquired, still examining the leaf skeleton.

Dallas hesitated. "No… that was my friend's book. He was always tucking things into books—slips of paper he'd written on, stuff he was pressing to save… I found a raven's feather in one of them a few weeks ago." Dallas's lower lip trembled as he recalled Channing's love of nature and books, his attention to detail. "These were pretty much all his books, and every now and then, I find stuff in them."

"Oh, I won't flip through any more of them, then." Samantha shut the book gently and replaced it on the shelf. "He must've had a real eye for natural beauty. It's kind of like treasures he left for you to find, isn't it?"

Dallas's breath caught in his throat at her observation.

"I'll leave them alone, just as he kept them," she continued. "You should frame that leaf, to display and preserve it. He must've been a brilliant reader, by the looks of all these… So, you're making your way through reading them all?"

"Slowly but surely, I'm trying," Dallas admitted, returning to the couch. "The Catholic ones in particular."

"You're religious, huh?" Samantha continued perusing the titles. "I thought so from that cross necklace. But some guys just wear those to look cool, you know? Or even as a gang sign." She turned and stared at the crucifix around Dallas's neck, her attention diverted from the books.

Dallas wrinkled his nose. "That's weird. I'm Catholic—that's why I wear it."

"Yeah," Samantha said dreamily, "how could I forget what you said in the bar that night?" She sauntered over and sat next to him on the sofa before he could get up and move. "You said my beauty was a gift from

God. That might just be the sweetest thing a man's ever told me before." She put a hand on Dallas's thigh.

His brain commanded him to brush it off, but his muscles refused as he was overcome by her attractiveness, long dark eyelashes accentuating aquamarine eyes against her china doll skin. She slid closer, ruby lips pert and inviting. His resolve faltering, he imagined slipping his arms around her waist. His right hand inched towards her, and as his fingertips brushed against her hip, he suddenly forced his hand to obey and instead push her groping fingers off his leg. Coming to his senses, he stared her in the eye.

"Look, Samantha — you said you just came over here to talk," he began firmly. "But I'm gonna speak plainly with you. You seem to be looking for something more. I'm not looking for a girlfriend right now, and I'm definitely not looking for some kind of cheap fling."

She scooted closer as he spoke and tried laying a hand on his forearm this time.

Dallas's skin tingled beneath her touch, and he sat immobile, even as he screamed silent commands at himself.

"Oh, I think you *like* it, even if you're not looking for it… We can take it slow. I know you're all gentleman-like, after all. You're so different from other guys. I know a girl like me doesn't deserve you, but you're just so good to me. I'm not seeing Mike anymore, you know. If commitment's what you want, I could probably give that a try…" She ran an index finger up his arm and onto his chest. "We could put on *The Rain Song*. It's so slow and romantic, and —"

Dallas jerked away from her wandering hand's self-guided tour of his body, and he sprang to his feet and backed away from the couch. "Samantha," he said with fire in his eyes, "I'm beginning to feel like you're harassing me!"

She threw back her head and laughed. "Oh, Dallas, you're too much!" she cried. "Women can't harass men! That's the funniest thing I've ever heard! You're just precious, aren't you?"

Precious?!? Dallas fumed, eyebrows lowered and face red. "What makes you think men can't be harassed? Here you are, making obvious advances on me, and I'm telling you *no*! I told you I'm not looking for a girlfriend in any way! I want you to keep your hands *off* me, do you understand?!"

Samantha's face crumpled. "Oh… okay, I understand," she quavered, eyes down. "But please, don't yell at me…" Tears glistened in the corners of her eyes.

Dallas's jaw dropped. He couldn't believe this! He hadn't yelled, but what choice did he have besides at least raising his voice? Was she really that sensitive to a man's anger, or was this just another part of her game? What if he really did lose it and yell at her next, and she turned *him* into the bad guy? He thought about calling the police, then decided he'd sound like an idiot. The police might agree with Samantha that a woman couldn't harass a man. What would he even say? *"Help, a woman who's coming on to me is trespassing in my apartment?"*

With a turn towards his bedroom, Dallas intended to grab his Divine Office book. If he sat down and prayed while ignoring her, she'd eventually give up and leave, right? He hesitated. What if she came after him into the bedroom? That was the *last* place he wanted her cornering him. The idea made him hot all over.

She followed his path with her eyes. "Is your bathroom in there? May I use it?"

Dallas grunted. "Why bother asking? You've already made yourself at home here." He looked away, unable to hide his contempt for her behavior any longer. *I tried. I tried to just talk to her.*

Samantha's tears streamed openly. She slipped past Dallas and went into his bathroom. Groaning, he flopped back on the sofa and covered his face with his hands, realizing he'd probably left the toilet seat up, and only half-caring. "Please, help me, God," he mumbled. He pulled Channing's Memorare prayer card from his back pocket and read it over and over, trying to calm his mind and gain some clarity before she came back out.

A few minutes later, he heard the bathroom door open. When Samantha didn't emerge, Dallas sighed and stood up. But he wasn't about to set foot in there with her. He peered through the bedroom doorway to see what she was up to. She stood flipping through the sleeve of old photographs that Dallas kept on his dresser. It took all his will not to cross into that room. She had no right to look at pictures of Channing and him!

"This must be your friend!" Samantha said brightly. "I'm real sorry, Dallas. He looks like a sweet kid. What was his name?"

"Can you please put those down?" Dallas's voice trembled. "I don't like to talk about him to anybody. Please."

Samantha glanced over at Dallas. "Oh, okay, I understand. I'm sorry; I can tell that you miss him." She set the stack of photos down respectfully but picked up the top one. Flopping herself down on the foot of Dallas's unmade bed, she held it up so he could see. "You haven't changed a bit!" she exclaimed.

The photo was one Channing had taken of Dallas leaning against the Isuzu, shirtless and hands covered in motor oil. He'd just finished working on his car in that picture.

"How old are you here?" Samantha drew one foot up, knee bent, the motion of her bare leg all Dallas saw.

He blushed. "Probably about 17." Everything had changed completely since that day.

"So young?" Samantha asked. "Well, then, you've been a man for quite a while, haven't you?" She looked him over intently from where she lounged in the tangle of his sheets, in that way he'd noticed her eyeing him in the bar. He shrank back from the doorway and stood in the den, facing away from her, willing away the tantalizing image of her making herself comfortable on his bed.

"Aren't you coming out of there?" he finally called over his shoulder.

"Why don't you come and make me?" she teased.

Dallas tensed, spun halfway around, then quickly retreated across the den, running both hands through his hair. He was certain she could hear his drumming heart.

She giggled behind him a moment later. "I was only kidding, Dallas! Goodness, you're so serious!"

"Yeah, that's the way I am," he snapped, spinning to face her and sticking his hands deep into his pockets again. He narrowed his eyes. "You don't seem to like that, so I'm not even sure why you're here!"

Samantha returned Dallas's stare, her eyes wide. "I'm here because I *like* you, Dallas. A lot. Can't you tell?"

Dallas blushed crimson. Her comment on his seriousness had sounded like a criticism. "I… I'm not sure why…" His gaze dropped.

"Really, Dallas—I like you." Samantha's voice softened, shy for the first time. "I'm not totally sure why myself, but I do. I mean, I can't help it. It's *your* fault for being attractive to me!"

Dallas stared, baffled by her teasing.

"I know what you must think," Samantha continued, softer now, "with how much I've been seeing Mike, but Dallas… when I'm with Mike, I'm not always thinking of him." She gazed into his eyes. "I've been thinking more about—"

"Don't, Samantha—" Dallas cut her off, shutting his eyes against her temptations. *It's just lust!* he argued with his quickening pulse's response to the knowledge that she had been fantasizing about him. Dallas tripped over his tongue, unable to explain that to her.

"I just thought I'd like to get to know you." Samantha's voice was quiet as she twirled a strand of her hair around a finger. "I'm sorry if I've been coming on too strong. You're attractive to me, and not just physically. I… care about you." She took two steps into the center of Dallas's living room, hands clasped together at her thighs right at the hem of her dress, swaying as she eyed him. She was like a beautiful mythical creature, a wispy fairy newly emerged from the unfurling petals of a flower. Dallas's brain was radio static as he fell into the sparkling blue pool of her gaze.

"You're all alone, and I feel so bad for you, knowing that your friend died," Samantha continued. "You two were close, huh? I could tell by the look on your face when you first mentioned him. Sometimes it helps to talk…"

Samantha lowered herself onto the edge of the couch and gazed up at Dallas with a tenderness that made his heart ache inside. She waited, eyes inviting him to trust her somehow.

She can tell that I miss him… Channing… Dallas sank into the chair he'd pulled out from the table and rested his chin on his hands, elbows on his knees. He shuddered and shook the sound of the tractor-trailer squealing to a stop from his mind. His temples throbbed. How could he ever stop reliving this, dwelling in this pit all alone? Dallas inhaled. He was going to let her in.

"Channing was like a brother to me," Dallas began in a faraway monotone, staring at the wall as he spoke. *I need to talk about him; I really do, and it's better than talking about... us...* Dallas gulped allowed his mind to shift to memories of his friend. "He was two years younger than me, and I kinda made myself responsible for him."

"Channing is such an interesting name," commented Samantha. "I like that a lot. Channing—I've never heard it before. His parents must've been real creative."

Dallas stiffened at the mention of Channing's parents. "Actually," he said, looking at her pointedly, "*he* was the creative one. His parents, they were..." Dallas paused, trying to be both charitable and truthful. "They abused him terribly. He deserved so much better. I was always getting into scuffles for him 'cause kids would prey on him, too, like they could just sense his weakness—"

"Is that how you got that scar?" Samantha interrupted, pointing at the faint mark above Dallas's eyebrow.

Dallas shivered at the sudden reminder of the prison guard who had slammed his head against the wall mercilessly, leaving the gash that had resulted in that particular injury. He imagined his shame if Samantha had seen his face right after Hudson's abuse of him or if she even heard the story behind it, and he brushed the mark off as unrelated before adding, "I got this one in a fight with a kid who was always picking on him, though." He turned his lower lip down with an index finger, revealing a distinct white line. "That was in middle school, maybe early high school."

Samantha gave him a winning smile. "Well, it's true what they say—chicks dig scars. It means you're not afraid to stand up for yourself and other people you care about."

Dallas felt his ears grow warm, and he shrugged it off. "Well, the girls must be all over that punk now, because he got the worst of it in that fight." Dallas turned his hands over subtly in his lap to hide his knuckles from Samantha's line of vision. In actuality, he had more visible evidence of a lifetime of battle wounds himself than he'd ever given to Paul.

Samantha didn't notice his fidgeting hands and laughed. "So, you're a real tough guy, huh? That's good. A man should be physically strong. It must've been hard for you to see what Channing's parents did to him... So, they beat him badly, huh? That's so wrong! He looked like such a precious kid in those photos—how could they not have absolutely adored him?"

A warmth touched Dallas deep inside at her concern for Channing as Samantha leaned forward, hands in her lap. He opened up to her without trying.

"His dad beat him all the time when he was little," Dallas said. "He left for good when Channing was six. Never saw him again. That was before I met him," Dallas added, glancing up at Samantha's face, rapt with attention. He went on. "It made me livid, the things he told me had been done to him. But his mother—she was nearly as bad. And her boyfriends after his dad ran off… I still can picture some of the massive bruises and broken finger they gave him."

Samantha made a quiet gulping sound. Dallas glanced up again, and she whispered, "Oh, how awful. Poor Channing…"

"It made him really on edge, having to be worried about whether his mom would flip out and attack him," Dallas continued. "She'd get mad and throw things at him, heavy things, and, well—she was his mother. He still loved her as best he could, and Channing wouldn't ever have fought back. He told me, 'It's objectively wrong for a guy to hit a woman.' I agreed with him, but man, I still nearly wanted to kill her sometimes. Her boyfriends beat up on her, too, in front of Channing." He sighed. "She had some mental illness going on, but she wouldn't always take her medications or get help for it when things got really bad."

Samantha listened quietly. She even had the start of a tear in the corner of one eye, and Dallas noticed. He pushed aside his conflicted thoughts about her and delved into the catharsis of spilling his guts.

"One time, I remember we were in high school… well, I was. Channing had dropped out by then. We were at his house…" Dallas furrowed his brow, trying to bring back all the details in clear view of a day long-buried in his subconscious. "Channing was checking over a paper I'd written—even though he'd quit school, he was brilliant, always reading…" Dallas waved an arm towards the collection of books on the shelf. He furrowed his brow, mentally calculating that it had been over five years since that day.

"Suddenly, the lights went out," Dallas continued. "His mom hadn't paid the power bill. So we climbed on the roof of the house to look at the stars. Channing liked sitting up there for the solitude and view. He always sat in this one spot near the chimney…"

Dallas paused and glanced at Samantha, wondering why he was telling her all this. He blushed and averted his eyes. "I'm sorry, this is probably the most boring story ever."

"No, go on." Samantha's voice was almost reverent as she scooted to the edge of the couch.

The details spilled out of Dallas involuntarily now, his pent-up ache opening like floodgates. "So, we were looking at the sky. I didn't know much about the stars and stuff, but it gave me this melancholy feeling, thinking of how they'd been there for thousands of years, observed by past people long gone from this world. My own insignificance was so real, like I was lost... that probably sounds weird. But Channing knew the names of everything, and who had first discovered stars and when, using them for navigation, all kinds of facts. When I told him about feeling so small, he said, 'We're only blips in time.' Ironic, huh?" Dallas sighed with a sad smile. "To think that when he'd said that, I had no idea he'd die a year or two later." His stare was distant as silence filled the room.

"Insignificant blips in time..." Samantha's voice was far away. "It sounds like sad song lyrics."

"I'm sorry; I'm not trying to be all depressing." Dallas bit his lip.

"No, it's okay. I like those kinds of thoughts, like comparing our lives to something as eternal as the stars. We have such a short time to shine, to live our lives to the fullest. Nothing like the endurance of the universe."

"The constancy of the universe gave Channing a lot of peace after he'd grown up in such a chaotic way." Dallas put his elbows on his knees and focused on the rug. "Me, I was always more of a skeptic. Blow up and burn out, the end. But realizing that something so big can appear not to change over such a long period—even though we know it really is ever-changing—well, it brings a kind of security. He was figuring all this stuff out on his own. I finally got it, and I owe my faith in God to his influence." Dallas paused, subconsciously fingering the medals and crucifix at his neck.

Samantha sighed. "Wow, that's all so... deep. You're brilliant, Dallas, and it sounds like Channing was an amazing person. How terrible that he died so young. So, had his mom finally stopped abusing him by then?"

Dallas closed his eyes again and recalled how the stillness of that night had suddenly been shattered. He clearly saw Channing in his memory, sitting bolt upright and squinting at his watch in a panic.

"No, it's just that he was learning how to cope with it," Dallas said slowly. "But the abuse left this uncontrollable reaction, like a kind of panic attack. Sometimes Channing would start shaking and then just freeze, trying to make himself as small as possible   it's how he'd tried to protect himself when his father was beating him. Anyway, we were still on the roof when his mother got home, raving and probably drunk—a frequent occurrence. When she wasn't drunk, her mental illness made her just as bad to be around…"

"Did you manage to get away without her seeing?" Samantha's eyes were wide, hands clasped in her lap.

A warmth was chasing away his loneliness, spreading through Dallas at her genuine concern. He found it easy to go on with the story.

"He was terrified that she'd see him if he jumped down." Dallas talked with his hands now. "Practically frozen with fear. I had to coax him towards the edge of the roof. I promised him I wouldn't let her see us."

Dallas was back in his mind, the seconds unfolding. Channing had nodded, his resolve strengthened by his friend's confidence and control of the situation, waiting for Dallas to make the call. *I did take care of him, I did…*

"When we heard the door slam, we dropped to the ground and rushed around the house, my keys in my hand. We both scrambled through the passenger-side door, and then I peeled out of there quick. Channing was freaked out that she'd follow us. He stayed over at my house the next few days. It was always best to keep him away from his mother's instability…"

Dallas trailed off, and his cheeks warmed as he glanced at Samantha. He'd really rambled on. "I'm sorry, that was probably a pointless story… I mean, it doesn't even scratch the surface of everything his parents did to him."

Samantha's damp eyes softened. "No, it's okay. I'm glad to listen, if it helps you to remember him… and I'm so sorry he had such a rough time growing up. My father drank heavily at times, too. It sucked, but he never physically abused me, at least. Channing was lucky to have you for his friend."

Dallas bit his lip as he thought the opposite. Channing had given him so much—most importantly, his faith. He prayed Samantha wouldn't ask again about how he'd died—he could never tell her that. How it was his fault. But why had he shared that detailed memory? Dallas knew. Her sympathetic words and demeanor had pried him open, exposing his hunger for human connection. His emotions were a raw jumble now that he'd let her in, struggling in the tide of his memories of his best friend.

He had to banish those feelings back inside, safe from Samantha. Dallas sat up and attempted a half-grin at her. "Bet you weren't thinking you'd be spending your Friday night listening to my sob stories, huh? I'm okay now…"

But she remained stoic. "No, Dallas, I'm just so sorry about it all… that he's gone, and you miss him so much…"

Her eyes glistened with almost-tears, and Dallas felt them well up in his own as he nodded, biting his lip. The tender concern of a woman had evoked the response he always suppressed in front of other people. He swiped at his eyes with the back of his hand. *Man up! Stop moping in those memories that are over and gone.*

But he hadn't been able to prevent a lone tear from running down his cheek. Before he knew what was happening, Samantha had crossed the room and was seated sideways on his knees, hanging on his neck, murmuring into his ear, "You poor thing… I'm so sorry… Let me stay with you tonight and take care of you…"

Dallas's tears cascaded and soaked into the shoulder strap of her dress as he was caught in a tug-of-war between melting under her sympathy or prying himself away from her embrace. His heart raced at the smell of her. The feminine compassion he'd never known before enfolded and melted him before sudden bitter memories of his mother coursed through him, and he shoved them aside before they could build. His hormones were going haywire inside him. *It'd be so easy to just give in, to drown myself in her…* Samantha was a wrapped gift hand-delivered into his lap. Did she really care, or was she manipulating him? Dallas's tears ceased, fireworks and alarm bells going off simultaneously inside his head as her weight pressed against him. Was he too weak to resist? His heart thudded with each justification: *she's gorgeous and she likes me and she listened about Channing and… NO!* He squirmed to draw back from her, but she stroked his cheek with one hand and pulled his head back to her shoulder with the other, swaying rhythmically on his lap. She slid one hand straight down his chest, pausing at his belt buckle and hooking two fingers behind it. *NO, NO, NO!* argued something deep inside of Dallas, and the place where her fingers had crossed his scapular under his shirt scorched like it was on fire. He jerked his head away from her shoulder and put both hands on her waist, pushing her off his lap and bolting up from the chair. Dallas made for the door, gulping, "I need some air." He stumbled outside without looking at her.

Trembling on the sidewalk under the awning to his door and inhaling the humid night air, Dallas's fiery response to Samantha's intrusiveness resurfaced. She'd gotten to him! What had he been *thinking*, telling her all that? Fuming, Dallas kicked himself for losing his focus, for hiding in his memories of Channing. That insistent thought of becoming a Catholic priest bombarded his mind again. He had to end this—*now*. If that was his calling, he couldn't fall prey to her sympathies, real or manipulative. *I can't let her entice me anyway—it's not right! I know better than that! I'd regret everything the second I woke up tomorrow! I know how to respect her and myself. But I can't resist this alone! Please, God, help me!* The old stubborn opposition enkindled his will as he clenched his fists tighter, and then he turned and strode back inside.

Samantha stood inside the doorway, watching him with a look in her eyes that Dallas couldn't quite decipher.

"I'm sorry, I shouldn't have gone there with all that talk about Channing," he said flatly, sidling past her and into the apartment. "I shouldn't burden you with my past problems."

"I'm glad you told me," Samantha said, trying a bright smile at him. "I just want to help you feel better. You know, a man showing his vulnerability like that… it's *very* attractive, Dallas." She gave him that coy look again. "Kind of like the scars — do you have any more to show and tell?"

Dallas set his jaw, unmoved. Samantha had pulled a display of weakness from him, but his aloof confidence was back in full force. "No. And you should leave now." He stalked to the door and pushed it wide. The rain had slowed to a light mist. He stood solidly by the open door, arms crossed.

"Gosh, don't you like me, Dallas?" Samantha sniffed slightly. "I just wanted to comfort you. I thought I was finally getting to know you, seeing your tender and protective side… You wouldn't want to drive me back to Mike and his type, would you?"

Dallas steeled his will and wouldn't back down from glowering at her. She was playing him, taking advantage of his protective instinct! "I'm not in charge of you. You're the one who decides who you hang around. If you don't want anything to do with Mike, then don't see him anymore."

"Hey, maybe you can help me with that!" Samantha tried to pull Dallas back into the room.

He jerked his arm from her grasp. "Here's how I can help you." Dallas leaned towards her, keeping his voice calm. "I'm telling you to stop hanging around jerks like Mike. And to stop throwing yourself at men. If you want to get a good guy, then you can't act as if all we care about is your body. Respect yourself, go home and put on more clothes, and start acting like the lady that you are."

Samantha stared at him incredulously, then gave a little chuckle. "Oh, Dallas, I don't know if I can believe any of that old-fashioned talk. Here's what I meant about you helping me." She ducked back into his bedroom and snatched a t-shirt off the floor. "I'm going to take your shirt, see, and make Mike jealous." Her eyes twinkled with mischief.

The pale tan shirt with bold logo waved before Dallas like a battle flag. *Channing's old Flying J truck stop t-shirt.* "You can't have that shirt," Dallas said firmly, taking a step towards her and lunging to grab it.

"Oh, I thought you wanted me to leave?" She dangled the shirt just out of his reach, both eyebrows raised. "I'll be gone if I can take it with me. Wouldn't you like revenge on Mike yourself, hmm? You *know* what he'll think if I have some of your clothes…"

"No, I don't want any revenge!" Dallas spat. "And you're *not* going to go making those guys think something happened between us, so *drop the shirt!*"

"Make me," she said, lowering her eyelids. "They'll believe what I tell them whether I have your shirt or not."

"It's not even my shirt," Dallas muttered, running both his hands through his hair. "It was… his."

Samantha looked tender for a moment. "This shirt was Channing's?"

Dallas glared in response.

Samantha let out a long sigh. "I really was touched by all you said about him, and I'm truly sorry he was abused and that he died… but Dallas, I just don't get you at *all*. But I'm *not* such a terrible person as to take your dead friend's stuff. Really, and I hope you wouldn't think of me that way." She carefully folded the t-shirt as she spoke and set it on the arm of the sofa.

Dallas shot her a fiery accusation with his eyes. "Yeah, but you're terrible enough to want to spread rumors about me, huh? Make people think something went on here between you and me?"

"Oh, *Dallas!*" She laughed, rolling her eyes. "Guys don't care about that! What, you don't *want* those other guys to think something happened? All men like to have that kind of reputation!"

"Sorry to disappoint, but not me," Dallas snapped. "You're right—you *don't* get me at all. I think you've insulted my honor plenty for one night. I want you to leave now. Goodnight." He held the door open wide and didn't budge.

Samantha rolled her eyes and huffed as she slipped her shoes on, making a show of leaning way over to retrieve them. Dallas swung his eyes towards the ceiling, exhausted from trying not to watch her body on display.

As she buckled the straps of her shoes, Samantha said, "You know, there's such a thing as being *too* good." A sneer flashed across her face.

Dallas bristled at the putdown and then felt surprised at himself that it had stung. Why should he care what she thought of him—she'd been fawning over how nice he was, and now she was mocking him for being morally upright? He'd had more than enough of this confusing mental exercise.

She sauntered towards the open door and paused, going up on tiptoe to lean close to Dallas's face. She shot him that look of admiration again, practically batting her eyes at him. "I still think you're just adorable, Dallas," she murmured as she brushed her lips against his cheek, bringing them to rest against his mouth. Stunned and suddenly light-headed, Dallas found himself kissing her for a split second, and then his legs were going to Jell-O. He flinched and snapped his head to the side, breaking the connection between them. He glared at her, unable to find words.

Undeterred, Samantha lifted her eyebrows. "When you get lonely enough, I hope you'll come find me. Goodness knows, I'm lonely enough myself." She ran a hand across Dallas's chest as she walked out. He fell against the door and locked it behind her, tingling all over.

Dallas whirled to punch the wall, stopped himself short just in time, and instead, turned his fists on his pillows in his bedroom. Then he collapsed on the bed, facedown. He couldn't stop shaking. He tried to shut out the image of Samantha curled up on his couch, Samantha running her fingers across his arm and chest, Samantha on his bed and sitting on his lap, for crying out loud… She was there when he shut his eyes and when he opened them again. The enticing way she spoke his name echoed in his mind: *Dallas…* He pushed himself up from his pillow, where the red from her lipstick boldly affirmed the events of the evening like a flare. Dallas flung the pillow against the wall and got into the shower, letting the cold water hit him like it was putting out a fire.

"This is so messed up, God!" he choked out. "How can she want to be treated so cheaply? And what makes her expect *me* to treat her like that? Is she so resigned to being used that she thinks it's the only way to get any attention?" Dallas slumped against the wall, the cool tile against his forehead, water running in streams down his body as he scrubbed at his cheek and lips with a washcloth. The hidden circumstances of his own conception suddenly invaded his brain, and he shuddered, critical of the character of his unknown father. He ground his teeth with vehemence. *I can never let myself be like that sorry excuse of a man, NEVER.*

Dallas dried off and settled into bed with his prayers. He read through Vespers, breathing in each word as balm for his soul. Then he tried to go to sleep. He lay awake for hours, stomach in knots as he tormented himself over the incident of that evening. He'd done nothing to invite Samantha's advances on him, so why did he feel so dirty and ashamed? *I did the right thing…* And yet he couldn't drive the temptation of the images away. His heart pounded faster at the thought that Samantha may have gone to find Mike after she'd left. Was she with him right now? What was he doing to her? The thoughts ravaged his mind. Was he a jerk to have kicked her out? Should he have tried to keep her here, to protect her from going to Mike or some other creep from the bar? But if she'd stayed, he knew what might've happened. Dallas's perceptions of his manhood were all muddled in his mind, his instinct to defend on high alert. He clutched his scapular with one hand and Channing's prayer card under his pillow with the other, reciting the Memorare repeatedly. He finally fell into a restless sleep.

When he awoke the next morning, it was after nine. Dallas rubbed his temples, noticing the headache he had developed overnight. He wandered to the bathroom sink and splashed cold water over his face and hair, then toweled himself off and stared into the mirror, scrutinizing his face for any faint trace of Samantha's lipstick. The man he saw staring back was broken and weary. He regretted all he'd told her about Channing the previous evening, as if he'd somehow betrayed his friend. He went to the kitchen and started the coffee, realized he was starving, and got out the eggs.

After breakfast, with the headache starting to lift, Dallas could think more clearly. He prayed the Rosary and read through the morning prayers, his internal storm stabilizing as his anger at Samantha for trying to seduce him turned to pity. Dallas's natural deep-seated aversion to sex outside of a marriage commitment surprised him, but he suspected it had to do with growing up fatherless, and now his Catholic faith informed the complete picture of its rightly ordered purpose and beauty. He remembered his mother's only real advice to him as a young teenager, and he closed his eyes and whispered, "I'm not gonna disappoint you in the one expectation you ever made clear to me, Mom. I'm gonna do what's right, but my own weakness is obvious to me now. I'll always have to fight against myself." He closed his prayer book, guilt fading. *Please, God, help Samantha see her true worth.*

Still, Dallas was restless. He paced his apartment. He had no job, no friends. Temptations of apathy, sloth, and the flesh surrounded him. *I've gotta get out of here. But to where?*

The seminary.

No. Dallas froze and clenched up inside. *I'm not good enough for that, at all.* His mind flew to last night, and he scowled at himself for feeling Samantha's temptations. He forced the memory from his thoughts. Then he thought of the two awful accidents and his prison sentence, and he cringed. *Definitely not good enough.*

It was a rash decision, but Dallas left the apartment that morning and went by the rental office to drop off payment in advance for the next three months. He stopped at the sporting goods store and bought a frame backpack, then went home and packed only what he needed into his car: the tent, the camp stove, a sleeping bag, some clothes. His purposeful frenzy of activity cloaked his edginess. He consulted his road atlas and marked a route to the start of the Appalachian Trail in Georgia, bought a few grocery supplies, and got on the road.

The last thing Dallas did before leaving town was to stop by the Catholic church where he'd been attending Mass. He found the priest in the sacristy. "May I go to confession with you before I leave?" he asked. It was a bit early, but the priest had the time.

Refreshed with a clean soul, Dallas drove out of town with plans to attend Sunday Mass somewhere along the way the next morning. He always liked to visit other Catholic churches. The stability of participating in the same ritual and with the same scripture readings regardless of location was deeply comforting in a way Dallas couldn't quite put into words. He headed east, finally stopping in a Walmart parking lot after 10:00. As he settled down to sleep, the delicious thrill of doing nothing but hiking and sleeping along the trail tingled inside him. He was finally more in control, his own man again. Dallas yawned.

The next morning, driving towards his goal of the southern terminus of the Appalachian Trail, an inkling that he was trying to outrun his problems twitched at Dallas. But he couldn't outrun his own thoughts. He tried arguing with them: he was being prudent, getting away from bad influences. His blood boiled over being run out of his own apartment, but now that Samantha knew where he lived, Dallas couldn't relax there. He stared through the windshield at the road ahead. *It's myself I'm so mad at.* Dallas remembered his words in confession. *I don't trust that I can maintain my self-control if she comes back again.* His concerns about the toxic environment were accurate, but there was more to it than that. Dallas didn't know how to face his relentless calling, and he didn't know how to continue dealing with his past.

He turned up the volume of the album he couldn't remove from the tape deck. The more angry-sounding songs had garnered his appreciation over the past few months, helping to vent his own emotions. The words that Dallas rarely considered yet were ingrained in his subconscious came wailing out of the speakers. Suddenly, he was Channing, whose opinion of poetry as well as song lyrics had been that you could glean meaning and truth from them because at the heart of every difficulty was a longing for God and Truth. The lines from their favorite album ironically voiced exactly what Dallas was asking God. Could God save him from the world? From himself? And he'd tried patience, but it wasn't working. He couldn't just sit around doing nothing!

Raw rhythm guitar chords surrounded by silence reverberated in Dallas's ears. Was he really taking action now? The lyrics admonished him for his indecisiveness. That image of the priesthood barged into Dallas's mind again. Was that really the decision God wanted from him? Dallas tapped his fingers on the steering wheel. But it was *God's* decision — he only got to decide whether to cooperate with it or not.

You're a quitter. The accusation snaked through Dallas. He gripped the wheel tighter. He'd quit his job, quit his life in Texas, and now he was running away. Samantha came to his mind again, and his face flushed. *I didn't quit on her — I had* to kick her out! She'd only drag me down with her! Dallas couldn't help her — not the way she wanted. But was he less of a man for not being able to keep her away from her own bad decisions and for being tempted by her against his will? He took a deep breath — he was forgiven for feelings of lust and anger and contempt, and as long as he could keep himself from dwelling on her allure… He exhaled slowly. *God is love and mercy.* The memories slunk away from his mind.

Dallas's call dragged his thoughts back. If answered, it would be for eternity — *forever.* "I'm going away," Dallas said aloud. "Where I can feel your presence and nothing else. I trust you, God — I *have* to. You can show me your will for my life if I surround myself with silence, right? I'll have no peace until I figure out if you're really calling me. It's time for me to take action, if that's your will for me."

With a pang, Dallas cast a glance over his shoulder at the thick blanket folded up on the back seat. All those cold nights they'd slept in the car, how he'd always made sure Channing was covered with that blanket…

"Channing," Dallas whispered. "Are you trying to get through to me? Make me pay attention and focus on what God wants me to do? There's reminders of you everywhere, Chan… like right now, through this music. Did you pick this album out on purpose for me all those years ago? I kinda think you did, because it's unreal how it's talking to me directly. Man, I miss you so much. I wish I could talk all this through with you. Maybe I'm crazy, but I feel like you're pushing my thoughts in the right direction, towards God's will. I'm gonna go into the woods for some serious discernment. I'm gonna find out if I'm supposed to be… a priest. Thanks, Channing."

Forever… The concept was butterflies inside him. *Forever is longer than the longest time. Unending!* But Dallas craved the security that forever offered. *And it's what a priest promises, how he gives of himself…*

Dallas sat up tall. *Father Benedict!* The priest would be worried about him. Dallas pulled off the interstate and found a pay phone.

"Where are you calling from?" Father's voice was concerned when Dallas had told him he had given up his job and left Wichita Falls.

"Mississippi, headed for Georgia. I'm planning to hike the Appalachian Trail awhile, try to gain some clarity on the direction my life needs to take. I'm hoping a strenuous extended hiking trip will clear my mind. But I realized I'd be an idiot to run off without telling anyone. I don't want you worried if you call my apartment and never get an answer."

"You should get a cell phone," Father Benedict advised, not for the first time.

"They make me uncomfortable for some reason." Dallas brushed off the advice, fidgeting with the silver phone cord. "I promise I'll keep you updated on my progress along the way."

"Dallas…" The priest's tone was grave. "This all seems rather sudden. I knew you might quit your job, but has something else happened?"

Dallas sighed. He might as well tell him. "Samantha, the woman at the bar who kept calling me… well, you remember how I told you she was coming on to me, and you heard her message yourself. Two evenings ago, she showed up at my apartment! It was stupid of me to even let her in, but I didn't really mean to. I felt so confused and out of control—I'd start feeling bad for her, and she seemed really concerned about me, and we even seemed to be getting along as friends—but then suddenly, I realized what she was trying to do. I guess that spurred me to action, made me get out of there quick. And just to feel that temptation she was putting on me, even though I knew I wasn't going to give in, it still just, well… it felt really, really rotten." He bit his lip, unable to admit his weakness to the priest, that he feared she could break his steadfastness if she came over again.

Father Benedict's reply was soft. "In a way, you were protected from the world while you were in prison—"

"Exactly!" Dallas exclaimed. "I feel so unprepared!"

"There are many worldly temptations for a man, so much pain and corruption and brokenness—the results of sin, all of it. But," said Father, his voice rising in optimism, "there are still people in the world trying to do what's right and follow God's way. You are one of them, Dallas, and when you realize you are too weak to do it alone, you know you can turn to the Lord for strength."

"Thanks for the encouragement, Father," Dallas said. "It means a lot to be reminded and reaffirmed in what's right and true. I don't know if leaving so abruptly was the best choice I could've made, but I know I had to do *something*." He flipped the edges of the dangling phone book with his free hand. "Will you please pray hard for me? I can't focus back in the city. I need to discern what God really wants of me. I hope getting away can help with that."

"I will double down on my prayers for you, Dallas," the kindly man replied. "Sometimes meeting God in nature can give you a fresh perspective. Are you planning to keep up your prayers and attend Mass at towns along the trail?"

"Yes, I'll get a map and mark out my route based on getting to Mass on the weekends," Dallas responded. "You know, Channing and I used to go out exploring and camping, and it was one of the only times I really… just felt *free*."

"I can understand that," the priest replied.

"Father Benedict?" asked Dallas after a short silence.

"Yes?"

"How do you know for sure if you're being called to the priesthood?"

Dallas thought he could feel the priest smile, even though that was impossible. "You'll just know, Dallas. You will realize there is nothing else you *can* do. You are still feeling that tug months after your release, yes?"

"I am." Dallas gazed out at the interstate stretching past. "I need to make a decision that'll impact my life forever. I think I've been trying to run away from it. But maybe now I'm running *to* it instead. Anyway, I'm gonna figure it out."

Dallas stood at the trailhead with his map, his gear, and a plan. As he took the first steps of his hike, he thought of the nickname he'd picked up in prison. *Yep, here goes the Hermit, off into the wilderness.*

Early spring was a perfect time of year to start the Appalachian Trail. Dallas was alive, all the world surrounding him and nothing to do besides conquer this trail and figure out his own path at the same time.

He covered ten miles the first day, and it was with a satisfied weariness that he pitched the tent in the early evening. Dallas built a small fire, and as the sun set, he read his evening prayers by the firelight, adding more fuel as night grew darker.

Dallas crawled into the tent early that first night, not yet acclimated to the daily exertion of hiking. But after three days, he fell into a steady rhythm. He was covering 14-15 miles per day, trekking in silence broken only by the friendly greetings exchanged with other hikers as they crossed paths. Dallas was mostly alone with his thoughts, focusing on all the natural beauty around him, the fresh air that invigorated him, the dappled sunlight streaming through the new leaves on the trees overhead, rosary beads slipping through his fingers, swinging with his steps at least once a day.

The steady pattern of his footfalls on the trail made a backdrop for his thoughts, allowing them to run through his mind as a sequence of events. From his childhood in Nevada through his prison term and his current life, Dallas's path had led him here, to this moment, to this urgency of decision. He focused on his calling in life in silent meditation.

Late afternoon on his first Saturday, he came to a town and got a cheap hotel room. Almost as blissful as his first one post-prison, the shower beat down on him as Dallas washed away the grime and campfire smoke from the first five nights on the trail. Just when he was finally getting used to good beds again, the hotel bed had become uncomfortable now that he'd been sleeping directly on the ground.

Back at the fireside the next evening, following the early morning Mass and a full day of hiking, Dallas stared into the flames after praying Vespers. His mind ran through song lyrics about fire and burning as he fixated on the flames before him. Fire was mercy, as a purification for the soul, like the words of Saint Paul: "But if someone's work is burned up, that one will suffer loss; the person will be saved, but only as through fire…" The smoke of his campfire curled up into the air like captivating incense rising towards God. Flame and smoke heightened his senses: sight, smell, and touch added to the sound in his mind of both the lyrics and the scripture verse. Dallas closed his eyes and was in the cathedral in Denver, Channing alongside him reciting poetry that made him think of the magnificence of the building, his words rising up in that thin, clear voice of his, like smoke. How amazing that humans could string words together that, somehow, pointed out truths that could have only come from a Creator. *Channing showed me the truth that God is everywhere in the works of human hands and minds, regardless of the mortal artist's intent.* Dallas breathed in the smoky smell and marveled awhile at how the world worked. If he looked for it, he could find God's handiwork in everything.

Dallas sat up late by the fire, finally dragging himself away to get some sleep. In the tent, he stared at the domed ceiling with his flashlight. Way too spacious for him alone, even in his typical sprawled-out sleeping position, the tent had sheltered Channing and Dallas repeatedly. He smiled faintly at the past, then shivered at the memory of their close call with the mountain lion. Dallas swallowed. It would always hurt, but he remembered without crying now. The powerful emotions still simmered underneath the recollections, but that was a good thing. Maybe he was learning how to coexist with his memories of Channing. Maybe he was almost healed.

As he hiked the next day, Dallas squinted at stationary figures in the distance. A family was seated on a log along the edge of the trail, the father standing alongside.

"Hey." Dallas gave a nod to the man, then halted. Something seemed off. "You guys doing okay?"

"Our son just twisted his ankle about a half hour ago," the father replied. "It doesn't look broken, but it's pretty swollen. We're trying to decide if we can carry both Thomas and his gear for a few days to the next town. I know the ankle will heal up, but I'm not sure how long it will take and if our food will last until then if we stay put."

Dallas saw they had already bound the ankle and elevated it. He mentally assessed his own food supply and recognized it was far too small to make a difference to a family of four.

"If you'd like, I can help carry something," he offered. "Either your son or his gear. I don't feel right leaving you here."

"Dad, can I ride on his back?" Thomas asked, eyes bright. "Then you can carry my gear, can't you?"

Thomas's mother nudged him and whispered something to him.

"It'd be no trouble," Dallas reaffirmed. "I'm not in any hurry."

The father studied him. "I really appreciate the offer, but you don't think he's too heavy?"

"I weigh 85 pounds!" piped in Thomas.

"I think I can manage that." Dallas grinned. "Let's give it a try."

Thomas gripped tight to Dallas's shoulders, his hurt ankle dangling in front as Dallas took a few steps. "I have a rope, so maybe I can rig up a kind of seat for him. We'll have to figure out what to do with our packs. Can we divvy up our gear?"

The family set to dividing things so that most of Dallas's and Thomas's gear went into the other three packs. They strapped Dallas's mostly-empty pack to the frame of the older son's, and Thomas wore his own lightened backpack.

"Please let us know if you need to rest," Thomas's mother said to Dallas. "I'm sorry, we didn't even get your name. We're the Bryans. I'm Tammy, and my husband is Pete. Our older son, James, and you've already met Thomas."

"Nice to meet you all. My name's Dallas."

"Are you Catholic?" Tammy nodded towards his crucifix necklace.

"I am."

"So are we," Pete said. "Are you hiking all alone?"

"Guess I'm not anymore." Dallas forced a grin against his initial reaction. He really needed to be by himself right now, but how could he just leave them without help?

The new pace was much slower than what Dallas had been covering. Thomas sat in a sling-style seat tied from rope, one leg on each side. Dallas's solitude of being alone with his thoughts was soon forgotten as Thomas kept up a running dialogue as they walked. By the time they stopped for lunch, Dallas knew where the family lived, that they hiked sections of the Appalachian regularly on school breaks, the names of the family pets—everything. He sighed. He hadn't been able to think for a single minute about his decision since Thomas had first opened his mouth. But this was the right thing to do, even if it was a distraction from figuring out his life.

"How old are you, Dallas?" the boy asked as they set off again after lunch. "Are you a grownup?"

Thomas's mother was right behind. "Thomas, yes, he is an adult, and it is impolite to ask adults their age. Dallas, would you prefer him to call you Mr.... I'm sorry, I don't know your last name."

"It's Malone, Dallas Malone, but no, you can all just call me Dallas. I'm not *that* old, at least I don't like to think so at 23 years."

Dallas felt Thomas's fingers running over the chain of his necklace. "You're Catholic, just like us," Thomas reiterated the fact.

"Yep." Dallas shook his head to deter Thomas's fidgeting. "Becoming Catholic a little over a year ago was the best thing I ever did in my whole life."

"Wow, you mean you weren't born Catholic?"

"No," he answered. "I had to find out about God on my own. You and your brother are lucky to have the gift of faith from your parents."

"We go to a Catholic school," Thomas said. "Well, James goes to the Catholic high school now. Our dad always tells me that too, that it's a gift to get to go there." Thomas spent the next half hour telling Dallas about school, their church, and their priest.

Late in the afternoon, they came across a clearing big enough for all the tents. Dallas helped the two boys pitch theirs first, Thomas fumbling about and needing reminders to keep off his bad ankle.

"Can we help you pitch your tent, Dallas?" asked Thomas.

"You better sit right there on that log," Dallas directed, "and you can watch. Better yet, tell your brother and me what to do."

Thomas enjoyed giving Dallas and James directions, doubling over with hilarity when Dallas joked around by doing exactly what he said literally, with unintended results. Pete gathered firewood in the area while Tammy purified water and unloaded food to make dinner. Dallas pulled out his hatchet and joined in the search for fuel and to get a break from Thomas's incessant chattering.

"I sure appreciate your help," Pete said when they were out of earshot of the others. "Thomas can talk your ear off, so I apologize for that. You're very kind to put up with him."

"He's a fun kid, and certainly not shy at all." Dallas stooped to grab a stick. "And helping you all out is the right thing to do."

"What's your line of work, Dallas?"

"I was working in construction," Dallas began, "but I'm taking a break to hike the trail. Not sure how far I'm going yet."

"Where are you from? We live in Virginia."

"I'm from Nevada but have been living in Texas recently," Dallas replied.

"And you're out here hiking all alone?" Pete asked as they returned to the campsite, carrying the firewood they'd gathered.

"That makes me just a little worried, from a mother's perspective." Tammy set a pot of water beside the fire James was building. "What if something happens to you on the trail?"

Dallas cracked his knuckles and avoided eye contact. "I see your concern. But I don't have any family to speak of, so I'm on my own anyway. I'm trying to figure out what I'm supposed to do with my life, actually."

"Are you going to hike the whole thing by yourself?" asked James.

"I might." Dallas added a stick to the fire. "I won't know until I figure out what God's will for me is. Maybe he'll let me know soon, and I'll be able to turn around before I get too tired," he joked.

Dallas and James added larger logs to the flames, Thomas giving the running commentary. "I can tell you've built fires before, Dallas. You know just how to do it. Wow, you have lots of matches. James is really good at building fires—he always makes them for us. Do you like roasting marshmallows?"

Before long, the fire was roaring. Dallas was into it, encouraged by the boys' enthusiasm. "It's a bonfire!" Thomas cried.

"I don't think we'll have any trouble boiling water over this fire," Tammy said. "Very impressive, boys. I see you like fire-building as much as James does, Dallas."

They cooked dinner, Dallas contributing some of his own food. As the sun set, they ate around the fire.

Finishing up, Thomas said wistfully, "Kevin would've liked Dallas, wouldn't he, Mom?"

She met her youngest son's eyes with a sad kind of smile. "Sure, Kevin would have liked him." The family was quiet, and Dallas felt like he'd intruded on a private secret.

Pete broke the silence. "Kevin was our oldest, would have been 19 now. Hiking was his love, so we continue doing it as a way to keep his memory alive."

"He wanted to hike the whole Appalachian Trail," James added. "He would've done it, too, if he hadn't died."

"I'm sorry that you lost your son and brother." Dallas's eyes moved from face to face as a lump welled in his throat. "It's beautiful that you honor Kevin's memory this way."

"I'm sorry, we don't want to make you uncomfortable." Tammy brushed aside a tear.

"No, not at all. Actually, I lost my best friend almost four years ago in a terrible accident. It can help to talk about the person you lost, I know. Don't feel bad about bringing him up, because he was important to you."

"Thank you, Dallas," said Tammy. "It's been hard on us all. And I am so sorry about the loss of your friend. Kevin died in an accident also. You said you don't have any family to speak of?"

"No." Dallas stared into the flames as he ached inside. "Channing, my friend… he was like a younger brother to me. We were mostly on our own. My mother, I'm not sure where she is now. So, yeah, it's just me, myself, and I." Dallas glanced at the two boys sitting across from him. "You guys stick together, okay? You each have a best friend for life. I bet your big brother would be proud to see you helping each other out."

Tammy's eyes were misty, and a moment later, she told the boys they should get some sleep. As they said goodnight, Dallas's wristwatch alarm interrupted them.

"What's that for?" Thomas asked. "Is it your bedtime, too?"

Dallas chuckled. "Sort of. It's a reminder to say my evening prayers before I go to sleep."

"Sometimes we pray the Rosary," James said. "Kevin liked to lead it…"

Dallas had retrieved his prayer book from his tent.

"What prayers do you say, Dallas?" Thomas pulled at the book.

"Thomas, let him say his prayers in peace," his mother said in a warning voice.

"It's okay." Dallas lowered himself to a log. The boys craned to peek at the book as they sat down on either side of Dallas. "See, I read here, for the evening prayers. These are the ones I said this morning." He tapped the page. "It's all laid out in here, and you get to read different psalms, hymns, Gospel readings… I do it several times throughout the day."

"Cool, look at all the bookmarks," said James.

"If your parents will let you stay up a few more minutes, you can read them with me," Dallas offered. He met their mother's eyes. "But if they need to get to sleep…"

"No, go ahead." Tammy nodded. "It sounds like a lovely end to the evening."

They all made the sign of the cross, and Dallas began with the words of the hymn.

"Now that the daylight dies away,
By all thy grace and love,
Thee, Maker of the world, we pray
To watch our bed above.
Let dreams depart and phantoms fly,
The offspring of the night,
Keep us, like shrines, beneath thine eye,
Pure in our foe's despite.
This grace on thy redeemed confer,
Father, co-equal Son,
And Holy Ghost, the Comforter,
Eternal Three in One."

Dallas pointed out the psalms and responses, and the brothers read along with him. The firelight flickered, giving just enough illumination to make out the words on the pages. Dallas let each boy read a section aloud, resisting the urge to help Thomas with the longer words and allowing a peacefulness to creep in. At the final "Amen," they thanked him and said goodnight. Thomas turned back at the entrance to their tent.

"Dallas?" he called softly.

"Hmm?" Dallas turned his head towards the boy.

"You're not all by yourself. You're friends with God."

A broad smile spread across Dallas's face as Pete helped Thomas get settled into a comfortable position for the night. Maybe Thomas wasn't so annoying as he'd first thought. And what a massive responsibility, raising kids…

When Pete was back out of their tent, he sat alongside Tammy and took her hand in his. "I can't get over what a blessing it has been for our family to meet you today, Dallas. You get on so well with the boys."

"I think you remind them of their older brother," Tammy said, tears welling in her eyes again. "Kevin used to help James build the fires, and he was always the one to remind us to pray as a family each evening. He had a very mature faith for his age. His brothers miss him so much, and your kindness to them today—it just means so much to us. Thank you."

Dallas stared into the fire, the dull ache of missing Channing settled in the pit of his stomach. He looked back up at the man and woman across from him. "I admire the closeness and the faith of your family. It gives me hope, because sometimes everything seems so bad out there in the world." Dallas bit his lip and tried not to think of his own mother.

"The kindness of a stranger has reminded us of the good in the world," said Pete. "I'm grateful you were sent our way today. I truly think you've helped the boys in more ways than one already."

After solitary prayers by the dwindling fire, Dallas slid into his tent an hour later. God sure had a sense of humor—he'd gone from being alone to camping with a family of four. Dallas chuckled. *But I suppose God knows what I need more than I do.*

The next morning, Dallas was up at sunrise, stoking the fire. He sat absorbed in the morning prayers, Lauds, while the coffee brewed. After a few minutes, he heard the unzipping of a tent. The family was starting to stir and wake.

At the scent of the coffee, Tammy and Pete brought their own cups from their gear. As Dallas motioned for them to hold out their mugs, Tammy exclaimed, "What a surprise to wake up to this!" The warmth on her face made Dallas feel like a million bucks.

As the three adults sat around the fire sipping their coffee, Dallas, for the first time, consciously realized he was another one of the grownups in a group. Even when visiting Mitchell or spending time with Father Benedict while getting himself reestablished into society, he hadn't felt like a full-fledged adult yet. Turning 21 in prison had made the transition seem unreal. But here, he had made coffee and offered it to other adults who viewed him as an equal. Dallas's thoughts went to the construction crew — it had been like an extension of high school. This hiking trip was a prompt to grow up the rest of the way.

They had breakfast, and Dallas, Pete, and James got the tents down quickly. They examined the trail map.

"I think we can make it to this point by late afternoon." Pete pointed out the spot. "It's about eight miles. Only five more miles to town the next day, then you can be relieved of your packhorse duties."

Dallas chuckled and reiterated that he really didn't mind.

As they hiked, Thomas prattled on about various topics. Dallas again craved solitude so he could focus his mind and figure out his life's direction. *But I'm probably right where I'm needed.* He prayed for the answers as to what he was supposed to be learning from these few days with this family.

"Hey, Dallas?" Thomas asked suddenly. "You need to decide what you wanna do, after you finish hiking the trail, right?"

"That's right." Dallas shifted Thomas a little higher. He ached from the boy's weight plus the additional fifteen pounds of gear attached to Thomas.

"What stuff do you like to do?" Thomas asked. "I like to build stuff and ride my bike… so maybe when I grow up, I'll build stuff or fix bikes. So, you're grown up, but you still don't know what you want to do?"

"That's right," Dallas answered. "I like to work on cars. I sort of like building things, so I was on a construction crew… but we mostly destroyed old things so they could be rebuilt, newer and better."

"That sounds fun!" Thomas exclaimed. "Like, smashing stuff?"

"Pretty much," replied Dallas with a smile. "It's satisfying to smash stuff up, but I feel like there's more to life than that, something more purposeful that I could do."

"Do you have a girlfriend?" Thomas inquired. "You could get married and have kids."

Dallas laughed right out. "Nope, I don't. I'm not sure that's God's plan for me. I'm sort of scared of girls, you see." Dallas was only half-joking.

"Really? Me too!" Thomas said. "Well, not really *scared* of them… I just don't like them much. But they're good for becoming moms. If you want to have kids, Dallas, then you have to not be scared of girls so you can get a wife."

James spoke from behind them. "People don't always like to talk about that kind of stuff, Thomas. It's kind of a private topic."

Dallas suppressed a chuckle. "I'm sure it's a big decision to get married and take care of a family. You guys are fortunate. I bet you're going to grow up to be good young men, in part because of your parents working together to raise you as dedicated Catholics who love God and others."

Inside, Dallas bristled at the reminder of his own absentee father. It was amazing he'd been able to keep from snapping at Thomas all these hours on the trail—he had no idea how parents did this and certainly had no good example.

"I just thought most everybody got married and had kids when they grew up," Thomas said.

"Not priests," his brother corrected him. "Dallas, our brother Kevin said he might've wanted to become a priest when he grew up."

Dallas was silent a moment and miraculously, so was Thomas. "James, how old was Kevin when he died?"

"Seventeen." James had fallen into step alongside Dallas. "He'd mentioned maybe being a priest since he was really little, Mom says."

Seventeen. Channing was seventeen, too.

"My friend who died… I thought maybe he would've become a priest, too. He discovered the Catholic faith on his own, and he told me about it a lot in the last months before his death. Because of him, I met a wonderful priest and learned a lot from him, and then became Catholic myself. It was a beautiful gift my friend gave to me, my faith, even though he died so young."

"So maybe *you'll* become a priest, Dallas!" Thomas said in his ear.

"I have certainly thought of that possibility," Dallas replied with a private smile.

"But I think it'd be boring to be a priest," Thomas lamented. "All you do is pray all day."

James shot back at his brother, "It wouldn't be boring. Kevin wouldn't have thought of doing it if it was boring." Dallas could hear the defensiveness of his big brother in James's voice.

"Do you think priests can still go camping?" Thomas asked. "I bet they have to live at the church all the time."

"Sure," Dallas told him. "You know, I read something once about the pope, Pope John Paul II—"

"Yeah, that's our pope, too!" Thomas said.

"Of course, he is, dummy," James scoffed. "All Catholics have the same pope."

Dallas tried to de-escalate the argument. "Anyway, our pope, after he became a priest but before becoming pope, he liked to take camping and hiking trips with his college students. If the pope did it, I bet any priest who wanted to could continue hobbies like camping and hiking."

"Dallas, can you stop a minute so I can get my trail mix? Hiking makes me hungry!" Thomas declared.

James caught Dallas's look and rolled his eyes, but Dallas smiled and said nothing, eyes twinkling.

At their camping spot, Dallas extended the stick into the flames, staring at the tip as sugar caramelized into golden-brown perfection. He wistfully recalled the last time he'd roasted marshmallows—with Channing—and he stared brooding into the flames as he reflected on the memory. He felt a tear start in the corner of one eye but didn't allow it to fall.

He was startled out of his semi-trance by Thomas, who was trying to tell him goodnight.

"Oh, goodnight, Thomas," Dallas answered. "Tomorrow's the big day to get your foot checked out and rested up better in a real bed."

"I hope it heals fast," James said, "so we can get back on the trail again soon. Maybe we'll catch back up with you, Dallas."

Pete broke in quickly. "Dallas will likely be far ahead of us by then, boys. We were lucky he came along when he did. I'm not sure if we're going to make it back on the trail on this trip. We'll have to see what the doctor thinks."

Both boys' faces fell, and then Thomas said, "Well, I'm *glad* I hurt my ankle, 'cause if I hadn't, then we wouldn't have met Dallas!" Everyone laughed, and they all said goodnight to the boys.

Once they were zipped into their tent, Pete said, "I heard some of the boys' conversation with you while we were hiking earlier."

Dallas glanced up, unsure if he'd overstepped his bounds in talking to the boys about such serious topics.

"About Thomas asking you if you wanted to get married or become a priest..." Pete folded his hands under his chin. "I'm sorry if his questions were getting too personal. James understands how to put things more tactfully, but you can see that Thomas is a work in progress."

Dallas's eyes reflected the firelight as he stared deeply into it. "No, it's okay. It's funny because they had no way of knowing it, but... I've been discerning the priesthood, actually."

Tammy and Pete exchanged glances. "You'd make a good one, Dallas," Tammy said softly. "You have a way of being open about God but in a very comfortable and relatable way. And you've done nothing but serve us since we met you along the trail. You're good with people, and we certainly do need more priests. I heard the boys telling you that our Kevin had talked about being a priest since he was a little boy. We'll never know now, but we like to think he might have followed that path."

Nobody said anything for a few minutes. Then Dallas spoke up. "I want to thank you for letting me spend time with your family. I don't know if you could tell, but I'm kind of an introvert usually. It's good for me to focus on other people's needs instead of myself because... well, truthfully, I can get really wrapped up in my own feelings and worries. Part of my discernment is to figure out if I'm kind of resisting the call to the priesthood because I'd have to give up my privacy, in a way, my tendency to be a loner. Meeting up with you folks has been serendipitous because it's helped me see that firsthand, which is something I need to pray about a lot while I'm out here."

"Serendipitous, now there's a word you don't hear used every day," Pete commented with a laugh.

"Especially not from somebody so young as you are," added Tammy.

Dallas blushed. "Well, yeah. Sometimes words just slip out of me, and I'm not entirely sure where they come from." *Channing*—that's who they'd come from. With a sigh, Dallas speared another marshmallow.

The next morning, Dallas let the boys finish off his apple cinnamon instant oatmeal for breakfast. It had rained overnight, dampening everything, but they'd gotten the water boiling over the fire. Dallas got his tent packed up quickly and offered to help Pete pack his family's gear.

"Aw, I want to show Dallas this log over the stream that me and James found!" Thomas said. "Can he come see it, Dad?"

"Sure, I've got the rest of this stuff handled here." Pete slid a pole out of the tent and began collapsing it. "But you still need to stay off that ankle, remember."

James helped support Thomas as they walked down the stream. It was in view of the campsite, and Thomas was being good about leaning on his brother and keeping his weight off his injury. James helped Thomas sit on a tree stump and then crossed the stream on the fallen log. "Look, we found the perfect vine to swing on!" he exclaimed, grabbing hold of the end and showing Dallas.

"Looks fun," Dallas said.

"I wish I could do it!" Thomas lamented.

"Let me see how strong it is." Dallas grabbed hold of it and tested to make sure it would bear his weight.

"Okay, Thomas, just once now," Dallas said. "If you can hold tight on my back, I'll swing one time with you. But you have to promise not to beg to do it more than that, 'cause I don't think we should push our luck, huh?"

"Okay, I'm ready!" Thomas was standing up gingerly on his sore ankle. Dallas crossed back over the log and hoisted Thomas to his back, then walked back across the log with him and took hold of the vine. He lifted his feet and swung out alongside the stream, Thomas cheering gleefully, then back again and landed.

"Okay, my turn!" announced James. He grabbed hold of the vine and ran a few steps, then leaped out over the water, swinging far out above the stream, and then back to the shore again.

"Is that vine sturdy?" called Tammy as she looked on from the campsite.

"Yes, Mom!" James replied. "Dallas checked, and it can hold him and Thomas!" He tried the vine again, this time starting on the log and swinging over to the shore. "Want a turn by yourself?" He offered the vine to Dallas.

"Sure." Dallas took the vine in his hands. "Think I can swing across the stream and land on the other side?"

"Hmm, maybe..." James studied the opposite bank.

"Go, Dallas, go!" cheered Thomas. "He can do it!" he said to his brother.

Dallas took a running leap and swung out across the stream, then let go and dropped to the bank on the other side at the point where the vine was extended its farthest. Both boys cheered. James tried and was successful. Then Dallas swung from the shore up to the log, making a balanced landing while keeping his grip on the vine.

"Aww, I wish my ankle wasn't sore, 'cause then I could do some awesome stunts!" complained Thomas.

"How 'bout you think of some challenges and I just do them for you," Dallas offered, full of energy and fun now. *Fun*—he was actually enjoying himself. *The story of St. John Bosco mentoring the boys...* Dallas straightened up, feeling as if he were outside himself looking in.

Thomas thought a moment. "Swing back and forth across the stream twice, and then drop back where you started!"

Dallas did so, and James said, "That's too easy. How about this: swing up to the log, but let go of the rope when you land there!"

Dallas accepted the challenge and got a running start, swung up to the log, then let go of the vine and dropped onto the slippery surface, barely keeping his balance. Thomas shrieked with excitement and clapped his hands. Then James tried it, but at the last second, he kept hold of the vine to keep from falling off the log into the stream below.

"Okay, I've got one." Dallas rubbed his hands together. "I'm gonna stand on the log, and James, you swing the vine up to me, just throw it hard, and I'll jump off and catch the vine as it goes by and swing back to the shore where you're standing."

Both boys were full of enthusiasm and encouragement as Dallas stepped back out on the log. "Here it comes!" shouted James.

The rope came within range and Dallas jumped out for it, caught hold, and swung across the stream and dropped next to James, landing neatly on two feet.

"Again!" cheered Thomas, beating his fists on his thighs. "That was awesome! Again!"

Dallas stood again on the center of the log, ready. James swung the vine, and Dallas leaped towards it. He caught it with one hand but missed with the other, and, unable to keep a good grip, lost his hold and fell into the stream below. Tammy and Pete came running and found Dallas sitting up to his waist in the water, laughing hysterically. Thomas and James were doubled over as well.

"Are you okay?" Tammy asked Dallas.

"Just a little wet is all." Dallas stood and shook out his arms. "Nothing a towel won't fix." He waded to the shore and climbed out, his half-zipped boots squelching with each step.

"Did they put you up to that?" Tammy eyed her sons with stern suspicion.

"No, no, that one was all me." Dallas chuckled. "My idea."

"That was an awesome fail!" James high-fived Dallas.

"Do it again, Dallas!" Thomas shouted.

"I'm sure once into the water is plenty," Tammy said with a little smile. She turned to Dallas. "Well, if you were anything like these two are when you were younger, then I'm sure this is nothing new to you, Dallas."

He grinned. "Reminds me of some of the crazy stuff we used to do when we went to hang out in the woods near where I grew up, climbing and jumping off anything we could. Yeah, we were nuts. And apparently, I still am." Dallas slipped off a boot and poured the water from it.

After Dallas had changed into dry jeans behind some bushes, he pulled James aside while Tammy and Pete were busy examining and rewrapping Thomas's ankle.

"You'll have to keep helping your brother out for a while," Dallas told James quietly. "I'm sure your parents will appreciate it. And he will, too, even if he doesn't tell you so. But they'll all rely on your strength for a while."

James smiled, affirmed in Dallas's assurance of his abilities. "I broke my leg when I was eight," he said. "My dad and Kevin had to carry me upstairs every day. I'm probably bigger enough than Thomas that I could carry him up the stairs on my back."

"I can tell you care a lot for Thomas." Dallas clapped a hand on James's shoulder. "He's fortunate to have you for his big brother. You're a good example to him." He realized he was saying the kinds of things he would have liked to hear as a young teenage boy himself. Other than Channing's appreciation, he hadn't gotten much encouragement in his process of growing into a man. Dallas turned towards the others, and James followed.

"I don't wanna go," Thomas whined as they put on their packs. "If we go, then we'll get to town soon, and then we won't see Dallas anymore!"

"We'll all be sorry to part," Pete agreed, pulling Thomas to his feet. "But I'm eager to get there myself so we can get a cold drink and maybe some ice cream."

Thomas, encouraged by the possibility of a treat, got on Dallas's back and they started off. They were mostly silent as they trudged along the last leg.

A few hours later, everyone was licking ice cream cones on the sidewalk in front of a small cafe. Dallas had noticed a hotel they'd passed and planned to get a room there for the night. The Bryans would head further into town to get to the doctor.

Tammy scrawled their address and phone number on a scrap of paper. "I hope you'll keep in touch, Dallas," she said as she handed it to him.

Pete shook his hand and again expressed his gratitude. "My old back couldn't have carried him so far," he said with a laugh. "Don't ever take your youth for granted, Dallas!"

Dallas shook his hand back firmly. "No, I won't."

Thomas and James gave Dallas various high-fives and playful shoves and slaps on the back.

"Okay, okay!" Tammy laughed. "Enough roughhousing on the sidewalk. Let's go, boys."

"Bye, Dallas!" they shouted and waved as they headed up the road. Dallas turned and headed back to the hotel.

Refreshed and clean after showering and shaving off the several previous days' stubble, Dallas headed out of the hotel towards the Catholic church. He slipped in the side door and found an empty pew in the transept. Mass wouldn't start for another fifteen minutes, so Dallas knelt, crossing himself, and went through a list of prayer intentions in his mind. He pulled out his book and prayed Vespers, then leaned back with his eyes closed.

Dallas welcomed the peaceful time with God in this small-town church. Mass began, the building only half-full. An older lady sitting in a nearby pew stared at Dallas. Squirming in his seat, he examined his clothes and wished he'd at least packed a pair of khaki pants. He was in his cleaner pair of jeans and a plaid flannel shirt. He'd tucked it in but had no belt… *or maybe it's my earring.* His hand went instinctively to the little silver ring, a piece of his past self that he couldn't quite part with, but Dallas wondered if his wearing it made little old religious ladies suspicious of him. Dallas focused on the priest and pushed out the concerns of whether other people were looking at him or not. He was here to participate in the sacrifice of the Mass as the highest act of worshipping God.

Kneeling for the consecration, the ringing of the bells made Dallas's heart jump into his throat. The visceral reaction had persisted at every Mass he'd attended. An invisible force plucked him up and dropped him back into a different time and place, right back to that Oklahoma convenience store and the jingle of the bells on the door, and then to Mitchell's shop, when the police entering the building had sounded the door's bells there as well. Going back to Mitchell's shop and confronting those bells again hadn't made a difference. Those bells had signaled the event that began the worst day of his life. Dallas couldn't shake the ominous feeling brought by the physical reminder. But he'd have to get over it eventually—whoever heard of a priest who had panic attacks every time bells rang? Doubts crept into Dallas's heart, and he squeezed his eyes shut tight and gritted his teeth behind closed lips.

Lord, please deliver me from the grip this memory has on me. Dallas made himself stare at the bells as they were rung the second time, forcing himself to see that these were not those bells from his past that had ushered in such tragic events. "I'm not there anymore," Dallas whispered to himself.

After Mass, Dallas wandered over to the prayer candles. He liked to light a candle for Channing in every new church he visited. It was comforting to imagine that prayer remaining, going up to God in the church for hours after he'd left. He lit a second one and dropped a few more quarters in the slot, adding another prayer for Kevin and the family who missed him so much. The loss of another potential priest felt like a stab in the heart to Dallas as he recalled his inklings of Channing's future. Dallas knelt in a nearby pew and gazed up at the old wooden crucifix hanging in the front of the church. The words "It was you, not Channing" kept running through his mind. *Me, God? You really want me? Me, with a felony on my record, an aloof loner, to serve your people for you as one of your priests?* Dallas closed his eyes and bowed his head to his folded hands, slumping forward. He couldn't make himself feel worthy.

But it's not about my worth, is it? If you're all-powerful, God, then I gotta believe you can do anything, and use anyone, for a higher purpose. Dallas's mind returned to that question he still hadn't fully answered: had he forgiven himself? He believed that God could forgive him. He had to keep working to extend that same consideration to himself. With a sigh, Dallas resolved not to give up. He stayed on his knees in the church long after everyone had left.

Back on the trail the following day, Dallas hiked rigorously, stopping only for lunch. The sky, overcast since midmorning, was an ominous prediction of bad weather. When he stopped for the evening, Dallas built a fire and got the tent up as quickly as he could. Four hot dogs and an apple made his dinner. He wished he had some mustard, a wistful reminder of Channing. The complete solitude of being alone hit Dallas acutely after the constant hubbub of being with the friendly family of four. Thoughts of Samantha wormed into his imagination, and how she had tried to use his loneliness to prey on him—and how he'd secretly liked it, sort of. Dallas lowered his eyebrows, disgusted with himself again. There was no denying it—Dallas was lonely. He was done with self-pity, however.

The sky opened up as soon as he pulled out his prayer book. Dallas tucked it inside his shirt and tried shielding the fire with a large trash bag. Success nominal, he gave up and crawled into his tent for the night. Dallas removed his combat boots and stretched out on his sleeping bag. He folded his hands behind his head, gazing up at the last light of early evening as the rain pattered on the fabric. When Dallas opened his prayer book, the paper that Tammy had handed him fluttered out. He was suddenly struck with the guilty thought that maybe he should try to find his own mother.

Families were important. Dallas wasn't sure where things had gone wrong for his. Try as he might, he couldn't conjure up any feelings of warmth for his mother. But there was something to be said for family duty, and regardless of how emotionally dry she had been to him, Dallas knew he'd try to help her if ever she reached out to him, now that he was an adult. He shut his eyes tight and wrapped his arms across his chest. *Does she ever think of me, wherever she is?* After observing a mother's love for her own sons in the past couple days, he ached at how his own mother could have prevented herself from showing any of those feelings towards him. Dallas reached under his shirt and fiddled with his scapular. He was under Mother Mary's protection, but he hadn't fully figured out what that looked like for him. Discovering that there were families who did things together and talked and joked gave Dallas a weird sensation underneath his usual resigned numbness. He saw God's plan for families—but understanding it on a personal level? He couldn't.

Studying a water mark on the tent's ceiling, Dallas furrowed his brow. What was he supposed to take from his interactions with Thomas, James, and their parents? He'd wanted solitude, but, just like in prison, it hadn't stopped him from giving a listening ear or a helping hand to someone in need. Dallas was exhausted more than just physically from the encounter, but he was becoming a better person each time he gave his time to others. *And… I kind of miss their company now.*

"Maybe that's it," Dallas said aloud. "Maybe I'm supposed to be learning that my life is not my own." He thought back to his pre-prison days and saw it there, that, yes, he'd felt a duty towards Channing. *Don't focus on how you failed at that.* Dallas rubbed his temples, trying to concentrate. *I don't always want to help people, don't want to go out of my comfort zone… and yet, I'm driven to do it. What's making me do it?* It was more than just a sense of obligation. It was the power of the Holy Spirit urging him on to do good, to fulfill his purpose in life: to serve other people.

Dallas sat up. He would be serving people, a lot of people, as a priest. As a monk, he'd be alone; well, alone with other religious brothers, but alone with his thoughts, too: *alone with the temptation to fall into selfishness, self-pity, and despair.* The priesthood: a true and noble purpose, serving others, always directed away from oneself. *And the Eucharist…* Dallas's breath caught in his throat as he again thought of his recurring dream, his unworthy hands being used by God to bring the Body of Christ to others, and for the first time, he murmured aloud, "God, I think I know that you want me to do it. I know what I'm supposed to do. I just *know* it." Shivers ran up and down Dallas's spine as he knew with certainty that God was calling him, for real. He lay back again and smiled up at the calming sound of the rainfall above him, all around him.

Dallas fell asleep peacefully, a weight lifted from him.

The next morning, he studied the trail map. *Should I head back yet?* A nagging feeling still urged him on, and Dallas wasn't sure if it was from God or from his own selfish desire to be alone. He estimated the time needed to cover the distance marked off by his finger-length measurements. He could make it to Sunday Mass in the next town. It would give him a few more days to sit with his decision, pray on it, and make sure. Doubt hung at the back of his mind—would he really be allowed to become a priest? He folded up the map and pressed his hands to his face, inhaling a slow breath. *I need to actually forgive myself, completely. If there's nothing holding me back, will the bishop see that? And will it make a difference?*

The solitude of constant rain for the next three days was a sarcastic answer to his introvert's wish. Dallas passed very few hikers on the trail. He built a small fire once, but otherwise, everything was far too wet. He hiked all day in the rain, then pitched the tent in as sheltered a place as he could find each night. Everything was a muddy mess. Eternally grateful for Ziploc bags, he spent his long, quiet evenings praying and reading *Orthodoxy* and *Les Miserables* inside the little yellow tent.

Dallas stared at the page late on the third night of torrential downpour. The bishop in *Les Mis* could've been Father Benedict, and he could have been Jean Valjean. Dallas had never been entitled to Father's treatment of him — a criminal — but the priest had looked beyond that.

His experiences in solitary confinement coursed through Dallas in a shudder as he revisited prison through the fictional pages. Those days had filled him with despair and come close to stealing his very soul from him. To be dehumanized was to make a man into an animal, and there was no doubt in Dallas's mind that he could have become completely hardened and hate-filled if he'd been put into solitary more frequently or for longer periods over the course of his prison term, especially without Father Benedict's support. Unlike Valjean, Dallas had cried so much that he was unrecognizable to himself after awhile. He'd never been one to cry before Channing's death, but it would have been far worse to have become so deadened as to never have permitted one tear to fall from his eyes.

As Dallas read, his mind jolted to a standstill, his crimes stripped down and exposed for exactly what they were: *wrong*. Valjean had stolen a loaf of bread for his poor sister and her children, and Dallas had stolen to feed himself and Channing when they'd had no food or money. They wouldn't have died of hunger. What he had done had been flat-out *wrong*, plain and simple. Dallas despised his past actions, but he couldn't get enough, devouring them in print on repeat. It was exactly what had happened to him. His decision had been worse for Channing in the long run.

And this was Channing's book. He'd picked it up in Minnesota, a few weeks after they had settled in there, at an estate sale. But he'd never said a word about this. Surely, he'd seen the parallels, given his intelligence and intuition. Gratitude for his friend washed over Dallas as he realized what Channing must have seen in this story, yet he hadn't piled more guilt on Dallas over something that was in the past, unable to be changed.

Could Dallas forgive himself? He closed his eyes and listened to the rain beating on the tent outside. *Yes. Yes, I can forgive myself. I have to. Channing would have done it. God already has.*

He'd done wrong. He'd been stupid, impulsive, immature. But Dallas was not that 19-year-old boy anymore, the one whose rage had controlled him, the one who'd struggled desperately to grow up despite having had no adult examples for himself, the one who'd thought the entire world was against him and especially Channing, the one who had felt like he was the only one who could take on their problems, the one who'd been a slave to his fight-or-flight instinct, the one who hadn't believed there even was a God. And yet, his inability to do anything of worth on his own struck him now more than ever. *And that*, thought Dallas, *is why I have to forgive myself. Because it's not me — I'm nothing! It's God. What an insult to the Almighty if I refuse to do for myself what he's already done for me.*

Dallas unzipped the tent and gazed through the streaming rain, the ancient trees towering above, surrounding him. The slightest edge of the last of the evening's dim light melted away, far in the distance through the trees. He pulled off his socks and shirt and stepped outside the tent and into the deluge. Mud oozed between his toes, and he stretched out his arms, allowing the rain to soak him. Water streamed down his face, into his eyes and mouth and ears, down his chest. He felt his jeans soak through as the rainwater ran down his body. Muddy water soaked up into the cuffs of his pants.

The power of the surrounding world invigorated him. Here he was, a speck on the surface of a vast earth, an amazing planet teeming with life and wonder and miraculous occurrences all around him, and he was allowed to witness it all, revel in it, experience it. There was a Creator who saw him as deserving of taking part in this great dance of life in an immeasurable universe, and Dallas dizzied at the enormity of it all. He turned his hands palms up and surrendered to the driving rain, remembering his baptism. All at once, he sensed the unexplainable of what had drawn him to nature from his earliest days of childhood.

Finally overcome by chills, Dallas retreated into his tent, trying not to drip water on his sleeping bag or pack. He reached for his towel and dried himself off, slipping out of his soaked jeans and transferring all the water on his body into the now-saturated towel. Shivering, he slid into his sleeping bag and huddled there to warm up while he read his evening prayers in the glow of his flashlight.

Once he was warm, Dallas was drowsy and comfortable. The rainfall on the tent had a white noise effect. Dallas unzipped the sleeping bag and threw it off himself so he wouldn't overheat, then was lulled to sleep in the cozy enclosure of his old tent.

As wet as everything was outside, Dallas woke completely dry. The tent's waterproofing had held up well over the years, plus he'd been tarping it during rain for extra protection. As soon as he stepped out to pack things up, it was a different story. Everything was wet immediately, and Dallas gave up on trying to keep his clothes dry. His poncho was devoted to covering his pack and sleeping bag as he folded up the tent as quickly as possible in the rain. Only a mere inconvenience, the weather was tolerable because the temperatures were well above freezing. Dallas had a vague feeling that the whole experience was making him stronger. After all, he'd been through far worse. He was the one choosing to be here. After the years in prison where he had so few choices, Dallas held power in his grateful hands.

The sun had finally chased away the rainy days, and Dallas welcomed the downhill slope as he descended from Clingman's Dome late afternoon. Reaching his campsite for the night, he rubbed his aching feet. The wet weather which had soaked his boots had given him blisters. Dallas built a roaring fire and sat with his bare feet propped up near the warmth of the flames. Everything had dried out in the past couple of days, and he was taking full advantage of the change by building good fires and sitting up reading Channing's old copy of *Orthodoxy* fireside.

He had been on the trail for three weeks and had anticipated being out here for months when he left Texas, but now… Dallas knew he wouldn't need that long.

The quiet evenings solidified the conviction that he knew what it was he was meant to do with his life. *It's the only thing I can do*, he realized, as the last few days of silence, of being alone with his thoughts, had only confirmed his calling. A deep sense of peace swelled within every cell of his body. *I need to turn around. I know what I have to do, and I've finally fully forgiven myself*. His last stopping point would be in the next town. Then he could return, heading back towards the rest of his life. Dallas couldn't run from this. He didn't want to.

On a Saturday afternoon, he arrived at the next town ready to rid himself of the grimy accumulation of sweat, dirt, and smoke. He got a hotel room and cleaned up quickly, skipping shaving, before walking back to a restaurant he'd passed. Dallas's stomach burned for food. Hiking so extensively and continuously had increased his usually light appetite a lot in these few weeks. He ordered two sandwiches and a bowl of cheddar potato soup, along with a cup of coffee. The warm food and drink were bliss, and Dallas decided to finish off the meal with a piece of cheesecake. He motioned the waitress over to him.

"Big appetite today; you must be a hiker," she observed. "You're hiking all alone?"

"I am," Dallas acknowledged. "Could I please have another coffee refill, along with a slice of cheesecake? Used up my coffee on this last leg of the trail, so I'm recaffeinating today," he explained.

"Sure thing. I'll be right back," she answered with a wide smile before heading towards the kitchen.

Dallas gazed through the window at the great view of the hills above the town, where he knew the AT wound its way through the landscape. He pulled a small notebook out of his shirt pocket and started jotting down notes. He would track some of his experiences, like how he'd recorded memories of Channing during the long years in prison. Never much of a writer, he paused and chewed his pen cap, grasping for accurate words to describe what was happening inside him. He barely noticed the waitress refilling his coffee for the third time until she silently touched him on the shoulder. He jumped, and she nodded towards his full steaming mug. "Oh, uh, thanks," Dallas said.

He read over his last words again: "I know where my future lies. I know for sure." He closed his eyes and let the words stream through his mind, then glanced at his watch. It was just past three, so he paused in his writing to pull out his book and read the afternoon prayers for the day. Afterwards, he went back to his journaling, more thinking than writing. How could paper and ink contain what this was, this answer to his life that was bigger than himself?

While finishing his fifth cup of coffee, Dallas allowed his mind to turn over those days when he and Channing, teenagers who had thought they had all the time in the world ahead of them, had sat in places like this for hours on end, imbibing copious quantities of coffee. Dallas set the pen aside and stretched the fingers of his right hand.

The waitress approached and smiled. "Are you planning on a sixth cup of coffee? You seem to be on a roll there."

Dallas met her stare. The way she was looking at him was unnerving. "Uh, you've been counting?" was all he could think to say.

"Don't worry, refills are free," she replied. "But, if you stay much longer, I'm going to have to sit down across from you and get to know you, since it looks like you might plan to never leave!" She laughed, and Dallas's ears grew pink. *She's just joking around, isn't she? She's too old for me anyway.* Still, his recent experiences with Samantha had him on guard. *Maybe this is my cue to leave.*

"Actually, I'm finished," he replied. "Finally. May I have the check, please?"

She stared at him a second longer, then turned to go get the check.

Dallas sighed with relief. He was most likely overreacting, he wanted to avoid those kinds of situations completely. *Besides, I'm probably being egotistical. Not all women are going to throw themselves at me just because one did. I mean, I'm not really that attractive, am I?* Dallas realized he knew very little of this topic and what women found to be desirable in a man. *This waitress is probably just being friendly. Still, I don't have to hang around chatting with her to find out.*

As she approached with the check, Dallas occupied himself by flipping back through his notebook. He kept his eyes down as she laid the check on the table, then he pulled out his wallet and set a few dollars on the table as tip. He handed over his cash at the register, received his change, and turned towards the door. The waitress passed him on the way.

"Thank you," Dallas mumbled with a quick glance before dropping his eyes.

"Sure thing," she replied as he slipped out the door.

On the sidewalk, Dallas blew out the breath he realized he'd been holding. The waitress hadn't meant anything. She was just being friendly, and he'd better learn how to do likewise but without ever sending the wrong impression. He glanced over his shoulder as he walked away. Figuring out how to balance that hadn't been made easier by being in prison so long, without seeing a female for years. His mind roamed to his mother again as he neared the hotel, hands in pockets. *Maybe I'd understand women better and be more comfortable around them if she had…* He paused, chewing his bottom lip and staring at some children on a swingset across the road. His mother had always kept him fed, clothed, and sheltered as a child. Wasn't that enough? He kicked a rock as he continued down the sidewalk. *…if we'd had an actual relationship, that is. Or if I'd ever had a chance to see a man treating her well.* But Dallas couldn't change how she was, or how life had gone for her. He sighed as he unlocked his room and slipped inside. One thing he was sure of in discerning his own future: it couldn't be marriage. With no example of what a marriage should even be, all of his past baggage would be an unfair load to place on any woman. But God could take it. Dallas exhaled in relief as he flopped down on the bed. *Only God is strong enough to take all of this junk from my past, and I don't have to feel bad about dumping it on him.* Dallas pondered the endless supply of mercy he had found. That warmth of rightness settled inside him again.

Picking up the phone in his hotel room, Dallas dialed Father Benedict's number.

The priest greeted Dallas. "How has your journey been?"

"I think it's over." Dallas's voice was calm. "I'll turn around and head back tomorrow. I'm in Tennessee, closer to the top of the state than the bottom."

"So, you have had some productive time to pray and think and be alone outdoors?" Father questioned.

Dallas laughed and related the story of meeting up with the lively family and helping them out for two days, and how that experience may have taught him more about his calling than the time on his own.

"I know that I'm supposed to serve others," Dallas stated with surety. "My life isn't meant to be my own. If I made it my own, I'd become more and more selfish. I know my own personality, and that's what would happen over the years if I just did what I wanted to please myself all the time. I feel called to give my time to other people, especially to help them get closer to God, to really know him and understand the Church he left here for us all to grow closer to heaven through Jesus. I…" Dallas took a deep breath. "I know now that I'm supposed to become a priest."

Silence came from the other end of the line. Dallas's heart pounded quickly with the declaration, and it seemed like minutes instead of seconds before Father Benedict spoke.

"You sound genuinely convicted on this, Dallas, with a kind of light in your voice," the old priest said gently. "It is not an easy path to take, but I can personally vouch that it is an excellent one, and one many young men ignore the call to because they don't always know to listen for it. God is calling you in such a unique way, and He will use the hardships you have endured to help you be a leader for the people you will serve. I already saw that in you during your incarceration, the way your past problems allowed you to humble yourself and see the humanity of others. That is going to be your most powerful asset as one of God's priests, Dallas — your love of your fellow man despite their weaknesses and sin, knowing that you can help broken people turn back to him for healing and to find their way to their true home in heaven."

Dallas smiled. "You have a real way with words, Father. You describe my feelings on this so well. And you were right — I just *know* it now. I know this is the only thing I can do with my life! I've never been so at peace with a decision before. But Father Benedict… who gets to decide if I'm good enough to be a priest with my background?" Dallas wound the phone cord tight around the fingers of his free hand. "Can you really be ordained with a manslaughter conviction in your past?"

"An *involuntary* manslaughter conviction," Father Benedict reminded him. "All the details of that will need to be laid out to a bishop before he would allow you to enter. And I will help you, Dallas," the priest assured him. "I'll vouch for you as being an excellent candidate for the seminary. Would you like to go through my archdiocese? You would have to move up here if the archbishop agrees to accept you. You've had no college at this point, is that correct?"

"That's right." Dallas paced the room as far as the phone cord would allow. "I'd be in the seminary for eight years, wouldn't I? And do I have to apply there, get accepted, like applying to college?"

"Yes, but if the archbishop approves you, acceptance to the seminary will be easier, so don't worry about that right now. I know you've told me that school was something you muddled through without much enjoyment, so eight years may sound like a long time. But it is a good period of preparation that gives young men time to be sure they are doing the right thing."

Dallas ran a hand across his face. "How will I even pay the tuition?"

Father Benedict's soft voice came through the line. "Easy, Dallas. Don't worry about all these things. The archdiocese helps you in everything. If God wants you to enter the seminary, you *will* enter. Enjoy your time hiking back, and call me again whenever you'd like, but certainly after you make it back to Texas. Would you like me to go ahead and speak to the archbishop on your behalf?"

"I'd appreciate that very much," Dallas answered. "And you can tell him anything about my past, my conviction, everything. I'd rather get everything out in the open before I get my hopes up."

"Pray, hope, and don't worry. All will work out for God's plan."

Dallas could almost see Father's serene smile through the phone. He exhaled slowly, and they said goodbye.

On his way to the grocery store, Dallas stopped by the Catholic church. He checked the confession and Mass schedule for the next day, then sank into the back pew of the empty church and stared at the tabernacle before him. *Pray, hope, don't worry...*

Only one more week on the trail. As Dallas hiked, he was drunk on the wonder of his natural surroundings interwoven with the peace and hope flooding his mind. Channing's way of not taking any little thing for granted lit him up inside as he reveled in the beauty all around him in the simplest things, even an insect or a leaf. The ordinary, everyday things were really little miracles. *Chesterton's thought that we are so obsessed with novelty when the real miracle is that the sun should rise every day, again and again, that a pattern in nature should repeat over and over through a species of flower...* Contentment, stability, assuredness washed over Dallas with that promise of miraculous repetition. It was like the repetition of the liturgy, the never-ending cycles of the Church year, Christ's sacrifice made present again through the Mass, always, past and present combined. He had finished *Orthodoxy* and realized that he could reread it and gain still more insight from it. It was obvious why Chesterton had been Channing's favorite author: Channing, who pretty much memorized everything he read, who needed some serious depth of thought for a book to capture his attention and draw him back to reread it again.

The steady rhythm of prayers by the fire that evening had become a ritual since he'd turned around on the trail, firmly cementing his vocation in his being with each passing day. The flames and his prayers rising up, side by side in the silence of the solitude of night, lighter than air, imbued Dallas with a true manliness, a confidence like steel. He'd never felt so right before. God's purpose for his life had him on his knees in awe, speechless.

The campfire's movement and light bounced off his skin, its warmth permeating him in the setting sun. Dallas glanced at the date on his watch. Exactly one month until Channing's birthday. A pang of longing flitted through his heart. "He'd be turning 22 years old," Dallas said aloud into the flames. "I can't even imagine him as a fully grown adult. He's perpetually seventeen in my mind." The sadness would always be with him, the dates coming as yearly reminders. The anniversary of Channing's death had fallen at the start of the trip. Dallas blew out his breath slowly, the pain no longer a gut-wrenching stab. *I just have to endure the pain and keep on going. It's my cross to bear.* He whispered up a prayer for Channing's soul, sorrow offered up on the smoke to be used for good.

If Channing would have turned 22 soon, then that meant Dallas was almost 24. He quickly did the math in his head—if he got accepted into the seminary, the path to the priesthood, he would be nearly 32 at his ordination. *I can't fathom being that old.* The priesthood suddenly seemed a long, long way off. *More than double my time spent in prison!*

Pushing aside his brooding thoughts, Dallas said his evening prayers and did some reading before crawling into his tent just after 9:00. It was so easy to fall asleep each night after these days of physically challenging hiking. *Maybe this is how it feels to die after a life well-lived.* He yawned. *Like you could just comfortably slip away in peace after all the good, hard work that you did on your journey through this world…* He shivered—was the thought disturbingly morbid, or a deep spiritual comfort? Maybe both. Channing had lived a good life in his last few years, Dallas knew in his heart. *And if my own journey is gonna last far longer, then I'm willing to do it well in whatever time you give me, God, and for your purpose.*

Sprawling himself out across his sleeping bag, Dallas fell into the delicious sleep of satisfied exhaustion.

Dallas's map indicated only six miles until he reached the place where he'd begun nearly seven weeks ago. His insides quivered as he packed up his tent for what would be the last time on this journey. The eagerness to move forward with his life mingled with a dread that his past would prevent him from being allowed to seek ordination to the priesthood. What if he was totally upfront about everything, and the door was shut to him? *But it* can't *be; God's calling me!* Maybe Father Benedict had already spoken to the archbishop of Denver.

As each step brought him nearer to the trail's end, a nostalgia about leaving the AT tingled inside despite his readiness. Dallas paused and gazed up at the trees with a bittersweet smile that he had a new special place to add to his memories: a place he had found without Channing. Maybe it was a healing step—proof that while it wasn't what Dallas would've chosen, he *could* do it without Channing.

As he trudged onward, Dallas's thoughts drifted to the place in the woods where he and Channing had explored and camped several times in their teenage years. It had been five years ago or more that they'd last gone out there. *And with this same camping gear…* One stray tear ran down Dallas's cheek. He wiped it away, rough stubble under his fingers evidence of how much he needed to shave at this point. It had been over two months since his last haircut. Dallas ran a hand through hair too heavy to stick up much like it normally did, being longer than it had ever been in his memory. *A haircut will be one of the first things I do back in Texas.*

Texas. Dallas supposed he should keep up his lease until he was sure the archbishop would allow him into the seminarian program. Nervous butterflies filled his stomach. What would he do with himself while waiting for an answer? Dallas pulled his rosary from his pocket and prayed in silence as he treaded along the last leg of the trail.

An hour later, his car came into view. *The end of the trail.* Dallas halted, hardly believing he was already back here at the parking lot where he'd begun. He took a deep breath of the forest air, then strode to the Isuzu with conviction in his step. He propped his pack against the car and fished into one of the pockets for his keys. Unlocking the trunk first, Dallas lifted his gear in. Then he got into the driver's seat, eager anticipation tugging at him like it always did when he hadn't driven in a while.

I'm heading towards the rest of my life now. He turned the ignition and gave the gas pedal a few revs. *This is the real deal. My life is yours, God.* With one last look out the window at the surrounding forest, Dallas pulled out of the parking area and got on the highway, heading west.

It was dusk when Dallas drove into Wichita Falls. He had slept in the parked car overnight and, still exhausted from his backpacking trip, hadn't awoken until after nine in the morning. He'd only spent a few minutes cleaning himself up, shaving with the help of his car's rear-view mirror, and after driving all day, Dallas craved a hot shower in his apartment. Checking the time, he decided against stopping for groceries. Despite his physical tiredness, Dallas was more at peace mentally and spiritually than he'd been in a long time. *Deciding to say yes to my vocation is the right thing to do.* He smiled in certainty. *The archbishop's gotta say yes. God wouldn't lead me to this point for nothing.*

Passing the familiar grocery store and stifling a gaping yawn, Dallas racked his brain to remember if he'd left a pizza in his freezer. What better Friday night plans could there be than showering, eating, and lounging around a bit before crashing for the night? The bar where he'd gone after work with his old co-workers drifted past through the passenger window. Dallas gave it a haphazard glance.

He did a double take. *Is that who I think it is?!* It was Mike, and with chagrin, Dallas acknowledged that it was indeed Samantha with him. Mike's truck beside them in the parking lot left no doubt. The angry expressions on both their faces were discernible even from this distance, and Dallas hadn't imagined what he'd seen—Mike had just struck her across the face with the back of his hand.

The lowlife jerk! Dallas squeezed the steering wheel hard, arm muscles taut. He should pull over and, so help him, the punishment he'd inflict on Mike… But his distrust for Samantha brought a scowl to his face. "She can fend for herself, that—" A pang of guilt stabbed him before he verbalized the rest of his thought. *I didn't mean that, God.* No matter how she'd acted towards him, she didn't deserve to be hit by a man. He had to turn around.

"Why me?" Dallas grumbled as he made a U-turn. But his pulse raced with a worry for Samantha that he couldn't ignore. Maybe he could just call the police. For the first time, he wished he owned a cell phone.

Dallas made a left turn into the parking lot, scanning the area to see if anyone else was out there—no one. The shadowy figures of Mike and Samantha, arms flailing, drew him to the end of the lot, their shouts audible through the glass. Dallas's body tightened, and his stomach churned in disgust, recollections of Mike's physical strength from their days of working together on the crew magnifying the cruel injustice of Samantha's dainty body being overpowered by the jerk's aggression. When he saw Mike shove her up against the hood of his truck, large hands gripping each of her wrists, Dallas lost it. He threw his car into park and leaped out, rational brain flooded by instinct. Heart pounding and face hot with fury, he strode up to them and grabbed Mike by the back of his shirt, wrenching him away. "Leave her alone!" he shouted, putting himself between Samantha and her attacker.

Mike spun to face Dallas. His face registered shock at the interruption, then disdainful recognition. "Get the hell outta here, Malone," he sneered.

"Dallas," gasped Samantha, "he hit me! He hit me!"

Mike shoved Dallas hard in the chest with both hands. "I said get lost and mind your own business!"

Dallas gritted his teeth and returned a fist in Mike's gut. Mike barreled at him again, Dallas's fist colliding with his face this time. Mike staggered back between his truck and the car parked alongside it, breathing hard with nostrils flared, hesitating.

"You can go on home, Samantha." Dallas, fists still raised, didn't take his eyes off Mike. "I'm not gonna let him follow you."

"My car's not here," Samantha said from beside him with a little sob. "He drove me. I... I don't know what to do..."

"Come on, Sam, I didn't mean it," Mike said in his typical laid-back voice, taking two steps towards her with hands out to the sides. "You know I didn't mean it. Come on; I'll take you home myself."

Dallas glimpsed the hint of fear on her face as she inched back. "You better watch it, Mike," he growled in a low voice. "If you so much as even touch her again—" He glanced sideways at Samantha. "Do you have a phone? Call a taxi."

"N-no, I don't have my cell phone on me." Her voice trembled. "I have money, though..." She stepped forward and squatted down for her purse, knocked to the pavement in the scuffle.

In the dark, Dallas hadn't noticed if there was a pay phone in the area. Could he risk taking his eyes off Mike to go find one? No—Mike, still on his feet and nursing his bruised jaw, rubbed the spot where Dallas had hit him, glaring. Dallas's eyes flitted to Samantha. "Go get in my car. I'll take you to the police station so you can report this."

Mike jolted forward and opened his mouth as if to threaten her not to go to the police, but he held back when Dallas tensed and widened his stance. Dallas had the upper hand, and he was sure Mike didn't want to get punched again.

"I... I don't know if, um... if the *police* are necessary," Samantha stuttered. She backed up beside Dallas again, who stepped in front of her protectively as she studied Mike with a conflicted expression on her face.

"Just go get in my car if you feel threatened by this bastard," Dallas said, eyes narrowed at Mike the whole time. "You don't need to stay with a guy who's assaulting you."

Samantha made no reply but edged her way back to the still-idling Isuzu, hesitated as she glanced back at a glowering Mike, and slowly sank into the passenger seat. Dallas, veins pumping with adrenaline, glared back at Mike. "If I had a phone, I'd call the cops to come down here right now," he snarled. "So I guess you just got lucky. If you're smart, you won't contest any charges Samantha brings against you. 'Cause I'll be there to testify against you, and if you hadn't realized before, this bar has security cameras out here." Dallas jerked his head towards a camera mounted high up on a nearby light pole. Mike's face registered worried surprise at his oversight.

Dallas backed towards his car, seething at Mike. He jumped in and threw it in reverse, then turned out onto the road.

"Oh, Dallas, thank you!" gushed Samantha as she leaned across the seat and hung on his shoulder. "You came at just the right time to diffuse our little disagreement. Sometimes Mike gets a bit out of hand—"

"Samantha," Dallas interrupted as he shrugged her off his right arm, "I'm driving you to the police department, and you're going to file a report against him. That wasn't just 'a bit out of hand.' I saw him slap you across the face and slam you against the car! You need a protective order to keep that jerk away from you!"

Samantha laughed nervously. "Oh, it'll all blow over by tomorrow or the next day." Her small voice sounded nonchalant, but Dallas thought he detected anxiety there. "He'll be mad the rest of the night, but it'll be fine after that. But, um, I would ask you to just take me home and drop me off, but Mike might show up there while he's still mad... And, if he thinks *you're* there, he'll be *really* mad, like *jealous* mad, so—"

"Which is why I'm headed to the police station." Dallas's eyes were set unflinching on the road in front of him. *Unbelievable—after what just happened, and she's still trying to play us against each other with herself as the prize?* Dallas inhaled slowly. "I haven't given Mike any reason to think I'd go to your place at all. You don't think you're hurt badly enough to need medical care, do you? If so, we should go to the ER instead."

"No, of course not; he didn't hurt me *that* bad. I don't think it's really a big deal, Dallas," she said, voice slightly annoyed. "But, I mean, I *do* appreciate so much how you stepped in. Maybe it would've gotten worse if you hadn't shown up..." She leaned closer, tone softening. "Could you take me to your apartment?"

Dallas was pierced by that alluring charm she put into her voice. Did it just come automatically to her when she talked to men?

Samantha put a hand gently on his upper arm. "Mike doesn't know where it is, so I'd be safe there for tonight."

Dallas cringed. *Liar.* If the other guys on the crew had told her where he lived, then their buddy Mike probably knew too. But maybe Samantha was too rattled to be thinking rationally. *Be charitable. But don't let her manipulate you!* Dallas gripped the wheel more firmly. "Absolutely not. I'm taking you to do the right thing, to report his violent behavior, and that's all. There's nothing to debate." He drove on in silence, his jaw set, thankful that the police station wasn't much farther down this street.

In the absence of conversation, Samantha noticed the music coming from the car speakers. "The Toadies!" she squealed. "You like the Toadies? Of course, most people around here do. We're loyal to our local bands. Did you know they finally put out another album earlier this year? I bet they're touring to promote it now. Hey, we should go to a concert together! Clearly, we share the same taste in music. I'll find out when they're going to be playing somewhere near here, how about it?"

Dallas stuttered a noncommittal response. Unnerved that Samantha had commented on the music at all, he glanced at the cassette deck, the tape that Channing had been the last to touch still running on its endless repetitive loop. It was clear she was trying to make an emotional connection between them, but Dallas didn't want to concede that the music was something she could share with him and his best friend. Still, the thought of reveling in the shared interest of a concert with another person… he imagined himself and Samantha pressed in by the energy of a crowd all in sync with each other as they sang along with the band.

Samantha turned sideways in the seat and studied Dallas with a playful gleam in her eyes. "Your hair looks cute, Dallas! It's longer than when I last saw you! So where have you been? It's been a while."

Dallas prayed silently for guidance on how to respond. He couldn't believe her upbeat attitude. She should be more upset after being abused like that! And what was she doing back with that scumbag, anyway? His biceps in both arms tightened. "Look, I'm not feeling chatty right now. You were in trouble, and that's the only reason you're in my car now. He was *abusing* you, Samantha, and you need to report that to the cops. You can't just tolerate that kind of treatment and brush it off like it's no big deal."

They had pulled into the parking lot. Dallas got out of the car, hesitated a second to wait for Samantha, then dragged his feet around and opened her door. She was crying as she stood, knees shaking. "You're right, Dallas," she sniffed. "He hit me. Three times. And he pinned me against his truck. You saw that yourself."

"And has he treated you like this before?" As Dallas stared at eyes that wouldn't meet his, he dreaded the answer he knew was true.

"Um... well, he's been a little rough before," she admitted.

Dallas cocked one eyebrow. "A *little* rough? He's hit you like that before, hasn't he?"

Samantha stared at her feet, avoiding an answer. She finally lifted her head slowly until her glistening eyes met Dallas's. "Yes," she whispered. "Yes, he's hit me lots of times now. I... I don't know what I want. He's good to me sometimes too..." Her voice trailed off and she gazed into the distance, fidgeting with the bracelet around her wrist.

Dallas swallowed and forced a calm voice, focused on taking action so he wouldn't notice his heart threatening to shatter. "Okay, let's go in the station now. You can tell them everything, so he won't be able to hurt you ever again." He slammed the passenger-side door and started towards the steps. When Samantha didn't follow, he paused and turned. "You can do this, and I'm going to help you. You're a strong person. You can stand up to him and protect yourself. You've gotta believe in your self-worth, okay?"

Samantha looked up at Dallas as if she didn't really believe what he'd said. But a little light had come into her eyes, and she lifted her head and straightened herself up, taking a deep breath and a step forward. "Okay, yeah." She brushed the tears from her eyes. As Dallas turned towards the building again, she caught his arm. He spun around. Samantha dropped his arm quickly and glanced side to side, as if suddenly remembering their last encounter. She sighed and walked towards the entrance, and he fell into step beside her, hands in his pockets. "Why can't all men be like you, Dallas?" she asked wistfully into the air. "You're just so... *nice*."

Dallas pulled the door open, and they stepped into the building. After a lengthy wait under glaring fluorescent lights in a sterile hallway, Samantha was seated across the desk from the on-duty officer while Dallas leaned against the doorframe, still agitated and unable to sit still in the cramped office. While recounting exactly what had happened, Samantha's voice quavered, and Dallas closed his eyes to the pain. The hint of shame in her voice wasn't quite covered up by her tough outer appearance. Dallas noticed. *Just like me.*

After taking photos of Samantha's bruised face, the officer questioned Dallas about his involvement.

"I saw him hit her as I drove by. I used to work with Mike and had heard him speak about women in a derogatory way before. But I would have stopped regardless of who it was because I couldn't keep driving by after seeing physical abuse like that, not if I could try to stop it. It wouldn't be right."

Dallas admitted to punching Mike twice, and Samantha was quick to defend him. It was self-defense because Mike had shoved Dallas, and because he was restraining her when Dallas first laid a hand on him.

"So, in short, she needs a protective order against this thug, and she needs a police officer to take her home," Dallas concluded. "If you need me to testify against Mike, you know where I can be reached."

The officer stared up over her glasses and yawned, appearing unaffected by the incident. "Look, we're pretty understaffed right now. We can get an officer to drive her home, but it will be several hours from now. She's welcome to wait here, but can't you just take her home? You brought her in."

Dallas shifted from one foot to the other, torn. Samantha hadn't flinched. She stared at the floor, dejected and weary, her toughness finally cracked. Having to recount the abuse she'd endured had reduced her to something Dallas didn't recognize.

"It's okay, Dallas. I can wait," she murmured, not bothering to take advantage of the situation or even making eye contact with him.

Dallas sighed. He wanted desperately to do the right thing, but he was no longer sure of what that was. He glanced at the officer seated behind the desk, who was staring at him with a disapproving, if not bored, expression.

"Come on," he finally said. "I'll drive you home so you won't have to wait. It's after midnight already."

Samantha's eyes skittered to meet Dallas's, and she looked as if she wanted to say something, but she quickly closed her mouth again and dropped her gaze.

"It's no trouble, really," he added. "You should get home as soon as possible and get some rest."

Samantha slowly rose. "Okay. I do have to work the evening shift tomorrow, so yeah, I could use some sleep…"

Dallas stepped out of the office and held the door wide for her.

"Thank you for your assistance, Mr. Malone," called the officer as Dallas turned on his heel and followed Samantha down the hall, his shoelaces dragging along behind him on the slick floor, a picture of the way this night had turned out.

She was uncharacteristically quiet as they pulled out of the police station parking lot and headed across town towards her apartment complex. Dallas assumed Samantha would resume her talkativeness along the way, but she did not. All she said was, "Thanks for driving me—you really didn't have to."

The music at low volume and the vibrations of the old car combined with the darkness of night and the exhaustion of her earlier ordeal lulled

Samantha to sleep after a few minutes. Dallas glanced over, observing her head resting against the glass of the passenger-seat window. His heart lurched in his chest. Now Channing was no longer the last one to have slept in that seat. Dallas's face flushed in anguish and anger, replaced immediately by guilt. *Give her a break. She's been through an awful ordeal tonight. Just like Channing.* He couldn't begrudge her this. It was a chance to be more selfless anyway, to stop worrying about things of this world. It's what a man with his calling should do. Dallas slowly blew out his breath through his lips and let it go.

Samantha started as the car halted in her apartment parking lot ten minutes later. She mumbled an apology for falling asleep as she blinked her eyes and squinted through her window.

"Don't worry about it." Dallas tried to sound kind yet detached. "You've had a rough night. Just show me which door is yours. I've already circled the lot to make sure Mike's truck isn't here."

"I appreciate you looking out for me like that. My apartment's down on this end, number 126." She pointed through the windshield.

Dallas put the Isuzu in drive and pulled into a vacant parking space along the sidewalk. Samantha, her purse and cardigan sweater gathered in her lap, peered through the windshield towards her door but didn't budge. Dallas couldn't tell if it was due to fear or her desire to drag out every minute possible with him. He gave her the benefit of the doubt again, remembering how her demeanor had fallen as she reported Mike's physical abuse in the police station.

"I'll walk you to the door," Dallas found himself saying as he stepped onto the pavement. He strode around to the other side, eyes alert to his surroundings almost subconsciously. He needed to see her safe inside for his own peace of mind, anyway.

Samantha opened her door, and Dallas met it, swinging it back for her. Samantha gazed up at him as if admiring a superhero. But she hesitated, and Dallas couldn't tell if he read fear hidden in her eyes.

"Come on," he coaxed, "I'll make sure you get locked safe inside."

Samantha dropped her eyes. "Um… that's just it. I… well, it won't matter if I'm locked in or not." Her voice became hushed. "Mike has a key."

Dallas's stomach lurched. That predator could just come over and let himself in? And after what he was doing to her earlier... "You need to have the locks changed," he insisted, crossing his arms. "As soon as possible. Tomorrow morning, first thing."

"I guess that would be smart, but I have to check with the landlord," began Samantha, "and I might have to wait a week, until I get my paycheck—"

"No, you need to get it done immediately," Dallas repeated firmly. "I'll deal with the landlord afterward if he has a problem with it. You don't need to get permission to protect yourself. And I'll pay for it if you can't afford it now. I'm not going to feel okay about it until the locks are changed if that scumbag has a key." He bit his lip to prevent himself from asking Samantha what she had been thinking to have given him one at all.

Her wide eyes darted around the parking lot as she put one foot on the pavement, then glanced up at Dallas. "What if..." she whispered, "what if he comes here later tonight?"

Dallas had already thought of that and the dilemma it put him in. "Let's just get you inside and then figure this all out," he said, rubbing his left temple and trying to conceal a sigh as he gestured for her to get out of the car.

Samantha stood up, Dallas shut the car door, and they walked down the sidewalk to her front door.

Reaching in her purse for her key, Samantha glanced up at Dallas with a little smile. "So," she began, "I guess I'm inviting you inside, then... and you're accepting." The playfulness in her voice faltered as she perceived Dallas's expression of steadfastness and purpose.

"I just need to make sure you're safe," he stated, eyes serious and arms crossed over his chest.

They entered the apartment. As Samantha locked it back behind them, Dallas brushed past her, asking, "Where's your phonebook? I'm gonna see if there's a 24-hour locksmith who'll come rekey the door now."

"Dallas, relax a bit!" Samantha tried to laugh him off. "Don't you want a tour of my place first?"

"No." Dallas was abrupt. "I want the phonebook." He held out a hand.

Samantha gave him a withering look but retreated into the living room and rummaged through a drawer. "I don't think they'll do it in the middle of the night," she called. "I think that's only if you're locked out, and they have to come get your car open, that kind of thing." She returned to the foyer, handing over the White Pages. Dallas took the book and headed for her phone, its location on the kitchen wall already on his radar.

He dialed the first number he found that indicated a 24-hour emergency service. Samantha was correct—they wouldn't rekey a door at night. Dallas tried two more numbers with the same result. Sighing, he replaced the receiver and put an elbow against the wall, hand on his forehead.

"Dallas, I'm sorry you're having to go to all this trouble." Samantha stepped closer. "Really, I'll probably be okay until morning. I promise, I'll call one of these numbers first thing tomorrow, at eight a.m. We can just hope Mike already came by here and left when he saw I wasn't back yet." She picked up the scrap of paper where Dallas had jotted down each number and stuck it under a magnet on her refrigerator. "Hey, I have that same album you had on in the car, right here!" She walked into the den to put the CD in her stereo.

Dallas opened his mouth to stop her and then changed his mind. He'd been listening to it for months straight already but didn't want to have to explain something so personal. He closed his eyes and saw Channing frozen in time in the seat across from him, twirling a string of cheese from his pizza slice around his index finger, that moment when Dallas had been hit over the head with what the depths of true friendship meant, unconditional love and loyalty, his first conscious realization that he could sacrifice his very life for another person...

Samantha's voice broke into his memory. "Want to stay awhile and listen to music, have a beer or two?"

Dallas, refusing to be swayed from his goal, ignored her question. "Do you have a family member or close friend who can come stay with you for the rest of the night? I don't want you alone here when Mike has access to your apartment."

"My mom lives an hour away, and I'm not sure she'd even come." Samantha waved a hand. "She doesn't like Mike, from what I've told her, and she's probably a bit scared of him—"

"As she should be!" Dallas slammed a fist down on the kitchen counter with more force than he'd intended. "And as you should be, too. I meant maybe a male relative who could come stay with you—a brother or cousin, a neighbor, anything..."

Samantha gulped at Dallas's display of anger. "I... I *am* a little scared of him, Dallas. But it's my fault for getting involved with him. I'll probably be okay alone. I have a gun."

Dallas jerked his head up. "And you know how to use it? Does Mike know you own a gun?"

Samantha nodded to both questions as she rounded the kitchen island.

Dallas breathed out, releasing the tension held inside of him. "Well, that might deter him from even coming over here… you think?"

Samantha cast a glance to one side and toyed with the hem of her dress. "Well, Mike owns some guns, too. So, I don't think… well, I want to believe he wouldn't threaten me with one, but he can hold a bit of a grudge when he's mad. And I don't think he's intimidated by me, even if I'm armed…"

Dallas's hopes sank. He couldn't see a way out of this now, all alternative options a blank to him. He tried to reason with himself mentally. *You're not her savior. But how could you leave her alone, as prey for that lowlife excuse for a man? You'll have no rest from worrying if you do.* Anger towards Mike burned through his body, and irritation rose at Samantha for having wormed her way into his life in the first place. Dallas clenched his fists at his sides. "I shouldn't have even stopped," he grumbled under his breath before he realized he'd said it aloud.

Samantha turned away, tears springing to her eyes, and Dallas was immediately miserable with regret.

"Samantha, I… I didn't mean that." He took a faltering step towards her and dropped his head. "I'm sorry." He turned and paced the small space between the foyer and kitchen, talking with sweeping arm gestures. "I'm just so pissed off at Mike right now that I could punch a hole through the wall! I promised to get you home safe, and I'm *not* going to break my word." He stopped and stared at her, but her damp eyes were on the floor.

Samantha wandered into the living room. Dallas followed a few steps, leaned back against the other side of the island, and studied the mess of a girl sunken down on the couch. Low notes drifted from the stereo, filling the apartment with their steady hum. She raised her wide, teary eyes to meet his. Dang, they were so glittery blue. "So… you'll stay?"

It was the decision Dallas had already made but didn't want to admit out loud. Dedication to his calling, his assured discernment of his vocation to the priesthood, assailed him mentally. *Why, God, why, right as soon as I'm ready to follow your call?* Dallas shook out one arm and then the other. He had to do the right thing — *things*, rather. He had to make sure Samantha was safe from Mike for tonight, and he had to be true to God, and true to himself and Samantha both, by respecting the truth about her femininity, his masculinity in light of his calling, and what he knew to be right about human relationships and sexuality. *She doesn't see things the same way I do.* He bit his lip, jealously guarding his discernment as something far too special to share with her. She wouldn't understand his vocation, anyway. But he could handle this. The excitement burned in him over the certainty of his calling. And God would keep him safe from temptation. *I just have to make it clear to Samantha why I'll stay.*

"I don't want you to read anything into this," Dallas began, fidgeting with Channing's glass ring on his finger. "But I won't be able to sleep if I leave you alone, knowing Mike could get in. Since you don't have anybody else to come watch out for him, then… I'm going to stay. You're going to sleep in your room, and I'm going to sleep on the couch—if I sleep at all, that is. Do you feel safer keeping your gun with you, or do you want me to keep it out here, with me?"

Samantha rose from the couch, relief and gratitude flooding her face. "Oh, Dallas, thank you so much!" she gushed. "You really don't have to, but of course, you're such a gentleman that you wouldn't leave me if there was any chance I wouldn't be safe. Yes, you keep the gun. Maybe it's old-fashioned of me, but I feel better with a man having to use it rather than me." She turned and went into her bedroom and returned a moment later with the handgun.

Dallas accepted it gingerly as he recalled his very limited experience using a firearm. Images of Channing and himself shooting empty cans with his old BB gun flashed through his mind, his heart sinking with the knowledge of his poor aim, and he wished his friend were here, although he knew deep down he wouldn't have ever made Channing be the one to protect them despite his being the better shot. Swallowing down his concerns, Dallas examined the pistol with cool eyes and tucked it into his pocket. He locked up the accidental shooting in the safe of his mind and prayed he'd have no need to use this gun. Ever since the unintentional manslaughter crime, he'd felt sick at the idea of having to shoot anyone, even in self-defense.

Almost as if she had been reading his thoughts, Samantha said with a furrowed brow, "I hate that you could be in a dangerous situation if Mike comes over here armed." She stepped towards him, eyes tender, and stopped a few feet from where Dallas leaned against the kitchen island, arms folded across his chest. "I mean, I trust you completely that you can protect yourself… and me…"

"It's okay, I don't mind danger," Dallas broke in. It was true, but he realized as soon as the words had left his mouth that it might have come across as cocky. "I mean… really, I don't think about it, and so I'm not afraid of getting shot or killed or anything. I just act when needed. If you need protection, I don't care if it endangers me." He swallowed. *And I went to confession just this past Saturday, so I'm ready…*

Samantha gaped. "You… Dallas, are you saying you'd be willing to *die* for me?"

He focused on the scuffed toes of his boots, not wanting to answer her question with the firm and automatic *yes* that was the truth. But he hadn't detected any kind of manipulation in it, only a sincere amazement that he would risk his life for hers. He glanced up and saw she expected a response.

Dallas straightened himself and took the gun from his pocket, placing it on the counter behind him. He cracked his knuckles and tried to think of something else he could do to buy time before replying. Coming up with nothing, he stammered, "I... don't really know if, uh, I should answer that, because I don't want it to come across the wrong way..."

Samantha's eyes welled with tears as she nodded quickly. "I understand. I couldn't expect you to be willing to die for somebody who's treated you the way I have." She broke eye contact and caught a tear with one finger as she tried to hide her face.

Dallas snapped his head up, eyes wide and sincere. "No, that's not what I meant at all—it's... it's just the opposite. And it's not connected to how you've treated me, but just because... well, because a man should be willing to take a bullet for a woman." Samantha met his eyes as he was speaking. Dallas glanced away again, reddening at the admiration written on her face.

Samantha was chipper as she bounded into the kitchen and flipped on the light. She opened a cabinet. "You'll want some coffee if you're going to try to stay awake, huh? Hey, are you hungry?"

"Um, yes to both." For the first time since stopping at the bar parking lot, Dallas thought about his missed dinner and how the last thing he'd eaten was a couple granola bars as he was driving back towards Texas earlier that afternoon, now seeming like weeks in the past. "I haven't eaten since about 3:00."

"Oh, Dallas!" Samantha froze, appalled. "I'm so sorry! You've been so concerned for me, and you haven't even had dinner! Here, let me make you something. I think my appetite's come back too, now that I'm getting past my little scare from earlier." She opened the fridge and stooped, rummaging inside.

Dallas decided against arguing that it wasn't just a "little" scare. "Don't go to any trouble for me—it doesn't have to be a real dinner. I'll eat most anything at this point."

"Leftover Chinese takeout?" offered Samantha. A couple of Styrofoam containers sat on the counter while she took plates out of a cabinet.

"Uh, yeah, that sounds great." Dallas stood awkwardly on the other side of the island while Samantha busied herself dishing up food. She started the coffeemaker while one plate of food was microwaving. "Want a drink of water?" she asked over her shoulder. "You just get comfortable at the table, okay? I'll bring it all to you in a jiffy."

Dallas's eyes, drawn to her form from the back as she bustled about the kitchen, snapped down as he averted what had been a subconscious gaze driven by drifting thoughts. His stomach tingled, and not from hunger. *She's beautiful, and I'm standing here staring and that's all I can think about...* Dallas shook his groggy head and sat down at the nearby kitchen table, staring into the living room and fumbling to get control of himself. He bent to take off the boots he'd been wearing for the past twenty hours. His fingers hesitated at the zipper. Running around in his socks would be too comfortable in Samantha's apartment — the last place on earth he'd expected to be tonight after the certainty of his vocational decision. He kept his boots on.

Samantha broke in with a heaping plate and a glass of water set down in front of him. "Go ahead and start, I'm sure you're absolutely famished! Don't wait on me." She was already back at the counter, putting another plate into the microwave. Dallas breathed in the steaming dish in front of him gratefully and closed his eyes, crossing himself and mumbling the blessing before digging in.

With a much smaller portion on her own plate, Samantha sat across from him a minute later. They made small talk as they ate, Dallas pacing himself as he fought the urge to scarf down the meal like a wolf.

Samantha seemed to be enjoying watching him. "I just love feeding a man," she said, face smug. "It's so satisfying somehow."

Dallas fumbled with his fork and made no reply. He ate more slowly, feeling scrutinized and disliking it immensely. *I have absolutely no clue about women.* The realization warmed his ears as his childhood flashed into his thoughts — had his mother derived satisfaction from feeding him? He didn't think so. *Should* she have? Dallas hadn't even considered this before. Maybe it was his mother who was weird, not Samantha.

As he finished his food, Samantha stepped back into the kitchen and grabbed a mug. "How do you like your coffee?"

Dallas swallowed his last bite. "Just cream." Then he reconsidered. "But I don't mind it black, either."

"Is milk okay?" asked Samantha. "It's one percent."

"Sure, that's fine." Dallas stood up with his plate, feeling like he should help somehow. He stepped to the sink and rinsed the plate. "Should I put this in the dishwasher?"

"Don't you worry about it." Samantha turned, exchanging the coffee for his plate. "Here you go, just make yourself comty." She smiled brightly.

Dallas realized with chagrin that she was thoroughly enjoying this. *Please, God, don't let her read anything into this whole mess of a situation. Please, help her not to get her feelings hurt even more than I've probably already hurt them... and please help me, God, give me strength and resolve to get through this... just six hours...* Dallas scanned the parking lot through the window before going back into the living room. He reached into his back pocket and pulled out Channing's prayer card. He gazed, bleary-eyed, at the image and murmured the words to the prayer, and he was suddenly spinning, a whirlpool of Channing in that same pose, prayer card in one hand and coffee in the other. A tear involuntarily slipped down Dallas's cheek. He quickly tucked the card back into his pocket, sat down, and leaned back to take a sip of his anti-sleep aid.

The clanking sound of dishes ceased, the water in the sink stopped, and Samantha came around the counter. She sat down at the other end of the couch, facing Dallas.

"Ooh, I love this song!" she commented at the sound of the opening guitar chords. "It's my favorite on the whole album. It's so romantic, don't you think?"

Dallas nearly choked on his coffee. "*Romantic*? It's a stalker song, Samantha. Listen to the words. The guy's a total creep." After what she'd gone through tonight, and that it could be Mike creeping around, letting himself into her apartment and waiting outside her bedroom... Dallas shuddered at the idea.

Samantha was quiet, listening to the lyrics. "Oh gosh, Dallas, I think you're right!" Her eyes widened, then she laughed. "I totally missed that before! You're so smart!"

Dallas muttered, "Nah," as he chuckled slightly at the compliment.

"What, you don't think so?" Samantha leaned towards him. "Reading all those books you have in your apartment—of *course*, you're smart!"

"Well..." Dallas tried to paint an accurate picture of himself. "Those were Channing's books, after all. I wouldn't be reading any of them had it not been for him."

Samantha's face softened at the mention of his friend, and with a quavery warmth Dallas remembered the concern she'd shown when he'd told her Channing had died. But the way she had then used it to her advantage surged through him, drowning the tingling, and his face flushed with anger. He stared at the mug nestled in his lap, hoping the subject would change. As he flipped through the pages of his brain for something unrelated and neutral to say, Samantha spoke again.

"I bet it makes you feel close to him to read his old books, huh?"

Dallas closed his eyes helplessly. *How does she do that?* The funny feeling ignited and spread inside him, the vague sense that he didn't understand feminine compassion yet had somehow craved it all his life. "Yeah," he answered quietly. *Don't let your guard down!* a voice argued inside him. *But I miss Channing*, another voice seemed to respond.

"I'm sorry again, that he died," Samantha said gently.

Dallas nodded, staring straight ahead. He took a sip of his coffee.

"Does it help you to talk about it?" Her pillowy voice was soft compassion.

Dallas closed his eyes again. Fighting off stress and exhaustion always compounded his emotions over Channing's death. The coffee would help. He needed to stay alert in case he had to deal with Mike. Dallas glanced up at Samantha and was surprised by her tears.

"What's wrong?" A lump rose in his throat. He knew why she was crying.

Samantha attempted a smile. "It's just so sad... I can picture how you must've been with your best friend who was like a little brother to you. It's clear how you felt about him, and that shows me how incredible a person he must've been..."

Dallas felt a surrender of agony inside. *Why is she doing this to me?* Samantha's sympathy was spot-on, and despite rational brain urging him to do otherwise, Dallas relented and answered her.

"He was definitely an incredible person." Dallas's voice cracked slightly, but he refused to cry. "It was four years ago that he died, but it seems like less because when I was in prison, well, it felt like he was just out here, waiting for me, and getting out after so long and starting to live my life again without him..." Dallas trailed off.

"It must've been a kind of shock to you." She inched closer.

He could fall into her embrace right now. Dallas wrapped his arms around himself.

Samantha touched his shoulder. "Did he die while you were in prison?"

Dallas shook his head. "He died the day I was arrested." Instant regret was too late to retract the statement he saw had shocked her. He jolted up, paced the length of the room, and stared out the window beside the front door.

Samantha silently crossed the room behind him and paused. Dallas cradled his coffee mug against his chest and squeezed his eyes shut, trying to block out the sounds of Channing being hit by the truck.

Finally, Samantha spoke. "I don't mean to upset you, Dallas. You can tell me as little or as much as you want, whatever is better for you. I have no right to know; I only want you to talk if it makes you feel better. But I'm glad you had that kind of friendship, because it helped make you into the kind of guy you are today. I bet you would've died to save him, too, if you could have."

Dallas couldn't tell Samantha how her words were like a painful but necessary surgical procedure to his broken heart. Instead, he took a deep breath. "Thanks for being understanding about him. You know, I want to try to keep my focus right now, in case I need to be ready for…" He stepped away from the window and towards the gun lying on the counter, then picked it up and carried it to the end table beside the couch. He sat back down and tried to refocus his thoughts.

"I'm sorry." Samantha sank down alongside him. "I didn't mean to bring you down. Hey, know what I do to cheer myself up sometimes?"

Dallas lifted his head, half-hoping for another round of Spades. "What?"

"Sing along to music, but really loud and silly. You know the words to all these songs—do you ever sing along when you're driving?"

A smile twitched at Dallas's lips. "Yeah. Or, at least, I used to."

"And it was fun, wasn't it?" Samantha's eyes danced, and she nudged him with her elbow. "Come on, admit it!"

"Yeah, sure." A smile broke out on Dallas's face. "Me and Channing, we sang terribly, but the louder we got, the more fun it was."

Samantha hopped up and advanced the CD to another track. "This one's fast and fun!" She spun around and sang along, trying to match the vocalist's sound. Her feminine voice rang with more talent than Dallas had expected, yet it was still exaggerated enough that he couldn't stifle his laugh.

"Okay, you too!" Samantha pointed a finger at him as she plopped back down on the couch. "Can you imitate the echoey microphone effect in this part coming up?"

Dallas knew exactly what she was talking about. He drew in a breath and then imitated the voice along with the music, one hand muffling his lips to try to get the effect right.

Samantha burst out laughing. They sang along to the rest of the song together, Dallas loosening up with the antics. This was better than moping over Channing, anyway. When had he last let himself go enough to really enjoy the music?

"Oh, gosh!" Samantha put a hand to her mouth as the song ended. "It's so late—we probably should keep it down!"

Dallas checked his watch. "Oh—yeah." He cleared his throat. Had he let his guard down too much? But it sure felt good to just be silly for a few minutes. He stretched and yawned. "We should both get some sleep soon, anyway."

Samantha nodded. "It's past two. If Mike hasn't come here by now, then I'm hoping he won't at all. I do appreciate you wanting to be ready just in case, Dallas." She laid a hand on his.

They were quiet a few seconds before Dallas pulled his hand away. Rubbing it absently and staring at the carpet between his feet, he blurted, "What were you and Mike fighting about?" He clenched his jaw shut. Why had he asked? It wasn't his business.

Samantha inched closer, but she left a small gap between them. "Mike wanted to leave, and I didn't." She dipped her chin and was silent again.

So, that was all. Dallas's shoulders slackened.

"He was acting all controlling." Samantha's voice trembled beneath the bitterness. "Said he didn't like how I was looking at this other guy in there. That guy looked at *me* first. But Mike coerced me outside before I'd even finished my drink. If you hadn't showed up, I probably would've given in and gone home with him."

Instead, I've come home with her. Dallas shut his eyes and willed it all away to numbness, all the rush of emotions and exhaustion and conflict. He let his breath escape slowly. "You should get some sleep. It's been a rough night." He turned his head towards her and scrutinized the swelling bruise on her cheek where Mike had struck her. Dallas bit his lip.

Samantha studied her hands in her lap and sighed. "I suppose you're right. I'd rather stay up and chat, you know, be a good hostess—"

"We both could use some sleep." Dallas inched back, the hair raising on the back of his neck. "I'll still be on alert even if I do fall asleep, though. I don't sleep deeply when I've had caffeine this late."

Samantha jumped up and headed for a closet. "I'll get you a pillow and some blankets. Get up. I'll make you a bed there on the couch."

"Don't worry about it," Dallas replied, "I'll do it…"

Samantha returned with arms full of sheets, blankets, and a pillow, and Dallas stood to take them from her.

"No, you've done so much for me already!" She brushed him off. "The least I can do is wait on you as my guest." She spread a sheet across the cushions, and Dallas looked away, trying not to notice her low-cut top made more obvious by the way she was crawling across the couch. Maybe that wasn't even her intention. Dallas felt his cheeks reddening. *Please, Lord, let her go to her room and go to sleep after this…*

"Do you need a toothbrush?" Samantha stood from the finished makeshift bed. "I have an extra one that's new. There's just the one bathroom." She motioned towards an open door behind her. Dallas could see that it had entrances from both the living room and her bedroom. "If you need a shower, there are extra towels in there, too." She flashed a grin. "Or are you a morning shower kind of guy?" That slight seductive tinge to her voice zinged Dallas reflexively by now.

"I've got a toothbrush in my car," he said, ignoring her second offer. The idea of a shower was tempting, though. He'd been longing for one after his time on the trail.

Samantha laughed. "Well, aren't you Mr. Prepared! You're just great, Dallas—I've never known anyone like you!"

"I was on a camping trip, so I have one packed up in my stuff, is all." Dallas shrugged and headed towards the door. "Be right back."

When he reentered the apartment, Samantha's bedroom door was closed, hopefully signaling that she was getting ready for bed. Dallas stepped into the bathroom, toiletry bag and clean clothes in hand. He examined himself critically in the mirror, running his fingers through his greasy, too-long hair and staring back into tired eyes—dark spots underneath, drooping eyelids. He checked the date on his digital wristwatch for confirmation—he hadn't showered in five days. Maybe he should, especially before sleeping on her clean sheets. Indecisiveness stirring in his gut, Dallas glanced over his shoulder at the door behind him and went for the knob. He clicked the lock into place, then crossed to the other door and locked it, too. There, that was better. Uneasiness melted away to relief with the anticipation of feeling clean again.

Through the secured bedroom door, Dallas called, "Uh, which towels did you say I can use?"

Samantha's voice filtered back to him. "Any of those that are folded on the shelf. They're blue," she added.

Dallas pulled a towel and washcloth off the stack, turned on the water in the shower, and hung the towel over the rod. He stripped his smoky t-shirt over his head, undid his jeans and let them fall to the floor, and stuck a hand behind the curtain to test the water temperature.

The knob of the door leading to her bedroom rattled. Dallas spun to see it opening and, to his horror, Samantha stepped into the bathroom. As his stomach leapt into his throat, she stared him down, her eyes dancing.

Dallas snatched the towel and frantically wrapped it around his waist. "Get out, GET OUT!"

Samantha didn't flinch. "Sorry. I picked the lock since I heard the water running and thought you were already in. Just had to get my pill." She stepped to the counter, eyes diverted to the package she picked up. "I'm supposed to take it at the same time each day, and I'm a few hours late."

Dallas retreated to the living room and slammed the door behind him. He stood shaking, his back pressed against the door as he inhaled rapid breaths. *Did she see anything?* His heart pounded. His clothes were still in there!

"Hey, can you get out of there so I can get my clothes?" he called, blushing.

"I thought you were going to take a shower?" The door opened a crack. She passed pants and then a shirt out to him. "Where's your underwear?"

Dallas grabbed the clothes and mumbled, "I, uh… don't wear them," and shoved the door closed again. It was true—he didn't see the purpose other than the rare occasion that he wore shorts. Her giggles through the door at his response made him want to die. He yanked his jeans on hastily, trying to maneuver them under the towel. He pulled his t-shirt over his head. Samantha had passed him the clean shirt, but the jeans were the ones he'd just removed. He didn't care—she'd just have to have his dirty jeans and unwashed hair on her sheets—that is, if he stayed at all! He stood fuming, heart racing.

A moment later, Samantha sang through the door, "Are you decent?"

Dallas opened it with burning ears, and she waltzed into the room as if nothing had happened. "This yours?" Samantha handed him his lighter. "I think it fell out of the pocket of your jeans. You don't smoke, do you?"

Dallas shook his head and avoided eye contact.

"So, why do you carry a lighter?"

"Comes in handy sometimes." He didn't feel like explaining to her that he just liked fire.

"But not for smoking?"

"No. My mom smoked, so that killed my appetite for it real quick." Would she just stop talking to him so he could recover from his shame?

"I know exactly what you mean." Samantha gazed into his face.

Dallas squirmed and shifted to turn his back.

"My mom smokes like crazy, and my dad did, too, and so, after I tried it a few times, it just wasn't something I wanted to do." Samantha rounded Dallas and flashed a smile over the similarity they shared, then seated herself on the end of the couch.

Dallas stood against the opposite wall, shifting his weight from side to side and scowling.

"So, you weren't circumcised, huh?" Samantha said without missing a beat. "I thought most guys were, but I don't mind…"

Dallas felt his face go beet red. "That's not any of your business!" he spluttered as he turned to the wall and wished he could sink into the floor, still feeling completely exposed. He clenched his fists at his side. *How much more mortifying can this night get??*

"Oh, Dallas, I'm sorry," Samantha crooned, rising and approaching slowly. "I didn't know you were sensitive about it. You have no reason—"

"I'm NOT sensitive about it." Dallas whirled to meet her eyes. "What I'm sensitive about is my privacy being invaded! You had no right to break in!"

"You're right, Dallas; I'm sorry." Samantha bowed her head. "I wasn't thinking; I just remembered I needed to take my pill."

Birth control pills. He'd read about their possible side effects in the Theology of the Body materials Father Benedict had brought him to study. "Those pills aren't good for you," Dallas blurted, crossing his arms. "They can increase your cancer risk."

Samantha lifted both eyebrows. "Well, having a baby wouldn't be good for me, either. What else am I supposed to do?"

"I don't know, maybe not have sex?" Dallas sniped, staring her in the eye.

Samantha blushed.

"If you stop taking those things, and you tell Mike you're not taking them, then you know he'll be less likely to pressure you for sex, right?"

Samantha gave a small eyeroll. "Oh, my gosh, Dallas, you're so…" She huffed and pursed her lips. "Things aren't as black and white as you make them out to be. And, he doesn't really *pressure* me—"

"I just don't want you to have nasty side effects to your health or get used by jerks," Dallas added, "and both are consequences of the Pill."

"You're just trying to change the subject," Samantha interrupted, "but really, I'm sorry I embarrassed you by walking in on you. I didn't mean anything by it, and I was only commenting because I was more curious than anything—"

"Well, if you're changing the subject back," Dallas said hotly, "I'm gonna tell you that you don't get to do things like that and then talk about it as if it's nothing!" His eyes blazed as he made wide gestures with his arms. "It was violating and degrading!"

"Degrading?" Samantha wrinkled her nose. "But you have nothing to be ashamed of. You've got a nice body, Dallas…"

"Are you saying that as long as you like what you see, it's okay to look without permission?" Dallas maintained the hostility in his voice to cover the subconscious goading of his ego.

Samantha stared at him quizzically.

"Like, if a man came and stared at you through the window while you were changing clothes," he went on, "you'd think it was okay as long as he admired your body?"

Samantha shrugged. "I guess I kind of see your point, Dallas. I'm sorry; I didn't even think of how it could make you feel violated. And I wanted to make sure you knew I wasn't teasing you because of not being circumcised."

Dallas raised an eyebrow. "I didn't think you were."

"You mean other guys didn't tease you about it growing up?" inquired Samantha. She'd assumed what Dallas could only interpret as a motherly voice, eyes wide and sympathetic. She settled back down on the sofa again. "I hope they didn't, but I've heard..."

Dallas shrugged. "It's somewhat common in Nevada."

"It's rare here in the Midwest," Samantha interjected.

"Yeah, I realized that in prison," Dallas replied before he thought to check himself.

"Where was the prison?" Samantha asked softly.

"Outside Oklahoma City." Dallas's eyes were suddenly occupied by the dirt under his thumbnail. He'd said too much. "Look, could we not talk about it?" None of this was remotely appropriate for conversation: his prison horror stories, his anatomy, none of it. And he could never tell her about his own close call with sexual abuse.

Samantha didn't press for more. Dallas leaned back against the wall and studied his bare feet, the flames of embarrassment still licking at him.

"So, really, *cancer*?" Samantha asked skeptically.

"Yeah, read the package insert that comes with it." Dallas met her eyes with his. "All the side effects are spelled out there. Not to mention the fact that you're putting a drug in your body that breaks your God-given, normally functioning fertility just so men can have their way with you, with little risk or consequence to themselves, and—"

"The cancer thing just doesn't seem right," Samantha stammered, "that doctors would prescribe—"

"What reason would I have to lie to you about it?" Dallas interrupted. His eyes penetrated Samantha's, and a spark of pain flashed through him. *I really do care for her...*

"I guess you wouldn't have any self-interest in making it up, no..." Samantha's voice trailed off, and a silence hung in the room.

Dallas squatted down and stared at the locked front door. *Please, God, let her realize her own dignity.* Even the violation of her eyes against him couldn't induce a grudge against her, couldn't keep him from wanting what was best for her... But she'd seen him naked! Dallas's skin tingled with a mixture of shame and primal pleasure. He pressed his fingers to his temples. *I don't need to think about that! Please, God, keep my eyes on my path, the one I know in my heart you have laid out for me...*

Feeling Samantha's eyes on him, Dallas glanced up and saw she was watching him with a subtle smile. He cleared his throat and turned his head, but before the thoughts could bombard him again, the harsh ring of the telephone made Dallas jolt upright.

Samantha gave a surprised gasp and jumped to her feet. "Now who in the world…"

Adrenaline pumping, Dallas beat Samantha to the phone and fired off the number flashing across the caller ID. He raised both eyebrows at her.

Samantha's face went white, and she put out a hand to steady herself against the wall. "It's Mike," she whispered.

Dallas pressed his hand against the receiver and narrowed his eyes. "Don't answer it."

With a sick expression on her face, Samantha sank into a kitchen chair as the answering machine picked up. Mike's crude words exploded into the air, threats laced with vulgarities. Dallas winced and ground his teeth.

The tirade lasted thirty seconds before Mike slammed down the phone. Dead silence hung in the room.

Samantha stood up. "I... I'm sorry you had to hear that." She unplugged the phone from the wall and leaned against the wall.

Dallas's jaw dropped. *She* was sorry? She'd just been cussed out and threatened, and now she trembled all over, scared to death in her own home. He flexed his arms, his entire body tense. "You have nothing to be sorry about." Dallas felt heat surge through him. "That effing bastard..." He whirled to face the phone again and somehow suppressed his urge to tear it off the wall. That did it. No way could he leave now.

"Hey, he's probably full of hot air." Samantha's hand on his shoulder brought Dallas's blood pressure back down a notch. "I'll get the restraining order against him tomorrow. He didn't actually say he'd come over here right now. I'm sorry I dragged you into all this, Dallas."

He turned towards her, and his face softened. "Yeah. It's okay." It was anything but okay, but what else was he supposed to say? He pulled at his shirt collar and shook out both arms, then followed her back into the living room.

"So, you like to go camping?" Samantha asked as she settled onto the couch. "I've never been."

"Yeah." Dallas tucked his hands in his pockets. He wasn't sure what else to say.

"I always wanted to go when I was a kid," Samantha continued. "My dad... he was going to take me once. He promised he'd come get me one weekend, just before he moved out when he and my mom were divorcing..."

Dallas held his breath and tried not to look at Samantha as her words hit close to home. He clenched his jaw. Had a man *ever* treated her right before?

"But, well, he never did. I reminded him once, and he put it off, saying we'd go someday..." She popped up from the couch and opened a cabinet door next to the stereo, tucking a Led Zeppelin record under one arm. "This was his album, the same one he used to play for me. And here's his picture." She turned to reveal a framed photo clutched against her chest.

Dallas stared, but words wouldn't come.

Samantha held out the photo at arm's length and gazed at it. "That was nearly fifteen years ago now that he promised. I thought maybe... maybe you'd kind of understand..."

"I'm sorry." Dallas followed the frame back to where Samantha held it close again. "I guess maybe it's harder for you, 'cause you remember. I never even met my father, and I just try not to think about it." He drew his lips together tight and examined his fingernails again to hide his clenched fists.

"What's it like, camping?" She rocked back on her heels. "My dad said cooking over the fire was fun, that we'd roast hot dogs on sticks..."

Dallas shuffled his feet, eyes locked with the image of Samantha's liar of a father through the glass in the frame. "Yeah, the fire is the best part. And the quiet. The solitude." He cracked his knuckles, looking for some way to end the conversation and quell his desire to smash the picture frame. He didn't want to talk about either of their deadbeat dads, nor did he want to appear to be making her a camping promise that he'd never keep.

When Dallas said no more, Samantha set aside the photo and turned towards her bedroom with a yawn. "I guess I'll get ready for bed." She shut the door behind her.

With a sigh and a stretch, Dallas retrieved the rest of his clothes from the bathroom floor. He dropped them in a pile beside the couch, then returned to the bathroom and applied toothpaste to his toothbrush. He scrubbed vigorously and spat a mouthful of foam into the basin, then rinsed his mouth.

As he was chasing the toothpaste lather down the drain with handfuls of water, the other door to the bathroom opened. Dallas jumped, and Samantha stepped in behind him. Her reflection in the mirror caught his eye and he blushed, sidestepped to get out of her way, and bumped into the doorframe in the process.

Samantha giggled. "Sorry, didn't mean to scare you." She picked up her own toothbrush.

"Uh, I'm just..." Dallas stuttered. He commanded his eyes away from her figure, covered by a nightgown that left little to the imagination, but he couldn't help but notice that she was using his toothpaste. He hesitated, trying to decide if he should say something or not, but his conscience was ordering him to get out of that little room and away from her skimpy lingerie right now.

Dallas escaped to his bed on the couch, stifling a snarl as the heat rose in him. He shook himself and opened his Liturgy of the Hours book to the day's office of readings. He forced his concentration on the lines in front of him, but the words ran together. The coffee didn't seem to be doing anything. *I must just be beyond exhausted.* Dallas strained to open his eyes wide.

The next words jumped at him, and he sat up straight. *"I find woman more bitter than death; she is a snare, her heart a net, her arms are chains; He who is pleasing to God eludes her, but the sinner is her captive..."* Dallas's heart thudded in his chest. *Help me, God, please protect me... How is this happening to me?! Remember, O most gracious Virgin Mary...*

"I like your toothpaste flavor!" Samantha called through the doorway, breaking Dallas's manic prayer. He closed his eyes. So she *was* using it on purpose.

"Um, since you're about ready to go to sleep," Dallas said, "I'll be on guard out here. Lock your bedroom door just in case, but try not to worry. Just get some rest."

Samantha emerged from the bathroom and stalked across the room, seating herself next to Dallas on the sofa, closer than before. He bolted up, the warning words from Ecclesiastes ringing fresh in his mind.

"Oh, did I surprise you?" Her voice dripped with innocence. "I just thought I'd help keep you awake..."

"We already went over that, remember?" Dallas moved as far across the room from her as possible and pretended to examine a picture hanging on the wall.

Samantha made no move towards her room.

Dallas had to put his foot down. This was unfair of her—she was taking advantage of the situation! Keeping his eyes on the artwork, he said flatly, "Goodnight, Samantha."

She rose and sauntered across the room to the doorway of her bedroom.

Maybe he'd gotten the point across. Dallas held his breath.

Samantha paused, hanging on the doorframe with her cheek pressed against it, studying him in silence.

Dallas finally threw a glance her way and had to pull his eyes back again because of the nature of her nightgown. Why did she have to be so attractive? He blushed and turned away, hands in his pockets. *She sees your struggle,* the thought burned in his mind.

"What's the matter, Dallas?" crooned Samantha's voice right behind him. He pivoted, and she was there, one hand on each of his arms. Dallas gulped and squeezed his eyes shut, his brain shouting orders at him as she pressed up close to him, his skin burning beneath her fingers. *O Brave New World...* Dallas was flooded with Channing's lucid reading voice from a distant past, scenery slipping by through the windows, motor vibrating as the car was propelled forward, *just a story...* but now Dallas was inside the scene, backed against a wall, *Dallas the Savage...* His hands moved to stop her but instead slipped around the small of her back and clasped there. Samantha yielded under his touch like melting butter, and Dallas sensed a tender power he didn't know he had. She stood on tiptoe and brushed her lips against his neck. *Stop, STOP!* screamed his brain. As he ran one hand up her back to her shoulder, Dallas desperately fought the urge to pull her in closer, tighter, heart racing inside his trembling body. The old dream flashed like lightning in his mind, the priest dream. But what if the archbishop told him no? He saw himself rejected, retreating back to Samantha's comfort, to her fire that would consume him... *To lose my soul and destroy hers, too...* Suddenly Dallas pushed her back, tucking his arms in close to shield himself, cowering with a helpless whimper he could hardly believe came from himself. "N-no... please, please stop. Please, Samantha, I'm begging you..." Dallas's face burned at his admission of weakness and his realization that he could fall completely under her spell in one instant of faltering.

She followed him a step, studying his resistance. "I thought maybe you were starting to change your mind. I... What's wrong, Dallas?"

Her gaze tried to reel him in like a hooked fish, and Dallas practically flung himself back to widen the distance, rounding the kitchen table and fumbling into a chair. Seated behind the table for a buffer, he ran both hands through his hair and mustered up all his will. Sickened at how quickly he'd almost fallen, Dallas swiped the stack of napkins off the table before clenching his hands over his face. *"The sinner is her captive..."* He had to take control! She couldn't do this to him!

Samantha lowered herself into the chair across from him, eyes moving hesitantly between the scattered napkins and Dallas's face. The table blocked his view of most of her body, and he made himself look her in the eye.

"Samantha, listen to me," he commanded. "You need to go into your room and stay there, because this isn't some kind of slumber party — got it?"

Samantha cleared her throat and glanced at her hands in her lap. "I don't mean anything, Dallas," she stammered. "This is just what I always wear to bed —"

"And you're not in bed yet," Dallas interrupted. "Look, I've put myself in an uncomfortable situation, and I'm doing it in *your* best interest. But my being in here in the middle of the night has the potential to give scandal. Maybe you don't care about that, but *I* do. And based on past events, you haven't given me much reason to trust that you won't use this as evidence to spread rumors or imply certain things about me."

"For a moment I was starting to think that it wouldn't be a 'rumor' anymore, Dallas," she said coyly.

He cut her off. "I'm really sorry I touched you like that—I didn't mean to, and it was wrong of me. But you running around in that thing and cornering me… you're trying to tempt me intentionally! You're making this incredibly difficult for me." He challenged her with unblinking eyes.

Samantha's voice faltered. "I… I know, Dallas, what you've said about not wanting a relationship… I just like you so much…" She fell silent, twirling a strand of hair around one finger. Suddenly she stood up. "But you can't be saying you don't like my nightgown." She made a mock pouty face and took a step towards Dallas.

She was taunting him, he knew it. She'd seen his weakness, his crumbling resolve, and seemed intent on exploiting it. Dallas cursed himself for having put his arms around her for those few seconds. She needed to understand how serious his "no" was. She'd only been encouraged by his moment of hesitation. "I'm saying I *don't* want to see you in it." A harshness crept into Dallas's voice.

"Liar." Samantha stared Dallas down with the accusation she had thrown at his feet.

He exploded. Leaping from the chair and knocking it flat, Dallas raised his voice and nearly shouted an accusation of his own as he realized she was technically correct. "You know *exactly* what you're doing!" he snarled. "Of course, you know I *want* to see it, and you know that's *not* what I meant! I'm saying it's *wrong* for me to see you this way. I swear, Samantha, if you don't get into your room and shut the door *now*, I'm *leaving*!" He kicked the chair, punctuating his threat. "I'm trying to help you, and your thanks is to flaunt your body at me?! It's out of my hands what happens to you then because I *refuse* to stay here just letting you try to tear my will apart intentionally!"

Samantha ducked her head and choked out something indiscernible before slipping into her room.

Breaths heavy, Dallas watched her go, then righted the chair and retrieved fistfuls of napkins. He gripped the edge of the table and inhaled slowly, praying his shouts and the clatter of the chair hitting the floor hadn't woken the neighbors.

Samantha returned in a fuzzy bathrobe drawn closed up to her neck. Dallas still seethed inside but had regained control of his violent impulses.

"I'm sorry, Dallas," she said softly. "See, I'm covered up now."

"Sorry about the chair," he mumbled, arms crossed and eyes on the floor.

"If you really need me to go stay in my room now, then I'll do it. Please, Dallas, don't be angry. I really am grateful to you…" Her voice trailed off, and she backed towards her bedroom. "Goodnight," she called meekly as she closed the door.

Dallas buried his face in his hands, shaking as he flopped down onto the couch. He couldn't see straight. Exhaustion beating him down, Samantha's seductions being forced upon his imagination, his natural protective instinct being provoked and now taken advantage of, all on top of his newly determined vocation being at the forefront of his mind, and Dallas was a wreck. He took up his book again and murmured the prayers to himself once, twice, and began a third time when his head drooped, and he had to snap it back up again to stay awake. He glanced at the gun. He was in no state to defend anyone, let alone somebody he wasn't even feeling like protecting anymore. Then Dallas was flooded with guilt. He saw Mike abusing Samantha in his mind, and the wrath against his former co-worker bubbled inside him. Staying was still the right thing to do. *I can't stand the thought of anyone hurting her like that…* Dallas glanced at his watch. The alarm was set for 8, when he could call a locksmith, ensure that the door was rekeyed, and then get out of here. He got up to peer out the front window into the parking lot, one last check to make sure he didn't see Mike's truck, and then he returned to the couch.

A corner of paper, bright white in contrast to the dim room, caught his eye from where it protruded from beneath the couch. Dallas pulled it out as he sank down, intending to set it on the coffee table. Maybe it was something Samantha had dropped. The blue inked words grabbed his attention, and he paused. There was a title and what appeared to be verses beneath. *Poetry?* Dallas skimmed the words, and he remembered Samantha saying she'd written some song lyrics. An uncomfortable heat tickled inside him—maybe this was private and he shouldn't be reading it. But he couldn't tear his eyes from the soul-baring lines.

When you block it all out
When you put on an act
It's not who you should be
But you've made it your fact
When you hide who you are

When you form a new truth
Just pretend you're so strong
But inside you're aloof

An ache welled in Dallas's throat. The simple, raw lines — was this the real Samantha? Was the control she exhibited all a ruse for her pain? The thought of her father made Dallas bite down a snarl. He set the paper aside, picked up his prayer book, and rubbed his eyes. Maybe, after some sleep and his brain was functioning with better clarity, he'd ask her about these lyrics she'd penned. But he was run ragged. He returned to his fatigued recitation of his prayers, but his eyes drooped shut in the middle of each sentence. Unable to fight off sleep's insistent hammering at his body, Dallas set down his book. He reclined on his back, settling into the softness, and dropped off, the deep, plush cushions cocooning his weary body.

Dallas was dreaming, the setting fuzzy but pleasant. A voice he couldn't decipher murmured through thick fog. He smiled at the liquid words of incoherent comfort. The wind was tickling his ear... or was it rain? He shifted in his sleep and his eyes fluttered, then closed again, and he was semi-conscious of a soft blanket covering him. *I'm warm... too warm.* Dallas shifted again, opening one eye with a yawn. He saw Samantha's face in a hazy blur, her seductive smile like sugar. Head still in his dream, Dallas returned the smile, feeling a little dopey about it. More words he didn't comprehend but nodding slightly as if in agreement, his head bobbing to the beat of some ethereal instrument. Her face vanished, and he involuntarily mumbled something. *Her name...* He was trying to call her back, but his tongue was heavy and useless in his mouth, eyes both shut again. *I'm asleep...* But she was still there, enclosing him somehow, and... Were they outside in the rain? But how was he touching her leg? He moved his hand clumsily. *Her skin...* It was silk beneath his fingers. *My ear's wet, and my neck...* Dallas squirmed from the tickle, and the whispering in his ear morphed into discernable words: "You like that, Dallas? Mmm, you smell so good..." He turned his head towards the voice, returning an affirmative drowsy mumble that was drowned by lips against his. His mouth kissed back, eyes still closed and head floating in the bliss of the dreamworld. As his brain struggled to understand the next enticing words, the hand belonging to the voice caressed his chest and fiddled with his scapular under his shirt, wrapping the cord around a finger...

Dallas's eyes flew open at the sensation as he was suddenly roused from his torpor. He lurched upright in an instant and scrambled up from the couch, where he'd been nestled deep in the jumble of pillows and blankets on his back with his right hand behind his head, fast asleep. Samantha tumbled to the floor. She gaped up at him, wide-eyed, hands scrambling to adjust her nightgown hem. She quickly averted her eyes from Dallas's inflamed ones.

"I can't *believe* you!" he exploded, nostrils flaring, as full awareness of what had been happening struck him.

Samantha opened her mouth and stumbled over her feeble attempt at an explanation.

"You *conniving, manipulative,* little..." Dallas barely bit his lip in time, preventing the hostile slur that he was about to hurl upon the woman who was getting to her feet and cowering simultaneously. Music throbbed low from the stereo, registering in the background of Dallas's blowup.

"Dallas, just let me explain—" Samantha's voice was worried and guilty.

"There's *nothing* to explain!" he spat contemptuously, throwing his arms wide. "It's obvious to me already; I'm not a complete moron! I'm here trying to protect you, and in return, you take advantage of me and HUMILIATE me! I should've left the second you started prancing around in that thing!" Dallas slammed his feet into his boots, not bothering to zip them even halfway. He snatched his prayer book from the bedside table, ignoring Samantha's pistol alongside it, and stormed to the door, fuming.

"Dallas, wait!" Samantha cried breathlessly. "I'm sorry, I just... I woke up, and I was so scared by myself, and... and you *did* seem to like it..."

"I'll be in my car," he said gruffly, glancing at his watch. "I should just go home! But I don't break my promises, even if you've given me no reason to keep them. In an hour, I'm calling the locksmith, and then I'm *done* accepting your version of hospitality! Lock the door behind me, the little good it'll do." He couldn't hide the sarcasm spewing from him as he slammed the door violently on his way out.

As the muggy air hit him, Dallas rotated and stretched his right shoulder, ridding himself of the tingling from where the weight of Samantha's head had compressed his upper arm. He kicked through the shrubs along the edge of the parking spaces and yanked his keys from his pocket, then got into his car. His heart pounded out the beat of the Led Zeppelin song he recognized that she'd turned on in the background. Dallas seethed in humiliated rage. *How dare she!?* His muscles twitched to start the engine and drive away for good—she could just deal with Mike herself! The sensation of her snuggled against him under the blanket pulsed through him, and he pounded a fist against the steering wheel to smash the memory from his mind. As if he needed another seductive temptation of her to fight off? Samantha's words echoed in his ear: *"You smell so good..."* Dallas self-consciously sniffed at his arm. *I smell like dirt and campfire smoke!* He wrinkled his nose. Had she really said that? How could she even think... And he'd been about to return the compliment in that half-awake moment. The chemical attraction between them was magnetic and irrational. Dallas shook himself and bowed his head, itching with a deep desire to throw himself into the confessional.

The unconnected metal square of his belt buckle caught his eye, and Dallas's mouth went dry. *She undid my belt!* His face flushed hot in furious degradation. *What if I hadn't woken up when I did?! Did she...* Dallas's eyes widened as he was transported back a year to prison, and the disgusting horror of Hudson, the abusive guard, burned into his past, the unknowns of what he'd done to him while unconscious in that storage closet... Dallas couldn't breathe. He fumbled with the door handle, Hudson's violations bombarding him as if they had just occurred. He stumbled to the nearby bushes, gulping for air and control, and vomited, shaking and sweating. He climbed back into the driver's seat again, cool and clammy, talking himself down from his past assaults. "Samantha doesn't know all that, she doesn't... It's no excuse, but she really wasn't trying to traumatize me..." He relented to the hot tears.

"What am I supposed to do here, God?" he pleaded. "If I leave, and Mike comes and lets himself in and hurts her, I'll regret it for the rest of my life. But she's waging a battle for my soul! And she's so hurt herself. Why, God?" He leaned back against the familiar headrest and waited, straining for God's will, his breathing evening out as his temper cooled. *Life is enormously difficult. You're still hurting, too. Resist temptation while treating her with respect. It seems almost impossible, but you can do it. You* are *doing it.*

"Jesus, I trust in you," Dallas murmured. *I resisted. I made my answer clear to her, and that's all I can control.*

Dallas watched through the windows with darting eyes. Just past seven now, the apartment complex had come to life as some of the residents left for work. Dallas was edgy with the rev of every engine, alert to the last chances that one might be Mike's truck pulling in. His anger at Samantha dissolved, giving way to contempt for Mike again as the image of him pinning her against his truck rushed through Dallas. *Wouldn't you like to get revenge on him, hmm?* came Samantha's smooth voice in his memory. Dallas tried to brush it away. All the wonderful, terrible things he'd like to do to her—and that she was inviting him to partake in—stampeded through his thoughts like a herd of wild horses. The sensation of her pressed against him, lips moving from his ear to his neck, then their mouths locked together, drew him like a moth to the flame to crawl back in there with her, give up, surrender himself to be overrun by passion and feelings. If it had been a few minutes more, what would he have awoken to? A warmth flashed through Dallas's body instead of revulsion this time, and he shook his head and blinked, but he couldn't keep from picturing himself bursting through the door and pulling her close, back onto that couch, and... His eyes flew open. *I can't think like that! The spirit is willing, but the flesh is weak... God, remove the images from my mind, please!* Dallas commanded himself to open his breviary, and he consumed the morning prayers desperately. His fingers moved across the crucifix at his neck, and he whispered a silent thank you that he'd awoken when he had, in spite of his primal desire otherwise. *It was because she had my scapular in her hand...* He drew it by one cord to his lips and kissed it. *Remember, O most gracious Virgin Mary...*

The overwhelming urges subsided, flames dwindling and cooling. He had to tell Samantha about his vocation. Maybe it would help her get why he was saying no to her. *Help me keep saying no, please, God, and then get me out of here.* Dallas prayed the Rosary slowly for the next half hour.

At eight, his watch beeped. Dallas took a deep breath, opened his car door, and stood, shaking out stiff legs. He walked to the door of Samantha's apartment and gave a short knock. The door opened. Samantha backed up, holding it ajar for Dallas and looking subdued. To his relief, she was dressed in jeans and a t-shirt.

Dallas headed straight for the phone, ignoring her attempts to talk.

"Dallas?" she said as he dialed the number. "Dallas, I need to tell you something—"

"After I get off the phone," he replied curtly.

Samantha stuck out her hand and pressed the hook, hanging up as Dallas pushed the final digit. He stared, mouth hanging open, the receiver useless in his left hand.

"Dallas, I can't let you throw your money away. Don't call anyone."

He set the receiver down and crossed his arms across his chest. "Okay, what's going on?"

Samantha's gaze skittered to the floor. "I have to be honest with you," she choked out in a whisper. "Dallas, you're so good to me... I deserved for you to just leave, and still, you stayed... I can't bear to lead you on to the point that you'll spend that much money on something unnecessary, especially when you're out of work. I..." Tears filled her eyes. "Oh, Dallas, I'm so ashamed of myself!"

He bit back the urge to tell her that she should be. Praying for patience and understanding, Dallas motioned for her to sit down in the nearest chair of the kitchen table. She did, choking out a thanks, and he rounded the table and sank into the other chair.

"Okay." Dallas struggled to keep his voice calm. "Tell me what this is about. I thought you agreed that changing the lock was necessary. Don't tell me you're thinking of letting that scumbag back in here?"

Samantha's eyes flew up to meet Dallas's. "No, I don't want him back—really, I don't!" she said emphatically. "It's just... I have a confession to make, and you're going to be *so* angry with me... The truth is..." She took a deep breath, then spit out, "Mike can't get in. He..." Her voice dropped to a whisper and she ducked her head. "He doesn't really have a key."

A fuzzy silence surrounded Dallas. He should be enraged, but only a stabbing sense of betrayal cut him deep inside. He wrapped his arms around his abdomen and dropped his chin with a dry swallow. *She* lied *to me.* Her total manipulation of his trust threatened to suffocate him. Samantha had systematically dismantled each of his good intentions and turned it into her own self-serving plot to get something from him —*and I've let her do it.* He thought he should hate her by this point, so why did it hurt so badly to know she had intentionally deceived him?

Samantha's tears were a flood. "Dallas, I'm so, so sorry!" she sobbed. "I've played on your good nature, and I *lied* to you! But I can't keep the truth from you —I like you too much to do that. It would guilt me forever if I let you pay someone to change the locks for nothing! I'm sorry I misled you, Dallas, really—"

"Why'd you do it?" His voice was low, head still down.

Samantha was silent other than her sniffles. "Because..." she started, then paused. "Because I didn't think about anything other than wanting you to stay! I had to see how much you really cared about me, and so I knew if you decided to stay to protect me..."

Dallas raised his head as she spoke. Samantha's eyes were red, her face streaked with tears. He couldn't hide the defeated misery in his own eyes, and he swallowed again. "And you did it all on purpose..."

"I'm so sorry, Dallas!" she blubbered again. "It means so much to me that you would care about me like that, and... and... oh, I don't even know *what* I was thinking! I just couldn't bear to have it end! I really *was* so scared earlier, with Mike, and after you saved me, I just wanted to keep you with me for as long as I could because... Oh, you must *hate* me so much! And I lied about something else—"

Dallas stopped her short. "I don't hate you, Samantha," he forced each distinct word through his tight, pained expression. "If I hated you, I wouldn't be so torn up that you lied to me." His voice was heavy with his effort not to break down in front of her.

They sat with eyes locked until Dallas had to pull his gaze away. "What... what else did you lie about?" Dallas fidgeted with the medals on his crucifix necklace as he awaited the answer.

Samantha took a shuddery breath. "About the coffee. It... was decaf."

Dallas almost snorted, but as this second confession sank in, the depth of what she must have been plotting made the coffee as much of a betrayal as the lie about Mike having a key. Samantha had *wanted* him to fall asleep. His cheeks reddened with degraded mortification. *How long was she lying there on the couch with me? How could I have put myself in this situation?* He dropped his head.

"Samantha?" Dallas finally looked across the table. She had her face in her hands, shoulders convulsing with silent sobs. "Why? I feel totally humiliated. How could you do this to me?"

"Oh, Dallas!" Her hands dropped from her face, and she jerked her head back up, her gaze skewering him with her version of tender devotion. "Please, believe me. That's not what I meant at all! I *never* wanted to humiliate you! I swear I won't tell anyone anything, either!"

Those blue eyes threatened to haul Dallas in, but his self-respect won out. "What did you *think* I was going to feel once I realized you'd completely duped me into staying overnight?" He threw both arms wide. "You were just hoping I wouldn't figure it out?"

"I... no, Dallas, deep down, I guess I didn't think I'd be able to fool you." Samantha toyed nervously with a napkin. "You're too smart for that."

"Well, you made a fool out of me." Dallas crossed his arms on the tabletop. "You let yourself into the bathroom *on purpose*, hoping to catch me like that, didn't you? Don't lie to me again."

Samantha nodded and avoided the fire in Dallas's eyes. "I... Yes, I kinda timed it so—"

"And then," he cut in, "to wake up to find you in bed with me, kissing me, and... I..." Dallas put a hand over his face, unable to complete the thought. He felt tears trying to form in his eyes and stubbornly held them back, not wishing to expose his weakness even further. "You unbuckled my belt!" he shot out as he smacked his palm against the table. "You *violated* me *again*! Did you—"

"No, Dallas, I swear! I... I would *never* have touched you like that while you were asleep, I *promise*!"

He bolted up from the chair and ran a hand through his hair. Could he even believe her? "Yeah, right!" Dallas glared at her. "Why else would you open my belt buckle?"

Samantha clamped her jaw shut and dropped her eyes.

Dallas was close to exploding with an instinct to flee, his heart exhausted from the unbearableness of it all. He turned towards the door.

"Do you want to know why?" Samantha sniffed, wringing her hands in her lap.

Dallas paused beside the table. He couldn't look at her. "Because you were trying to lure me into sleeping with you." His voice had a bitter edge. *And she was probably with Mike just yesterday, even…* Dallas fought the anguished thought from his mind.

Samantha continued as if he hadn't answered for her. "It's because of how I'm attracted to you, of course, but also… I know I don't deserve your kindness, and I knew I needed to thank you, and…" She swallowed. "That's the only way I know to thank a man for anything. They've always liked it when I've offered — until you…"

Samantha's words squeezed Dallas's heart, and then he bit back resentment, unable to tell if she was being honest with him.

"If that's true," he said slowly, "then I'm sorry. You don't owe that kind of thanks to any man, *ever*. Just saying thank you would suffice."

"It doesn't feel like enough," she whispered.

He wanted to shake her by the shoulders and shout some sense into her. Dallas bit his lip and held his breath instead.

"And, well, you know how I feel about you, and… I knew you'd *like* it, once you relaxed, and —"

"But it doesn't matter what I'd 'like,' speaking solely in terms of physical pleasure," Dallas interjected, flinging his arms out in exasperation as he grasped for accurate articulation. *Does she even understand at all where I'm coming from?* He rubbed his forehead. "It belittles me when you try to rope me in like that, try to get me to betray my principles — which are based on respect for both of us as human beings — because I don't believe in *using* a woman that way. Don't you get that my rejections of your offers of sex are supposed to show you my *respect* for you?" Even as the blunt words fell from his lips, Dallas recognized how weird they probably sounded to this doll-faced girl whose history was already so colored by experiences vastly different from what he would wish for anyone.

Samantha simpered. "But I wouldn't feel used by *you*, and I'd feel respected just as much, and maybe more, because you're such a good guy —"

"I wouldn't be a 'good guy' anymore if I gave in," Dallas interrupted.

"That's not true!" Samantha insisted. "And, Dallas, because you're the way you are," she added in almost a whisper as she gazed up into his eyes, "I thought that if I could convince you, that you would be so gentle… and I think that would be so nice…"

Dallas needed to escape. He almost couldn't breathe, his stomach churning with disgust as he pictured Mike being rough with her. He was beyond his breaking point—Samantha's pain was becoming his own. *But this isn't my war to fight—it* can't *be, 'cause I know I'll lose. She really, truly doesn't get it, not even a little bit...* The tornado within could destroy Dallas if he didn't back out now. *I really want to hunt that jerk down and kill him!* Dallas squeezed his fists tight, as if inflicting damage on Mike would erase all shame that this night had heaped upon his psyche. Instead, he told his rational brain to get control of himself as he paced beside the table.

"You really will keep away from Mike, report him if he violates the protective order, won't you?" Dallas wondered why he was asking. Her answers couldn't be trusted. He added quickly, "I just really hope that you do. You don't deserve to have a man hurt you, *ever.*" The last word carried such conviction and power that Samantha looked obediently into his eyes and nodded. "You can do it," he encouraged her in a serious, calm voice he could only attribute to the strength of God. He told himself not to think of those raw lyrics she'd written as he turned and strode to the bathroom for his toothbrush and toothpaste. His vocation burned inside like a fire, driving him away. At the front door, he muttered, "I better get home now." The explanation of his calling stuck in his throat as he stepped through the doorway and paused outside.

Samantha followed him to the door. She gazed at him, her damp, remorseful eyes shining from her porcelain face. "I'm so sorry, Dallas. I really am." Her voice softened to a cracking whisper. "Thank you. Thank you so much." Her eyes were like two deep pools, clinging to an impossible wish.

Spellbound by her expression and those trembling lips, Dallas lingered a couple seconds longer. "I'm sorry, too," he responded thickly. He tried to say more, but his tongue was paralyzed. *Tell her you forgive her. She apologized, so just say it...* Dallas couldn't force the words and bit his lip instead. He stepped back a pace and stood watching as she shrank inside the doorway and turned away, glancing over her shoulder at him with large eyes, and shut the door behind herself. The lock clicking into place sounded a finality, and Dallas turned and escaped to his waiting car. The broken look on her bruised face was suffocating him, and he inhaled deeply as he moved through the early morning air and slid into the driver's seat. *I forgive you, Samantha, I do. I do...*

Back in his own apartment another fifteen minutes later, Dallas collapsed onto the sofa, tugging his boots from his feet. The drama of the past ten hours had sapped him, body and mind craving relaxation. *God,*

I wonder about your timing. There was a reason he was put where he was last evening, but had stepping in been the right decision? Dallas couldn't—and shouldn't—set himself up as Samantha's defender, and he couldn't bear the thought of going through the emotional turmoil and temptation he'd just experienced on an ongoing basis. He felt like he'd been led into a trap and had barely escaped. He bit his lip. *I'm too weak to keep getting involved with her. I need to trust it to the law now, and to God.*

The doorway bar accepted Dallas's pent-up agitation, accustomed to his frequent manic pull-up bouts by now. Then he got into bed to grab a few more hours of sleep before he could function. He fell asleep immediately.

Awaking midday to sunlight streaming through his window blinds, Dallas sat up and rubbed his eyes. His stomach growled, a reminder of what had happened to last night's late dinner. He never wanted to eat Chinese food again. His feet hit the floor, and he stretched on his way to the kitchen. Dallas opened a cabinet, spying a box of cereal while realizing he had no milk. He desperately wanted a cup of coffee, caffeinated coffee. Remembering the pizza, Dallas opened the freezer and pulled it out. He preheated the oven and started some coffee.

In the shower, hot water beat against him. *I do forgive her...* Dallas thought about Samantha's father and ground his teeth. He couldn't blame her entirely for being the way she was. He had to find a way to let her know he accepted her apology without falling into her traps. He closed his eyes and let the water drum its pelting rhythm over his face, and he saw Samantha with her bruised cheek in his mind. *"I think that you would be so gentle..."* *I would; I would...* He forced the tempting fantasies of the mystery of her body from his mind with a shake of his head and resolved to get to confession as soon as he could.

Dallas returned to the kitchen in his towel and slid the pepperoni pizza onto the top rack of the oven. He glanced at the clock and returned to the bedroom to shave and get dressed, mug of coffee in hand.

After consuming half the pizza, burning his mouth on the cheese in his impatience, Dallas grabbed his wallet and headed outside. He drove in the direction of the grocery store, pulling into a gas station along the way to run in for another cup of coffee into which he gratefully poured a few half and halfs.

In the store, Dallas pushed the cart with one hand while sipping his coffee with the other. He stocked up on the basics as he moved mechanically through the aisles, willing himself not to think about last night.

In the checkout line, magazine headlines teased him with their self-centered messages. *What would've happened next, if I hadn't woken up when*

I did? The pleasantness of his dream-like state came back to him. Her alluring voice taunting, *"you like that, don't you,"* the way she'd said it, how she was wrapped around him, her hand... *Stop it!* Dallas tore his eyes away from the magazine rack and instinctively touched the crucifix around his neck. Channing's Saint Francis medal alongside it brought his thoughts to a time when Channing was the one huddled up against him, hidden under a blanket in the back of a pickup truck as they fled from the police... Dallas saw two scenarios side by side in his mind, so similar yet completely paradoxical, and he glanced again at the magazine covers next to him. *What He Really Wants — Ten Tips to Drive Him Crazy*, one headline read. He tapped his foot, the urge to move growing within him as he fought off the fact that he had liked the sensation of Samantha next to him on the couch. *And I kissed her back, half-aware... I should've stopped myself somehow!* He could feel the magazine models staring at him even as he kept his eyes forward, and Dallas knew he was living a countercultural life, one that was under constant attack. He would have to fight against this for the rest of his life. *But you* like *to fight, you know. You can do this, but only with God's help. And if you could make it through Channing's death and prison, then you can make it through anything. Lord, give me strength...*

Dallas unlocked the car with one hand while gripping three bags of groceries in the other. As he pulled the door wide, a blunt force hit him out of nowhere in the side, knocking him off balance. Before he could react, Dallas felt his arms wrestled tight behind his back, and he was spun around and forced halfway into his car, groceries spilling everywhere. The door's crushing weight made it clear that somebody had slammed it on him intentionally, and he winced and gasped while thanking God it hadn't been his head. Dallas threw himself back against his unknown assailant before he was turned around and pinned against his car. One of the biggest guys Dallas had ever seen had him by both arms, and sneering beside him was Mike, bruise shining on his jaw. A fist flew at Dallas's face, and he was unable to protect his eye from Mike's punch. Dallas saw a bright light before regaining his vision, Mike's raucous laughter ringing in his ears.

"That's payback for last night!"

Heart racing, Dallas struggled to free himself, but whoever Mike's friend was, he had a grip like steel. Mike got up in Dallas's face, shouting obscenities and waving his arms around. Then he delivered another punch to the jaw.

"Mind your own damn business, ya punk!" Mike ordered as he glared into Dallas's eyes. "You said you don't want Sam, so stay the hell out of it!"

Dallas's eyes were fiery as he growled, "She wants nothing to do with you anymore, you abusive bastard, so you better—"

Mike hit Dallas once more, a jab to the gut this time, and the guy grabbing Dallas's shoulders yanked him away from the car as he doubled over. Dallas felt the huge hands throw him to the pavement, where he gasped for air and gripped the parking tie to make the earth stop tilting. He felt a kick in one thigh and saw cans and apples strewn across the asphalt with two sets of retreating shoes getting smaller as the laughter and taunts faded.

Dallas pushed himself upright and bellowed in Mike's direction, "She's getting a restraining order on you, asshole!" His head pulsed in violent pain with every spewed syllable. *Shut up, you bonehead!* But there was no shout in return. Dallas touched his eyelid, blinking and looking from side to side without moving his head. It would bruise, but no real damage. He tried to stand up but wobbled, so he grabbed his car door for support and felt his stomach churn. *Please, God, not another concussion...*

Across the lot, Dallas saw Mike and his unknown friend jump into Mike's truck and peel out of the exit. The horn blared and unintelligible shouts peppered with profanities rained on Dallas through the window as they roared past.

How did they know I was here? Probably followed me. Dallas squatted down and gathered the spilled food. So, Mike had some tough friend to fight his fights for him. Dallas sighed and shook his head. *Loser. But I better be on my guard. And Samantha...* She had promised to get a protective order, though. Dallas had to believe she would be okay. He tipped his chin towards the clear spring sky. "I can't walk back into that trap." Tossing the last of the cans into his trunk and slamming it, Dallas rounded the car and slid into the driver's seat, then checked his jaw and eye in the mirror. *St. Michael the Archangel, defend us in battle... literally.*

The blinking light of his answering machine greeted Dallas as he set down his grocery bags. The insistent green flashing had gone unnoticed in his exhausted state when he'd first gotten home earlier that morning. He put the cold food away before hitting the button to play the messages.

The first two were telemarketers, and Dallas deleted them partway into each message. Next was a hangup. The last message was different.

"Dallas, this is Mark, your mother's brother," came an unfamiliar voice through the speaker. Dallas froze and almost dropped the leftover slice of pizza he'd picked up. He had met his uncle once when he was about four years old, and the memory was vague. "Sorry to call you out of nowhere like this, but I got some bad news yesterday that you should know. Um, here's my number, so give me a call back when you can..." The receiver clicked, then a beep and the date sounded through the machine.

Yesterday's date. The message had been left only yesterday. A brooding darkness settled over Dallas. He sensed what the bad news was already. *My mother...* He'd never been in contact with his uncle in twenty years, so what other reason would there be for the guy to track him down now?

Dallas paced the living room, unwilling to pick up the phone right away. His mother's half-brother was nearly ten years younger than her, born to her father and his second wife. Dallas knew his grandparents had divorced when his mother was a child, and he'd never met his grandfather, who had died before he was born. His mother's half-brother was rarely spoken of throughout Dallas's childhood. He hadn't even been aware of what part of the country the guy lived in. *How did he find me?* Dallas rubbed his temples. *And how did Mark hear this bad news, if it is what I think it is?*

Steeling himself to get it over with, he punched in the number his uncle had given. The man's voice answered, and Dallas gulped. "Uh, this is Dallas. I got your message."

"Hey, I know this is weird," his Uncle Mark said distantly. "I had to look you up. I hate to have to be the one to tell you—"

"My mother's dead, isn't she?" Dallas's hollow voice seemed to come from outside himself.

Mark sighed. "Yeah, she is. Her body was found and identified a few days ago, off a rural road in Idaho. Apparently, she'd been missing a while... they said her body had probably been there over a year. They think maybe it was foul play, but it could be drugs or suicide. Did you know she was missing? Hey, how old are you now? All grown up, right?"

Over a year. She must've died when I was still in prison. Dallas was blank for a moment before responding, "I haven't known where she was for several years now. I was 19 the last time I saw her, and I'm almost 24 now. I..." Dallas hesitated, unwilling to say where he had been for most of that time.

"Well, again, I'm sorry to have to break the news," his uncle rushed. "So, they need somebody to… claim the body. They looked up all her records and stuff, which is how they connected her to me, on some old paperwork from our dad's will from years ago. She'd apparently bought a cemetery plot next to her mother, right after she'd died, so that's already taken care of. They just need somebody to claim her and have her buried there, and I figured, as her son, you know, that you'd want…"

"Yeah, I'll do it." Dallas grabbed a pen and paper from the counter. "Tell me who to contact about it."

Dallas scribbled down the information as Mark relayed it to him.

"Again, I'm real sorry. Hope you get it all sorted out."

"Wait," Dallas said, sensing his uncle getting ready to hang up. "You want me to tell you after I get arrangements made for her funeral? I mean, if you wanted to come—"

"No, I wouldn't be able to take off from work," Mark responded quickly. "I'm in New York; too far away, anyways."

"Can you think of anyone else who would want to know?" Dallas asked desperately, realizing how isolated he and his mother had truly been for most of his childhood.

"Hmm, not really." Mark's voice was vague. "Our dad's dead. His brother's dead, too. He had some kids, but I never really kept in touch with them. Did you ever meet any of them?"

"I don't think so." Dallas slumped against the wall and rubbed his face. "I don't even remember her mentioning her father's brother. And her mom was an only child—"

"So yeah, I gotta go now," Mark cut him off. "Good luck."

"Yeah, thanks," Dallas said as the click came through the line. He returned the phone to the receiver and stood in the center of his apartment, numb.

Dallas was not surprised that his mother was dead. But her lack of family connections, her seclusion, hit him like a ton of bricks. Had she had any friends; other people she would do things with years ago? Dallas's search of his memories came up empty. She never had people over, and if she would meet up with anyone else when she was out, she never spoke of it to Dallas. He couldn't even come up with the name of one co-worker she may have mentioned. *Because she rarely talked to me.* Dallas gritted his teeth.

He wanted another cup of coffee. Dallas went into the kitchen and scooped grounds in the coffee maker, the one his mother had left in the house, the one he and Channing had brewed coffee in outside the public library. Dallas bit his lip. He didn't know what his mother had gone through her whole life, and now that she was dead, it was no good to be angry at her over their lack of relationship. Hadn't she fulfilled the main role of a parent—providing for his physical needs? Something deeper had been lacking, something that didn't bother Dallas in his conscious mind most of the time… but now that she was dead, it was as if he'd been holding his breath his whole life suddenly. *I have this coffee maker because of her.* Dallas stared at the gurgling machine as the coffee started to drip. It had to be the lamest thing ever that a son could be grateful to his mother for after just learning of her death. Guilt crept in, alongside the numb broodiness in another part of his mind. *But she fed me, sheltered me, raised me with some basic standards…* Dallas blew out a deep breath, unable to feel a proper response to the news.

But as her only child, Dallas's duty to his mother was clear. She finally needed him—needed something that only he would step up to do. And it was a corporal work of mercy to bury the dead. But could he extend mercy and forgive her? Harboring a serious grudge against his mother hadn't been conscious thought, but the deep bitterness towards her that lay buried inside suddenly opened him up. *Samantha…* He tingled with the memory of her doting on him last night. Dallas whirled and kicked a kitchen cabinet forcefully with a loud crack as he played the blame game with his mother, pinning his current problems on a ghost. The split wood gaped like his soul.

The coffee was done. Dallas dumped it into his mug and thought maybe he should have a stiff drink instead. He strode away from the damage his boot had inflicted and stood at the window, taking sips of the steamy beverage and trying not to think.

After downing the cup, Dallas picked up the scrap of paper on which he'd written the phone number of an office in Idaho. He dialed the number and set his mouth in a tight line as he wondered exactly what he was going to say.

Dallas muddled his way through transfers and the relaying of details until he had the needed information. He sank onto the couch. He needed to get a certified copy of his birth certificate to prove his relationship to his mother. He scrubbed a hand across his face. *Why, why didn't I grab that file folder of documents when Channing and I left Nevada?* Dallas knew why—because he was still just a kid then with no idea of how life worked. He grabbed the phone book and flipped open to the government offices, looking for one that sounded right. Once he jotted down a number, he picked up the phone to first call Father Benedict.

After laying out all the details about his mother, Dallas listened to the priest's response. Father Benedict asked Dallas to come through Denver on his way and stay over one night.

"I have this strange numbness tinged with annoyance, Father. Is it awful of me to be *annoyed* that I have to take care of this?" Dallas asked.

"Feelings are a tricky thing, Dallas," the priest said, "and in your situation, ambivalence is not an unexpected response. It's your actions that count, especially when you act in the way you know is right despite your feelings that are urging you to do otherwise."

Dallas squeezed his eyes shut and tried for the millionth time not to think about last night with Samantha.

"Would you like me to come for the burial?" Father Benedict asked.

"You would do that?" Dallas raised both eyebrows. "I mean… *can* you do that? Like, she can't get a funeral Mass… I don't even know if she was baptized."

"If you would like, I can say some general prayers for her," Father replied. "Not a Mass—you're right that those are for baptized Catholics—and it won't be a full funeral rite either, because that doesn't fit the situation. But everybody deserves to be buried with respect and our prayers for their souls."

Dallas hung up, shoulders sagging and eyes closed. He wouldn't have to do this alone. He dialed the number he'd looked up about obtaining a birth certificate to figure out what his next steps would be.

Two days later, Dallas got on the road early. The former excitement and freedom of a road trip eluded him, and Dallas sighed at the vanished former hobby from his more carefree days. This trip had such a dark purpose, and road trips weren't the same without Channing, anyway. He stopped at a Catholic parish along the way and found a priest, spilled his guts in confession, and continued towards Denver feeling much lighter.

When he arrived at the basilica, Father Benedict welcomed him with a warm hug and showed him to the guest quarters.

"What happened?" Father Benedict pointed to Dallas's black eye.

"Kind of a long story, but I'm fine," Dallas brushed him off. "I'll explain some other time."

The priest studied Dallas a moment through squinted eyes, then dropped the subject. "Are you hungry?"

"Yeah, getting that way," Dallas replied. "I had coffee and two bagels for breakfast and haven't eaten since."

"Then I'm taking you out for dinner," Father Benedict decided.

At the restaurant, they discussed choices of prayers and psalms that could be included at the burial. Unsure when it would take place, Dallas hesitated to make firm plans, but at least the format was laid out now. The reality of everything was setting in, and Dallas was at least glad for the distraction that kept thoughts of Samantha at bay.

"You have everything needed to claim her remains?" the priest asked.

Dallas nodded. "I got a copy of my birth certificate yesterday, looked up exactly where this office is in Idaho, too."

Dallas allowed Father Benedict to buy him a drink, struck boldly with choosing something hard. Learning that your mother is dead seemed like a good enough time as any for drinking whiskey. Dallas downed each bourbon on the rocks in close succession. The tingling warmth crept through his arteries, a relaxing burn, numbing him from the conflict swirling inside.

An hour and a half later, riding back to the church in Father Benedict's car, Dallas pressed his forehead against the glass of the passenger window. *Don't talk, don't...* The road tipped and wobbled again, so he shut his eyes tight. A lightheaded freedom mingled with a despairing emptiness inside him. Dallas pressed a hand over his face until he saw red through his eyelids, keeping his head turned towards the window. *I... I'm drunk off my...* He heard the drone of Father's murmuring Rosary being prayed aloud and hid himself behind the words.

In the parking space outside the rectory, Dallas coached himself and practiced his speech silently, hearing it slur inside his mind. *Open the door... Steady...* He gripped the handle and planted his feet firmly on asphalt, rising upwards and leaving his stomach behind him in the car. *You're totally wasted, Dallas...* He slowed his ascent and clamped his lips tight. *Don't puke; don't do it...* The night air offered a touch of relief, and Dallas followed behind Father Benedict, the sidewalk wavering and undulating like a waterbed.

In the hallway, Dallas felt along the wall to his bedroom door and paused, holding the doorknob with a death grip to keep it from floating away. As he saw the priest turn towards him, he somehow got through the doorway. "I'm real tired, so goodnight." His practiced words were foggy, but Dallas shut the door and dropped onto the bed, squeezing his throbbing-hot skull with both hands and imagining himself passed out in the grave with his mother.

The next morning, Dallas awoke with a splitting headache, a sensation previously unimaginable. At breakfast, Father Benedict eyed him curiously. The Irish priest always appeared unfazed after a few drinks himself.

"I've never had four whiskeys in a row before." *Or was it five?* Dallas held his face in his hands with his elbows on the table, embarrassed in front of the other two priests of the basilica. He fought the fading feeling that he might still throw up.

"Never had a hangover before?" one of them asked. "What do you normally drink?"

"Coffee," was Dallas's honest answer. Everyone laughed.

After the other priests had left the kitchen, Father Benedict pulled his chair closer.

"Dallas, I didn't realize how quickly you were consuming those drinks. You looked like a pro, so I didn't even think—"

"No, it's okay; you didn't know I was such a lightweight." Dallas forced a weak grin. "It's my own fault for not taking it slow—it's not your responsibility. I think I've learned my lesson. This is no tradeoff for the brief mental escape."

Before Mass, Dallas wandered into the gift shop off the narthex of the church, examining the various Bibles, statues, and prayer cards. One caught his eye: the exact same prayer card as the one in his back pocket! Channing's Memorare prayer card, with the same picture of Mary and the Infant Jesus. Dallas picked one up and gazed into the serene face, the tender eyes focused on him, expressing the love of her son and the Savior of the world. This card had sustained him in prison. He would buy copies for Smith and Pedro. At the register, he laid down five copies of the Memorare card and pulled out his wallet.

An hour later, he was in the church, right near the place he and Channing had sat that day so long ago. Through the pounding in his head, Dallas grasped for the meaning in Father Benedict's homily. He slogged through the responses and wondered if he'd feel better soon.

After Mass, Dallas and the priest sat outside near a plaque commemorating Pope John Paul II's recent visit for World Youth Day. The fog in his head was lifting, but Dallas still wasn't ready to make the 12-hour drive the rest of the way to Idaho.

"That's perfect, because I can tell you what the bishop said when I told him about you," the old priest said with a smile.

Dallas snapped his head up and saw the twinkle in Father's eyes.

"He wants to meet with you," continued Father Benedict, "and he sounded very interested. He believes that you sound like a very dedicated young man, and that's what we need in our seminarians pursuing the priesthood. We can set up a time for you to meet with him after you get through this current situation. You need to devote whatever time you need to this right now."

Dallas sighed. "I honestly hope it won't take too long. Ideally, I can get the burial taken care of before I leave the area, so I don't have to make a return trip."

"Where is the burial plot located?" asked Father Benedict.

"In the town where I grew up, northern Nevada."

"Once you get to Idaho and make arrangements to have your mother's remains sent to a funeral home near the cemetery, call and let me know. I'll come up there as soon as you need me for the burial."

"Father, are you sure?" Dallas cocked an eyebrow. "It's like eleven hours from here."

"I'll need to drive it over two days, but yes, I will be there," he assured Dallas. "I know you want to treat your mother with humanity and will be glad to support you in that. You've said she didn't really have anyone, and that's a sad thing, very sad. I want *you* to know that you have somebody."

Dallas nodded, eyes on his boots.

"And Dallas," the priest continued, "the seminary will be so good for you if you go. There is a kind of camaraderie, a brotherhood, among the men studying for the priesthood. I know you had that with Channing, and that you began to form those kinds of relationships with a couple of the others in prison. It's a wonderful blessing to have friends, especially if you don't have family."

"I should have tried to find her," Dallas said with a shrug.

"You couldn't have." The priest laid a gentle hand on Dallas's forearm.

Dallas frowned. "I guess not. I was in prison, after all. But you offered to try, and I told you no. And when she first disappeared… I don't know, I guess I didn't think she wanted me coming after her. The note she left made it clear that I was on my own. Yeah, I suppose you're right. She's the one who left, and without any way to be contacted."

"It's natural for you to feel regrets over what did and did not happen between you and your mother," Father Benedict said.

Dallas nodded, then tried a smile. "Thanks for talking to the archbishop about me. I should sound more excited about it, that he might give me a chance. That's great news. I mean, I don't want to get my hopes up, but…"

"With the difficulties you are having to take care of right now, I understand why you don't seem more excited," Father replied. "You need to focus on your mother right now. But I wanted to give you something positive to keep in mind."

Father Benedict had to go make a hospital visit, so he left Dallas with directions to a nearby coffee shop. Once Dallas was there and had finished a cup, his head felt clear. He pulled out a few sheets of paper and a pen and began writing letters to Smith and Pedro in prison. Smith's sentence was up in a few months, and Pedro's in another year. He'd meant to go visit them or at least write, and he was feeling guilty at not having gotten around to it. He knew what some encouragement could do for them.

Father Benedict had also asked him to be thinking about and writing down references and past work experiences, kind of like a resume. Dallas's list was embarrassingly short. A concern nagged at him that he wouldn't be seen as seminary material. *Priests probably come from more normal family backgrounds…* With a sigh, he pushed those thoughts aside and focused on the upcoming unpleasant task.

Dallas spent the late afternoon back in the basilica, praying through the chaos in his mind. He studied the same windows Channing had marveled at, stabbed in pain at having lost most of the stained glass artwork his friend had made. But it was time to tear himself away… He could drive a few more hours this evening now that he felt better.

Dallas declined Father Benedict's invitation to stay for dinner. "Tomorrow's Friday, so I need to get there before the office closes. I'm a little concerned about money since I've not been working. I don't want to spend a bunch on fast food and hotels."

"Dallas," the priest said, "I want to make sure you know that money is not an impediment to entering the seminary for a man who truly has a calling and desires to follow it. The Church will always work with those who cannot afford it all on their own. While you should certainly be frugal, I don't want you to have anxiety over your finances. I realize you have the burial expenses now, although having the plot already taken care of should bring some relief. God does provide."

Dallas smiled. "Yes, he does. I know that. Still, I question the timing. As soon as I stepped back into my life after hiking the AT, he sure hit me hard with some crazy problems. Maybe it's meant as a wake-up call, having to put others ahead of myself," he added. "But I feel really beaten down right now. I'll have to tell you later about what happened as soon as I drove back into town. I haven't had a moment's peace since I got back!"

"We'll talk more soon," the priest said, embracing Dallas. "Call me when you know details and need me."

Dallas drove towards the sunset and kept going until it was past ten, when he pulled off at a Walmart and parked the Isuzu in the middle of the lot. He killed the engine, sprawled out in the front seat, and fell asleep.

Dallas glanced out the passenger window before making his left turn out of the parking lot the next morning when the realization struck him like lightning: he hadn't even thought of Channing when falling asleep alone or waking to the empty passenger seat. He bit his lip. He was growing more and more accustomed to these daily actions absent Channing. How should he feel about that? Dallas adjusted the volume. *Still can't eject our album...*

The growing dread in the pit of his stomach demanded his attention as Dallas neared his destination. He didn't want to think about it, but the questions came regardless. *Will they make me physically identify the body? Will they be able to determine the cause of death? Was my mother mixed up in something so bad that she was murdered over it? Did she just wander off and die? If it was suicide, should I have noticed signs of depression in her?* Dallas's memory was jarred back to his own attempt in prison, and he suddenly couldn't swallow at the thought of having sunk to such a low. *Is there a genetic predisposition for that sort of thing? Should I be paying more attention to my own mental health?*

Pulling over to the side of the road, Dallas got out and tried to shake it off. His heartbeat raced like a sped-up drum. *None of this matters in the long run,* he told himself as he walked briskly into the nearby field, breathing deeply and kicking rocks along the way. *God only suffices.* His personality, with all its foibles and flaws, was only a temporary state on earth—it didn't control his destiny. But anxiety consumed him. He stretched, then jogged back to the car. *I just have to put one foot in front of the other... rather, put one mile behind the other, and just get there and do the right thing. She was my* mom, *for crying out loud...* He got back into the Isuzu and pulled back on the road.

After a couple pauses to check his route in the atlas, and once to again fill up the gas tank, Dallas pulled into the small town in Idaho, searching for his turn. About to tackle the task at hand, his unease was replaced by determined purpose.

Once he'd spotted the building, Dallas parked and went through the main door, identifying documents in hand. He was directed down the hall to an office and asked to sit on a bench outside the door. As he waited, Dallas scanned the birth certificate in his hands. *Father's name, blank. Mother's name, Sharon Louise Malone.* Dallas had no middle name. *August 3, 1977, Elko County, Nevada.* He stared at it so long that the words ran together in a black blur. He blinked and flipped the paper over in his lap.

Finally, he entered the office and sank into a chair across the desk from the man he'd spoken with on the phone, Mr. Collins, who greeted Dallas and expressed his condolences at the unfortunate situation which had brought him all this way. Dallas tried a smile in return but knew he only looked grim. Mr. Collins examined Dallas's license and birth certificate and explained how the body had been identified. It was not advised for Dallas to try to identify the remains himself so long after death, for which he was relieved. He had no reason to doubt the accuracy of the DNA matching.

"You may hire a lawyer, if you wish, to track down whether a will had been made," Mr. Collins explained. "There was not one uncovered in the other legal documents which were found and linked to Ms. Malone."

"I doubt she had one, so I'll just handle it on my own," Dallas responded. "You said you couldn't find a record of another residence past this Nevada address?"

Mr. Collins nodded an affirmative.

"Yeah, that's the last place she lived that I knew of, and it was three or four years before she died that she left there. Who knows where she was living after that..." A pathetic image of his mother staying in cheap hotels and her car came to Dallas, and he wondered if she'd lived the same kind of life as Channing and him in those early weeks after they'd left Nevada.

Dallas called a funeral home and arranged to have the body sent to Elko, and he quickly agreed to schedule the burial for the following Wednesday. The sensitivity of the funeral director's phrasing of questions contrasted with the morbid thoughts swarming inside Dallas. He shuddered and got queasy at the gruesome image of finding human remains months after the death. His mother's body, lifeless, and—Dallas shook himself. All these complete strangers: the police, the funeral directors, everyone who had to take care of the messiness of his own life's tragedies. Were they used to it after years on the job, numb to the morbidity, or did they see their jobs as callings to help families through the realities of accidents and gruesome deaths? His last view of Channing ran through his mind on a loop until he blinked it away and focused on the papers being handed to him.

After filling out forms and providing his signature on a few documents, Dallas received a copy of his mother's death certificate. He asked if he could use the phone to make one more call. Father Benedict said he was able to arrive in Nevada by Tuesday evening. Dallas filled out a death and burial notice to send to the Elko newspaper via email. Everything arranged, Dallas shook hands with Mr. Collins and exited the building. He stopped at the bottom of the steps and stood unmoving, realizing that it was not even a two-hour drive back to his hometown, and he didn't have any idea what he should do with himself until Tuesday.

Dallas's feet were glued to the concrete. Part of him was pulled to go back "home," but there was a bad taste in his mouth from all his and Channing's negative experiences there. He'd been saving them both when they'd left Nevada. What did that town have left for him? The 14 years Dallas had attended school there were light years in the past, as if it were a mere fraction of him, even though it represented more than half of his lifetime. And somehow, he had no friends, no connections there.

Unsure of what else to do, Dallas got in his car and opened the road atlas. On the page that included southern Idaho, he pinpointed what he thought was the approximate location where his mother's body had been found, based on the information shared with him. He left the city limits and pulled over at the spot about twenty minutes later. Stepping out of the car, his boots hit dry, dusty earth on the shoulder of the lonely highway. Dallas waded into waist-high vegetation that brushed against his hands.

It was somewhere right around here… Did she die here, or was she dumped here after… He gazed overhead, a cloudless and blue expanse with an unrelenting bright sun creeping lower in the late afternoon sky. Dallas couldn't make himself feel. Feeble attempts to pray tripped over his mind, dull and uncooperative. All he could manage was a murmured, "May God have mercy on her soul."

His tent was in the trunk. Wondering if it was private property, Dallas searched the area for some indicating sign. Nothing. He found a spot where he could park his car so it wouldn't be noticed from the road, drove it into the field, and parked along the tree line. Dallas unpacked his tent and sleeping bag, then ate some food that didn't require a fire.

By the light of his flashlight, Dallas read his evening prayers and offered them up for his mother. Still unable to conjure any meaningful feelings, he knew the action itself would count for something. He set the book aside and sat staring into the darkness beyond the mesh door of the tent.

After yawning several times, Dallas reclined on his sleeping bag, kicking off his boots and wishing he'd remembered a pillow. He passed a restless night in this place near his mother's end. Why wasn't it evoking any kind of emotional response to help him through? *I'm not upset or any normal feeling, only restless and agitated. And mad at myself. Feel, Dallas, feel! Why can't you be sad over this?!* He slept off and on, then got up with the sun, packing up and giving up.

Dallas stopped at a gas station for coffee and doughnuts. The white powdered sweets almost forced themselves on him—Channing had loved the things. Dallas checked the map and headed south towards the state border.

As the landscape became familiar, Dallas's chest tightened. He was stepping back into his past, his childhood. The familiar McDonald's came into view, and then Marino's, the pizza restaurant he and Channing had liked. Both were just as he'd last seen them. Dallas drove down the main road and turned in at the little convenience store outside Channing's neighborhood, where Dallas and his mother had also lived for a while and where Channing's mother had still been occupying their rental house at the time when they'd left town for good. In middle school, he and Channing had walked together to this store frequently, and it was where Channing's mother had sent him to buy her cigarettes. Dallas idled, staring at the old building with the grimy-looking walls.

Not knowing what he was doing or even what he wanted to do, Dallas sat paralyzed. Thoughts attempted to form, like bubbles at the bottom of a pot of water that hadn't yet boiled. Finally, he pulled out again, repelled by the demons of his past, accelerating down the main road. His old street came into view, and he made the turn. There it was—the rental house where Dallas had last seen his mother. Where he had found the note that had changed his life. A pickup truck was parked in front. The lawn was unmowed, and a couple of the shutters hung askew. Dallas slowed and then stopped at the curb, slumped against the wheel and staring. His former life held him captive, trapped inside frozen memories.

The front door opened. A man emerged, striding straight across the narrow lawn towards Dallas's idling car. He jolted upright and ran his fingers through his still too-long hair. *Don't drive away. That'll just look suspicious. You don't want your license plate called in to the local police.* Dallas rolled down his window, and the man called out, "You lost or something?"

"I used to live here," Dallas said, "about five years ago. I had business back in town, so I was just driving past some old places."

"You rented this place?" asked the man, the vaguely familiar figure now towering above the driver's door. "Five years ago?" His eyes narrowed.

"W-well," stammered Dallas, "my mom did. I'm really sorry. I wasn't trying to be a creep or anything."

"Malone?" the man asked.

Dallas's throat went dry. "Uh, yeah, that's our last name. How—"

"I was your landlord." The man crossed his arms across his chest. "I live here now."

Dallas sucked in a breath, mind racing with the one time he'd seen the man when he'd come to collect the overdue rent as he and Channing made a mad dash for Dallas's car. "I realize my mother ran off and left this place on pretty short notice, and so, um… if she'd missed any payments, then… well, I'll make good on them."

The man's eyebrows shot up as he met Dallas's steady gaze. "Actually, yes, she did miss the last couple months as I remember. I have the paperwork somewhere, so I can look it up. You knew she was behind?"

"Well, I was only 19," Dallas answered, "and barely knew my mom's financial situation, but I suspected something was wrong. She moved out without telling me where she was going, and I was stuck not knowing what to do with the house, unable to afford the rent myself—so I left, too. You saw me and my friend leave. Uh… sorry about that." Dallas left off the part about his mother being dead now.

"Well, I'm dumbfounded." The landlord ran his hands through his thinning hair. "Never expected I'd see that money. You really want to pay it now?"

"If she owed it, then it's the right thing to do."

The man eyed him with furrowed brow.

He probably thinks I'm crazy… might as well make him continue to think so. "Did you, uh, happen to clean out the basement after we left? This car was all I had to fit stuff in, and so I took what I could that she'd left here—"

"Your mother abandoned you?" the landlord asked point-blank.

Dallas shifted in his seat. "Well, I was technically an adult by then, so—"

"But she was paying for this place, you were living here with her, and she just split? Dumped the rent on a 19-year-old kid who couldn't afford it?" The man's bewildered expression made Dallas squirm.

"I guess when you put it that way," Dallas said, cheeks warming, "uh, she sort of did, yeah."

"There was loads of stuff in the basement, yeah," the former landlord acknowledged. "There's a small pile still down there. Didn't quite know what to do with some of it. Some interesting artwork—didn't think I should throw those out, and didn't seem the kind of thing to donate, either. Are they yours? There are a couple pieces of stained glass art that are real talented."

Dallas's eyes lit up. "You still have the stained glass? My friend made those! Could I… could I look at them, if you don't mind?"

"Sure," the man answered. "They've just been sitting, and I have no plans for them. Guess they were meant to be found by you. Come on in."

Walking on clouds, Dallas followed his mother's former landlord to the basement door. Inside, their eyes adjusted to the dim light as the man walked over to where Dallas knew there was a ceiling light with a pull chain. Suddenly, the room was flooded by brightness, and Dallas blinked, eyes scanning the remembered layout of the unfinished basement, mostly cleared out now. Vague old paint cans still on a shelf, the familiar yard tools including a rake and shovel, and there, in the far corner past the stairs: a pile of Channing's artwork.

Dallas glided across the room and dropped to his knees, hardly daring to believe it. His fingers caressed the surfaces: three large stained glass pieces and four painted canvases. Channing had spent countless hours on them. Holding up one of the 12x12 inch frames to the light, studied the swirling mosaic of yellows, oranges, and greens. His tears flowed freely. *The dragon… this was one of Channing's favorites.* He'd mentioned once after they'd left that he should have remembered to bring it, but they had been in such a hurry… The familiar lump rose in Dallas's throat.

"You can't know what these things mean to me," he said in a quavering voice. "If you don't want them, then I'd sure love to take them."

"Absolutely," the man answered. "Let me look up those missed back payments for you. The paperwork's in a file upstairs." Dallas heard the familiarity of the creaking stairs as the former landlord ascended to the main floor.

Dallas handled each piece as delicately as crystal, marveling at his good fortune in retrieving these special few of Channing's years of work. A conversation came back to him suddenly, from when Channing was reading aloud from Dante's *Inferno* at the beach: *"This says sinning against nature is sinning against art,"* Channing had explained, *"because it's unnatural to sin against creation, and creation is the art of the Creator, so when we ourselves make art… wow. Dallas, have you ever stopped to think about how we ourselves were created, yet we are the only creatures that can intentionally create?"* Dallas recalled that he had then joked with Channing if it was a sin against art for him to have destroyed his own work of art, the huge sandcastle he'd spent half the day creating.

He sat back on his heels, closing his eyes and breathing in the old smells from a time and place where he and Channing had worked on his projects in the comfortable silence of camaraderie. Dallas's hands assisted, but it was all Channing's vision, all from his mind and his inborn skill and his willingness to experiment. *God gave Channing that gift, his ability to create art… Hour upon hour spent crouched before the kiln, right there on the floor... If I open my eyes, just a slow peek, will he still be here beside me?*

A few moments later, returning footsteps on the stairs chased Dallas's reminiscent thoughts away.

"I'm sorry, I never introduced myself," the man said. "I'm Darren Olson."

"Dallas Malone," he said, extending his hand. "I remembered something else — is there any chance you might have found a couple folders of old documents? I don't know what papers my mother might have left, but my birth certificate was in there, for example."

"I did find one folder of documents, yeah," Darren replied. "Not sure if any were birth certificates. I put them through a paper shredder, though, so they wouldn't fall into the wrong hands. I didn't read through them, figured it wasn't my business, but seems like I remember they were bank statements and bills and stuff. Sorry about that."

"No problem, it's probably better that way." Dallas lifted the stack of artwork and hugged it to his chest. "I appreciate that my identity didn't get stolen or anything." *Bank statements...* The wheels started turning in Dallas's frugal mind. If he'd known any better, he might have taken those in case they'd help him access his money — the money he'd earned that his mother had deposited into her account. *Stupid, stupid me. Then Channing and me wouldn't have been so desperate that — stop it, stop doing this to yourself! You can't change the past.* The money must be long gone now, anyway.

They looked over the rental contract and payment records. Two months' rent had been missed when they had abandoned the house, totaling $900. Dallas asked Darren if he would accept a check.

They walked together to the Isuzu, where Dallas pulled his checkbook from the glove compartment. As he handed Darren the payment, he asked, "So did you... do you remember my mother?"

"Met her maybe twice," he answered. "She always mailed the payments. She was real quiet. Didn't get to know her at all."

"I don't think anybody got to know her, really." Dallas sighed.

"So did you find out where she went?"

Dallas shook his head. "Haven't seen her since." He turned away and busied himself with stacking Channing's art into the trunk between old newspapers. Then he stared at the old house one final time.

As he got into the driver's seat, Dallas said, "I really appreciate you letting me get this artwork. And I apologize again for how we all ran off."

"I'm just amazed somebody came back wanting to make it right," Darren responded. "You're a good son, Dallas, and if you ever find your mother, she'd better be darn sure to be grateful to you."

Dallas bit his lip and gave a departing wave, then drove back to the main road. He passed Marino's again, resisting the tempting smell wafting through the window, urging him to go in. "That was where Chan and me first heard this album," Dallas said aloud as the same songs repeated in an endless monotony. He couldn't handle going in there now, and after dropping over a month's worth of savings on that back rent payment... Dallas sighed.

He took the turn towards the wooded recreation area as if on auto-pilot, trailing the ghost of his past self. He and Channing had taken this route countless times. In the parking area, Dallas schlepped his gear on his back and hiked up the trail. Where the path flattened out, he watched for the place where they used to cut through the woods towards the stream. His heart sank as he scanned the trees. Nothing looked familiar. Dallas headed off-trail based purely on instinct and, a few minutes later, was rewarded by the faint sound of the bubbling creek. He reached its edge and estimated that he was a little downstream from their old favorite camping spot. He followed along the bank.

A moment later, Dallas nearly tripped over a primitive-looking and overgrown low rock wall. He stopped, stunned—he and Channing had built this! *Man, it looked so much bigger and better back then.* Dallas stared at the ruins miserably. He began clearing away fallen sticks and pinecones to make a place for the tent. Backing up, he almost stepped into their old fire pit, a hollow to match the one swelling in his gut. It was full of leaves and almost hidden from view.

As Dallas pitched the tent, he couldn't jump over the hurdle in his head: *I don't want to be here. I don't want to be in Nevada.* He was losing his grip, sinking into a slump. Trying to remind himself of his good fortune of the miracle of getting back some of Channing's artwork did nothing to raise his spirits. Channing was still dead, and his past life was coming back to haunt him here. He stood, numb, tent stakes in one hand and mallet in the other.

Dallas tried arguing with himself. Channing had loved being out here—why couldn't he just enjoy it? Dallas knew why—he was avoiding driving past Channing's house and their old schools with their mostly negative memories.

With a sigh, Dallas studied his surroundings. This place used to be such fun. Maybe he could force himself to kick back for a few days out here. Blocking out the thoughts of what lurked nearby in the town of his past and what lay ahead on Wednesday were Dallas's challenges.

Hands deep in his pockets, he walked off to find the nearby boulders they had liked to explore. Large rocks rose out of the ground before him. He walked the perimeter of the cluster, discovering a place where somebody had constructed a stick shelter between two of the rocks. A smile played at the corners of Dallas's lips as he thought about some other boys coming up here and doing the kinds of things he and Channing used to do. Dallas ran a hand across the bumpy lichen-covered rock surface beside him. He climbed up on the boulders, smaller now and somehow less magical and mysterious.

Dallas went back towards the tent, pausing at the spot where Channing had built his elaborate lean-to out of large sticks and branches. It was gone now, although Dallas thought that he could make out part of the structure among the disorganized piles of sticks at the base of the tree if he used his imagination. He pulled out some of the larger sticks and scooped up heaps of the leaf litter and twigs that had collected there over the years and tossed those aside. Then he propped some larger branches against the tree, the way Channing had done, and tried half-heartedly to reconstruct the fort. He got partway done and kicked it down, disenchanted with its lack of authenticity.

"Sorry, Channing," Dallas grumbled as he cracked a branch under his boot. "I just don't have the heart of a kid anymore. You always had more of that spirit captured within you than I did, anyway. Wish I could build it back for you, or at least enjoy the attempt." With slumped shoulders, Dallas trudged back to the tent and couldn't muster the will to build a fire. Let the last fire he ever built in this spot be one he'd made with Channing. Dallas sat down on what was left of the old log alongside the fire ring, leaning to clear the leaves from the center of the ring of stones. His hands brushed across cold gray ashes, and he dipped his fingers in, stirring up the remains of their now-dead fires. That last song, the one after which he still hadn't been able to eject the tape... He looked up at their crumbling stone wall as the lyrics sunk in. Dallas shuddered. He didn't want to think of Channing as a spirit roaming around here in the woods, but there was no doubt that the place was brim-full of reminders of him. Dallas closed his eyes and took deep breaths, ashes running through his clutched hand. *Channing's not here; he's in heaven. Please, God...*

Dallas pulled out his book and read his prayers, then ate a little food and got ready for bed. He splashed off his face in the stream and crawled into bed in the familiar yellow tent. As he fell asleep, he prayed, "Lord, please give me endurance and strength for these next few days." He wrapped his arms tightly around himself, a mirage to mask his isolation.

When he woke, Dallas realized he would have to clean up better before going to Mass. It was Sunday morning, so of course, he would go. He scarfed down some peanut butter on bread and then headed to the interstate and went to the Pilot truck stop right off the exit. He remembered they had showers in most truck stops, thanks to Channing's random and extensive knowledge of the truckers' havens.

With his bottle of soap on top of the handful of ashes from their fire ring that he'd sentimentally tucked into his pocket, Dallas got in and out unnoticed—the showers were reserved for "professional drivers only," according to the sign. Being clean and heading for Mass lifted his spirits, and Dallas drove off in the direction of St. Katherine's.

In a cool wooden pew towards the back, Dallas sat in the dim light, eyes closed. Mass wouldn't begin for another 45 minutes, and he absorbed the silence and the atmosphere, two lit candles for his mother and Channing flickering alone in the nearby rack. Dallas prayed, fiddling with the glass ring on his right ring finger and wishing he'd put his rosary in his pocket. He had Channing's prayer card, as always, and pulled it out instead, smiling at the worn edges and creases it had picked up over the years. *The miracle prayer card.* The silent reverence surrounded him, blessings of his formerly haphazard life sinking in firmly, and Dallas whispered a thank you to God for the recovery of Channing's artwork. Maybe he'd be hanging the paintings and stained glass up in his room at the seminary in just a few short months... A shiver ran down Dallas's spine.

The Holy Mass transcended reality, elevating and grounding Dallas's soul simultaneously as it always did, unexplainable. Participation in Christ's sacrifice and a humble reliance on God's strength and perfection brought Dallas to his knees, rippling through his body, carrying him in that one solid thing he knew of his own life: *I'm hearing God calling me. He really is. Please, Lord, make me worthy of this.*

Dallas trotted down the church steps and got in his car. Driven by the strength taken from the Mass, he straightened his shoulders. As he neared the public school complex, he observed that some of the buildings had been replaced with modern structures. He couldn't even get a bead on where the main entrance had been, even the parking lot had been redone in a different way.

Would he need a high school transcript to get into the seminary? Dallas's grades hadn't been excellent, but he'd passed, and since he was already here and was presentable... well, clean, anyway... *What've you got to lose?* He accepted his own challenge. Dallas glanced at his reflection in the mirror and pulled into the high school lot, wondering if there was any chance somebody might be here on a Sunday. No cars were in the lot. He'd have to come back tomorrow or Tuesday.

A tug at Dallas's heart begged him to drive past Channing's old house, and he argued with it. It's not like they had spent lots of time there, only hanging out there to watch TV when nobody else was home. Channing had never wanted to stay around the potential turmoil that came with his mother's presence, especially when she had one of her boyfriends around.

You're too chicken to drive by there. Dallas bit his lip and headed back to the woods instead and carried his stuff back to the tent, this time grabbing a couple books from the car. One Father Benedict had just loaned to him, a brand-new text that explained the catechism. Dallas sprawled out on his sleeping bag and read for the rest of the day. Washed in reassurance, especially by the section of the book related to death, Dallas escaped from his current discomfort—all but that tiny nagging inside him. *You don't give up; you don't cave to your fears. You* have *to drive past Channing's old house.*

Dallas looked all around at his and Channing's special place, cushioning him as a haven from the world. It was so quiet and removed from the town that he would have to go and face soon. He could camp two more nights, only get a hotel on Tuesday when Father Benedict would arrive in town. But he'd have to go into town tomorrow for that transcript. And maybe he could track down his mother's bank account.

After successfully obtaining a copy of his high school transcript the next morning, Dallas pulled in at the first bank he saw, ready for a random hunt-and-peck search. His mother had been desperate, though—it was likely that she'd cleaned out her account, taking any money she could. He shouldn't get his hopes up. Dallas still wondered if she had owed money for something illegal and hadn't been able to pay. Was that how she'd ended up dead—murdered?

The folder of identifying documents clutched in his hand, Dallas strode through the door. He assumed his confident and collected persona without effort.

"I'm looking around to see if I can find any bank accounts belonging to my mother, who is deceased," Dallas explained to the teller when he'd stepped up to the counter. "Her name was Sharon Malone."

The teller spent a couple minutes searching on the computer and then turned to Dallas. "No, I'm sorry. I don't see any account history for anyone under that name." Dallas thanked her and left.

It was the same story at the next three banks. Not all of them could see the history of an account that may have been closed, and Dallas knew he might be chasing after nothing. He might never find where she used to have her money—and his—if she'd withdrawn it all. Dallas racked his brain for past memories of a bank she'd been to while he was in the car with her. He had a fuzzy idea of one location, but when he drove past, there was no longer a bank, if there had ever been one there at all.

Getting back in the car and about to give up, Dallas spotted another bank sign further down the road. *Okay, last one, but only since it's right nearby.*

Dallas entered the bank and waited his turn in line. When he approached the teller, he cleared his voice and smoothed his hair with one hand.

"May I help you?" asked the man behind the counter.

"I sure hope so." Dallas's tone covered the grimness underneath. "I'm looking for any bank accounts that belonged to my deceased mother, anything under the name of Sharon Malone." He waited a moment as the man entered information into his computer.

The keyboard clicks paused. "We do have an account under that name."

Dallas perked up.

"It hasn't been active for several years. Can you tell me what her address was to verify if this was the same person?"

"I can tell you where she last lived that I know of." Dallas recited the address of their rental house.

"That's it," replied the man. "Looks like you found her. In order for me to give you any information regarding this account, you will have to prove your relationship. Or perhaps you know the other name on the account?"

Dallas's hopes soared. "Is the other name Dallas Malone?" He held his breath.

"It is," the man said, "as the secondary name on the account. Is that you?"

"It is." Dallas sagged with relief, pulling his license out and showing the man. "I also have my birth certificate on me if you need it. And my mother's death certificate," he added.

"Yes, those documents would be very helpful," the man responded. "If she were still living, I wouldn't be able to help you, actually, so a death certificate will be required to access the account. She is the primary account holder. Your name being on it helps you out, though. You'd need to deal with a lawyer otherwise, and sometimes that isn't worth the trouble. I'll print off the last few transactions and the balance after checking over these documents with my manager to make sure everything's in order here. Please take a seat while you wait." The man turned to find the manager.

Dallas, too restless to sit, paced the lobby. He fiddled with his ring and realized he'd been doing that more and more lately. *Stress.* Then he saw the manager and teller returning to the counter together.

"Mr. Malone, condolences on the passing of your mother," the manager began. "It appears that you have the documentation needed in order to view the account and take any actions you desire regarding the money."

"Thank you." Dallas gripped the edge of the counter in anticipation.

The teller made a few clicks with the mouse and then retrieved paper from the nearby printer and handed it to Dallas. He scanned to the bottom line to find the balance.

Twenty-five bucks! Dallas's face fell. *That's nothing compared to the rent payments I just made for her!* He swallowed and excused himself, sinking into a nearby armchair with the paper gripped in tight fingers.

The final transaction, dated January 26, 1997, leaped at Dallas in bold type — the last day he'd seen her. She had withdrawn just over $3,000 that day. He felt dizzy. That might've been some of his own money, the money he'd earned as a teenager. Or maybe she'd already blown through that. But money was money, and Dallas's last hope of regaining his rightful earnings had been dashed. He inhaled, but it was like the wind had been knocked out of him. He slowly moved back to the counter.

"I'll just withdraw the total in cash and close the account. Thanks." If Dallas's voice betrayed his dismay, the teller didn't let on. After a few moments, Dallas's hand moved pen across paper in the scrawl of his signature, and he grasped an envelope containing the bills that had just been counted out in front of him, the pithy compensation for a lifetime of his mother's transgressions. He tucked the envelope into his wallet.

More meaningless condolences echoing in his ears, Dallas turned on his heel and left. He pulled out of the lot, numb, and drove west, heading towards nowhere. Dallas had completely lost his appetite. He lowered his eyebrows, a deep, hollow bitterness consuming him. The music shrilled loudly through his car speakers, and he turned it up and rammed the accelerator under his foot, a tightness squeezing his chest. Dallas was part of the machine that propelled him at high speed out of town. The music screamed out a hostile accusation, well-aimed at his mother. "That's just what she was, a QUITTER!" Dallas's pitch and anger met the singer's, exceeded it. He repeated the charge with profanities attached, the worst things he could possibly say spilling out of his mouth as he pounded the steering wheel with a fist. Uncontrollable white-hot anger erupted from him as he smashed the eject button with his hand and flung the cassette tape over his shoulder to the back seat. Dallas strangled the steering wheel in his grip and raced down the empty highway, then suddenly jerked the car off the pavement into a field. He plowed through shrubbery and stomped the brakes, threw it in park, and flung open the door, stumbling in blind rage out of the car.

The seething monster of unbridled fury and anguish had Dallas in its throes. He stormed away from the car, kicking and tearing at the sagebrush in his path, until he collapsed to his knees, letting loose a guttural wail. Everything was red. The torrent exploding from the now-man at this final blow in his treatment from the woman who had birthed him was unequaled since his last prison fight. For three years now, he'd nearly choked on the reactions he'd been swallowing whenever he'd been insulted, taunted, or placed in situations in which he felt he had no say. "I've fought to be nice, I've turned the other cheek, and now… THIS!" Dallas yelled into the emptiness. "My own mother, my flesh and blood, the only relative I've ever known—the landlord was right! She *abandoned* me! My mother left me, and kept my money, and never tried to find me when I was in prison, and now she's gone and *died!*" Something he'd always brushed off, regarded as unimportant, was suddenly all too much for Dallas, opening a gaping hole in him. His mother hadn't loved him.

He tore at the plants around him, the smell of the sagebrush flooding him with recollections of Channing's love of the scent, making him angrier. Dallas flung rocks, yelled, and cussed through his choking tears. He stood up and kicked at clumps of dirt and hurled sticks, everything around him a target for his destruction. He threw a rock that hit his car, followed by ripped-off boots flung at the Isuzu, the violent thud they created against the metal echoing across the barren landscape. Dallas stormed towards the car to continue his attack against the possession that had once been his mother's. He brought a fist down on the hood, instantly regretted it in a howl of pain, and slumped down on his knees, sobbing and leaning against the side of the car, breath heaving in his chest.

After a few minutes, Dallas pushed himself upright and glanced around for his boots. One lay a few feet from him. He opened the passenger-side door, crawled over to the boot, and flung it into the car. The other was on the ground behind the car, where it had bounced off the trunk. Dallas stood up and dragged his feet to it, tossed it into the open door as well, then climbed across the passenger seat and put his head down on the steering wheel, his tantrum giving way to a broken misery.

Dallas's shoulders shook with silent sobs as he slumped against the wheel. *It hurts so much!* He wrapped his arms around the steering wheel, head throbbing hot, and released all the pent-up agony over a whole lifetime of feeling motherless.

Finally, Dallas was drained of every tear and angry impulse. Emptied out, he breathed steadily, eyes focused on the gauges in front of him. "God, please heal this part of my heart that I never realized was so broken," he whispered. Silence and stillness ushered in a peacefulness as his heart rate steadied. Dallas made himself sit up. He pulled his wallet from his back pocket and slipped the note out, holding it between trembling fingers. He knew it by heart from that first reading so long ago, and it had remained a time capsule in his wallet until now. Dallas unfolded the paper.

He stared at the hastily scribbled words in front of him:

Dallas –
Had to leave town suddenly. Big money problems and rent is past due. I'm not coming back this time. You're old enough to take care of yourself now, and capable, too. Find a job and make a life for yourself. I'm sorry for everything.

No signature. No emotion even coming close to touching on love or tenderness. And yet, an apology. He had to accept it. Dallas blew out a slow breath. *I've got to forgive my mother, especially since she attempted to ask for it in this pathetic way.* He stepped out of his car and rummaged in the trunk for his metal camping pot. He walked several paces away from the car, placed the pot on the ground, and pulled his lighter from his pocket. He dangled the paper above it in his left hand and flicked the lighter with his right. The corner of the note caught, then the flame grew as he dropped it into the pot. Dallas stood and watched his mother's words go to ashes, murmuring the words of the Memorare under his breath.

"Eternal rest grant unto her, O Lord," he ended once the flame died out. "I forgive you, Mom." Dallas meant it. He might never know all the whys about her… and that would have to be okay. He picked up the pot and flung the ashes of the letter to the wind, watching them drift away and scatter across the sagebrush, a weight suddenly lifting off him.

"Thank you, Jesus," he murmured, watching the last few ashes disperse. He pulled Channing's prayer card out and stared at the comforting image it held. *"I even have a real mother now…"* With a sigh, Dallas walked back to the trunk and set the pot inside, then climbed into the back seat and retrieved the cassette tape that had taken some of his misdirected aggression. He slipped it back into its case and said, "Well, something finally got me to take that thing out after over four years of it being in the tape player." He was half relieved, half saddened at the break in Channing's last interaction with the cassette deck, and so he focused on the relief and told himself that now he could listen to another old favorite. He pulled Channing's Deconstruction tape from the shoe box under the seat and smiled at the irony of how it was Channing's favorite album and not his that had a picture of a car engine on the front of it.

Before leaving, Dallas pulled out his prayer book for Vespers. The routine grounded and soothed him, and he ingested the words of the prayers and psalms slowly and allowed them to fill his heart and soul. *This is all I need. I am not my own. I belong to God, and that's all that matters.* A peace washed over him, a miraculous transformation, and Dallas marveled at it in awed silence for several minutes after closing his book.

The Isuzu propelled Dallas along its once-home main road, back to the woods for a final night. He scanned the main strip for a cheap hotel for tomorrow, then pulled over to a gas station, fishing in the cupholder for loose change. He grabbed a quarter, started to get out, then remembered that pay phones had increased to 35 cents while he was serving his prison term. *Still can't get used to that...* He reached into his pocket for more coins and approached the booth. As soon as he picked up the receiver, he realized he was making a long-distance call and would need even more money. Maybe Father Benedict was right about getting a cell phone. Dallas calculated the cost and pumped coins into the slot, then dialed the number.

Father Benedict picked up his cell phone after a couple of rings. "Dallas, glad to hear from you. I'm about halfway there. I've stopped at a hotel for the night."

"I'm going to get a room here tomorrow," Dallas replied. "You want me to get one for you too, or do you want to share a room with two beds?"

"We can share one," he answered. "Save on money that way."

They hung up after agreeing to meet at the hotel around five the next afternoon. Dallas dreaded the coming morning when he had to go to the funeral home to make sure everything had been taken care of as planned. Payment for their services would be due, too.

Once back at his tent, Dallas stared at his little camp. *I don't know if I'll ever come back here again, even just to visit for the day.* It was a bittersweet sentiment. He tried to push his concerns aside—namely, the amount of money it was going to cost for his mother's burial expenses. Cremation had been the more affordable choice, after checking with the cemetery to be sure that was okay. The plot was for a casket, but they would allow cremains to be buried there instead. His thoughts went to Channing's grave, and Dallas sighed—it would be quite a while before he could buy him a decent marker. He'd needed that trip hiking the AT to figure out his life, but not working for two months in the meantime had cost him, literally. Hopefully, that was the last time he'd need to follow one of his wild impulses to figure things out while neglecting what would be the more logical decision. Remembering Channing's praise of how practical he was, he gave a half-snicker. "You should see me now, Chan," he said to the wind. He prayed he still had enough for his mother's burial expenses.

Dallas ate dinner and took another walk through the peaceful wooded area. The stream was babbling, the evening birds were singing, and the sun was beginning to set. Dallas breathed in the chilling night air with gratitude. He headed back to the tent and sat up awhile by the fire ring, picturing the huge fire he'd built in this same spot to ward off the mountain lion, and reading his evening prayers.

Afterward, he lay back and gazed at the stars overhead. "Channing," Dallas murmured, "life isn't easy — at all. I thought we knew that back then, but it seems even harder now. It *is* harder, especially without you. But, somehow, by the grace of God, I'm getting through. I'm resigned to life being challenging, because God must know I need it. The knowledge that we aren't made for this world but for heaven — that helps me. I don't think I'd ever make it there if all these things hadn't happened to me. I still miss you, Channing, and I always will. And all my struggles, I'm offering them up for your soul, and now for my mom's, too. If you can hear me in heaven, 'cause that's where I hope you are now, please pray for me. I have to do a difficult thing in two days, although I think maybe I've already faced the worst of it. And then, my biggest concern right now is whether I'll be allowed into the seminary. I still don't know if the archbishop will really let somebody with a felony on his record become a priest. But Father Benedict has high hopes, so I'm trying to do the same. Thanks for leading me to him, Channing. He's been a mentor to me, a father figure, the one who got me through your loss and my incarceration. I don't know what I'd do without him."

Dallas crawled into the tent, heavy with acceptance. He closed his eyes as the quiet noises of night in the woods surrounded him outside the tent, and Dallas relished the memories they brought. As he drifted off, in his mind he and Channing could have been there camping again back in the mid-90s, lives so different despite the problems they'd faced, a near-innocence about them compared to the present moment.

The next day, Dallas packed up his tent and drove into town to the funeral home. The cremation was complete, and there would be somebody at the cemetery to take care of the burial tomorrow following the service that Father Benedict would conduct. When asked whether he wanted to go ahead and take his mother's remains, Dallas declined with a shudder. It would be weird to keep them with him even over one night. The exact opposite emotional reaction had consumed him regarding Channing's death. *Staying so long at his grave, the torture of not being there through his entire death and burial process...* Dallas shook his head and looked at the man addressing him from across the desk.

"Here's the paperwork regarding the services provided," the funeral director said, passing a sheet of paper to Dallas. "You can either pay now or in the morning when you come for the cremains."

After whispering a prayer, Dallas found the bottom line and its higher than expected number. With a resigned sigh, he said he'd pay it in the morning and stood to leave. It was likely the last sacrifice he could make for his mother, besides praying for her. Dallas would worry later about how he was going to eat and pay for rent somewhere. *It's no use letting it get me angry. She's dead. I released my rage. It's over and done with, and there's nothing that can be changed about it. I'll just offer it up for her soul. Thy will be done, Lord.*

Dallas drove to the old neighborhood. He stopped the car on the edge of the road, idling for a moment, and then killed the engine. Relenting to the pull of an invisible magnet, he stepped out, locking and closing the door. Hands deep in his pockets, he headed for the bridge that crossed the river. Dallas paused on the bridge and studied the tangle of shrubs, trees, and vines along the bank. The worn path where Channing used to slide down the embankment to be alone was overgrown now. It appeared that nobody had gone down there in years.

Passing the house where he and his mother had lived for a few years when he was in middle school, Dallas scrutinized it with lowered eyebrows. The house looked worse than he'd remembered: smaller, cracked window, broken porch steps, garbage in the yard. Funny how he hadn't noticed all that back then. Those had been the years of playing football in the street with the other poor neighborhood kids.

He walked on, turning at the next road. *Channing's street.* This was where they had first met, while Channing was sitting in the front yard of the house where the football had bounced out-of-bounds. Kicking an empty plastic bottle along the curb, Dallas tried to reimagine the scene from that day as the house came into view.

Slowing his pace, he glanced up at the prison that had kept Channing's abuse hidden in its depths. *That same nasty recliner is* still *sitting there on the porch, all these years later – how gross.* Dallas stopped and stared warily at the house. He closed his eyes and took a deep breath. *Channing, tossing the ball back to me clumsily, and those pinpricks I felt all over when the other kids laughed at him – it had to be the Holy Spirit telling me there was something special about him, making me scoff at them to leave him alone, because I could be a real jerk back then…* He opened his eyes again, hardened face examining the house in its current state.

He hadn't heard the car coming down the road as he stood in a trance, face condemning this place that had been Channing's hell on earth. *That was his bedroom window, the one beside the front door. Come out, Channing; I'm waiting for you like always...* Dallas's eyes begged the front door to open, for the thin figure to emerge into the daylight and cross the yard, escaping...

The approaching car turned into the short gravel driveway, and before Dallas could move, the driver had stepped out, studying him with suspicion.

Channing's mother! Dallas's skin crawled, his stomach lurching with stunned shock. He'd never expected her to still live here. Now they stood fifteen feet apart in a twisted joke of a staring contest.

Channing's mother dropped her cigarette onto the gravel and took a step towards Dallas. "You!"

Dallas hadn't prepared himself for this. *Crap, she recognizes me!* She was thinner than when he'd last seen her, unhealthily so. She wore a shabby dress and no makeup, and Dallas detected an off look in her eyes—drugs? Or just her mental illness?

"You!" she said again. "Dallas! Channing's friend—my Channing, who's dead!" She stumbled towards where Dallas was frozen on the curb. He took a deep breath and made himself find his tongue.

"That's right, it's Dallas. I was just back in town visiting and wanted to walk through the old neighborhood."

The woman's stormy anger zeroed in on Dallas, replacing her surprised expression from a few seconds earlier. "What are you doing looking at my house?" she sputtered. She had stopped about four feet from Dallas, where he could examine her face closer. She looked terrible.

"I've just been remembering the past." Dallas glanced side to side for an escape. "I... I really miss Channing. All the time."

Her eyes narrowed, and he squirmed as she analyzed the remains of the bruising around his eye. "You killed him—*you*! He went off with you, never to be seen again, and he *died*!" She pointed a bony finger at him, and Dallas shrank back. "How dare *you* miss him! Channing was *my* son, and he went with you and got killed!" She shed angry tears at Dallas.

The instant defensive reaction ignited inside him. She hadn't even cared that Channing had left! How dare *she* even act like this after she'd never wanted him in the first place? After she'd refused to even accept his body to be returned here for burial? Dallas swallowed hard, trying to stifle his anger. *Acknowledge your own role in this. Humble yourself... even to her.* He took a breath, glancing at her face and then down, and forced the words. "You're right. And I'm so, so sorry. He meant everything to me. I loved Channing like a brother."

Her eyes widened as if she hadn't expected this.

Dallas continued in a choked voice, "I made some really stupid decisions, and Channing being with me... well, he got caught up in it, and you're right — it cost him his life. *I* cost him his life. I regret it with every fiber of my being. Like I said, I loved Channing. He wanted to come with me, and... well, I know I let him down, and I've hoped and prayed for years that if he could, he would forgive me for my reckless choices." Dallas, tears welling up behind his eyes, stared at his boots on the cracked asphalt.

It was Channing's mother's turn to be speechless now. She gawked at Dallas with mouth agape, almost as if she couldn't believe it was really him standing there and apologizing.

Finally, she spoke again, voice softening. "You were his best friend; I remember that. What happened to your eye — get in a fight?"

Dallas nodded. "Yeah, but it's nothing."

She stared at him, lips pursed, then her posture relaxed. "Um, won't you come in?" she lamely offered, motioning towards the house. "It's been so long..."

Dallas cringed but accepted the invitation. He followed her across the weedy yard to the door. It was a wreck inside. She brushed a pile of clothing off the couch and offered Dallas a seat. He sank down onto the old couch with the stuffing coming out, aware of the strong odor of what must be cat or dog urine. Channing's mother sat on the other end of the couch, facing him. Her demeanor had flipped completely, and Dallas wasn't sure if it was because of his meek and apologetic response or because she was crazy.

"I shouldn't have yelled at you outside." Channing's mother fiddled with the corner of a blanket draped over the couch, eyes cast down. "I didn't mean you actually killed him. The police, they called and told me. He ran away from the police with you, and... and it was an accident. How long ago was that now, four or five years?" She looked up.

"Five years," Dallas answered numbly. "Five years and about two months."

"I got the phone call, and they told me he was dead. I didn't believe it and hung up on them." She paused as if trying to remember, and Dallas waited for her to go on.

"But when they called me back, I realized it must be true. They said I could have his body sent home, but I couldn't afford that. I told them I couldn't. I almost asked my boyfriend — I think that was Joe at the time — but I knew he wouldn't help pay. So I told them to bury him themselves. They mailed a death certificate to me..." She trailed off and stared out the window.

Dallas swallowed. "I visited his grave finally, last year. They buried him in the back of a cemetery right under some big trees. I... I think he would have liked the spot."

Channing's mother snapped her head up and looked Dallas squarely in the eye. "*Liked* it?" she echoed. "He's dead—he can't *like* anything!" She scowled at the floor, then lowered her eyebrows at Dallas. "Just last year? They buried him right away, I hope. Why didn't you go sooner?"

Dallas gazed straight back into her eyes. *They're just like Channing's eyes...* He jerked his gaze to his hands to cloak his emotion. "I was in jail," he answered flatly.

Channing's mother shot him a scornful glare. "That's right, the police must've caught *you* alive. But my boy died while you got lucky! I shouldn't have let him run off with you," she mumbled. "He—"

Just then, a man's accusing voice interrupted them. "Joan? Who's in there with you?" Footsteps thudded from down the hallway. Dallas's defenses went on high alert, every muscle tensed as he jumped to his feet.

The man stepped into the room, and Channing's mother threw herself in his path. "Oh, Brett, did we wake you up? I'm sorry!" Her voice was so different that Dallas could hardly believe it came from the same woman. "Brett, this was Channing's dearest friend in the world, Dallas."

Dallas nodded towards the man. "Nice to meet you, Brett."

Brett grunted, then turned to Channing's mother. "You know I'm sick to death of hearing about your dead kid," he said. Dallas could smell the alcohol on his breath from across the room. "But if you two want to have a little girly cry fest over him, then go right ahead. I'm goin' out."

"Oh, Brett, when do you think you'll be back?" Channing's mom asked in a desperate voice. "I was just going to get lunch—don't you want to eat? Dallas, would you like to stay for lunch? We're just having cereal, nothing fancy, I'm afraid... Brett, oh, wait a minute!" She skittered after him into the next room. Dallas could hear the exchange of frustrated words and wondered if this was his cue to slip away. Before he'd decided what to do, the door to the carport slammed, and then Channing's mother was back in the room as a car engine started up outside and then faded into the distance.

"I'm sorry about him; he's just like that," she excused her current boyfriend with a wave of the hand. Her eyes brightened. "But you can stay for lunch, Dallas! I don't think Brett would be mad if you did. And you being here reminds me of Channing..."

Dallas's discomfort muddled with a deep pity for the woman. She had ignored, abused, and neglected Channing, and had allowed his father and all her boyfriends to do the same, and here she was, acting as if she missed him. And maybe she did, in a way—maybe she'd learned to regret the past the way he had. Or maybe not, but that wasn't the point. *As hard as it is, I've got to show her mercy.* Dallas followed her into the kitchen, trailing after the woman for whom he'd held an angry contempt in his teenage years because he'd seen what the emotional and physical abuse had done to his best friend. He prayed for charity.

Channing's mom cleared space at the counter and took two bowls down from a cabinet. The room was a worse mess than the living room. Dallas wrinkled his nose at fly-swarmed garbage overflowing from the trash can and what appeared to be a week's worth of dirty dishes piled in the sink. Newspapers and junk mail were heaped on the kitchen table, and she bustled around to make space for them to sit. Dallas felt a funny quiver as he watched her efforts on his behalf. He prayed she would stay on this more friendly note rather than reverting to hostility. *It's all part of her mental illness. Just ride it out if she changes her mood again.*

She set a box of cereal on the table and retrieved the milk from the fridge. Sitting down, she said to Dallas, "You really were my Channing's favorite person ever. I know he wanted to go with you. And I know I was a bad mother to him a lot of the time. His father, though, he just… well, he messed me up bad. *He's* the one I truly blame for Channing's death, not you, because if he hadn't left us when Channing was little, then our lives would have been different, *very* different. Oh!" she said, her eyes lighting up in the same way her son's used to when he was struck with a deep revelation. "That's Channing's shirt!"

Dallas glanced down, amazed that she remembered the shirt and feeling foolish for having worn it here, as if he were some kind of thief. "Um, yeah… it is. I hope it's… well, wearing some of his old things makes me feel closer to him."

"Oh, of course, he'd want you to have *all* his things!" Channing's mother said with more enthusiasm than was appropriate, Dallas thought. "I have some of his old clothes still—maybe you'd want them?" She didn't wait for an answer and was out of the room. Dallas waited, tense on the edge of his chair. A moment later, she returned, carrying a stack of clothing. They were Channing's clothes from when he was probably about four. Dallas's fingers curled under the edges of the seat of his chair. *The crazy must be kicking in…*

"Oh, of course, these are too small for you!" she said with a nervous laugh. "But maybe you'll have a son one day. Or do you have children already?"

Dallas shook his head.

"I want you to take them, then, and save them for your children!" she gushed, thrusting the clothes into Dallas's hands.

"Oh, I couldn't…" Dallas held the stack of tiny outfits at arm's length. "I mean, these are your own memories of him. You should keep them, really. I probably won't ever have kids, anyway."

"Well, you're probably right." Channing's mother took the clothes back. "I would regret giving them away. This was my very favorite pair of his little overalls." She held the striped overalls up, admiring them with a wild-eyed grin on her face. She folded them neatly and set them aside. "Well, let's eat!" she said with relish.

Dallas shifted in his seat and silently crossed himself, then poured the offered cereal into his bowl.

Channing's mother was watching him closely. "You're Catholic? I didn't know that."

"Uh, yeah." Dallas wondered how much he should tell her. Would it offend or please her to hear that his conversion was Channing's doing? He cleared his throat. "I became Catholic when I was in prison. Channing had actually read a lot of books by Catholics. He used to tell me about them, and that got me interested."

Channing's mother unscrewed the milk cap. "That's right, he was *always* reading, wasn't he? I'd forgotten until you mentioned it." Suddenly, her demeanor changed again. She'd caught a whiff of the milk. She poured a small amount into her bowl, tasted it gingerly with her spoon, and grimaced in disgust. Then she lost it. She snatched the jug of milk off the table violently, clattering Dallas's bowl of cereal to the floor. He flinched back at her whirlwind.

"Dammit, Channing, you never get milk when we need it!" she screamed. Storming into the kitchen, she raged on. "It always goes bad! You were supposed to go to the store and get more!" She slammed the jug into the sink, where it crashed down on the dirty dishes and sent some of them flying in a spray of sour milk.

Dallas bounded up. Should he help her or flee?

"You went and *died*, and now you never help me anymore!" In hysterics, Joan slid down against a kitchen cabinet and hunched on the floor, sobbing.

Dallas sucked in a deep breath. Against his will, he moved around the counter and squatted down in front of the miserable woman. He inched a hand to touch her shoulder. She met his look, and he thought he could see her heart melt.

"Oh, Channing, I'm so, so sorry!" she sobbed. "I'm *so* sorry!" She reached for Dallas, and he allowed Channing's mother to fall apart in his arms, crying and shaking. Dallas patted her back awkwardly.

"It's okay, it'll all be okay," he murmured the reassurances. "You can cry; that's all right." The last of Dallas's resentment at this pitiful, broken woman drained from him, washed out with her streaming tears.

She cried into his shoulder, soaking Channing's shirt and clinging to Dallas for dear life, crying, "Oh, Channing! Oh, Channing!" over and over.

Does she actually think I'm *Channing right now? I definitely shouldn't have worn one of his old shirts,* Dallas scolded himself.

Still sobbing, she pushed him back and scrutinized Dallas's face. "Oh, Channing, that eye!" she blubbered. "It looks dreadful! I didn't mean to hurt you, I promise!"

Dallas pulled her to his shoulder again. "You didn't do that," he murmured. "I was in a fight, remember? But I'm okay." He felt her head nodding against him as if reassured. Playing along with her crazy seemed wrong, but what else could he do?

After her cries had quieted, Dallas helped Channing's mother off the floor and guided her by the hand, avoiding stepping in the spilled milk. He led her to the couch and eased her down, observing her with furrowed brow. She was shaking like a leaf. "Just lay back and rest, and I'll bring you some water." She nodded, eyes closed.

Dallas found a cup in a kitchen cabinet and filled it from the sink. He checked the freezer for ice, but finding none, carried the cup of water back to the other room. He helped the feeble woman take a few sips and then set the cup down for her on a flimsy TV tray. "Can I get you anything else?"

"Yes, my medicine. It's on the bathroom counter. Oh, Channing, I need my medicine... He used to go get my medicine..." She trailed off, closing her eyes again.

Dallas retrieved the pill bottle. The prescription had already expired, but Dallas recognized the name of the anti-anxiety drug and figured they couldn't hurt. He opened the bottle and handed one to her. She swallowed it with water and dropped back.

"Just rest here, okay?" he said. "I'm going to clean up the milk." She gave a faint smile and nod in response.

Dallas paused in the kitchen doorway, surveying the wreckage with hands deep in his pockets. He cleaned up the overflowing garbage first and carried it all outside in bags. Next, he found some cleaner and sprayed down the milk on the floor and counter, then wiped it up with paper towels. He poured the rest of the milk down the drain and put the empty jug into the trash. Then he started on the dishes in the sink. There was no dishwasher, so Dallas washed and dried them by hand, doing his best at guessing where to put them away. He cleaned out the sink with the cleaner he found in the cabinet under it, scrubbing away months of grime along with the spoiled milk while trying to hold his breath. *The level of filth in this house is probably unhealthy.* The insides of the cabinets were greasy, and Dallas tried to wipe them out but ran out of paper towels. He glanced at his wristwatch. He should get going soon, to get the hotel room so Father Benedict could find him. Dallas swept up the cereal scattered across the floor. While he was at it, he swept the whole room, emptying the dustpan twice before he had finished. Giving the whole kitchen a final inspection, his eyes came to rest on a stack of papers on the counter. Dallas hesitated, then pulled one of the extra Memorare cards out of his wallet and set it on top of the pile. He didn't know what Channing's mother — or Brett — would think when they noticed it there. *But Channing would've liked me to leave one.*

Dallas peeked into the next room. Channing's mother was sitting up, color back in her face. The cup of water sat empty. "Are you feeling a little better?" he asked. The concern in his words surprised him. He didn't need to fake it.

"Yes," she replied. "I'm sorry, Dallas, we were going to have lunch." She moved as if to get up.

"No, don't trouble yourself, please." Dallas stepped closer.

"But I want to feed you something, and I'm hungry myself," she said. "Is just dry cereal okay? The milk's gone bad, you see."

Did she not fully remember what happened in the kitchen a half hour ago? Dallas scratched his head.

They walked into the kitchen again. Dallas sat down and poured her some cereal first, then filled his own bowl. *Apple Jacks.* They sat and ate the dry, cardboard-like cereal. Channing's mom beamed at Dallas as if he were a child to whom she'd given a special treat, so he shoveled in the spoonfuls and tried to look like this whole thing was completely normal.

"It's your favorite, remember?" Her eyes shone with enthusiasm.

Dallas shifted uneasily. His playing it cool was diffusing the situation somehow. *But she thinks she's talking to Channing again!* He tasted another bite of the stale Apple Jacks. It had indeed been one of Channing's favorites. Dallas nodded as she stared at him expectantly. Channing's mother hadn't been a total stranger to her son. She had noticed. Maybe she'd wanted to care, but she just wasn't capable… Dallas choked down the last bite. He hadn't been capable, either. They'd both failed Channing.

Uneasiness gnawed inside him, and Dallas had to get away. How would Brett react if he was still here when he returned? Praying for no more mood swings, Dallas stood and pushed in his chair. "Thanks so much for lunch. It was perfect. I need to be somewhere soon, so I better get going. I'm glad to have seen you again."

Her face betrayed her dismay at Dallas's attempted exit, but before she could erupt, he blurted, "Channing forgives you. He told me so before he died, and... he loves you."

Joan's eyes fell and she murmured, "Well, then..."

Dallas waited to see if there was anything more, but when she remained silent, he edged towards the door.

"Don't you want to see his room before you go?" Channing's mother scurried after him and motioned into the hallway.

Dallas stiffened. No, he didn't want to see Channing's room. He knew the hours upon hours of misery that Channing had spent in that room as a child. He had to leave now. He'd only become enraged if more reminders of Channing's abuse were forced on him.

"I'm sorry, there's somebody I need to meet soon, and I'm only in town a short time," Dallas explained. "I do appreciate the cereal—it was kind of you to invite me to stay for lunch with you." He was in the front doorway now, every nerve ending tingling with his flight instinct.

Channing's mother motioned for him to wait a moment, heading towards Channing's room and calling, "That reminds me, let me give you this." She reemerged, holding a sketchbook. Dallas recalled its cover as if from the description of another person's dream. The quote printed in Channing's script across the book jolted back to Dallas—it was one Channing had often recited aloud: *"All we have to decide is what to do with the time that is given us."* Dallas was sick to his stomach at how little time Channing had been given, how his best friend never could have known how short his life on earth would be. *But he* did *figure out what to do with the time he was given*, Dallas reminded himself. Channing had found God before the end of his life.

"I bet he'd want you to have this," Channing's mom said, holding the sketchbook out to Dallas.

He accepted it, a little suspicious, but with trembling hands. It probably contained things that would hit his memories in painful and profound ways once he had gained the courage to flip through its pages.

"There's a picture in there he drew of you," Channing's mother added. "Looks exactly like you. So you should have it."

"Thank you." Dallas meant it. He vaguely remembered that drawing now. It seemed like decades had passed since Channing had drawn it while the two of them had been in the car, on a road trip to some place or another. He tucked the sketchbook under an arm and reached for the doorknob.

"Oh, Dallas, you're like another son to me," Joan said in a cracking voice. "Here, let me hug you goodbye. You'll come back to visit me again?"

"Maybe I can," Dallas said through his teeth, obligingly returning her hug, "the next time I'm in town." There wouldn't be a next time if he could help it. His whole body itched as he stepped through the door.

Channing's mother stood on the stoop, her gaze like deep emptiness as he backed across the lawn.

Dallas lifted a hand. "Goodbye, and thanks again."

She didn't say anything more, her eyes haunting Dallas as he walked away.

Dallas quickened his pace as his feet hit asphalt, putting distance between himself and Channing's mother. Like another son to her? She'd barely spoken to him in all the times he'd come here looking for Channing. *But she remembered my name… She remembered Channing's shirt…* There was something inside, buried under years of mental illness and abuse from her former husband and boyfriends, and Dallas doubted it could ever be fully uncovered. He felt like dirt at the relief of his escape. *You've done the best you could for her. But it's like with Samantha.* He cringed. *Don't involve yourself further. I'm gonna have to get used to giving people the help I can but then letting go and walking away.* What Channing's mom needed was something only a professional would have any hope of providing.

Dallas was jogging now, throwing nervous glances over his shoulder, until finally, he reached his car. He slid into the Isuzu and checked his mirrors in case his eyes had played tricks on him. Dallas locked the door, started the engine, and drove away, heading for the hotel. He was still shaking as he pulled into a parking space.

Dallas entered the empty hotel lobby and waited for somebody to come help him. A radio behind the counter played at a low volume. Dallas's heart still raced from the disturbing encounter in Channing's old house. *He wasn't there for me to rescue this time.* A shiver coursed through his body. All those times he had gone there to pick up his friend assailed his mind, when he'd rescued him from that awful place so they could go anywhere else… Dallas wished Father Benedict would arrive soon, but the clock on the wall said it was barely 3:00. He had a couple more hours with himself as his only company.

Where was the hotel clerk? Dallas tapped his fingers on the counter to the music's beat. He just wanted to lie down. The song coming from the radio snaked its way into Dallas's ears, the only sound to break the room's silence. As he recognized the voice, his eyebrows lifted. It was the Toadies, he was sure of it. Why did that band have to haunt him like this? A song he didn't recognize—off the new album, probably. Samantha's recent comments came back to him about the tape playing in his car. As the lyrics crooned through the speakers, Dallas felt the old familiar sensation of being sucked inside a dark tunnel, alone with hauntingly prophetic words in his ears.

He spun and banged the door open, nostrils flared as he inhaled the outside air. He wasn't going to sit in there and let the music torment him—not about Samantha, not about Channing. His hollow insides churned with the ache. Would this ever stop, the reminders of missing him so much? Channing, his best friend, whose death was like having a part of his own body ripped from him, a wound to be reopened, time and again... As much as Dallas loved Father Benedict and cherished the elderly priest's friendship, it wasn't the same as having a best friend close in age, raised under similar circumstances, to whom you could dump your darkest secrets and relate to regarding your deepest and most private problems. If things were different, he'd be telling his friend of his woes with Samantha, of his mother's death and how he was dealing with it, and of his deepest fear that he wouldn't really be cut out for the priesthood despite the unrelenting call. What insights might Channing pull from some deep place, likely a poem or song lyric or Bible verse? *Is that why the music gets to me so much now? Channing's not here to notice, so I do instead? Is it like some weird legacy he left to me?*

Tipping his face to the sky, Dallas tilted his head from one side to the other, stretching tense neck muscles. He blinked away the tears that had escaped and berated himself for losing it. *But this trip's been such a rollercoaster already... Maybe I have to cut myself some slack.* He tried to turn off his brain from the rapid barrage of anxious thoughts. *Please, God, please have Channing in heaven with you now...*

After finally checking in, Dallas took a shower, shaved, and then sprawled across the bed and immediately crashed. A knocking on the door an hour later wakened him. Groggy from his unexpected but welcome nap, Dallas greeted Father Benedict with a tired smile and helped him carry in his things. They talked over the next morning's plans for a few minutes, then Dallas asked the priest if he was hungry yet. It was only just after five, but the stale cereal lunch had left him ravenous.

"I brought us a picnic dinner." Father Benedict pointed to the cooler he'd brought. "Our housekeeper at the rectory put it together for me. Shall we take it to a park, if you know of one nearby?"

Dallas did. He and Channing had walked there occasionally after school when they were much younger, soon after becoming friends. Dallas remembered them trying to ride his skateboard down the stair rail and other daredevil-style feats at this park. He pointed out the rail and told Father Benedict the story with a laugh as they walked towards the picnic tables. Channing had ended up with a scraped-up elbow and twisted wrist, and Dallas with a bump on the side of his head. He'd forgotten all about it until now.

Father Benedict pulled out two plates, napkins, forks, even salt and pepper shakers, and set them on a table. There was cold fried chicken, hard-boiled eggs, pickles, cheese, crackers, apples, and a spinach salad. Dallas stared, mouth watering.

After they said the blessing, Dallas spoke. "You'll have to excuse my huge appetite at seeing all this food. Your housekeeper is amazing. See, all I had for lunch was a bowl of dry, stale cereal..." Dallas told him the whole story of his accidental run-in with Channing's mother.

"It was probably a stupid idea to walk through the neighborhood in the first place," Dallas admitted. "I was feeling sentimental, I guess, and figured while I was in town... I mean, I don't plan on ever coming back. I don't have any reason for it after this, and it's full of painful memories. Good ones, too, but it makes me feel kind of stuck in the past, and only in the bad parts of the past, if that makes sense."

"What are the funeral home expenses like?" Father Benedict asked. "Do you need help with it?"

"I can swing it," he replied truthfully, "and it's the last thing I can do for my mother, so I'll just grin and bear it. But it's gonna leave me nearly broke." Dallas told of meeting the landlord and offering to pay his mother's missed rent payments and the crushing disappointment of finding her nearly-empty bank account.

"Paying the rent was a sacrifice." Father Benedict dabbed his mouth with a napkin. "Was the landlord just dumbfounded over it?"

Dallas nodded. "It didn't feel right to not offer to cover it, especially since he let me come into the basement and get the last of Channing's artwork we'd left there. I'm telling you; it was a miracle he'd saved it. I'm so grateful to have those pieces back. A few of his best stained glass artwork... I want to give you one. Channing would've loved for you to have one."

"I'd very much like that," agreed the priest. "It will remind me of meeting the two of you in the basilica when he was admiring the stained glass. I can hang it in my window, and every time I see it, I will think of Channing and offer prayers for him. And his poor mother, too. What a sad, sad story."

"Yeah." Dallas nodded and picked at a chicken bone. "She's so messed up. She was fuming at me one moment, then the next she was gushing like she had always loved Channing and me both, talking about how I'd been his best friend and she thought of me as another son... I used to absolutely *despise* her, Father, like I hated her more than my own parents. But earlier today, she was so pathetic. Just shattered emotionally. For the first time, I could see that she had at least *tried* to care about her son. I'm not excusing any of the crap she put him through, because it had an awful impact on him. I saw it. And Channing was so good, so forgiving to her, always excusing her for abusing him because she was abused by his dad and then her boyfriends after that. I knew about all the things that she was doing to him, while he was going through it, and… and I just wanted to *kill* her. Truly, I did. But now…" Dallas sighed. "Now I just feel sorry for her. I don't know if I did the right thing or if there's anything else I should do for her. What if she tries to find me, contacts me somehow, now that she's seen me today? I don't want her to get all needy on me, because I really don't think I can help her." Dallas paused and rubbed the place between his eyes with both forefingers.

Father Benedict gave a little smile. "Well, Dallas, you certainly seem to have gained an ability for attracting desperate women lately, haven't you?"

Dallas was scrutinizing his empty plate, deciding if he should fill it up again or not. "Ha ha," he responded flatly, taking another chicken leg, "and you still don't know what happened the night I got back from my hiking trip." Dallas hadn't left a hint for the priest. His purpose in going to confession at another parish on the way had been twofold: his urgency for the sacrament, and his shame at admitting his weaknesses with Samantha to the priest he held in such high esteem.

"You'll have to fill me in in a minute, then," Father said, "but first, about Channing's mom." He paused and sighed. "You're right that you can't really help her, sadly. I think you did what you could in an unexpected situation. You showed her mercy and forgiveness, which took a great act of your will. She'll hopefully feel that blessing as something positive in her life, but no, you don't want her to become overly dependent on you. I'd honestly be concerned for you, not only due to her instability, but because of that boyfriend of hers."

"I don't get why she keeps dating these complete jerks!" Dallas scowled. "They take advantage of her; they push her around and intimidate her. There's no helping her if she keeps letting those kinds of parasites into her life." He tore a piece of meat from the bone and popped it into his mouth.

"It's a very sad thing," the priest answered. "Some people are so hurting and stuck in a pattern of bad choices and don't think they deserve any better, so there's no reason to hope to get out of the vicious cycle. They feel like they're already so damaged that nothing better will or should ever happen to them."

Dallas grimaced. "Sounds familiar. Like how hard it's been for me to forgive myself after Channing's death. I thought I deserved to just die. I think God allowed me to be able to sort of identify with her today. Maybe that's why I can't hate her anymore, even if I tried. I'll pray for her, too. I don't know what else I can do. Maybe send her a card each year on his birthday? I don't know. I don't want her to know where I live."

"A card might be a nice idea," Father Benedict replied. "Just don't include a return address on the envelope."

"Speaking of where I live," Dallas said, ready to change the subject, "I'm gonna need to make some decisions soon. I'll either have to make another rent payment, or move somewhere else, hopefully in Denver, on the chance I can join the seminarian program soon—"

"Oh, I have some news about that," Father jumped in. "I was waiting for a good moment to tell you. If you would be able, the archbishop can meet with you this Friday. I have hopes he's going to be understanding of your story, Dallas."

A smile broke out across Dallas's face. "Wow, I'm amazed you could get a time set up so quickly! We can get back to Denver from here by then, easy. Thanks so much, Father!"

The priest smiled. "I thought you'd be agreeable, and that's why I rented a car to come here. I can turn it in tomorrow afternoon. You'll drive me back if I give you the guest room at the rectory again, yes?"

"Absolutely, if you don't mind riding in a 19-year-old car with no air conditioning."

"I'll offer it up," Father Benedict quipped.

As they finished their meal, Dallas's mind wandered to what he would say to the archbishop. *How can I communicate this unrelenting pull, this burning vocation, and get him to see that despite all my awful past mistakes—*

Father Benedict interrupted Dallas's thoughts. "So, tell me what happened on the night you got back from your hiking trip."

Dallas brought a hand up to the bruised eye he still hadn't explained to Father. He relayed the details of what had happened with Mike and Samantha in the bar parking lot.

"I couldn't just drive on, after what I saw him doing to her. I was actually thinking, 'Okay, God, real clever, putting me in a situation where I have to get involved with these two again.' But I *punched* him, Father. I haven't punched anyone since before my conversion. What if he files charges?" Dallas sighed. "I just have a way of getting myself into trouble, don't I?"

"If he files charges against you, they'll be dropped," the priest said assuredly. "He was in the middle of assaulting somebody, and you stopped him. Is that how you got the black eye?" Father motioned towards Dallas's face.

Dallas blew out a sigh. "No, that was the next morning. He and some friend of his jumped me outside the grocery store; caught me off guard and did this to me. Said it was payback for getting into his business. He punched me a few times and then drove off."

Father Benedict frowned as he studied Dallas's fading bruise. "You were smart to insist that Samantha get a restraining order, too. That is more evidence against him, that she also sees him as an aggressor. Sometimes when put on the spot in a courtroom, a victim will downplay the abuse she's been subjected to, so her request for a restraining order will be good evidence. But let's just hope it doesn't come to that, shall we?"

"Yeah, no need to worry about things that might not happen." Dallas didn't believe his own words as he wadded his napkin in his fist and dropped it on his empty plate. Mike was still a threat to Samantha — period. "You're right — she did downplay the abuse to me, even though I saw how bad it was with my own eyes. I had to be very firm about her getting the protective order against him." Dallas sighed. "And then... Father Benedict, maybe it was a stupid thing of me to do, but... this is so embarrassing, and I already went to confession for my own failings in this, but..." He fidgeted with his plastic fork, snapping off the tines in a tiny pile.

Father Benedict looked at Dallas with open eyes.

Dallas cleared his throat and continued. "Father... Samantha lied to me, played on my sympathy towards her, and I... I *believed* her, ended up staying at her apartment overnight, to protect her... or so I thought. She told me Mike had a key to her place and that she was scared he might come let himself in. I didn't even guess that it could be a lie! She has nobody else to protect her, and she only told me this when I was dropping her back off, after we'd already gone to the police, and... well, I'm such an idiot! What did I *think* was going to happen?" He lifted his eyes and winced at what the priest might be thinking, and then details spilled from his lips about her advances on him. Dallas blushed in mortification as Samantha's enticement burned through his veins while he described his resistance. "It's hard to get the images out of my mind now. And I felt completely humiliated that she'd taken advantage of me, to get me to stay under the guise of keeping her safe from Mike. I can't let myself get into those kinds of situations, especially if I might be going to the seminary!"

The priest sighed and was silent a moment, eyes closed. "What a lost young woman." He shook his head. "Dallas, I know your heart is in the right place, but your instincts are accurate that Samantha is bad news. You cannot help the involvement you've had with her at this point, and of course, if Mike violates the order and you are called to testify, you will have to do so. But you must not seek out additional interactions with her. That will be easier if you do move to Denver, if you are preparing to enter the seminary, God willing. I know it's such a battle to be a good man in today's world. And sometimes you have to put measures in place to avoid temptation."

He knows. "Father, I..." Dallas couldn't raise his eyes from his lap. "I almost fell into her temptations. I could see myself just giving in, and... and what she wanted was very... um... I'm ashamed to admit that I... *liked* the idea of it." He forced his head up, eyes pained. "Does that mean... I don't have a true vocation?" The last whispered words burned in Dallas's throat.

Father Benedict's gaze communicated understanding. "Dallas, do you feel called to marriage at all?"

Dallas wrinkled his nose. "Not a bit. I think I'd be terrible at it. But that's not what I meant. It's just, the, uh, physical attraction aspect was very tempting..." His cheeks were warm again.

"Of course, it was," Father Benedict put in quickly. "That's quite normal, you know."

Dallas's mind fumbled with what the priest was trying to say. "But... well, yeah, I guess so, but priests aren't *supposed* to be normal, right?" Putting a hand across his face, Dallas backpedaled. "Oh, gosh, I didn't mean it that way. I just meant, priests are supposed to be holier and stronger than that, right?"

Father Benedict chuckled. "You *were* strong, from what you've described. To be tempted is one thing; to give in to those temptations is quite another. That's why I recommend you keep your distance from this woman. Priests are still men, Dallas, and we are physically attracted to women. It's as simple as that. What sets priests apart is our guarding of ourselves, the steadfastness of the decision to remain celibate and not to entertain and act on these temptations when they come to us. I asked if you felt called to marriage in any way because, if you did, it might mean your feelings regarding Samantha were coming from another place, one that would also require self-restraint, but that could end quite differently. If you don't think that is the case, then you may very well have a vocation to the priesthood instead of marriage. You've prayed so much on this, spent a lot of time in the presence of God's silence, and if it is the priesthood and not marriage that you are being tugged towards, then don't doubt yourself just because a pretty girl tries to make you fall. Of course, the idea is a pleasant one to us as carnal man, but it doesn't mean it is a call away from Holy Orders."

Dallas breathed out a sigh. As old as he was, Father still got it. "I understand what you're saying, I think. My feelings towards Samantha come on like a quick zap of lightning, an impulse that fades again afterward, but the call to the priesthood... it's a constant, like a longing ache in my soul. But ever since I came back from hiking on the Appalachian Trail — ever since I discerned that I'm truly called to become a priest — well, everything's blown up since then! It's like I'm under attack with all this crazy stuff hitting all at once."

"Spiritual warfare." Father Benedict's gaze was steady. "The devil doesn't want more priests, Dallas. If your difficulties lead to doubting your vocation, then he'll see that as a victory for evil. It's often precisely when we are doing the right thing that we run up against so many challenges. It's difficult. The path you have discerned isn't an easy one. You are a strong young man, and if you keep calling on God's assistance, you will be stronger. Keep fighting, Dallas."

Dallas stared across the nearby playground, brooding, lacing and unlacing his fingers in front of him. Then he glanced hesitantly at the priest again. "I guess sometimes I have a hard time figuring out what to fight for and how much. I can see that Samantha's on a path to self-destruction, and part of me wants to do whatever I can to stop her. She's made it clear that she's interested in a relationship with me, and, well... what if they won't even let me into the seminary? What if the door to the priesthood gets slammed in my face? My self-doubt, whether I'm really worthy of this calling, gets me wondering if I'm supposed to help Samantha away from these degrading men she gets herself involved with. Like, if I was dating her, could I help her develop better morals, help her learn to treat herself with dignity and demand the same of other people?"

Father Benedict made no reply, only eyed Dallas steadily.

Dallas sighed. "You want me to answer my own questions, right?" Dallas dropped his eyes to his empty plate. "I know it's probable that my weaknesses would eventually lead me into sin right along with her. And she's definitely not ready to discern marriage — she doesn't understand her own dignity and the purpose of sexuality. Sometimes I overthink myself in circles. I know, rationally, that I can't make another person change, and that it's not my job... that it's presumptuous of me to think I can 'save' her like that. You'd think I would've learned my lesson already by trying to be the one to 'save' Channing, huh?" Dallas shook his head. "Somehow, I'm gonna feel guilty if she goes back to that guy, or another like him, and gets hurt again, because maybe I could've prevented it. But God's in control, not me, and I've tried to be an upright example of a man to her. But if I'm not called to marriage, then it's not my place to keep being that for her. I've done what I could for her and barely escaped a fatal misstep. You're right that I need to keep my distance from now on."

"God will reveal his plan for you, but it takes patience." Father Benedict began repacking the picnic basket. "If the door to the priesthood is shut to you, then you will know it isn't your true vocation, and maybe time will give you guidance on the situation with Samantha and how to proceed. But this meeting with Archbishop Adams is on Friday, Dallas. I think you're going to receive an answer very soon. God is working in your life, and in a tangible way right now."

Dallas smiled up at the priest. "Yeah, I know he is. And I'm willing to submit to the hard stuff. But with my criminal record, I guess I'm nervous about anything that might be an impediment to the priesthood for me. I *know* it's what I'm supposed to do now, as much as I've ever known anything... at least, if I'm allowed in."

The priest smiled. "Then, if it is meant to be, it will happen despite any impediments."

Dallas nodded. "Thy will be done. Yeah, thanks, Father." He paused and glanced down at his hands in his lap. "There's just one thing..."

Father Benedict's eyebrows went up. "Oh?"

Dallas blew out a deep breath. "Samantha apologized to me for lying, and I didn't forgive her. I mean, I *do* forgive her, and inside, I already had even at that moment, but I guess I was still so burned up over everything that I couldn't tell her I accepted her apology. But what you say about keeping away from her is smart, so..." Dallas looked up helplessly.

"You want to tell her she is forgiven." The priest shut the basket's lid.

"Exactly." Dallas piled up the used plates and napkins. "And also, I never explained to her about my vocation. I was going to, but when I found out she'd lied to me, I was so hurt that I couldn't. If she knows that, and if I tell her I forgive her... Maybe I can write a note, mail it to her? I need to tell her somehow. I can't just leave it like I did." Dallas toyed with the broken fork pieces.

The priest reached out and patted Dallas's hand. "Of course, you should tell her you forgive her, because you do care about her and want an amiable parting. A note is a good idea. You'll find a way, Dallas."

The next morning, they stood inside the funeral home. Dallas received his mother's ashes in a simple container suitable for burial and wrote a check. He bit his lip as he printed the digits, telling himself to let it go, that it was just money. *Make it a free gift to her.* He closed his eyes and tried to allow the tightness to flow out of his body.

They arrived at the cemetery and found the burial plot alongside his grandmother's headstone. Dallas stood at the foot of her grave, trying to conjure up memories of his four-year-old self in this spot twenty years previous. He could not. It didn't look familiar at all.

Father Benedict was dressed in his clerics and had a prayer book and Bible in hand. Dallas glanced at his watch—ten minutes until eleven. He noticed a work truck parked down the drive. Probably the gravediggers. Dallas instantly felt like there had to be a better word that he wasn't coming up with offhand. There were two green tents set up in other areas of the cemetery, with piles of dirt beside them. Dallas had declined the tent and chairs; they were one more expense he didn't need, and he doubted anyone else would come, anyway.

A hole gaped wide in the plot alongside Dallas's grandmother's grave, a square of ripped sod lying haphazardly to the side by a small hill of freshly-dug earth. He wondered if he should put the cremains in the hole himself at the end. The paper he'd reviewed and signed verified that he'd paid for them to cover it with dirt, agreeing not to do it himself—it was their policy. A weird antsy sensation grew inside him. *I just wanna get this over with.*

At 10:58, Dallas nodded the go-ahead to Father Benedict. The priest began with the sign of the cross, Dallas joining him. He heard the spoken prayers, but he was watching and listening from somewhere far away. A static whoosh ran through his head, and he felt dizzy. *You're at your mother's funeral. This is important.* The facts remained out of his emotions' grasp.

Ten minutes later, and it was over. Dallas stood staring numbly at the box in his hands. He'd been holding it since they got out of the car because it didn't seem right to set it on the ground. But now he found himself squatting, gaze drawn down into the deep hole in the earth. He couldn't cry. The realization bothered him. He couldn't force himself to feel anything. Mechanically, Dallas kissed the top of the box.

"I'm sorry we didn't really know each other, Mom," he murmured. "You tried your best, being on your own and all, but I wish you'd let me into your heart a little. I wish I could've been something more to you, helped you out somehow. Nobody should have to die alone." Dallas still couldn't muster up one tear. "I'm here for you now, and maybe it's too late, but I'll be praying for your soul, Mom. I don't know most of what you went through your whole life, so I shouldn't blame you, really. Maybe you couldn't control everything that happened. I just wish things had been different between us. And… I love you, despite everything." With a sudden impulse, he pulled his wallet from his back pocket, withdrawing one of the Memorare prayer cards. He opened the lid of the box just enough to slide the card in on top of his mother's ashes. Then Dallas lowered his mother's remains into the ground and sat back on his heels, staring blankly at the darkness below. He sprinkled a single handful of dirt into the hole.

Father Benedict had stepped away to give Dallas some space and was ambling along a row of monuments nearby, pausing at each and reading the names. Dallas watched him for a moment, then looked back at the hole. *Nobody came.* Dallas fought the heaviness of his body to stand, then brushed the dirt from his hands onto his pants. His jeans and a button-up flannel were wrong for a funeral. But his mother had bought this shirt—he could see her pulling it from the shopping bag and handing it to his younger self—and that made it perfect. Swallowing the memory along with the lump in his throat, Dallas made the sign of the cross and joined Father Benedict.

"Thank you, Father," Dallas said, thumbs hooked in his pockets. "It means a lot to me that you could help lay my mother to rest."

"Are you okay?" The priest placed a hand on Dallas's shoulder.

"Yeah. I don't feel much of anything." Dallas shrugged. "Is that weird? I already had it out with her the other day—went out into the desert alone and just screamed and raged and threw rocks and junk. Got it all out already, and I can't find much left under that…" An ache welled in his throat. Would he ever know the whole story? "We can go now."

The grave lay far behind them, and both men paused and looked back. A uniformed employee was already there, filling it in with dirt. Dallas did a double take at another figure beyond the grave, back between some nearby trees and clutching a bouquet of flowers. Was that… *Channing's mother?* He squinted and shielded his eyes with a hand. *No, definitely not. I'm just paranoid.* Dallas's muscles slackened. The woman was of a different stature, and her hair was much lighter. Probably just somebody visiting another grave. Dallas turned to follow Father Benedict across the lawn straight towards the car.

"Should I have gotten some flowers?" Dallas wondered aloud as they approached the Isuzu.

"If you want to do that before we leave town, we can stop for some and come back to lay them at her grave," the priest responded.

Dallas thought about it half-heartedly and let the idea drop. He glanced back one more time at the man in work clothes tamping down the dirt, whispered a simple silent prayer for both his grandmother and his mother, and got into the driver's seat. He started the engine, and they drove out through the cemetery gates.

A weight lifted from Dallas as he gained distance from his former hometown and neared Denver in the early morning hours. He and Father Benedict had taken turns driving through the afternoon and night. The upcoming appointment with the archbishop had Dallas on the edge of his seat, butterflies swirling in his stomach. He so very badly wanted to make a good impression.

As Father Benedict washed dinner dishes Thursday evening, Dallas paced in the small kitchen.

"Do you think I should take out my earring?"

The elderly priest turned to scrutinize him up and down. "You should do what you think is best."

Dallas rolled his eyes and made an exaggerated huffing sound. "Okay, I will," he declared, removing the little hoop and pocketing it. "There, I probably look like less of a hoodlum already. I need to start a load of laundry — what should I wear tomorrow?"

"Just something casual but nice," Father Benedict said. "Not jeans."

"These are the only shoes I own." Dallas motioned down to his scuffed combat boots. "Are they too, uh… intimidating?"

The priest laughed out loud. "Dallas, don't worry. While you do want to make a decent impression visually, the archbishop cares far less about your clothes than about what you have to say and how you present yourself. And, most importantly, how much you love God."

Dallas blew out a deep breath and collapsed into the nearest chair. "I probably won't sleep a bit tonight."

"Oh?" asked Father Benedict. "I'll consider it an insult to my hospitality."

Now it was Dallas's turn to chuckle. "Okay, can I use your laundry room now?"

Father Benedict nodded, and Dallas stood to head for the door.

"Just a thought, Dallas," he called after him.

Dallas turned in the doorway to see the priest examining him with a scrunched expression. "What's that?"

"Maybe zip the boots up all the way," the priest advised. "And then make sure your pant legs stay all the way down over them. Just in case, you know. Looks a little more formal." He winked.

"Yes, sir." Dallas shot a mock salute as he went into the hallway. "Thanks for the tip."

The next morning, Dallas was up early. He combed his hair neatly and tried to decide whether to tuck his shirt into his khaki pants or not. He found his belt and tucked in his shirttail. He took Father Benedict's advice regarding his boots even though they felt strangely constrictive when zipped all the way to the top.

Dallas followed the smell of bacon to the kitchen and joined Father Benedict and another priest, Father Paul, for breakfast. Dallas nibbled a piece of toast. A mug of coffee was waiting at his seat, and he added some half and half.

"Don't be nervous." Father Paul reached for another strip of bacon. "People think of a bishop as intimidating, in charge, the boss. But Archbishop Adams is very friendly and down-to-earth. He's strong on the faith, absolutely, and doesn't compromise on issues of morality and doctrine. But he's a real people-person, and he's enthusiastic for new vocations to the priesthood."

"You can tell I'm nervous, huh?" Dallas met the priest's eyes.

Father Paul watched Dallas's moving hand. "Well, you've been stirring that coffee since you sat down. The milk's probably well incorporated by now."

Dallas froze, then withdrew the spoon with a nervous chuckle. "Okay. I'll try to relax a little."

Father Benedict was scheduled to celebrate the 9:00 morning Mass, with confessions available beforehand. Dallas went into the church and waited his turn. The tension in his muscles loosened following confession and the prayers of penance. At the rack of votive candles, he lit two: one for Channing, a flame in this church where they had first met Father Benedict, and the other for his mother. Dallas knelt in a pew near the front, reflecting on the cleansing power of the sacrament. Each day of his life was a continual letting go of his guilt and anger at himself. When he thought about it directly, he found that he'd made an incredible amount of progress.

In the minutes before Mass started, Dallas prayed for God's will to be done in the meeting with the archbishop. A sense of peace blanketed him. *Everything will work out in the end.* As Mass began, the sweet smell of the incense and the sight of the slowly rising smoke high above the gathered faithful invigorated Dallas's senses, and he closed his eyes, picturing the worship of all the saints and angels and the faithful communities over the last 2000 years all united in their praise of God through this ancient rite. The consistency and connection filled up the unidentified yearning within Dallas's heart that had been present since his earliest days.

Following the Mass, Father Benedict emerged from the sacristy and slipped into the pew beside Dallas.

"Feeling ready?"

"I am, actually." Dallas rose from his knees. "I'm just ready to do it, to tell the archbishop all about why I feel so strongly about this and why I know it's God's purpose for my life."

The priest smiled. "Tell him anything and everything that comes to your mind, as long as it is the truth. The good and the bad: it all has worked together to bring you to where you are today. He will likely ask you some specific questions, but mostly he's going to want to hear your story, what's happened in your life, and how you have been led to Christ. You'll do fine, Dallas." He gave him a few pats of encouragement on the back.

A minute later, they were walking down the hall to the archbishop's office. When they reached the slightly ajar door, Father gave a little knock.

"Come in," said a voice from within.

"Your Excellency," Father Benedict began, "this is the young man I've been telling you about, Dallas Malone."

Archbishop Adams rose to welcome them. "Dallas, good to meet you," he said warmly.

"Likewise, Your Excellency." Dallas was secretly grateful that Father Benedict had dropped the appropriate title for him.

"Please, have a seat." The archbishop motioned to a couch along one wall.

"See you in a while, Dallas." Father Benedict flashed a wink as he exited the room.

Dallas sank onto one end of the couch, and Archbishop Adams sat on the opposite end, turning towards Dallas. The man was tall and had short, graying hair. Dallas guessed he was in his late fifties. He held a folder of papers in his hand and laid it on the couch between them.

"I really appreciate you taking the time to meet with me." Dallas met the archbishop's eyes in the kind face and tried to appear cool.

The archbishop responded, "This is one of the joys of my job, to interact with men who are discerning a call to the priesthood. It is especially a joy when we have younger men hearing that call, as we have an aging clergy right now and need new young priests who will bring the sacraments to the people for the next generations. Tell me, Dallas, how old are you?"

"I'll be 24 in August."

"Wonderful. And you have been considering the priesthood for a few years now, I understand?"

"About two years, yes." Dallas nodded. "Since before I became Catholic, actually. I was baptized and confirmed a little over a year ago, and I spent about nine months before that studying and learning more with materials Father Benedict had sent or brought to me."

The archbishop's smiling eyes opened wider. "I didn't realize you were so new to the faith, but I hear from Father Benedict that yours was a powerful conversion. Tell me a bit about yourself—your family, your interests, just so we can get to know each other a little." He leaned nearer.

Dallas cleared his throat. "I have no family—anymore, that is. My mother passed away, um, recently. But we had fallen away from each other, and then I was in prison for three years and… well, I have a lot of regrets there." Dallas bit his lip—this wasn't getting off to a good start.

"My condolences on the loss of your mother," Archbishop Adams said, eyes gentle. "And you have no other living relations?"

"My mom had a half-brother who I never got to know. There's nobody else. I… I never met my father."

The archbishop stretched one arm across the back of the couch and changed the topic. "How about your interests? Hobbies, job?"

"I love camping and hiking," Dallas said, voice raising a notch. He tried to sound positive as he described building fires and tinkering with cars and his former construction job. "And I love to drive and have always liked maps and geography."

"Sounds like a well-rounded set of interests," the archbishop said with a nod. "You've been out of work a couple months now?"

"It was really important to me to focus and try to hear God's will for me, so yeah…" Dallas trailed off. He felt like a slacker as he tried to explain his seemingly wavering months since his release.

"Tell me about your first inklings that you might have a vocation to the priesthood," Archbishop Adams said.

Dallas thought back to his dream. "At first, I thought that it was my best friend who had the calling. Channing was his name, and he'd been reading all kinds of theological stuff since he was younger, around 12 or 13—he was really smart, just brilliant. Anyway, he was only 17 years old and would have joined the Church officially… had he lived." Dallas studied his hands in his lap and fought to keep his voice steady. "He told me, the night before he died, that he was sure he wanted to become Catholic. I thought for the first time that night—what if he's meant to be a priest? I had no real interest in religion at that point. And the next day, when we were in a dangerous situation, he insisted that I baptize him. I'm so glad I did because he died only minutes later." Dallas closed his eyes and took a slow breath. "When I was in prison, I read some of Channing's old books, including a copy of the Catechism—Father Benedict had given it to him. It gave me a lot of peace when I was struggling with specific things in jail. I started thinking maybe Channing was right about Catholicism—he was usually right about most things—and I decided to become Catholic, too. I'd been having this dream of following a priest into a beautiful church, and at first, I thought the priest was Channing. It tore me up inside that maybe he had a vocation and died before being able to follow it. But after several months, I realized the priest in the recurring dream was actually me. That was my very first thought of the priesthood, that maybe I had a calling. I scoffed at it then, that it couldn't be real… but it's only grown stronger."

"And how have you grown more convicted of this over time?" Archbishop Adams had an unwavering gaze.

Dallas shifted in his corner of the couch. "Well, I resisted it at first. I much preferred the idea of the solitude of a monk's life, to be honest. But that'd be selfish of me. I can't use a monastery to hide out from the world. In prayer, I kept feeling an urge to push my comfort level more, to put other people ahead of myself. I know I can do that—will *have* to do that—as a parish priest. It would combine my earnest desire to offer my life to God with the need I have to put others first, to stop focusing on my own problems, dwelling on the negative, really, and instead use my life to serve other people, to help them learn about God and grow in their faith. The idea of becoming a priest is like this slow-burning fire inside me, waking me at night, bursting into my thoughts constantly…"

"What would you say is the number one reason you believe you are being called to the priesthood?" The directness of the question made Dallas wonder if he'd been rambling. If he was going to make a decent impression, he needed to be straightforward and confident.

"The biggest reason is because I want to allow God to use me for good," he said firmly, "and I know what it's like to be adrift. I know it's my duty to help people who may be lost and don't yet realize that it's God they are seeking and that the Church can bring him to them. I want to offer the sacrifice of the Mass and to help save souls. I didn't deserve to be saved, Your Excellency, and yet a priest came to me in prison when I asked, and that changed my entire life! I want to help other people find God, too."

"Your earlier desire for solitude—has that left you?" asked the archbishop, leaning back and rubbing his chin with one hand.

Dallas pressed his lips together. "I've always been more of a loner, but that can lead me to selfishness and pride. So, while I might want to be alone sometimes, I know I need to step outside myself to be a better person, and as a priest, I would have to forget myself to help others. I'm really interested in getting involved in prison ministry. When I was in prison, there were several times when other guys approached me and asked me about God, about my faith, about Christianity… and at first, I didn't like the attention. I just wanted to keep to myself, keep my head down and skate through until my release. Somehow, they kept coming to me, like I was attracting them against my will. But it was really God they were being drawn to. So, I changed my attitude and listened more to people who came to me. Really, I guess I allowed God to change my heart and my will. I learned to give my time to people who needed it. And honestly, Your Excellency, I really don't know what it is about me that made these guys seek me out. I'm nothing special. I've gotta assume that God put them in my path for a reason—that it was God nudging them towards me." Dallas described some of his interactions with a few of the guys in prison and with the family he met on the Appalachian Trail and how his hiking trip had brought him such a sense of peace and assurance that he was truly being called to the priesthood. "And whenever I'm in church, in the presence of the Blessed Sacrament…" His lips trembled with his words. "…I'm just speechless at how God has changed me, how he wants to be here with us, and I just *know* I can do nothing else but this, to bring him fully to others in the sacraments."

"Can you talk a bit about your own personal growth over the past several years, Dallas?" asked Archbishop Adams. "How have you changed since your arrest?"

Dallas shifted in discomfort over the personal questions. A blunt answer would be best. "Honestly, I began as an impulsive, desperate 19-year-old with a jaded view of humanity. I wasn't a nice person, got into some violent situations while incarcerated at first. But after a year or two, I learned to turn the other cheek and see others as children of God in as much need of mercy and forgiveness and love as myself. I guess you could say I became a man over my prison term. And I was so torn up over Channing's death and being in prison at first that… well, I was on the verge of suicide."

The archbishop's eyes flickered at the word.

"But I didn't go through with it," Dallas rushed. "Turning to prayer saved me. Channing's example was what stopped me from my own ruin. Knowing that Channing had found truth in the Catholic Church encouraged me to persevere and seek that truth for myself."

"You mentioned violence," the archbishop said softly. "I know prison can be a rough place. Could you elaborate on any altercations there?"

Dallas took a deep breath and described some of the fights. "I know it probably sounds really bad," he admitted, glancing up into the bishop's face. "I take responsibility for my lack of self control back then. My last fight was over two years ago…" Dallas studied his fingernails to avoid the bishop's gaze. *Two years — that's nothing to somebody as old as him!*

"Do you think you have an anger problem, Dallas? I don't mean the question as an accusation." Archbishop Adams held up both hands. "I know that young men get into these kinds of physical fights from time to time, and they usually blow over. I was in a fistfight or two myself in my younger years. But sometimes there is a deep-seated problem beneath it, and since it has happened more than once…"

Dallas gazed out the nearby window and saw his temper tantrum in the desert from a few days previous. Heat rose in his cheeks. "I think I used to have a rage problem," he said slowly, pulling at one pants leg unconsciously. "I was ready to beat up anyone who insulted Channing, especially. I was mad at the whole world, kind of letting it simmer beneath the surface all the time. But becoming Catholic and remembering Channing's almost childlike optimism has gradually pulled me out of that. I knew I had to man up and take the high road instead of letting my passions rule me. I gained a lot of control over myself, focused on working out to release physical tension, and just constantly reminded myself that I couldn't go around beating up other people. I learned how to give the benefit of the doubt and to walk away instead of just instantly reacting." The image of Mike stumbling back from Dallas's punch flashed through him, and Dallas winced and clenched his fists. *Be truthful. You don't have complete control of yourself yet.*

The archbishop's expression showed Dallas he was waiting for that truth.

"Okay, I have to admit, I do still get mad. The other day, I was about to bury my mother, and all the baggage from my childhood hit me and got me furious at her. I went out in this field outside of town, all alone, and I screamed and threw rocks around, but then I stopped myself and let it all go. I also ran into Channing's mother. Her abuse of him had me hating her several years ago, but now I recognize her brokenness, and I sympathized with her. I know we all deserve forgiveness. Overall, I've mellowed out over the last two years, able to forgive people instead of harboring feelings of ill will and dealing with my anger in ways that don't hurt anyone. Except… well, I did punch this guy last week, when I saw him physically abusing his girlfriend. Guess I'm still working on my self-control…" Dallas pulled at his collar. He sent up a mental prayer that the archbishop wouldn't ask about the hardly noticeable bruising around his eye.

"Sometimes these deep scars need much attention and many years to heal," Archbishop Adams murmured, a gentle hand resting on Dallas's shoulder.

Dallas's eyes flew up to the archbishop's. *He can't trust that I'm stable.* The realization ground Dallas into the floor, and he tried to swallow, but his throat felt swollen.

"Your Excellency," he blurted, "I believe you know the details of my incarceration, and I've been concerned that it could be an impediment to my becoming a priest. I want to be completely honest with you about it." Dallas held his breath and waited.

The archbishop smiled at Dallas. "You are correct that it is something we must fully address. Before you give me the specifics, I want to be sure you know that I find your conversion story very moving, and I believe you are genuinely striving to seek God's will in your life, whatever that may be. I see in you an enthusiastic young man with a zeal for his faith — and such a history. After working through our own past battles, God can equip us to relate to other people who have gone through struggles of their own. I get the sense that you have a real heart for mercy and forgiveness, no doubt in part because you have seen mercy and forgiveness working in your own life. And," he continued, making his voice gentler and quieter, "I have no desire to make it feel like you are being put on trial again. But I do need to go over your charges so I can understand what happened. Due to the nature of public records, we must be able to one hundred percent stand behind our priests and have nothing to hide, to be able to assure anyone who asks that we know it all, that it has been resolved, and that we have no reasons for concern... basically, to be able to diffuse any gossip. Especially since your conviction is less than five years in the past, I need to give the details careful consideration and be sure that you have recovered from this serious recent history."

"I understand." Dallas, head down, forced himself to stop fidgeting with his ring. "The last thing I want is to cause the Church any scandal. I realize that while I've been forgiven for my crimes both by God and the State, the temporal effects remain."

"You put it better than I just attempted to do." Archbishop Adams smiled.

Dallas tried to feel at ease. "I guess I should describe my crimes: three counts of theft, two counts of fleeing from an officer and resisting arrest, and involuntary manslaughter. The thefts were shoplifting from a few gas stations..." Dallas delved into the sordid details, holding nothing back.

"In retrospect, I could have done things differently," he said, eyes hollow. "I mean, we tried begging; we tried asking at a food bank, but we didn't have much luck. Still, I could have swallowed my pride and taken us to a homeless shelter sooner, just until I got on my feet and started earning some money… but I was too scared we'd be separated. And I was too proud. I had a bit of a complex about being the only one who'd do a half-decent job of taking care of Channing. I've gone over and over all my mistakes and how I could've made different choices. I shouldn't have been so controlling, because he would have been 18 soon enough and into the men's shelter with me, but… he never made it to his next birthday because of my stupid impulsivity."

Dallas paused, blinking, and the archbishop sat in silence with him. He passed Dallas a box of tissues.

After dabbing his eyes, Dallas continued. The details spilled out: how he'd attempted to evade the police officer who had been blocking his way out of the store and how the man had drawn his gun, leading to its unintentional firing in the scuffle. Remorse poured over Dallas as he relived the event through its telling. Years ago, when the crime was fresh, he hadn't even been able to feel badly about it. Now overflowing with repentance, Dallas forever regretted his actions that had contributed to a man's death. His slumped shoulders shook as he willed himself to keep his composure.

Archbishop Adams had listened in silence. "Thank you, Dallas; you can stop there."

Dallas straightened, wide-eyed and relieved. He'd prepared himself to have to tell the most heart-wrenching part of the story in detail. "You don't need to hear about the second time I ran from the cops—my arrest?"

"You touched on that when you mentioned Channing's death, and Father Benedict related those details," the archbishop said. "He wanted to spare you the grief of having to talk about it again. I understand that it was terribly painful to lose your best friend in that way. I'm deeply sorry, Dallas, and I offer my condolences to you."

"Thank you." Waves of relief coursed through him. "It was the worst thing possible, thinking all your decisions were in somebody's best interests, only to find that they led to the opposite outcome. To have made myself responsible for Channing and then to tell him to run from the police with me… It made me nuts, going over it while trapped in prison. I hated myself for it. But my prison sentence gave me a lot of time to come to terms with what I had done, and it led me to throw myself on the mercy of Jesus. I had nowhere else to turn, and God was there, just when I needed him most, offering me stability. That's what I really hope most to communicate with you, how much God has changed me." Dallas's damp, serious eyes penetrated those of the archbishop.

"I see you have undergone huge changes in a short period of time," Archbishop Adams said. "And I appreciate your acknowledgment of the severity of these incidents."

Dallas nodded, eyes closed. "I understand how awful my mistakes have been. And yet God's been so good to me. I hear Him pursuing me, relentlessly, for this—"

"Your emotional response is strong, no doubt," the archbishop said.

Emotional response? Dallas sucked in his breath. *Is that all he thinks this is?*

"Well, I've enjoyed very much getting to talk with you today, Dallas." The archbishop stood and gave a little stretch.

Dallas's frantic gaze searched out the clock on the wall as he bolted up from his seat. *But we're not done yet, are we?* A nauseated dread settled in his stomach.

"Your interest in your faith and in the priesthood is clear," continued Archbishop Adams. "Of course, the archdiocese will run a background check, and because of the nature of your conviction, I will need to take some time to look over everything before making a decision."

Dallas's chin quivered, and he opened his mouth, but the question wouldn't come.

"No matter what I conclude, I will call to let you know. Can you please leave me a phone number so I can reach you?"

Dallas finally spit it out. "Your Excellency, please—tell me honestly. Do I have a chance?" His eyes, unflinching, bored into the archbishop's.

The archbishop sighed and took one step forward with his hands extended. "Okay, Dallas, I will be very upfront with you. It isn't a hard 'no.' But there are many factors: the seriousness of your crimes, the relatively recent timing of your conversion and your discernment of this calling, and the unfortunate circumstances of your past that contribute to the difficulties you've had with anger and emotional stability. I do very much believe you are in earnest. Your story is so compelling, and I believe you are listening for God and that he wants big things of you. You are willing to do big things for him, and that makes me want to jump with a definite 'yes,' purely as my first instinctual response. But I must consider: is this the right thing? And is this the right time? I will study your case closely over the next week because I don't want to leave you hanging about something I see is so important to you. I must make a thorough examination, then pray to know what actions God wants me to take. Dallas, due to how recently you finished your prison term, it may be that your answer will be: wait and see. Keep praying and discerning." He reached out and clasped Dallas on the shoulder. "God is with you, Dallas, whether he wishes you as one of his priests or not."

Dallas's eyes squeezed shut. *But I know God's calling me! What else can I do with my life? Nothing!!* He swallowed hard and forced himself to meet the archbishop's gaze. "Thank you for being straight with me," he managed the words. "I look forward to hearing from you whenever you're ready. Please, take as much time as you need because… because I really believe you'll hear that this is the one thing, the *only* thing God has in mind for me." He put on his self-confident expression, unblinking and firm.

Archbishop Adams gave a reserved smile. "I will most certainly pray deeply over this. I bet you're getting hungry for lunch, because I know I am." He motioned towards the door.

Dallas shook the archbishop's outstretched hand with his trembling one, then remembered himself and kissed the man's ring. "Thank you for taking the time to meet with me." The social norms covered his deep ache.

"It's been a pleasure, Dallas." The older man smiled broadly. "You are clearly a unique young man, and God has much in store for you."

Much in store for me. Dallas stepped through the door. *Just not the priesthood.* As he rounded the corner of the hallway, he broke into a jog to escape the out-of-control sensation. His breath caught in his throat. *Wait and see, wait and see*, the archbishop's words echoed in his brain. *But how? How, God, how can I wait and maybe even get told* no, *one day far in the future, and then…* then *what?* Dallas slipped into the basilica and hit his knees beside the altar rail, gazing at the tabernacle, each breath like a stabbing pain to his heart. "Please, God, please, God, please, God," was all the gasping prayer his tongue could formulate in the still silence of the place where he'd once ignored early promptings of his current fervency of faith.

CLEAN BREAK

"He told me he'd call to give me an answer, that he needs to fully understand my crimes and then pray about it to make a decision." This had been Dallas's only explanation to Father Benedict a half-hour after his meeting with Archbishop Adams. The priest's expression had remained one of hopeful joy, and Dallas had bitten back his visible doubts until now, driving home in the safety of his solitude.

He was almost out of money. Even though he could make the upcoming rent payment on his apartment, it would leave him scraping to cover the utilities and food. Father Benedict had known this. His gracious invitation pressed down on Dallas. Did he really want to move into the guest room at the basilica until he got his savings back up? If the archbishop told him no... Dallas swallowed the lump in his throat. Living there would be a stab to the gut after that. But Father Benedict was still so confident...

Dallas pulled in at the apartment where he had two more weeks' housing guaranteed before making that decision. He stepped out of the car, the humid Texas air hitting his face. He cursed it with a grimace. Then he blew out a sigh. *Remember, God's will, not yours. Be patient. If God wants you for this, he'll have you.* Dallas lifted his bag from the car and headed for his door with determined steps. He wanted to get inside and say his Rosary and pray Vespers before the serious decision-making would consume tomorrow's mental energy.

A paper taped to his door boldly welcomed him with his name in a bubbly script. The familiar feminine handwriting betrayed his suspicions that it was from Samantha. The trip had created plenty of distraction from her, and he braced himself for what this note might contain to frazzle his nerves more.

Fingers trembling, he unfolded the paper. Dallas scanned the words, brow furrowed.

Dallas,

I'm still so sorry for the way I've treated you. I know I don't deserve your forgiveness. I wish I knew how to have a healthy relationship with a man, but I don't, and so I've not been good to you. It was so wrong of me to lie to you. I'm really going to try to be better and am so thankful for all you've done for me. I just wanted you to know this.

Samantha

Dallas blew out a low sigh. Maybe this meant she really wanted to change how she interacted with men. *I just need to send her a note telling her I forgive her, and maybe that will be that and she'll leave me alone.* After taking care of the final arrangements for his mother and even making some peace with Channing's mom, Dallas wondered if this could be the icing on the cake of his success in navigating female relationships. But if the archbishop told him to wait, or just flat-out no... Dallas's insides quivered at the thought of staying where Samantha's temptations may inevitably find him. He stared at her note and thought of her pain expressed in those lyrics she'd composed. *These are just words — does she really mean them? Does she even understand how to change?* That's why he had to move to Denver, Dallas decided in that moment. Staying here would be setting himself up for the near occasion of sin. *And I know I'm going to be a priest one day, I know it... don't I?* Dallas sank onto his sofa with the letter still in hand. *But if I'm not... please, God, help me. I wanted so much to close the door on this chapter of my life, maybe with all the loose ends tied up nice and neat, too, if she really means what she says, but...* Her pretty blue eyes sparkled in his memory.

Dallas jumped to his feet and reached for his doorway pull-up bar. After exhausting himself, he flopped onto his bed for his evening prayers. As he leaned into his pillows, he caught sight of his dresser and its messy announcement that he should pack up the things sitting on top of it if he really was moving to Denver soon. *I am moving there.* Dallas's eyes were like steel, and he set his stubborn jaw. *I know I'm supposed to be a priest! I'm going.* He pulled himself to his feet and picked up the file folder of documents and some mail from the dresser and set them in an empty bin. The envelope of old photographs caught Dallas's eye, and he picked it up. His hand hovered over the bin, hesitant. He still hadn't looked through these...

Sinking back onto the bed, Dallas opened the flap and slid out the stack of glossy photographs. On top was the one of him by his car after changing the oil. He placed it underneath the stack to reveal the next photo: Channing, sitting barefoot in a tree, probably around age 15. Dallas lingered over each memory. One of him standing on the roof of his car — Channing had taken that one when they'd been goofing off one day. A few of Channing making stained glass. One of him painting, another of him in the driver's seat of the Isuzu wearing sunglasses and a ridiculous-looking hat, pretending to drive, an enormous silly open-mouthed grin on his face. One of Dallas acting the tough guy, eyebrows lowered at the camera. The next was from the same afternoon, taken by a neighbor acquaintance, of them mock-wrestling, Dallas with Channing in a fake headlock. *Goodness, the fun we used to have, doing pretty much nothing and everything, all rolled together…*

Then he came across the one he had known was in the stack somewhere, his favorite photo: Channing sitting by a campfire, staring into the flames rather than the camera lens, a deep, soulful expression in his eyes. Dallas sat consumed by the image for a long time. Finally, he set the stack of photos on his bedside table on top of Samantha's note. He squeezed his eyes shut tight and tried to subdue his thoughts of both Channing and Samantha as he fell asleep.

Dallas was a flurry of action over the next days as he zeroed in on his one goal: moving out and heading to Denver. And there were other dioceses, other bishops. He would try each one if he had to. Dallas pushed his cart through Walmart and dropped in a roll of packing tape. *I have a clear answer from God. I just have to find the path he wants me to take to get there — and that path leads away from Wichita Falls.* Doubts dragged at Dallas as he imagined himself wandering the country from church to church, but he fought them off as he tackled each item on his to-do list.

The bulk of the new cell phone in his pocket annoyed him, and Dallas resolved not to carry it around on him. He'd bought the most basic one possible and put a small number of minutes on it. Forwarding on his mail had been set up for the basilica's address. For his peace of mind, he wanted the authorities to be able to find him if Mike did attack Samantha again and his testimony was needed. He was leaving his apartment phone number set up until the last moment, anticipating the archbishop's answer that he hoped would come before he moved out. If not, he'd have to take it face-to-face. Could he handle the rejection?

Over a week had passed without a call from the archbishop, and Dallas was in limbo. He headed home and did some more packing up and loading of his car, leaving only the last essentials in his apartment. He'd sold off his furniture and would be ready to leave in the morning. Following a simple dinner, he settled down with a book on some pillows and blankets on the floor of his mostly bare apartment.

After reading for an hour, his mind wandered from the print, body restless. He needed to write that quick note to Samantha. Then he could drop it in the mail on his way out of town. Dallas had been putting it off, unsure how to explain his calling to her now that it was all up in the air. A voice in his head broke in: *You don't want to tell her. Because it's not happening, and so you need to leave your options open… and she's an option.* He squeezed his head between his hands and banished the voice of doubt, then jumped to his feet. Some fresh air would clear his mind.

Boots on his feet and keys in his pocket, Dallas shut the apartment door behind him and strode across the parking lot. The sky glowed pink from the setting sun. He followed the sidewalk along the main road, passing the gas station where he'd filled up countless times. Sentiment welled in him about leaving this town, the first place he had truly chosen to make his home, without the coercion of extenuating circumstances. His doubts followed him down the road. Going to Denver was a last resort, not because he had a firm plan. Was it his old pointless life, the one with no destination? If the archbishop said no, then what was he running to? He bit his lip as he passed the now-familiar buildings, having become so every day as to make his prison life seem far away and hazy, surprising him in how quickly he'd resumed life outside those walls. Dallas passed the movie rental store, lined with rows of DVDs. His years in prison, having taken him to the end of the year 2000, still made Dallas feel as if he had suddenly been dropped into another time, one in which DVD players had replaced VCRs, everyone had a cell phone in a pocket or purse, and cassette tapes were practically an archaic remnant of the past.

With his footsteps mechanical and thumbs hooked in pockets, Dallas drifted with the thoughts that suppressed his usual alertness until a sixth sense tingled the back of his neck with adrenaline. Was somebody following him? Mike and his goon? Dallas glanced over his shoulder with nagging suspicion. Several people were walking along the same sidewalk at varying distances. The weight of his knife in his pocket spoke to his fight instinct. *Okay, don't get ahead of yourself. It's probably nothing.* To assuage his discomfort, Dallas paused and sat down on the short cinder block wall that separated the Chinese restaurant from the laundromat, waiting.

In the distance, he discerned a familiar figure approaching. There was no mistaking it. She appeared as if out for a random walk, but Dallas couldn't help but think it was intentional. The tsunami her presence always brought surged inside. But this might be the last time he'd ever see her. Dallas tried to swallow the mixture of relief and anguish brought on by the realization. *I need to forgive her, and now I have the chance in person.* It wasn't like he could run and hide from her here. Regardless of the archbishop's answer, she deserved to know about his calling. Maybe that would end this once and for all. *But what if Mike's been bothering her again?* Ignoring the quavery feeling in his stomach, he offered it up silently.

Samantha was close, eyes pointed forward as if unaware of his presence. But this had to be intentional. Dallas kept his eyes on his boots, prayers for guidance chasing after the warmth that was rising through his body.

"Dallas!" She sounded surprised.

Dallas lifted his head. "Hi."

"Whatever are you doing sitting out here?" Samantha flounced over to him with a broad smile, her short sundress swinging.

Dallas's eyes were unwavering as they returned her look. "Waiting for you to catch up to me."

Samantha's mouth opened, but Dallas continued. "I hope that sorry excuse for a man hasn't been bothering you again. Is that why you've been following me?"

Samantha blushed and looked away. "Following you?"

Dallas bit the inside of his lip and gave her a penetrating stare.

Samantha sank down near him on the wall, subdued. "I told you I wouldn't lie to you again, Dallas." She played with her hands in her lap. "My car's parked back at your apartment complex. When I saw you head down the sidewalk... yeah, I decided to walk this way, too, hoping I'd bump into you."

"Well, you did." Dallas's suppressed giddiness was jostled aside by a reminder of humiliation. She'd been intentionally following him, and her first impulse was to tell him a lie—*again*. To diffuse his irritation, Dallas thought of the message she'd left him. "I found your note on my door. For your sake, I'm glad you want to act differently with men."

"So... you're not still mad at me?" Samantha's voice was hesitant as she risked a darting glance at his face.

"No, I'm not mad about that night anymore." Dallas sighed. "The past two crazy weeks have crowded out my anger. You apologized to me before I left, and I should've accepted it then and there. So I'm glad for the chance to tell you now—I forgive you, Samantha."

The sudden lightness in her face was all Dallas needed to feel a load lift off him. He added quickly, "But I don't like that you're following me. I thought your note meant that we could... umm... just close the door and be done with everything." As his hands twitched in his lap and he fought to keep them still, that voice invaded his mind again: *Is that want you really want, hmmm?*

Samantha gazed away and didn't respond directly. "I just wanted to see if you'd found the note, and what you'd been up to. I'm sorry things have been crazy. Like, in a bad way? Do you need to talk about it?" The warm sympathy in her eyes pulled at Dallas's will like elastic.

He tightened his posture. "No, I'd rather forget about most of it now." If he started talking to her about his mother and his doubts about the archbishop's decision, it would only arouse her womanly consoling that was like the tune of the pied piper drawing him to her. Dallas bit his lip.

"So, are you packing for a big trip?" Samantha asked brightly.

"You could say that." Dallas bent to rub at a scuff on his boot. How long had she been outside his apartment, watching? "Actually, I'm moving out of state tomorrow—and please don't ask me where, because I'm not going to say."

Samantha's face fell slightly, but she giggled. "You've anticipated me, Dallas! You knew what I was going to ask you next!" The flirty tone entered her voice so automatically that he wondered if she even recognized it in herself at this point. "You know me so well! But if you move away, who'll be around to protect me?" She leaned forward, studying his profile.

"The police, I guess." Dallas shrugged. "They can help you better than me, which is why I took you there after Mike hit you. I didn't always think so, but the police are better at protecting people than I am."

"Oh, that's right." Samantha's tone softened. "You never told me the details, did you? You know, I still can't believe it almost, that you were *arrested*. You're just too nice of a nice guy, Dallas! And it's like you don't even have to make any effort; it just comes naturally. How is it that you're so nice, anyway?"

"I'm not nice, believe me." Dallas crossed his arms. "Not by nature, anyway. I mean, you just saw yourself how long it took me to accept your apology. I have to make a constant effort to be nice every day, sometimes even every moment. It's been a challenge."

Samantha smiled at him and gushed, "I can't believe that, Dallas!"

"Believe it," he said flatly.

Samantha let the matter drop. "So..." She inched closer. "Did you get a job in another state?"

"Well, um, I'm hoping so." It wasn't untrue—Dallas had lined up interviews at three mechanics near the basilica in hopes of landing a summer job until... Still guarded at her initial dishonesty about following him, Dallas wasn't sure how to explain his vocation now that he had the opportunity. He bit the inside of his lip to keep it from quivering, and he gave her a side glance. *It still hurts like heck that she can't naturally be honest with me. I shouldn't let it bother me now that she's going to be out of my life...* He gulped. *She is, isn't she?* Dallas changed the topic.

"Has Mike been leaving you alone?" Turning to face her on the wall, he couldn't conceal the true concern he had for her despite everything. "Has he respected the restraining order?"

"Oh, yeah, and I'm *so* done with him," Samantha declared, her eyes narrowing. "I mean, I've seen him around a few times, but from a distance. He hasn't tried to talk to me or anything." She leaned in closer. "Actually, it's kind of funny when I've gone into the bar while he's there, because then he has to leave!" Her eyes danced, as if she delighted in this.

"'Funny' isn't exactly the word that comes to my mind. You shouldn't go to places where you know he might be, and especially not while dressed in clothing that's designed to attract the leering eyes of men," Dallas said bluntly.

Samantha waved off the advice. "I go where I want. And it's not the clothing's fault if perverted men look at me," she said with a toss of her head. "I wear things that I like and that make me feel pretty."

"Look, I know it's not fair, but we live in an unfair world." Dallas tried to come across as understanding. "I'm telling you this for your safety, out of concern for you. You've gotta make some sacrifices and not just go wherever you want if it's a place where Mike often goes. And about the clothes—it's not just perverts." Dallas, glancing down at her short skirt without even trying, immediately pulled his eyes away. "Clothes like that attract looks from men whether they're the type who want to look or not. Men are very visual, and certain clothing catches our notice. And I think you know that, based on what happened that night in your apartment." With all this, Dallas fixed his eyes on the road, concentrating on the passing cars in front of him, then turning to look her directly in the face. "I care about you, Samantha, that you get treated with the respect due a woman."

"After how I've acted... you *care* about me?" Samantha's eyes were wide.

Dallas felt the way she looked. *She couldn't tell?!* "Well, yeah," he mumbled. "Why else would I have been so concerned about your safety from Mike?" *And so torn up that you'd lied to me?*

She stared back at him, then dropped her eyes to where her fingers played with her skirt hem. "Actually, I've thought a lot about what you said. You're right that I knew exactly what I was doing, wearing that nightgown in front of you, and then..." Her face flushed at the memory. "But about how you said that I need to respect my own self-worth, too. I really should settle for committing to *one* guy, a *nice* guy, instead of jumping from one jerk to another, and to try dating somebody for more than the physical. But there aren't that many good guys in the world, you know... and, that's part of the reason I followed you tonight..." She stared into his eyes.

Dallas realized with a sinking feeling what she was getting at, and a sick sensation swirled in the pit of his stomach. He hated that she was not only attracted to him, but that it had become about more than just seductive glances and sexual conquest but also about the genuine way he wanted to treat her—*and I have to reject her. Would I give her a chance, in spite of her dishonesty, if it weren't for my vocation? If Archbishop Adams is calling right now to tell me no, would I...?* Dallas was silent, waiting to see if she was really asking him to be that exclusive "nice guy." She had only known casual flings, so could she really have a more serious kind of purpose in mind now, and could he even believe her? Could she really believe it herself? Dallas felt a pull in his chest, like his heart could be torn in two over the intensity of her interest in him.

Samantha spoke again. "I mean, you say I shouldn't dress this way, but what if I want to just look nice for *one* particular man—isn't that okay?" She leaned closer, her blue eyes sparkling. "Remember when I told you how intriguing I found you to be, Dallas Malone!"

Dallas's conscience bristled at the unnerving coyness in her voice.

"And to know that you care about me, even now..." Samantha's voice softened. "It's just that I've probably never in my life met a guy as good as you are, one that might be worth staying with." She scooted closer to him on the wall. "If I had *you* with me regularly, well, I could go anywhere without having to worry about jerks like Mike because you'd be looking out for me." She laid a hand on his forearm. "You could stay, couldn't you, and find another job around here? Or you could take me with—"

"I can't," Dallas interrupted in a firm voice, his heart racing in his throat. He pulled his arm away from her. "Look, Samantha, I can't be your savior, even if a part of me wants to." He closed his eyes and argued with his own ego. *Maybe she really does want to change, but she needs to want it for* herself, *not for me.*

"You *do* think a good man should commit to one girl and stand up for her and protect her, don't you?" Samantha glanced up hopefully.

"You're right that a good man should make a commitment." Dallas took a deep breath. *Here goes...* "And I've made a decision recently about what I need to commit my whole life to: I'm planning to become a priest, Samantha. A Catholic priest." Dallas paused to let what he'd just said sink in.

Samantha's jaw dropped. "A *priest*? You mean, you'd never have a girlfriend ever, or get married one day?"

"That's right." Dallas's gaze was steady.

"And you'll never have sex, like, *ever*?"

Dallas winced inside at what he knew she thought was a weakness, a failing of his manhood, and his mind played back the opportunity he'd passed up more than once. *"Ponder nothing earthly minded..."* He breathed in the words of the hymn that answered the doubts Samantha was casting on him. "It's a sacrifice I'm ready and willing to make."

"Do you know what you're giving up? Dallas, if you…" Samantha pursed her lips. "Are you a virgin?"

Dallas cleared his throat before meeting Samantha's gaze. "Only by the grace of God," he mumbled, all the possibilities of his unsupervised teenage years flashing through him. His aloof personality, along with his mother's one explicit directive, had largely kept him from those temptations, not to mention the three-and-a-half-year prison stint.

"Then you don't even know what you're sacrificing!" Samantha shot him a wide-eyed look.

Dallas's face felt warm. "Sure, I do. I'm a man. We think about it a lot. I *know* it's a big sacrifice."

Samantha leaned so close he could almost feel her pulse. She clasped her hands. "Dallas, if just one time, you want to… Then you'll know for sure…" Her clear blue eyes pierced him.

Dallas couldn't breathe for a moment. Sparks coursed through him, head to toe at the thought of her offer. *Third time's the charm, and this is your fourth and final chance – you can just go to confession after…* He shook himself and lowered his eyebrows. "I can't." He forced out the words.

Samantha slumped her shoulders and sighed. "I don't see how you could make that choice, for your *whole life*! That's really what you want?" she asked, nose wrinkled.

"Yes, it is." Dallas found his tongue and his stubbornness. "But more importantly, it's what *God* wants me to do with my life."

"How can you know what God wants?" Samantha asked skeptically.

Exactly! hissed the devilish voice inside Dallas. *Nobody's gonna want you as a priest with your history. Stay here with her – at least* she *wants you!*

NO! Even if the archbishop says no, you have to resist her! Dallas pressed his fingers to his temples and conjured the memorized words: *"If you act rightly, you will be accepted; but if not, sin lies in wait at the door: its urge is for you, yet you* can *rule over it." If God wants me for his priest, I've gotta master myself. I can't despair now. I* will *be a priest, I* will *make that commitment, I will…*

Dallas straightened up and summoned his courage. "I heard God calling me, clearly, during a long time of prayerful soul-searching. I mean…" Dallas hesitated, trying to muster the strength to expel the right words. *Don't tell her you haven't been accepted yet…* "Look, I'm flattered that you think so much of me, but…" He screwed up his determination and finished strong. "But I *can't* be that for you, or for any woman, because of this calling."

Samantha sighed, and her eyes glistened. "It's kind of a waste for you to become a priest, though. There are already so few nice guys out there for a woman to find."

Dallas didn't try to hide his grimace. "It's not a waste for me to do what God wills for my life," he said, the passion of his call filling him anew. "And it takes a good man to make a commitment, yes, either to a woman *or* to God. I want to be a good man, even though I know I have tons of flaws. I'm determined to give my life as a protector of the faith, committing to serve Christ in his Church. This calling is like a fire burning deep within me, Samantha. I… I don't expect you to understand, but to ignore it would be to ignore God, and then spend the rest of my life regretting it. I'd never have any peace if I did that. And you have a lot of promise yourself, you know. Your singing voice… you're talented, Samantha. And smart, and strong."

Samantha was quiet, gazing into the lit shop windows on the other side of the busy street.

A tightness constricted Dallas's chest. She was so dependent on men's responses to her, and now he'd hurt her feelings. Samantha's attentions to him had an appeal that touched at Dallas's primal self. He'd been startled to realize that he cared for her with an ardent tenderness. His throat ached. *I know how easily I could let myself falter. It's tempting to want a satisfying and co-equal relationship with a woman…* But Dallas knew his own past, his own temperament, and most importantly, his own deep-seated calling to the priesthood. It would be unfair to pile his own baggage onto a woman—another imperfect human being. That wasn't the path for his life. No romantic relationships could ever be perfect, but Dallas's attempt at one would fail even more miserably than most, he was sure. And Samantha wasn't even on the same page regarding God and morals, even though he hoped she was truly changing. He sighed. *I've been over all this with myself before—I'm simply not being called to seek marriage.* But these run-ins with Samantha had certainly complicated his feelings during his discernment. Dallas closed his eyes and gulped. *As painful as it is, I have to amputate her from my life—for the benefit of both of our souls.*

Dallas broke the silence before the dissenting voice inside could start another argument with him. "You deserve a man to treat you well and make a commitment to you, if that's what you really want," he began carefully. "But you should let God love you first. You don't need to rush into anything—it's okay for you to not be in a relationship right now. The most important thing you can do first is to look to God to be your savior and not a mere mortal man. Maybe none of this makes much sense to you, but I'm being genuine with you about my calling, I promise. I want to make sure you know I'm not making up excuses. I really do want the best for you." He stood up from the wall and turned to face her, hands deep in his pockets. If he didn't keep them contained, who knows what he might do with them. Samantha, small and alone, kept staring across the road. Her uncharacteristic quiet made Dallas ache inside.

"I should probably get back now," Dallas mumbled, remembering Father Benedict's advice as he stared at Samantha's shoe dangling from her toes, one bare leg crossed over the other as she bounced it mindlessly. The reassurance he wanted to offer her might be tempting things if he delayed the inevitable. He had to force himself towards a goodbye. The rhythmic movement entranced him. *I'm itching to put distance between us, but all I need is a split second and I could fall right into her…* He broke his gaze and pivoted towards home. "It's gotten dark, so why don't you let me walk you to your car on my way?"

Samantha nodded, then gazed up at Dallas with a guise of sparkle. "I can at least… *pretend* you're my knight in shining armor, this one last time." The distant pain in her eyes betrayed her true feelings, and Dallas had to look away.

They walked in silence until Dallas asked her how work was going. The small talk fizzled after a moment when Samantha didn't go into a lot of detail. Her deflation sank Dallas, making him feel as lowly as dirt.

Wobbling on skinny high-heels as she stepped off a curb, Samantha grabbed hold of Dallas's elbow. She'd sidestepped cracks and drains with skill, but her stride being shorter, Dallas slowed and allowed it. He forced himself not to think about how they must look. Nobody around here would ever see him again after tomorrow, so their appearance wasn't giving scandal. He was just trying to do a good deed for her. *And what kind of man would I be anyway if I let her walk alone over a mile in the dark along this busy street? Not a very good man. More like my father instead.* Alarmed at the sudden invasion to his mind of the man he'd never met, he tried to shove those thoughts down. *Is my being a "good guy" a subconscious response of trying not to be like my own father?* Raw compassion for his mother stabbed at Dallas. All that he'd been unable to feel for her earlier welled up inside at the parallels between her and Samantha. *Mom, I'm so sorry…* He blinked in case the tears began.

His attention was turned by two men approaching from the opposite direction. As they neared, one of them ogled Samantha and gave a low whistle. She returned an exaggerated eyeroll, but Dallas glared fiercely as they brushed past, knocking shoulders with the guy. He slowed and turned around halfway, teeth gritted and muscles tight.

"Oh, that was mild." Samantha tugged at Dallas to loosen his tense posture and keep him moving. "Guys like that, they don't mean anything. They're not exactly *nice* guys, but they aren't complete jerks, either. Like Alex, you know?"

Dallas held back from lecturing her again. He'd given her advice, and now he had to let it go.

As they approached the apartment complex, she stopped suddenly. Pointing at the lit-up cross atop the brick building down the street, she asked, "Is that the Catholic church? That's the one you go to?"

"Yeah."

"So, if you become a priest, will you be in charge of that church?"

"No, since I'm moving away, I'll be at a Catholic church there," Dallas explained. "I have to go to the seminary first, and after I've studied enough to become a priest, I get assigned to a church." He closed his eyes and prayed it would really happen, and soon.

"You mean you don't get to choose which church?"

"No." Dallas stared at Sacred Heart Church, a warm sadness rising into his throat. "When I'm ordained a priest, I'll make a vow of obedience to the bishop. That means I go to whichever of the Catholic churches in the area he chooses."

"Wow..." She trailed off.

Dallas forced his heavy feet towards her car.

"Well," Samantha said, falling into step alongside him, "I've actually never been to church before — I don't think even once in my whole life."

"I'd never been myself until a little over a year ago," Dallas responded with a small smile. "You could go to the Catholic church and visit sometime, if you want. You might find the Mass to be really beautiful and reassuring. I don't want to seem pushy or anything, but the Catholic faith... well, it's where I learned that God alone loves us perfectly. It's where I found Truth."

"Maybe I'll try it, then," Samantha said. "Maybe, someday. I still don't get it; how you could really want to become a *priest*..."

Dallas bit his lip. Nothing he could say right now would really make her get how he wanted it.

But you want her, too, came the voice in his head again. *If you're rejected from entering the seminary, just take something else you want.*

Shut up, Satan! Dallas commanded in his mind. *I'm staying the course, no matter how many years it takes me to get to the seminary!*

They were beside her car now. Samantha fumbled in her purse for her key, then unlocked the driver's side of the white sedan. Goosebumps rose on Dallas's arms as he opened the door for her, trembling at the knowledge that she was leaving for good — and that he was letting her. She paused, savoring the gentlemanly gesture.

"Well, I guess this is it..." Her eyes glistened as they caught the glare from the overhead streetlights, and Dallas felt sick again, a weight dropping to the bottom of his gut. He had to look away.

"Yeah." His voice was strained.

"Goodbye, Dallas." Her quavering little voice ran through him like ripples in a pond as she ran a hand lightly down the length of his forearm, where it rested on top of the open door that now separated them. He flinched internally, frozen under the enticement that came so easily that it was second nature to her. Dallas dipped his chin towards the pavement and closed his eyes, gulping to shake the feeling of that electrifying touch. This was why he could never tell her where he was going. They had to have a clean break, and it was now or never. *Last chance to change your mind, Dallas,* a taunt sounded in his head. *Your apartment's only fifty feet away; you could invite her in, let her be all sympathy for you...* He clenched his teeth behind his lips and fought back against the tingling heat running through his skin. *I'm weak without you, God! My life is yours and nobody else's. Please, strengthen me.*

When Dallas remained a statue, Samantha slowly sank into the seat and drew both her legs in after her. She started the engine and reached for the interior handle, the driver's door still in Dallas's clutching hands, and she ducked her head to hide the flowing stream before the deluge overwhelmed her.

"Samantha, wait a second." One hand darted to his back pocket for his wallet.

Samantha's breath caught, and she snuck a glance up through her running mascara.

Dallas held out a small rectangle of paper.

She reached to take it from his extended grasp.

"It's a copy of the prayer card that helped to save my life when I was in prison," he said, voice raspy. "Channing had one just like this, and I got it back miraculously after he died. I want you to have one, and if it helps you to know this, well... I'll be praying for you with the words printed on the back." He forced his eyes from the card in her hand to her face, despising the pain there that he knew he had caused. "I'll pray for you every day, Samantha."

She examined the Memorare card she now held in both hands. "I don't know if I can ever really change for the better, even with all the prayers in the world..." Her voice cracked as she gazed up at him for the last time through flooded eyes. "But... I appreciate it, since it's coming from you. Thank you — for everything." Her voice shook. "I won't ever forget you, Dallas Malone."

"Goodbye, Samantha," he said gently, the stoic expression on his face covering the conflicted volcano welling up inside of him. He gave her a quick encouraging grin in place of the burning desire to wrap her in his arms or break down sobbing — maybe both — and Dallas shut her car door and tore himself away, hands in pockets again, striding briskly towards his apartment.

He sensed Samantha's eyes watching him, trying to pull him back like a magnet, until he disappeared behind the shutting door. He hadn't looked back. A glance at his answering machine revealed no missed calls, and his shoulders sagged. Inside his apartment for the last night, Dallas clutched his nauseated stomach, trembling over the ties he had just cut. He collapsed onto his pile of pillows and blankets and released a torrent of silent tears, a jumble of frazzled emotion that he couldn't begin to logically understand.

Dallas awoke early the next morning with a raging headache. He'd cried himself to sleep, and for once, it hadn't been over Channing. Unsure whether that could be called progress, he squinted at his watch in the dim morning light: just after 6:00. He'd fallen asleep wearing his jeans and boots. A dread crept into his gut. *The archbishop hasn't called. But Samantha...* Her teary blue eyes stared him through when he squeezed his eyes shut. She said she wanted to change... Did God want him to help her do that? Was it a sign that he hadn't been given an answer? Or was it a test of his steadfastness? Dallas's lip quivered, and he tried to stifle the longing ache inside. *But I'm broke. I have to go to Denver and accept Father's charity, get a job and save up, and then, if the archbishop's decision crushes my deepest desire...* Dallas stared at the door he'd shut on Samantha last night. Her draw on him was so intense. Picturing himself chasing after her, he buried his face in his arms. *I can't believe I'm even considering the what-ifs after the things she's done to manipulate me...* Dallas jumped to his feet. *I don't need to be thinking of this now. I haven't been told no yet. There's still a chance... Stop wondering — just obey God.* He slipped the Memorare card from his pocket and stared into Mary's face. "*Do whatever he tells you.*" *Do what you know God is asking of you.*

Stumbling into the kitchen, Dallas turned on the coffee pot and stretched, then reached for his prayer book as extra fortitude. He had to leave, get as far from this town as he could. He lay on the bare floor and consumed the prayers, tension slackening.

Dallas closed the book with a sigh. *I'm not running away. I'm being called to this. Setting myself up as some kind of false savior for Samantha isn't my future. Remember what happens when you think it's all up to you to save somebody, to be everything to them...*

After pouring himself a cup of coffee, Dallas sat with it on his pillows on the floor and continued his prayers aloud. "God, strengthen me. Please keep me patient. I know how I'm supposed to serve you, and I can wait. I will wait for as long as you ask of me before I can become one of your priests. I'm humbled by the privilege, and it's worth waiting for, even if it's for most of my life..." Dallas opened his eyes as the determination swelled in his heart. He prayed the Memorare aloud for Samantha, as he'd promised he would, nothing but sincere words for her human soul. As much as it pained him to think that she might continue to make poor choices regarding men, he couldn't allow himself to go down the rabbit hole of guilt that he couldn't be what she wanted him to be. *God, please send her a good man one day, once she's ready — one far better than me. But please help her find contentment with herself first. Only you can bring that to her, if only she can be open to you.* Dallas sighed an amen. The previous night was becoming a hazy, uncomfortable memory now.

He lingered in the shower, his last in this apartment, still talking to God in his head. Finally tearing himself away from the beating water, Dallas turned the knobs and reached for the one towel he'd not packed. As he wrapped it around his waist, the phone rang.

Dallas slipped on the tile floor and caught his balance as he rushed to the phone. He snatched the receiver and put it to his wet ear. "Hello?"

"Dallas, this is Archishop Adams," came the friendly voice on the other end.

"Y-Your Excellency, how are you?" he managed through a dizzy sensation like he might throw up.

"Very well, and I think you will be, too." He chuckled. "Dallas, I have decided to take a chance on you and allow you to enter the seminary for the Archdiocese of Denver this fall. I want you in our program for priestly formation. I believe you are meant for the priesthood."

Dallas collapsed to his knees, and tears sprang to his eyes. He almost dropped the phone. His face felt hot, his legs shook, and he thought he was floating. He squeezed the damp wool of his scapular in his free hand and wept silently, trying to stifle the noises from going through the line.

"Thank you," he choked out. "Thank you so much! Thank you, God; thank you..."

Archbishop Adams continued, "Father Benedict tells me you are on your way today."

"Yes, I just have a few last things to pack up, and I can be out of here in a half hour." Dallas jumped to his feet. "I'll be there tonight!"

The archbishop laughed. "Your enthusiasm is contagious!"

"So, why? What made you give me a yes, and for this fall?" Dallas stumbled, trying to step into his pants as he cradled the phone between his chin and shoulder. "I prayed and hoped so much, but I thought—"

"Something happened here in the basilica yesterday which can only be attributed to the Holy Spirit," the archbishop's solemn voice answered. "Father Benedict will surely want to tell you in person. But it has been made clear to me that you were made for this, Dallas. Sometimes God reveals his will through others, and he has done so in what he wills for you. It was Channing who delivered the answer to us."

Dallas's stomach jittered as he drove through the gate of the Oklahoma prison in which he'd spent three and a half years of his life. He repeated in his mind, *I can do all things in Christ who strengthens me.* Reminders of the abuse he'd suffered here ran up and down his spine, and he knew this was part of why he hadn't come back to visit his friends sooner.

But the haunted memories couldn't deflate Dallas's giddy joy over his acceptance by the archbishop, and as he approached the prison, he smiled to himself that he'd be seeing his friends soon and could share the news with them. He wondered how they were holding up. *Seems like a lifetime ago when I was incarcerated alongside them, but it's only been six or seven months...*

Dallas parked in the visitors' lot and went through the main entrance, clearing security with no problem as he'd remembered to leave his pocketknife in the car. Father Benedict had dealt with this at every monthly visit. Dallas lifted his arms as he was patted down and passed through the metal detector.

The familiar visitation room opened to Dallas from an odd perspective. *I'm on the other side of the table now. This is surreal.* His comfortable jeans, his favorite boots, and his old gray t-shirt emblazoned with the faded words *Ralph Lauren Polo* were a far cry from the orange prison uniform he had always worn while in this room before.

Smith came in first. He looked older, much older than when they'd said goodbye in November, but Dallas greeted him with a wide grin.

"Keeping yourself out of trouble in here?"

"For the most part," returned Smith in his cocky voice. "Only been in solitary once since you left, so I'd say I'm getting on well. My term's up September first!"

"That's fantastic," Dallas encouraged. "I should've made it up here sooner to see you guys. I'm sorry about that."

"Now, I'm sure you've been busy enjoying your freedom!" Smith said, kicking back in his folding chair and resting a foot on the table in front of him until the guard reprimanded him. "How's Texas? How's life?"

"I'm on my way to Denver right now, actually," Dallas answered. "Said goodbye to Texas this morning. I worked there awhile on a construction crew. But I got restless, so I quit and then went and hiked part of the Appalachian Trail."

"No kidding!" Smith's eyes widened. "You *have* been busy, Malone! How far'd you get?"

"Only through Georgia and most of Tennessee, then I turned around and hiked back to the beginning. I was trying to get some peace and quiet and to find direction for my life."

"And I'm guessing that direction is Denver for some reason?" Smith raised his eyebrows.

"Yep." Dallas couldn't contain his wide grin. "I'm going to start studying to become a priest."

"A priest, I knew it!" crowed Smith as he beat a fist down on the tabletop. "Not a hermit monk after all, huh? So, your priest friend, the one who always came to visit you in here, he was from Denver, wasn't he? He's gonna teach you?"

"It doesn't quite work like that," Dallas explained. "I have to go to school, to a seminary. Father Benedict is kind of a mentor to me, and he's the one who put in a good word for me with the archbishop in Denver. It's a miracle he's letting me in. I'm still not totally sure what made him tell me yes, but he did, just this morning. It was such a relief!"

"Well, no kidding!" Smith shook his head. "How long you have to be in this seminary?"

"Eight years."

Smith's mouth hung open. "Whoa… that's, like, double the time you were in here, isn't it? Man, school was like a prison to me. How about you—did you do okay in school?"

"I managed." Dallas shrugged. "Even graduated high school. It wasn't so bad, and I expect this will be different. I have to get my undergrad degree—that's the first four years. So, how about you? Making plans for your big release date yet?"

"Yeah, my mom's lettin' me live with her awhile, so I can get my feet back on the ground," Smith replied. "Not sure about work yet, but I'll figure that out. My mom was skeptical about letting me live with her at all, and I can't say I blame her. I was such a slacker before, so this time I'm gonna make myself be better. I'm even gonna pay her for part of the rent and do some chores around the house to help pull my weight. It was the only way she'd agree to let me live there. Man, she's makin' a chore chart, like I'm a fool kid!" Smith gave a hearty laugh. "But it's all good, you know. I'm gonna try to not let her down again."

"That's great you have somewhere to go," Dallas said.

The two men chatted awhile longer. Smith told stories of other inmates Dallas remembered: fights that had broken out, who had bought and shared what from the commissary, their prison jobs, the cafeteria food.

"Speaking of food, you want a snack?" Dallas motioned to the vending machines. "Pick something out, a drink too if you want it."

Eagerly, Smith studied the choices. He selected a Three Musketeers bar and a Coke. Dallas put in money for two drinks and cracked open a can himself.

"So, you haven't asked me how your favorite two guys are!" Smith joked. "Aren't you wondering if Miller and Maddox miss you?"

Dallas rolled his eyes. "Oh, yeah, I'm sure they've been crying since I left."

"No, but man, those guys are pathetic," Smith sneered. "It's like they're still in sixth grade or something. Every time they pass Pedro in the hall or the cafeteria, they whisper, "Pedro loves Dallas!" And they think they're just hilarious. A few weeks ago, I heard them—you know Pedro wouldn't do anything; he's as good as you were, better even, at not letting things get under his skin. So, anyways, I heard them, and I got in their faces and told them since they were always talkin' about you so much all these months after you left, they must be the ones in love with you, and too bad for them that you hate their ugly faces and would never join in their sicko activities. Those guys are still jealous of you, as jealous as sin, man."

Dallas groaned. "This story isn't going to be why you got put in the hole, is it? I *told* you not to let them get you into trouble, and you promised you wouldn't!"

"I think I only promised I'd try," Smith quipped, "and no, I didn't go in the hole for that. I just walked off afterwards. I think they're both kinda scared of me. So that was the end of it. But they just aren't happy unless they have somebody to make fun of. Miller still looks like a damn fool of a jack-o-lantern with his missin' tooth. I think of you every time I see his ugly gap-toothed face." Smith grinned wickedly and took a swig of his Coke.

Dallas cringed. "I wish you wouldn't. Way to remind me of my guilt, man. You know that I feel bad for him."

"I still say he deserved it," Smith replied, crossing his arms across his chest. "You're right that it's Maddox who's the real bastard in here, and Miller just plays along. You and Pedro have more than enough sympathy between the both of you, though, so I'll take all the joy of jeering at the misfortune of people who were jerks to you guys."

Dallas couldn't help but chuckle. Smith hadn't lost his tough exterior, but Dallas knew he was more talk than anything else.

"Is the prayer group still happening?" Dallas asked.

"Oh, yeah, Pedro's all over that," Smith answered lackadaisically. "You can ask him about it in a minute, 'cause our time's almost up. Man, a priest! I can't believe it! Well, I can, of course, and I think you'll be a good one. Not that I know much about priests, but I'm guessing they have to be good guys who pray and turn the other cheek and all that holy stuff you're so good at. 'Father Malone, the peacemaking ex-con. Go to church, or he'll punch your teeth out!' Could be a good idea for a TV series, ha!"

Dallas laughed along with his old prison buddy. "It's been really good to see you, Smith. I hope next time it'll be on the other side of these walls and that you'll be wearing a color that's less glaring." He pretended to shield his eyes from the bright orange uniform.

They said their goodbyes, and Smith was escorted out. Dallas paced the room, stretching a bit, while waiting for Pedro's turn. Sitting in there alone, gray concrete walls surrounding him with nothing to do but remember his own imprisonment made his skin crawl. Dallas didn't like the feeling.

After a few minutes, Pedro was led through the door. With a joyful smile, he greeted Dallas, and the two of them sat down. Dallas offered him a snack from the machine, but Pedro politely declined.

"So, how's everything?" Dallas asked.

Pedro replied, "A lot of it's the same as when you left. I've got another year, and time is really dragging for me lately. But I'm still leading the prayer group. It's going real good. Like five guys come regular. Smith even comes sometimes, but I bet he didn't admit it to you, huh?"

Dallas chuckled. "Nope, he didn't mention he was staying involved. But I'm glad he is. You two keeping everybody else in line in here?"

"We watch out for each other," Pedro said. "I used to be kind of scared of him, you know, when I first got here. But he's a good guy. He acts tough. But he's loyal, like the kind of guy who would stick up for you no matter what."

"The two of you look like you'd be unlikely friends," Dallas said thoughtfully, "but I thought the same thing when I started to get along with him, too. Glad you guys each have a friend in here. How's your kitchen job going?"

They talked over Pedro's job and how a priest had started coming to offer Mass once a month at the prison. Pedro spoke of how he was gradually feeling drawn back to his faith more and more through the prayer group and the monthly Masses.

"My faith used to be something I just did, like, because it was there," he explained. "We would just go to church because that's what we did. But I've been thinking about it more than ever. If anything, prison's good for lots of time to think."

"Don't I remember that." Dallas cracked his knuckles. "This was where I started thinking on what my future was going to look like... I've finally figured it out, actually. I first felt it in here, and now I'm sure of what

God wants me to do with my life." He stared at Pedro in seriousness, about to tell him, when Pedro broke in.

"You're going to become a priest, I hope," he said as if it were the most natural and expected thing in the world.

Dallas's eyebrows went up in surprise. "Yeah, that's right. How did you guess that so easily?"

"I just know you'd be a good one." Pedro's eyes were glowing. "Just watching you in here, the way you were with other people. You'll make a good priest, Dallas. A real good one."

Dallas told Pedro he had brought a prayer card for both him and Smith and that a guard would give the cards to them later, since visitors were never allowed to hand things off to inmates directly. "It's the same card that some of the guys started calling 'the baby Jesus card,' the one I always had with me when I was in here."

"Your Memorare card?" Pedro asked.

"Yeah, I found several copies of the same card and bought some," Dallas answered, "and I want to give them to you guys. You know, some days, that card was the only thing that got me through."

"It's a real good prayer." Pedro nodded. "One of my favorites. I say it with the guys every time we have our prayer group."

"Yeah, I really like the idea of fleeing to the protection of the Mother of God, myself," Dallas added. "I still say it at least once every day now. It was my first prayer habit and the first one I ever learned. Hey, do you know much about the Liturgy of the Hours?"

Dallas explained some about the daily prayer rhythm to Pedro, and they talked a while longer on matters of their shared faith.

"I'm real glad we were in here together," Pedro finished. "With no other Catholics here, it was easy to start to ignore my faith mostly. But when I noticed you starting to get more and more serious, it was a real encouragement to me. Thanks for that, Dallas."

"I'm sorry either one of us had to be here in the first place," Dallas added, "but glad to see all the good that's come out of it. We've been given hope in lots of small ways here and there. I'm so glad we met and got to know each other, Pedro. Hey, let me give you my cell phone number—I gave it to Smith, too. Want you guys to be able to find me when you get out, wherever I'll be."

After Dallas bade Pedro farewell, he exited the prison and walked to his waiting car. He turned to look back at the concrete and barbed wire compound. The sun blazed overhead, throwing squatty shadows of the building and fence. Dallas, brow furrowed, stood locked on this former part of his life. He hoped he'd never come back. From somewhere in the distance, a mockingbird sang, and Dallas got in his car and drove away with a tingle of excitement about finally beginning his real journey.

The next evening, Dallas arrived at the basilica. Stepping into the church with his stuffed duffel bag over his shoulder, he was enveloped with welcome, a sense of home. His footsteps echoed on the marble floor, the altar drawing him forward. The trauma and confusion of the past few weeks — the violence, the bitter memories, the temptation, the mourning, the desperation and anxiety — all melted from him, and he was blanketed with peace. He lit prayer candles for his incarcerated friends, for Samantha, and for the souls of his mother, Officer Schmidt, and Channing, then knelt in prayer for them, wrapped up in his thanksgivings for being led to the certainty of his calling. Now that he was here, Dallas was bursting with eagerness to begin.

After pouring out prayers, Dallas slipped into the darkened rectory. It was after ten. He tiptoed towards the guest room and turned the corner. A sound behind him made Dallas whirl around, and he was looking into the delighted eyes of Father Benedict.

"Father!" Dallas shouted before he caught himself and dropped his voice to a whisper. "I'm here, I'm really here — I'm going to the seminary!" They embraced warmly, tears of joy streaming down Dallas's cheeks. Father Benedict pulled back and studied him at arm's length.

"I'm so happy for you, Dallas! I can see on your face how right this is. You look as alive as you did at the moment of your baptism!" An unconditional love shone on the face of Dallas's mentor.

"You've gotta tell me how it all happened!" Dallas bubbled, pulling the priest into the kitchen and seating him at the table. "I can't wait another minute to know! The archbishop said it was *Channing*." Dallas sat across from Father and gave him a stare that showed he wasn't letting him go to bed until he'd heard everything.

Father Benedict smiled his gentle, eyes-closed smile as he pulled an envelope from his pocket. The address of the basilica was printed across it in Channing's obvious scrawl. Dallas's jaw dropped, and he slid the letter across the table and bent to examine the postmark. *May 1997. The month he died...*

"I asked Channing, in our last telephone conversation, to write out why he wanted to become Catholic," Father murmured. "Go ahead. Read it."

With trembling hands, Dallas slipped the pages from the envelope and scanned his friend's prose.

Dear Father Benedict,

At the risk of this sounding like a trite essay written for a school assignment, I send you this letter expressing as well as possible my rationale for wishing to join the Catholic Church. While the reasons are enough to fill an entire set of leather-bound volumes, and far too complex for the brief letter format, I would like to focus on those most important to me, the events in my life that have contained so much meaning that I cannot view them as anything other than signs from an almighty, all-knowing, higher power — God.

Dallas skimmed over words about Channing's love of the continual presence of Christ through Catholicism, the sacraments, the ties to Old Testament history and its fulfillment in the New, to Eucharistic miracles and respect for human life, for the way God left a consistent form and structure for worshipping him alongside his saints and angels, present to all mankind at all times through the holy sacrifice of the Mass, with sensitivity to our limited human senses and how we can use them to experience Christ on earth before we are made ready to enter into his eternal glory... Then Dallas caught his name in the last section of the letter:

But now I must explain what brought me to all these deeper searches for meaning and truth, the only way that any of this heady theology can make practical sense in applying it to my own real life. To begin with, I had to know and accept that my life had any meaning at all. For most of my childhood, I felt worthless. I don't want to throw blame, but let's just say I experienced near-constant abuse, emotional manipulation, and bullying. I have forgiven those who hurt me, both intentional and unintentional. One person, however, was different. I met my best friend, Dallas, when I was eleven and he was thirteen. Dallas has always been stronger and bigger and tougher than me, a quiet leader. He was the first person who ever defended me against bullies at school, who told me that the way my parents treated me was wrong, who told me I was intelligent and creative and talented and didn't ever deserve to be treated badly. In short, he showed me my human dignity. As soon as I first started reading about the concept of human dignity in Christian sources — such as my favorite author, G.K. Chesterton — it was like a lightbulb went on. That's what Dallas has always shown me about myself, I realized. Human dignity was a real, true thing, not just meaningless words in a book, and I know it because I experienced it, and am still experiencing it, through the way Dallas treats me. I'm not saying he's perfect — nobody is, of course, which is why we need a savior — but he behaves in ways that prove that I have value, just because I'm me. Had I not had a friend like Dallas, I might not have been able to realize God's love, His fatherly care for me and all people as his created beings. If it weren't for Dallas, I might not have been able to believe in God the way I do. I think that God put him in my life as a way of revealing Himself to me in a small way, by having Dallas show me my own goodness. He's been an instrument of Christ on earth, acting as Jesus's hands and feet to me, and he doesn't even realize it! But he doesn't have to, because it is God working through him. God has written His truth onto our hearts — we don't have to acknowledge Him for that truth to shine through — and I pray one day Dallas will realize it, too, the way that I have.

Dallas's breath hitched in his throat, and tears sprang to his eyes. He read the words again, consuming the gifted beauty of Channing's descriptions, all the connections and intuitions that revealed the depth of his best friend's understanding of his very soul. Dallas lowered the letter to meet Father Benedict's eyes.

"You... you showed this to the archbishop? I never even knew he'd written..."

"Nor did I, until two days ago," said Father Benedict, eyes misty. "This letter had been misplaced — for over four years — and, well, Channing spoke up just when you needed him. I was cleaning out a desk where the incoming mail gets placed. I accidentally knocked a folder back behind it. When I pulled the desk out to retrieve the folder, I found this. It must have slipped down there after somebody brought it in from the mailbox all those years ago."

Dallas stared at the letter in his hands. He closed his eyes and dropped his head to the table, breathing in the ink, Channing's parting gift to him. "He had such a way with words," Dallas sniffled. "And he knew me better than I knew myself. If anyone could vouch for me to the archbishop, it would be Channing I'd want most. Everything happens for a reason, huh? Thank God this letter got misplaced until now!"

"The Holy Spirit placed it right where it was supposed to be." Father smiled. "Archbishop Adams said so himself, and I'm sure you can agree."

Dallas nodded vigorously, then he stood up with a whoop. "I'm really going to be allowed to be a *priest*, Father! God wants me; he really does!"

"I told you that if it was meant to be, God would make it happen." The older man clasped Dallas's shoulder with one hand. "You knew he was calling, and he was calling you urgently."

Dallas strolled down the back walk towards the basilica's mailbox. The July sky was clear, nearly turquoise, and the temperature had already climbed into the 80s. Dallas glanced at his watch. He had an hour before he needed to leave for work. Picking up five or six extra hours on Saturdays at the nearby mechanic shop was paying off — he was able to keep earning money while still having time to pull his weight around the church with his share of the chores. Thankfully, Father Benedict was letting him stay rent-free for the summer. Dallas smiled at the comfort of his own money as a security net. He would need it soon for any extras at school. *Just one more month…*

As he yanked open the mailbox, the seminary's return address jumped up at Dallas from the envelope on top. He gaped at what he prayed was the acceptance letter he held in his trembling hands. Dallas tore it open and skimmed the type… *YES!* Both Archbishop Adams and Father Benedict had told him not to doubt his acceptance, but it was the final piece he'd been waiting for to make everything official. He'd already passed his psychological evaluation—Father had assured him he would despite his worries. The emotions tumbled inside: relief, elation, and slight concern over whether he'd be able to cut it in his classes. He was eager to get to all the higher theology but knew he had to be serious about his gen ed classes first. *I need to approach learning as Channing did— something new and exciting to appreciate. If God is the giver of knowledge, then it's our duty to embrace it.* Dallas bounced onto the curb and jogged back towards the building, jumping to swipe at a branch dangling over his head, feeling light as a feather. He paused with a bittersweet sigh as his eyes caught the high stained glass windows. He'd been so busy that he hadn't thought of Channing in weeks now. This would have been an adventure the two of them might have enjoyed together, or at least Dallas knew Channing would've been there cheering him on. *Wouldn't it have been great to be able to talk about our faith together?* Those conversations where Channing had brought up deep spiritual thoughts he'd gleaned from books were becoming more and more distant. Dallas decided to write down more of them in his journal. The possibility of forgetting some of Channing's wise-beyond-his-years words was an uneasy thought.

The door banged shut behind him, and Dallas nearly ran into Father Benedict.

"Look, my acceptance letter!" He thrust the envelope into his mentor's hands. "Guess my high school transcript didn't scare them too bad after all."

"Of course not!" Father laughed. "When Archbishop Adams recommends young men for admission, the seminaries trust him."

"Yeah, I wasn't too worried, but just having it here in print…" Dallas held the letter up high and proclaimed the words: "Mister Dallas Malone has been accepted into the College of Liberal Arts Seminary Program at—"

"Well, if you're going, you need to buy yourself some decent clothes," Father Benedict interrupted.

"Like what?" asked Dallas, woefully ignorant of fashion and dress codes. He held both arms out and dipped his head to scrutinize his choice of wardrobe.

"A couple button-up long-sleeved shirts and another pair of nicer khaki pants," Father Benedict said. "Remember, all the seminarians meet together for both Mass and Vespers daily, and there will be other times in which you'll want to look a little more professional."

As the priest spoke, Dallas jotted down items on the back of the envelope.

"And you need a tie, a blazer, and a pair of dress shoes," Father Benedict added.

Dallas looked down at his boots, creased and scuffed with age and wear, and asked in mock belligerence, "What is it that you have against my shoes, Father?"

"They look pretty rough, son," he said with a smile.

"They have character!"

Still, he took the advice and went to a nearby shopping mall the next Saturday and got a pair of black dress shoes, khaki pants, and two more button-up shirts. He gave up on the blazer but picked out a tie, realizing as he handed over his money for it that he had never worn one in his life and didn't even know how to tie it properly. *Well, I guess I'll figure it out, and then, if all goes well, I'll be learning how to put on a Roman collar and all the vestments and never have to wear one of these nooses again.* The word "noose" reminded Dallas of his suicide attempt early in his prison term, and a shiver ran down his spine. Would any of the other guys at the seminary have past problems like he did? No parents who taught him how to tie a necktie or even took him somewhere that one was required, a criminal history, a low moment of despair in which he could have ended his own life… Brushing the fears aside as he drove away from the mall, Dallas resolved to try to just be normal and fit in, praying that he could overcome his past problems if he asked God to help him to persevere. Still…what would it be like to have a mother who would adjust your necktie or help you pack for college and move in? Dallas bit his lip.

In early August, Dallas walked into the kitchen to find Father Benedict and the other two priests with a birthday cake and a few gifts for him: some notebooks and pens, a couple of nice hardback books that would be useful in his religious studies, and a sport coat. The last one wasn't a surprise since Father had insisted on measuring Dallas when he had returned from the mall without one. Dallas had no family to send him off to school, but these people cared for him as if he were family anyway. He was less alone suddenly over his thoughts of moving-in day.

Father Benedict passed a huge serving of the ice cream cake to Dallas, whose eyes widened. "Father, are you sure you didn't mean to cut this one into four pieces?" He examined his slice critically.

"You could stand to be fattened up a little," joked Father Paul.

"It's your birthday, Dallas, so celebrate," Father Benedict added. "Lent will be here again just like every year, and the time for fasting and sacrifice will occur. Mother Church, in her great wisdom, has built in these rhythms for us — times of plenty and times of bare minimums. As Catholics, we feast and we fast, and now is a celebratory time. Your birthday, and then your big sendoff to the seminary in another week!"

"I'll expect another ice cream cake then," Dallas said with a straight face. "This really is delicious. I can't remember the last time anyone acknowledged my birthday. Thank you all so much."

Friday finally arrived. Dallas had ended his last half-day at his mechanic job with a bang — in his excited frenzy, a spill left him covered in motor oil, much to the entertainment of his co-workers. Entering the rectory, he passed by Father Benedict in the hallway and, as luck would have it, Archbishop Adams. Dallas held his hands up in a warning motion so they would stay back. The archbishop wrinkled his nose at the smell, then laughed when he saw the state of Dallas's work clothes.

"My last day, so I figured I'd get as filthy as I could before I had to start being clean all the time," Dallas joked.

"Oh, you don't have to always stay clean as a seminarian," the archbishop responded, "not when you come back here and can change the oil in my car for me."

"I'm not sure you want that, your Excellency," Dallas quipped back. "The floor around that car looked worse than me, to tell you the truth. Excuse me; I'll go get cleaned up before I track a mess all over the rectory."

After lunch with Father Benedict and the archbishop, Dallas received a blessing from Archbishop Adams before he left for a meeting.

"Are you all packed up and ready, then?" Father Benedict turned to Dallas once they were alone. "I'm going to miss having you around the place, Dallas."

"Yeah, who will do the dishes now?" He flashed a crooked grin.

"More like, who will keep me feeling young and light-hearted around here?" the priest responded. "Truly, Dallas, I have so enjoyed watching you grow into a man in the past few years. From the confused and skeptical youth who reached out to me from prison to the easygoing, dedicated man before me today, heading off to give his life for our Lord, wanting to do good for others and to share with them the sacraments you have come to love so… I thank God for bringing you into my life, Dallas. It has been a blessing to me I cannot express."

Dallas's mouth dropped open, stunned speechless. He always pictured himself as the taker, always on the receiving end. His throat felt dry. "You've done so, so much for me, Father. I can't even see that I've given anything to you. But if I have, I think it's through the grace of God, and because you took a chance on me, kept coming to visit me. I'm a better man because of you and all you've done to help me."

The two of them exchanged a hearty hug, and then Father Benedict helped Dallas carry a few more things to his car. "I hope we can expect you back here soon over a break?"

"Absolutely," Dallas replied. "I can't think of anywhere else I'd want to go."

"I know you will make good, lifelong friends in the seminary, because you will fit in with those other men in a special kind of brotherhood," the priest answered, "and I hope some of them will invite you to spend time with their families over many future holidays. But I'm calling dibs for this Thanksgiving." Father Benedict gave Dallas a wink.

Dallas smiled. "Have time for hearing my confession before I leave?"

About the Author

Erin is a Catholic homeschooling mother and a first-time novelist, following a childhood filled with writing creative fiction. She lives with her husband and four daughters in North Georgia. Her passion for vocations became strong when her youngest brother was ordained a priest. Her twenty years of Catholic adulthood have given her time to grow and see what really matters in life with a focus on the good, the true, and the beautiful, and she wants her characters to find and reflect the same. Reading the classics and Church Fathers and especially Chesterton alongside her homeschooled children has informed her current writings.

Erin initially created her characters, Dallas and Channing, over twenty years ago. She was prompted to pull out an old story about them to share with her teenage daughters and was dismayed to realize she had left the characters she loved hanging in hopeless despair. Dallas and Channing were always searching for something, and that something was God all along. The book's direction was suddenly clear, and Erin gave the characters depth and purpose, knowing she owed it to them to develop them further and give them hope amidst their hardships.

Erin is a member of the Catholic Writers Guild, and when she's not writing, she reads aloud to her children, organizes a moms' book club, builds community with her church family, and leads a forest school for local families to get out in the natural world. She enjoys traveling and photography. She can be found at www.authorerinlewis.com as well as on Facebook and Instagram - @authorerinlewis.

Published by Full Quiver Publishing
PO Box 244
Pakenham ON K0A2X0
Canada

www.fullquiverpublishing.com